Change of Pace

KAYLA GROSSE

Published by Kayla Grosse

Printed in the United States of America

First US Edition: April 2025

ISBN: 979-8-9923007-2-7 (paperback)

AISN: B0DV43VHYY

Editor: Mason Frey

Cover Designer/Artist: Andra Murarasu

Map Art: Francesca Weber

Layout: Nicole Reeves

To Sally
Thank you for teaching me to cherish every heartbeat.

Author's Note

Dear Reader,

This book is very near and dear to my heart, as I am a Kawasaki disease survivor and the proud owner of an ICD implant. If you don't know what these two things are, don't worry—you'll learn about them inside these pages!

   As with all my books, I'd like to take a moment to share the content you'll find as you read. If you don't want to know, you can skip this and move on!

- Talk of death and dying

- Near-death experiences

- Kawasaki disease rep

- ICD implant rep

- Past heart attacks

- Discussions of body image, weight loss, and disordered eating

- Talk of medications

- ADHD rep (medicated with a stimulant)

- Open-door spice (including dirty talk and oral)

- Light bondage

Please note: I've done my best to represent an accurate experience of living with a heart condition as well as ADHD. Not only do I experience these things myself, but I've had multiple people with varying experiences read this story. However, any decisions and representation given is my responsibility. As always, please take care of yourself and your mental health.

Now, it's time for you to fall in love with Jesse & Asher.

Xoxo,
Kayla

P.S. At one point in this book, Jesse & Asher take a trip to Cadillac Mountain in Maine. I'm aware that, during August, this is not the first place in Maine to see the sunrise; Mars Hill is. However, I took liberties since this is fiction and I liked this specific location! Just in case you plan a road trip someday, I don't want you to blame me for getting your information wrong :)

The Jesse Girl

Ingredients:

2 oz gin
3 oz cranberry juice (unsweetened or sweetened, depending on preference)
½ oz fresh lime juice
½ oz simple syrup
2 oz club soda
Ice
Fresh cranberries and rosemary sprig for garnish

Instructions:

Fill a shaker with ice, then add gin, cranberry juice, lime juice, and simple syrup. Shake well for about fifteen seconds, and strain into a glass filled with ice. Top with club soda and gently stir. Garnish with fresh cranberries and a sprig of rosemary if you'd like!

Change of Pace Road Trip Playlist

"Heartbeat Song" Kelly Clarkson
"Brave" Sara Bareilles
"Shots" LMFAO & Lil Jon
"Toxic" Britney Spears
"E.T." Katy Perry
"Radioactive" Imagine Dragons
"Perfect" One Direction
"Complicated" Avril Lavigne
"Torn" Natalie Imbruglia
"Quit Playing Games (With My Heart)" Backstreet Boys
"Stronger" Kelly Clarkson
"A Thousand Miles" Vanessa Carlton
"I Get Around" The Beach Boys
"Jessie's Girl" Rick Springfield
"Truly Madly Deeply" Savage Garden
"Can't Help Falling in Love" Haley Reinhart
"Cake by the Ocean" DNCE
"I Won't Give Up" Jason Mraz
"I Won't Back Down" Tom Petty
"Everything You Want" Vertical Horizon
"Dare You to Move" Switchfoot
"I'm Yours" Jason Mraz

Definitions

What is Kawasaki Disease?

Kawasaki disease is a rare inflammatory condition that primarily affects children under five. It can lead to serious complications if left untreated. The condition causes inflammation in the blood vessels, especially the coronary arteries, which supply blood to the heart. Without immediate treatment, approximately 25% of children with Kawasaki disease may develop coronary artery aneurysms, which are abnormal bulges in the vessel walls. These aneurysms increase the risk of blood clots, heart attacks, or long-term heart damage. *– Information gathered from the Kawasaki Disease Foundation*

What is an ICD Implant?

An ICD (Implantable Cardioverter Defibrillator) implant is a small, battery-powered device placed under the skin, usually under the collarbone, to monitor and regulate heart rhythms. If it detects a dangerous arrhythmia (irregular heartbeat), it can deliver an electric shock to restore a normal rhythm. In addition to defibrillation, an ICD can also act as a pacemaker, delivering small electrical impulses to help maintain a steady heart rate when it becomes too slow or irregular. *– Information gathered from Google*

Change of Pace Road Trip

Start: Madison, WI
1. The Corn Palace, Mitchell, SD
2. Yellowstone National Park, WY
3. Idaho Potato Museum, Blackfoot, ID
4. Florence, OR
5. Carhenge, Alliance, NE
6. World's Largest Ball of Paint, Alexandria, IN
7. World's Tallest Filing Cabinet, Burlington, VT
8. Cadillac Mountain, ME
9. Return to Madison, WI

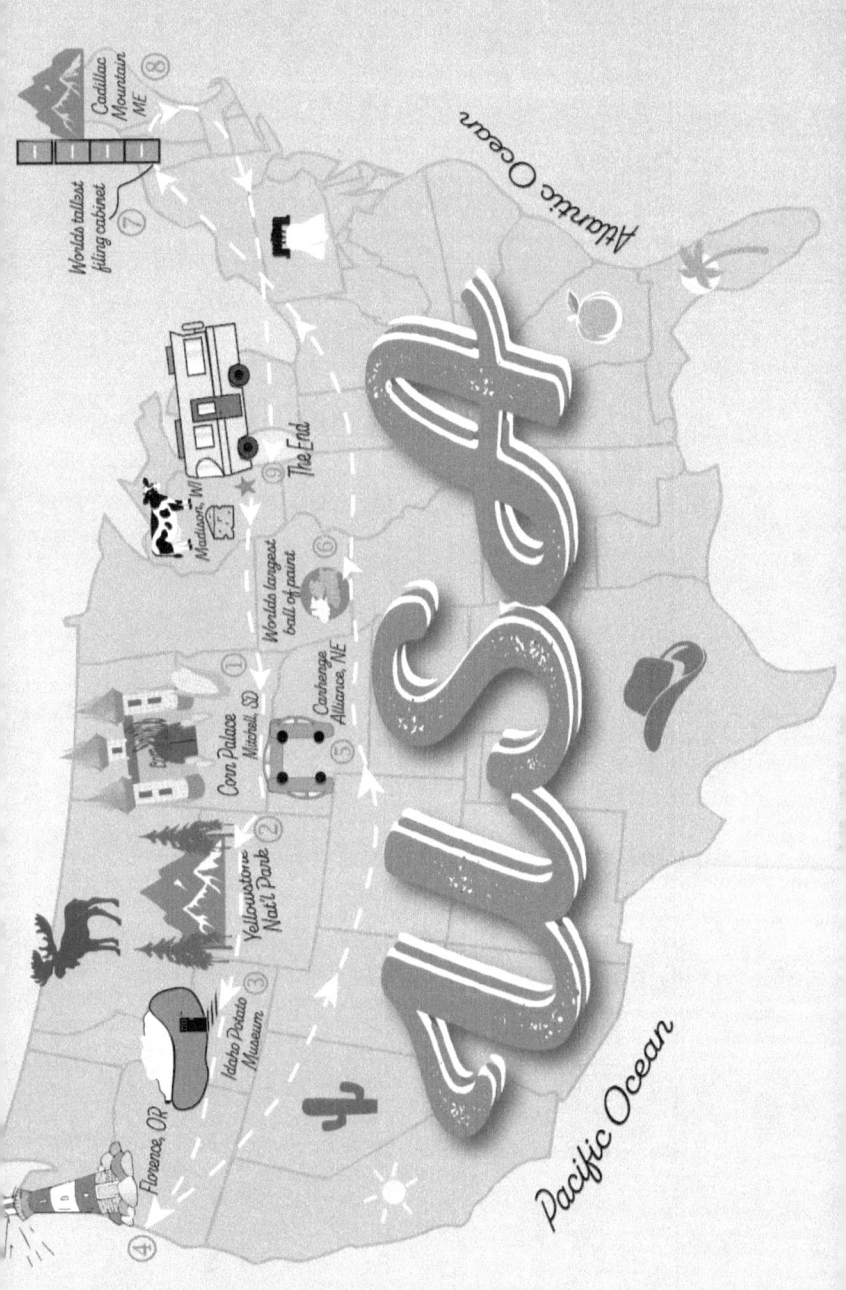

Jesse's Change of Pace Bucket List

~~~~~~~~~~~~

☐ A one-night stand *(It's okay to enter your slut era, Jesse. Remember, you don't have to be thin to get dicked down good! Xoxo, your best friend)*

☐ Get a tattoo

☐ Watch the sunrise at Cadillac Mountain in Maine

☐ Say yes to something you want to say no to

☐ Take a dance class

☐ Ride a motorcycle

☐ Crash a wedding

☐ Swim naked in the ocean

☐ See Old Faithful at Yellowstone

☐ Swim in a hot spring

☐ Find a decent gluten-free pizza

☐ Visit at least four new states

☐ ~~Dominate a man~~ *(Why did you scratch this one out, Jesse? Xoxo, your best friend)*

Chapter One

Jesse

"Remember, if his balls smell weird, leave immediately."

My face burns tomato-red from my friend's insane remark as I keep my eyes fixed anywhere but on the chuckling bartender. He sets down our second gin and tonics, and I think I die a little inside. Leave it to Kate to say something like that in public.

"Keep your voice down," I hush, the heat of embarrassment licking up my neck. "I don't need the entire bar knowing I'm looking for a hookup." I say the last part so only she can hear.

Kate turns, laughter coming from her pink-painted lips. "Isn't that the point, though? You'll have the first item of your bucket list crossed off by the end of the night. And I'm just giving solid advice every woman...or man...should adhere to."

"Kate—"

"Isn't that right..." She turns her attention to the bartender pretending to wipe the bar top down and looks at his name tag. "...Luke? You agree with me, don't you?"

I clear my throat and turn my attention to the attractive twenty-something blond man standing behind the bar. He's not looking at me, though—he's eyeing Kate like the beautiful snack she is. "Every Man's Girl-Next-Door Fantasy" is what the guys in high school called her. And with her brown hair, blue eyes, and thin yet toned figure, she's exactly that.

"What were you talking about?" Luke asks. "I heard what you said, but I think I need to know the context."

Kate sits straighter in her chair. I open my mouth to stop her from telling him and embarrassing me further, but she beats me to it.

"If your hookup's balls smell, leave immediately," she chirps.

Unlike me, Luke's cheeks don't turn red. He looks very interested and amused by the conversation. "I don't have experience with another man's balls, but I agree that not having smelly balls is important," he says before looking into Kate's eyes. A flirty smirk that matches hers tugs at his lips. "Can't say I've ever had that problem. I make sure to take a shower every day."

"And you wash all the important places, really get in all those crevices?" Kate runs her finger around the rim of her drink.

"*Oh my god.*" I groan under my breath.

Luke doesn't falter at her brazen question. "Of course. Happy to let you smell them, if you'd like."

The double meaning of his words is obvious—and gross—yet Kate giggles. I take a sip of my drink, eyes bouncing between the two of them. Am I watching them fall in lust in front of my eyes? Kate flips her hair over her shoulder and bats her eyelashes.

Yep. I am. So much for this night being about me and my bucket list, the bucket list I created after having one too many near-death experiences due to the lingering effects of surviving Kawasaki disease. Once you have two heart attacks and a subsequent ICD implanted to prevent another catastrophic cardiac event, you start to look at things differently. Or at least I did. Hence the bucket list and tonight's game plan to get me laid. Well, it *was* the game plan...

Kate laughs at something Luke says, making my attention stay on them. Luke's now leaning across the bar, and Kate is too. They look as if they're about to jump each other right here and now.

I grip my gin and tonic, the icy glass cooling my heated palm. I really should've known it was risky asking Kate to be my wingwoman. She's not only attractive, she's very good at flirting and loves to be spontaneous. Her ability to have men eating out of the palm of her hand is unmatched.

While her flirting prowess was the initial reason I asked her to help me tonight, my friend and roommate, Melissa, warned me about bringing her. Melissa was worried something like this could happen and wanted me to bring her instead. But her engagement party is tomorrow, and she has family in town from out of state.

I could have waited until next weekend, but I was eager to start crossing items off since I start a new job in a little over a month and want to accomplish as many as I can before then. Not to mention, Kate was really excited to help when I told her about my bucket list. She promised I would be the focus of tonight, so I agreed to let her be said wingwoman.

So much for that.

I pull my phone from my small purse and text Melissa. Kate is too engrossed in her talks about "hygiene" with the bartender to notice.

ME:

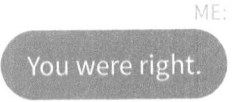

I expect it will take some time for Melissa to answer considering she's with family or her soon-to-be husband, but a message comes through before I can put my phone away.

MELISSA:

My gaze darts between the two flirts before I type out the next message.

ME:

Kate has already reeled in the bartender…but not for me.

MELISSA:

Do you need me to come? I can be there in thirty. Maybe forty-five.

ME:

You know you can't. You're busy!

MELISSA:

What bar are you at?

ME:

Seriously, it's fine. I just wanted to let you know you were right.

MELISSA:

poop emoji As much as I want you to get your freak on, you don't have to do this tonight. We can go out after my family leaves town. I will be the best wingwoman.

I lift my drink to my lips, the taste of pine needles strong on my tongue. Normally, I would have asked for more tonic—especially with the copious amount of blood thinners I'm on—but I'm grateful for the stiff drink right now. And as the alcohol burns down my throat, I'm reminded this is my first time drinking since I got my ICD implant put in two months ago. It's also my first night going out for more than a quick meal or something easy, like a movie. This should be a happy time, not one where I find myself annoyed at one of my friends for breaking her promise.

I text Melissa back.

> Okay, sounds good. I'll try again another night. Thanks for being such a good friend.

After I press send, I close my eyes for a moment to collect myself. I'm annoyed with Kate, but I'm also annoyed at myself. I know I shouldn't care so much about crossing this particular item off my list tonight. But I had this night all planned out in my head. Having a one-night stand is one of my biggest items, my scariest items, and I thought it would be the push I need to check off the rest.

I remember when Melissa first saw the item—she was curious why it was on there. My answer was easy to recite. For as long as I can remember, I watched my friends during college and throughout our twenties explore, hear them talk about the guys they hooked up with and all the fun they had while doing it. But I never allowed myself to experience it. I've always lived in a larger body, and I let my insecurities and hangups stop me from believing anyone would want me like that. It didn't help that men rarely ever approach or flirt with me.

After my heart attacks, discovering that I'd had undiagnosed Kawasaki disease as a child—which caused aneurysms in my heart—and then getting the ICD implant, the answer got even easier. Not only do I want to experience the thrill of a one-night stand, I want to take control of my body again. I want to feel alive and be carefree. Have unabashed fun.

When Melissa's response doesn't come through, I stuff my phone in my purse and look back at Kate, who is lost in Luke's blue eyes. I take another sip of my drink and let my gaze drift from the couple to a man standing on the other side of Kate. His lips are in a straight line, and he's glaring at Luke as if he wants to punch him across the face. *Same, buddy.*

I put down my drink, and my eyes drift over the bar. It's getting busier now that it's after nine, and besides Luke, there's only one other bartender working, and she's busy. The man next to Kate tries to wave at Luke but is promptly ignored. I should tell Luke he has a customer, but I get caught up studying the new stranger's sun-kissed profile.

He's got a slight double chin covered by well-trimmed golden-brown facial hair, the color matching the tapered curls with dusty-blond highlights mixed in. He looks to be around my age or maybe a little older given the frown lines on his forehead, though that could just be from his clear annoyance. I find myself smiling at the visible emotions on his face and wonder how long it's going to take for him to blow.

"Actually, Luke, maybe you could help my friend, Jesse, here."

At the sound of my name, I snap my attention from the stranger back to Kate. "What?" I ask.

Kate gestures to Luke then to me. "I was about to tell him how he could help you tonight. He gets off work in a few minutes." She waggles her eyebrows at me, and my stomach drops.

Is my friend really suggesting I sleep with the man who wants to sleep with her? Hurt and embarrassment flood my already annoyed body, driving me to stand. The action is so abrupt I nearly cause the stool I've been sitting on to fall over. I manage to grab it as I look at Kate, ignoring Luke's eyes on me.

"I'm going to go."

"What?" she asks. "I thought—"

"It's fine, I changed my mind."

"But your bucket list—"

"Another night." Without looking the bartender in the eye, I put enough cash to cover the drinks and tip on the bar top then down the rest of my drink. Kate stands to join me, but I stop her. "No, stay. You go have fun."

She frowns. "But I—"

I lean forward so my mouth is by her ear and only she can hear me. "He wants you. Go with him; it's fine." It's not fine. And I'm seriously questioning if Kate has ever been a good friend to me or if I've just ignored all the signs since we've been in each other's lives for so long. When I pull back, she's still frowning.

"You're upset," she notes.

I want to say "No shit, Sherlock" but manage to keep myself together. We're in public, and I don't want to cause a scene. I also know Kate, and I understand her enough to know she probably thinks she was being a good friend by even suggesting Luke "help" me. But he wouldn't be helping me, he'd be giving me a pity fuck. That's the last thing I want.

"I'm not angry." The lie comes out easy. "Please, go have fun."

"Jesse, come on. I'm trying to be your wingwoman here."

Still aware of Luke's curious gaze on the both of us, I shake my head. "Text me when you get home safe, yeah?"

She nibbles on her lip and glances back at Luke, who's still not helping other customers, including the stranger I was watching before.

"You're really sure? I feel bad," Kate says so only I can hear.

"Don't." I manage a smile. "I'll grab an Uber home and talk to you later."

I pat her shoulder and take a step away, but before I can leave, she grabs my wrist. Her eyes scan up and down the rose-colored wrap dress I'm wearing. "You should stay and dance. Trust me when I say men will flock to you in that dress. You're hot!"

"I'll think about it." Another lie, but I say it so she'll let me go. She plants a kiss on my cheek, and I walk off, leaving her to the night I was hoping to have and beelining it for the bathroom.

I sling my purse over my shoulder and weave through the crowd of people out for a good time, some already visibly drunk. I sway slightly as I head toward the restroom tucked off to the side of the packed dance floor. The drinks I had didn't hit me while I was sitting, but now that I'm moving, the buzz is undeniable. It's not enough to cloud my judgment or slow me down, but it's definitely enough to feel it.

I push open the door to the restroom to find both stalls are full but the sinks are open. Not needing to pee, anyway, but wanting to collect myself and give Kate time to leave with Luke, I wash my hands then stare at my reflection in the water-stained mirror. Kate was right about one thing: This dress does great things for me. Not sure if she's correct men would flock to me, but I do look good.

The simple wrap dress gives me the illusion of a waistline and cuts low on my chest, showing off my ample cleavage. I'm wearing heels that make my five-foot-ten frame almost six-foot and enough makeup that I look as if I'm wearing one of those face filters on social media.

I look like the enhanced version of me. Well, minus my new friend below my left clavicle, a thin red scar from my ICD implant that I've covered up with a skin-colored silicone bandage. I simply wanted to be normal for the night, to not have any conversations with potential men start with talking about my health issues.

The anger I felt at the bar returns and makes my eyes sting. I inhale a deep breath to keep my glassy eyes from shedding tears.

"Holy shit, you're so beautiful!"

I blink and lift my focus from my bandage in the mirror to see a woman coming out of the stall behind me. I turn my head as she walks up to the sink next to me, eyes on me as she puts soap in her hands.

"Me?"

She looks around with a wide smile on her face. "Yeah! Who else would I be talking to? Unless I'm so drunk I'm not seeing properly. Which could also be true! Those espresso martinis are *strrronggg*."

The way her sentence strings together in a quick cadence confirms she is drunk. I chuckle and grab a paper towel to dry my hands off.

"Um, thanks." I hand her a paper towel since the dispenser is behind me, and she takes it with a smile.

"Are you like an Amazon or something?"

I shake my head. "I wish."

"Yeah, I think you are one. You're tall and hot. I wish I was tall."

A second later, another woman comes out from the other stall. She stares at me, and her eyes go wide. "Oh, you are tall. Holy sexpot!"

"Miranda, I told her she's an Amazon. She is one, right?"

"Definitely."

A huff of laughter leaves my lips, and I find myself flushing from the attention of the two women. They look like twins with their dark-haired bobs and short stature, both dressed in sparkly black mini-dresses.

"Not an Amazon," I say. "Just tall."

The woman called Miranda pushes her friend or sister out of the way and washes her hands, swaying a bit as she does. "Oh man, no more espresso martinis, or we're going to have to go home early."

"Agreed. I'm Gina, by the way. And this is my bestie, Miranda."

"Nice to meet you, my name's Jesse."

"Hot name, too," Gina says. "Damn."

"Thanks." I flush harder. "Normally people don't have that reaction. Usually they think I'm a guy or ask if I'm named after the cowgirl in *Toy Story 2*."

"Those people are dumb," Miranda says. "Wait." She takes a step toward me, her green eyes boring into mine. "Are you crying?"

I blink again and curse my sensitivity. I'm a crier and always have been; I get it from my mom and grandma. I do my best to try to hide it because I hate crying. But sometimes it's impossible—especially when I've been drinking.

"I'm fine," I reply.

"No—nope!" Gina steps up to me so she and Miranda are in my personal bubble. "Who hurt you? Was it a man? Woman? Who!"

"I'm fine, really," I chuckle.

Gina's finger presses into my sternum, her face close enough I can smell alcohol on her breath. "You're way too hot to be crying in a shitty bar bathroom. Are you here with someone?"

"I was with a friend, but she left with the bartender." The information leaves me before I can think about it. Apparently the small amount of alcohol in my system is allowing me to give these two strangers insight into my night gone wrong.

Miranda and Gina both look at each other and nod before focusing back on me. "You're our friend now," Gina says. "We've adopted you."

I snort an embarrassing laugh, causing them to smile. "I was going to go home."

"You look way too hot to go home. Come dance with us!" Miranda adds.

Before I can tell them yes or no, Gina grabs one of my hands. "Us women have to stick together," she says.

"Yeah." Miranda takes my other hand. "It's a rule that you can't leave your fellow comrade in a bar bathroom sad. That's like...against the woman code."

"Woman code?"

She nods. "Exactly."

"I don't want to intrude," I say.

"You're not. We invited you. Now, come!"

Without waiting for me to speak one way or the other, they turn and tug me from the quiet of the bathroom. Gina pulls the door open, and the loud mashup of "Shots" by LMFAO and another song I don't recognize assaults my ears.

"I LOVE THIS SONG! Come on, Jesse!" Gina cheers, pulling me along until we're in the middle of the dance floor. The crowd almost seems to have moved out of the way so we have a prime spot.

Gina and Miranda let go of my hands, but we're in sort of a circle that reminds me of how I used to dance with my friends at high school dances. The two friends laugh and giggle, dancing with each other suggestively before turning toward me.

"Feel the music! No time for being sad when you're dancing!" Miranda yells, taking my hands again. She pushes me out and in, swaying her hips and telling me to mimic her. I enjoy dancing, but I always feel a little awkward, especially when I'm only tipsy and not drunk. It's much easier to let loose and pretend like nobody is watching when you're inebriated.

"Move your hips, Mama!" Gina adds.

My eyes shift around the room briefly, and I look at the spot Kate was in before. She's gone now, and so is Luke. My stomach sours a bit, but Miranda squeezes my hand, and I look back at her.

She grins at me then attempts a spin. It's awkward, and I laugh when we both almost topple over, especially since her coordination isn't exactly on point right now, and neither is mine. The song switches to a remix of "Toxic" by Britney Spears, and now it's me who's saying how much I love this song.

After a final glance at the barstool that's now occupied by a man, I decide I'm going to do what Gina and Miranda are suggesting—I'm going to feel the music and have fun. If anything, I owe myself that. And Melissa will be proud of me for making friends and going outside of my comfort zone by not having someone I know with me. Maybe that should've been the first thing on my bucket list.

With a laugh, I throw my hands up and swivel my hips, running my hands down my curves as I let the techno beats of the remix wash over me, making my new friends cheer with happiness. I guess this night has taken a turn.

Chapter Two

Jesse

I DON'T KNOW HOW long I've been dancing for, but I can no longer say I'm under the influence of alcohol. I've sweated every last ounce of gin and tonic from my body.

"We're gonna go get a drink and take a breather!" Miranda yells over the pounding music. "You wanna come?"

I shake my head, and they wave before they walk off the floor. I close my eyes, feeling the beat of the music in my soul. I don't know what's come over me, because never in a million years did I think I'd be out in public dancing like nobody was watching. And there are definitely people watching since not only is the dance floor crowded but so is the bar. Not surprising, since it's Friday night.

The upbeat song currently playing slows, and the futuristic chords of "E.T." by Katy Perry plays. I open my eyes and inhale a deep breath, thinking that maybe I should rest for a second now that it's a slower song. This is the most activity I've done since my surgery, and water does sound good, especially over alcohol.

After a pit stop at the bathroom to pee and freshen up, I make my way to the bar. I look for Miranda and Gina but don't see them. After some searching, I find an open space to stand between a man and a woman. I turn to look at the dance floor, my eyes scanning once more for my new friends that saved me from having a horrible night and find them back at it with drinks in hand. They're not alone this time. A guy is sandwiched between them, grinning like he just hit the jackpot as they grind on him.

Seeing them have so much fun, I wonder if instead of grabbing a water, I should just call it a night. I've had a good time, so I think I can call it a win. Maybe I'll add "dance in a bar like a lunatic" to my bucket list and check it off.

"Dance here often?" the man next to me yells over the noise of people and music.

I move my focus to him and immediately recognize the man from earlier that Luke wasn't serving.

Since the stranger is closer to me this time, I can see more than his profile. Not only is his hair curly, but there's also one perfect curl that has flopped on his forehead. His amused eyes look into my hazel ones, and I immediately get lost in them. They're brown but not just any brown. They're a sumptuous brown that reminds me of hot chocolate, the kind that tastes like a melted dark chocolate bar, not the powdered stuff. I think there are flecks of light brown in them, too.

"Sorry, what?" I ask.

His bowed lips tip into a lopsided smirk as he turns his body so we're face-to-face and his side is propped against the bar top. Even in my heels, he surpasses me, which must make him six-foot-four. I know because that's my dad's height.

"I asked if you dance here often?"

I shake my head. "Never, actually."

"Could've fooled me. You looked comfortable out there."

I raise a dark eyebrow at him. "You're joking."

"I'm being completely serious. It looked like a lot of fun."

"And why are you not dancing?"

He brings a dark-colored liquor to his lips and sips it. "I thought about it, but I didn't want to cut in. You and your friends were having fun."

I mull over his words, confused by them. It takes me a second to realize he wanted to dance with Gina or Miranda but didn't want to interrupt. I point to the floor where my new friends are still gyrating on the man between them.

"You could have asked them to dance," I say. "They would've."

The man beside me eyes them but then turns his focus back to me. "And if I asked you, what would you have said?"

"What?" I ask dumbly.

His smile gets wider. "If I wanted to cut in to ask you, what would you have said?"

"Me?"

"Yes, you."

"I—I, um—well, I—I wasn't—no—"

"Damn." He chuckles, the sound hitting me square in the gut and fanning warmth throughout my body. "Guess I'm not as cute as I thought. Glad I didn't cut in."

"No!" My hand darts out, and I grab his forearm before I can think about it. The moment my hand touches his warm skin, I pull back, red staining my cheeks. "I'm sorry, I shouldn't have done that."

"Done what? Touch me or call me cute?"

"I didn't call you cute...?"

"So I'm not cute?"

"No, you are, but—"

"See, you did. I'm not complaining, either—I think you're cute, too. No, I think 'hot' is a better word for you. Or stunning. Cute and hot are too average for what you are." His molten chocolate eyes flick down my body then meet my gaze again. "Yeah, I'm going with stunning."

I think all my breath has left my lungs at his words. Sure, I've dated. I've had sex before—with my ex who I dated for six months before my first heart attack two years ago. But never in my twenty-eight years of life has a random man at a bar called me cute—much less hot or stunning. Those words were always reserved for the conventionally beautiful women I was with. Women like Kate.

The nameless man stares at me, expecting me to say something, but I'm speechless. He runs his free hand over his bearded jaw and smiles again. "Are you okay?"

I swallow and finally manage a nod. "Yeah. I'm fine."

He leans on the bar, and an awkward beat of silence passes between us. I should probably say something.

Do you thank someone when they tell you you're stunning? Or do I call him handsome? Because while he is cute, handsome is a better word. Or rugged, with his beard and broad shoulders—more outdoorsman than a Calvin Klein model, which I prefer. I'd rather not have to take off my clothes and wake up next to Brad Pitt's muscular body and gleaming veneers. Men like that are almost too pretty.

I like what this man is: a sturdy Midwesterner, like most of the men I grew up with here in Wisconsin.

"Can I buy you a drink, Fine?"

It takes me a second to put together that he's calling me Fine because of what I last said and we don't know each other's names. A small laugh escapes me, and his lopsided grin makes my stomach flip over. He wants to buy me a drink and dance with me. This night has taken a turn, that's for sure.

"You're not here with anyone?" I ask.

"I'm here with you," he responds smartly.

My cheeks pull tight. "I see. And now you want to buy me a drink?"

"Seems like it."

I lean against the bar, and he takes that as a sign to flag one of the bartenders down. It's the female bartender this time. She's much nicer and more professional than Luke.

"Gin and tonic for my friend here and two waters," he says in a friendly tone.

The bartender goes about making my drink, and I stare at him, mouth agape. "How did you know what I was going to order?"

"I saw you here earlier with your friend."

"And you remembered my drink?"

He purses his lips and turns sheepish. "Fuck, that's weird, isn't it?"

I try not to laugh at his distress, letting him hang in another beat of awkward silence while he attempts to read my face for a reaction. When he shifts on his feet and clears his throat, I eventually give in. "Maybe a little weird that you remembered but also kind of sweet."

"Well, Fine, you're hard to forget. Which is saying something since I am forgetful on a good day."

If I wasn't already red from dancing, I'd turn red now. The man stares at me, and I get lost in his beautiful brown irises. His pupils are slightly dilated, and he's watching me closely for my reaction. For a moment, the noise of music and bar patrons fades, and it's only me and him.

"Here you go; do you have a tab?" the bartender asks.

I blink rapidly, but my new male friend doesn't look away as he says, "Yeah, add this and anything she wants until I close out."

I think the bartender laughs, but I'm not paying attention. The man's lopsided grin pulls into a full smile, his eyes even more penetrating as if he can see into my soul. It's disarming but in a good way. I don't think anyone has ever looked at me like this before.

"Here." He picks up the water and holds it out for me.

"Do I look parched?"

His eyes crinkle at the corners. "Always good to stay hydrated. Never know when you'll need the electrolytes."

My eyebrows shoot up. "Are you always this—" I trail off, searching for a word.

"Forward?"

"I was going to say flirty. But I guess that's a good word."

He reaches out and takes my hand, the warmth of it sending tingles up my arm. For a second, I wonder what he's doing, but then he places the glass of ice water in it and pulls back, picking up his own drink and eyeing me from over the rim of his glass.

"I'm only forward when I see something...or someone...I want." He takes a sip of the amber liquid, and my eyes track to his throat, watching the muscles work as he swallows. I wet my lips at the movement, and he does it again. When I meet his gaze, he's smiling.

My chin tips in embarrassment at being caught staring—at his throat, of all places—and I take a sip of the water. The chilly liquid leaves an icy path down my throat, shooting shivers up my spine.

"Was that too *too* forward?" he asks when I don't speak.

I take another drink and meet his eyes again while I mull over his question. Jesse pre-heart attacks and ICD implant would think his words and actions too forward. But I don't now. This nameless man is oddly charming. I can't explain it, but I'm drawn to him.

"Do you still want to dance with me?" I ask, letting the question be my answer. His pink tongue slips out to lick his lower lip seductively.

"I would love to."

Heat curls in my belly, and I set the water down. When I see the full drink he paid for next to it, I frown. I don't really want to drink it, but I also don't want what he paid for to go to waste. Call it the Midwestern girl in me who always wants to be nice and accept what's given to me.

His warm hand touches mine again, holding my hand in his. His palm is rough like a workman's hand. It sends shivers up my spine like the water did, but this time, it's not from the cold.

"Leave the drink," he says. "It's no big deal."

"Do you read minds?"

"In my downtime." A laugh bubbles from my chest, and he squeezes my hand. "You offered me a dance, and I'd like to collect. Screw the drink—unless you want it."

I shake my head. My gaze flicks from his warm eyes to his lips. "Okay, but first, I want to know your name."

"Asher, but call me Ash."

"Ash," I find myself repeating, enjoying the way it feels on my lips. It suits him.

"And do I get to know your name? Not that I mind calling you Fine."

I shake my head in amusement as he starts to play with my fingers in his grasp, as if he's done it before. The action is swoonworthy, and I have the impulse to kiss his lips. Instead, I give him his answer.

"Jesse. But you can call me Jesse."

Now it's his turn to laugh, his smile so wide it makes me smile. "Well, Jesse called Jesse. Shall we dance?"

"I'd love to, Asher called Ash."

He presses a soft kiss to my knuckles, his lips lingering just long enough to make my heart stutter. Before I can completely dissolve into a puddle on the floor, he tugs me toward the crowd of dancers, his lopsided smirk permanently settled on his lips.

Chapter Three

Asher

THERE ARE A COUPLE of things in life I'm very good at. One is technology, specifically software and app development. The other, and arguably more important, is an unshakable ability to hyperfocus on what I want. Once I lock onto something, it's like the rest of the world disappears, and I don't stop until I get it.

I've had this trait for as long as I can remember, one that became easier to define after my ADHD diagnosis when I was a kid, and it's a trait that is very much coming into play right now. Because the moment I laid eyes on the stunning brunette currently following me to the dance floor, I was sold on our future. I could see it from start to finish, and I wanted it. I wanted her. No matter what it took.

Undeniably crazy? Yes. But I felt it in my gut so strongly, it nearly doubled me over. The funny part is, I can't even explain how I know. Maybe it was in the carefree way she moved on the dance floor. Or how she looked so happy with her friends, as if dancing in this shitty bar was the best thing in the world. I truly don't know. The only thing I do know is I couldn't leave this place without at least speaking with her. And now that I have, I'm even more sure I want to get to know her.

With her hand in mine, I find an open space near the middle, bodies undulating around us. I gently tug her toward me, still keeping us at a distance. A frown marks her round features, and I want to soothe it away. "May I?" I gesture to her waist.

Her striking hazel eyes widen, and she nods. "Of course."

The smile that's been permanently on my lips since I saw her dancing from across the room grows. I came to this bar to grab a drink and catch a baseball game, but I haven't watched one inning. All I could see was the stunning woman on the dance floor, dancing like she was in her bedroom alone.

Her eyes were closed half the time, her round hips swaying to the beat, sometimes offbeat. I'd imagined what she'd feel like pressed into me, how her softness would meld with mine. I'd wondered if she'd smell like flowers or something sweet. But nothing I drummed up is like the real thing.

She's draped her arms over my shoulders, fingers linking behind my neck. My hands have found the subtle dip of her hips, and her breasts press against my chest. She's warm, searing even. The heat of her leaves a mark so deep, I know I'll always feel the phantom weight of her presence like a brand on my body.

Fuuckk.

My fingers grip her tighter on instinct. I breathe in, an attempt to keep my dick from making an appearance and potentially scaring her away even though I've made my intentions clear—I'm pursuing her. But instead of being calmed by my inhale, I'm hit by her scent.

I was right in my first thought that it's floral, but there's also a spice to it, maybe a perfume or a shampoo. It's mixed with the sweat of dancing and the faint smell of alcohol, but I couldn't care less. I pull her closer as the beat of the song changes to the slower, more seductive pace of "Radioactive" by Imagine Dragons and inhale again near the crown of her head. She lifts her chin and stares up at me with an amused grin as our hips move, and it gets harder for me to stop the reaction I'm having to her body.

"Did you just smell me?"

I should be embarrassed, but I'm not. "I did."

Her lips press together, and her cheeks turn a rosy pink that has me wondering if her entire body turns that color when she's flushed. By the color of her cleavage, I'm going to take an educated guess and say yes.

"What do I smell like?"

I'm not sure if it's purposeful or not, but she nearly grinds her heat against my crotch, matching the beat of the song. Stifling a groan, I touch my nose to the crown of her head again and drag in a long breath. The floral notes and spice of her sweat tickle my nose before I bend low enough for my lips to be at her ear.

"Like sex."

Her body stills in my arms, and for a moment, I debate if I've gone too far or not, if I really have been too forward and should have kept that thought to myself. Maybe we should have spent more time at the bar before I asked her to dance. Maybe I read our instant connection wrong, and she wants nothing more than a sexy dance with a stranger.

I pull back to apologize, but she grips me to her. Her eyes meet mine, and I find her pupils have dilated and her breaths are shorter.

"Would you like to get out of here?" she asks.

In my mental eye, I react by dragging her off the dance floor and finding the nearest flat surface to fuck her on. If we wouldn't get arrested, I'd ruck up her pretty dress right here and see if she's already wet and ready for me. The front of my jeans grows tight, and I reach up, pulling one of her hands from behind my neck and holding it.

"I would love nothing more."

Jesse glances at my lips before turning away, tugging at my hand as if she's in a hurry to leave before I change my mind. But nothing will change my mind about wanting her.

Before she can move me, I pull her back. She lets out a squeak of surprise when she hits my chest. Her eyes are lit with questions, and I use my free hand to cup the side of her face, running my thumb over her cheekbone before holding her chin in my thumb and forefinger.

"A kiss first, Jesse called Jesse." Her pretty eyes dance with mirth, and her pouty pink lips that match her dress gently part. "May I?"

"Yes."

The way she didn't hesitate to answer makes my heart stop for a beat, and I seal my mouth over hers without wasting another moment. Her lips part immediately for me, and while I want to delve inside her mouth and taste her, this is our first kiss. Our only first kiss, and I want to savor it. Memorize it and burn it into the fiber of my being so even when we're old and gray, I'll never forget it.

Jesse (last name unknown) doesn't know it yet, but this is our last first kiss. I've never been more certain of anything.

Chapter Four
Jesse

ASH TAKES HIS TIME exploring my lips as if we're alone somewhere tucked away behind closed doors instead of in the middle of a dance floor packed with people. And like when he took my hand at the bar, the sounds around us fade away, and I get lost in him. All that's left is the warmth of his lips and his strong hand cupping my head, fingers threading in my hair.

He tugs on my lower lip, and I gasp, my hands moving to his hips and pulling him against me by his belt loops. I expect him to seek entrance into my mouth, to tangle our tongues together, but he sucks and nibbles as if he's savoring me.

He goes on and on until I can't take it anymore. I've never been one to take charge, always letting my partners lead, but like most of this night so far, I find myself doing what I don't expect. The moment his mouth parts for air, I slip past his lips, our tongues finally touching.

Ash groans, his other hand reaching up to cup the side of my neck. He tastes like smoky whiskey and smells like woods and musk. He allows me to lead the kiss, not taking over or demanding more than I want to give. His soft yet strong body presses into mine, the bulge of his erection rubbing into the skin of my lower belly. The pressure of it makes this moment real, and his answer to my question returns to the forefront of my mind. He said yes. He wants to leave here with me, but he wanted to kiss me first.

"Yeehaw, Jesse!" a familiar voice hollers. "Don't stop, get it, get it!"

The room around us snaps back into focus as I pull away from Asher's lips, turning my head to find the twinkling eyes of Miranda. She pumps her fist then goes back to dancing with the guy I saw her and Gina grinding on before. But now, Gina is off dancing with another woman, one who she's about to kiss, from the looks of it.

A brush of Asher's thumb across my cheek brings my attention back to him. His lips are swollen and marked with traces of my lipstick, and his eyes are glossy with lust.

"You good?" he asks breathlessly.

I nod. "Yeah, you?"

"More than good." As he speaks, Miranda dances over and bumps into him, slapping him on the shoulder.

"You got the hottest girl in the room! Take care of her, or I'll kick your ass." Miranda shoots me a thumbs-up then goes back to dancing with her guy.

When my eyes meet Ash's, he's grinning like a fool while trying not to laugh.

"I just met Miranda tonight, but I think she's telling the truth," I say.

Ash leans forward so our lips are close again. "I think so, too. Especially the part about getting the hottest girl in the room."

My teeth trap my lower lip, and I stare up at Ash, the desire in his eyes growing. He leans down to kiss me softly before tucking a strand of hair behind my ear. "I promise to take care of you."

"Really?" I say. "And how will you do that?"

One of his hands presses against my lower back, and he brushes his lips over the shell of my ear. "By making you come so hard the word "fine" will no longer be a part of your vocabulary, Jesse girl."

The way he says the last part, as if my name is precious and unique, fully does me in. If I wasn't ready to strip and offer myself to this man before, I am now.

"Close your tab, and I'll meet you out front," I tell him as I pull away.

"Where are you going?"

"I need to use the restroom."

Asher studies me, as if he's afraid I'll use the moment to run. Maybe I would have in the past. Hell, I might've if he'd met me before I met Gina and Miranda and let loose on the dance floor. But now, there's no way I will.

I lay my hands on his chest and lean up to kiss him. "I'll meet you out front."

His lopsided grin returns. "You promise?"

"I promise."

Satisfied, he lets me go, looking back at me one more time before he heads to the bar. I quickly say my goodbyes to Miranda and Gina and send them a text so they have my number, words of approval leaving their lips as we part. It not only makes me wish I had known them before tonight but also burns the need deeper to evaluate my friendship with Kate—or, at the very least, have a serious talk with her about how she made me feel.

But it doesn't matter right now. Had she not ditched me, I wouldn't have ended up at the bar next to Ash.

Not wanting to make him wait, I rush to the bathroom, where I rinse my mouth and pat my face and under my arms with a wet paper towel. If this is heading where I want it to go, the least I can do is not be crusty with sweat.

After I spritz my face with some rose water Melissa gave me and reapply my lipstick, I check myself in the mirror. My eyes stare back at me and smile. For the first time since my diagnosis two years ago, I feel like things are looking up.

I pull out my phone and text Melissa, letting her know I'm going to invite Ash back to our apartment. She responds with a million emojis expressing her shock and excitement followed by a warning to use protection. I laugh and like the message before

I put my phone away, not wanting to wait longer and risk Ash thinking I ditched him.

With one last look at myself in the mirror, I send my reflection a cheesy double thumbs-up and give myself a pep talk. "You can do this, Jesse. You can freaking do this. He's hot. You're hot. This is what you want, what you came here for. You can do this."

I exhale a breath and leave the bathroom in search of the man who's waiting for me. When I spot him, Ash is out front, right where I told him to meet me. His lopsided grin is on full display when he lays eyes on me.

There are a few people loitering and enjoying the Wisconsin summer night along with the bouncer, but it's as if they don't exist as I approach him. He holds out his hand, and I put mine in his. Is it strange that this feels like something we've done a hundred times before? It's exactly how it felt when he played with my fingers in the bar.

He squeezes my hand. "You ready?"

"I am."

We stand there for another second, making heated eyes at each other before we both try to speak at the same time.

Asher laughs. "You go first."

"Would you mind going to my place? It's within walking distance."

"I don't mind." He brings my knuckles to his lips and ghosts a kiss on them like he did earlier. "I want you to be comfortable."

I smile. Where did this man came from? He's unlike anyone I've ever met, and there's a familiarity to him I can't place. "Well, I figure if you murder me, at least my family and friends will be able to find my body. I also have a security camera."

There's a pause before he barks out a laugh. I probably shouldn't have said that, but it just came out. Once he's finished laughing, he leans forward so only I can hear him. "The only thing I'm going to murder is that pussy of yours."

He pulls back so I can see his eyes, his lopsided smile more of a Cheshire cat grin. "Did you really just say that?"

He cocks his head to the side. "Too forward?" he asks, echoing his earlier questions.

"No, it's just...I've never met anyone like you."

He rubs his thumb over my knuckles. "I feel the same way about you."

I study his face in the dim light. His nose is rounded at the tip, and his skin is tanned, likely from spending time outside. I want to ask him what he means, because given the way he talks and his good looks, I'm sure he's met and taken home plenty of women. And despite my health issues in the last couple of years, I'm not a very exciting person. In fact, I'm average. Not that he's had time to learn any of that.

Ash squeezes my hand, and I meet his penetrating gaze. "If you don't want to do this, we can find a diner. Talk. I know I've been forward, but I want to do whatever you're comfortable with."

For the first time since I came here in search of someone to sleep with, I feel guilt pool in my stomach. Ash doesn't know about my bucket list. He doesn't know that, in a way, I'm using him. He seems like a really nice guy, very different from Luke the Bartender. Different from my one ex who didn't put much effort into our relationship or any of the few men I've dated. And despite us being mostly strangers, if I'm reading everything right, he genuinely seems to care about me.

"Jesse?"

My vision that had gone hazy refocuses. Melissa gave me advice before I came here tonight: She told me to go with the flow, that no matter what, I don't owe anyone anything even if I do sleep with them. It's not like I have any allegiance to a stranger, nor does Ash have any to me. But I still feel a little bad.

I move to speak, to trauma-dump the last couple of years onto him and make sure he knows tonight is selfishly about me. If he hopes there's more after tonight, he's going to be disappointed. But Ash takes the action as an invitation; he closes the distance and kisses me.

He kisses me differently than he did earlier. It's passionate. Raw. His tongue slides against mine in a way that shows dominance and strength. I melt into him as if I'm a willing lamb on its way to slaughter.

When a man smoking nearby wolf whistles, Asher doesn't stop—the audience only seems to spur him on. He squeezes my hand, still in his, sucking on my tongue and making me moan low in my throat. His kisses are like his personality: forward and overpowering. When he finally does pull back, we're both breathless.

"I'll take whatever you're willing to give, Jesse girl."

I want to comment on his mind-reading abilities again, but I melt at the name. All my prior reservations fly out the window, and I reclaim the strength I felt in the restroom. If I want to confess to Asher about the bucket list later, I will. But if he's willing to take whatever I can give, then I'll give him what I can: tonight.

"Let's go back to my place," I say.

Chapter Five

Asher

"It's NOT MUCH, BUT it's home," Jesse says as she shows me into her small bedroom. She's right; the space isn't much. It's big enough to fit a queen-sized bed and a small desk in the corner, but that's about it.

The one thing that strikes me about the room, and the living area she took me through to get here, is there isn't much personal stuff around to give me insight into what she likes. In the living room, I saw basic furniture and a television, and in her room, there are a few pictures on the wall, but that's it.

None of that matters to me, however, because I'm used to staying in spaces that don't feel much like home when I travel for work. Plus, had I chosen where we went, I would have gotten on my knees in the bar bathroom and ate her out until she screamed. Even I can admit the bed is better and definitely more sanitary. Not to mention more comfortable.

Jesse drapes her purse over the back of the desk chair and stands in front of me, lit only by the dimmed overhead light. She wrings her hands in front of her body nervously, and I take a step toward her, wondering what happened to the woman who danced freely at the bar. Her wide eyes track my movement, her chest heaving and nearly drawing my focus to the lush valley between her tits. But I'll have time to explore that area in great detail later. Right now, I need her to be comfortable like she was before.

My gaze stays focused on her face as I gently take her hands in mine. She swallows, the muscles of her throat working. Her lips, swollen from my earlier kisses, gently part. I place her hands flat on my chest, then step close enough my lips skate over the crown of her head, making a soft sigh leave her. The sound is like music to my ears. I inhale her floral-spiced scent and continue my path of kisses down her cheek until her lips are captured in mine.

Now that we're familiar with each other's kisses, we deepen it without hesitation. She grips the cotton T-shirt I'm wearing, pulling me closer so there's nearly no space between our bodies. My hands find her midsection, and I grip her there, but a gasp leaves her mouth. I gently pull away.

"Ticklish?"

She nods, so I drop my hands lower to her hips, pulling her into me so she can feel the evidence of what she's doing to me. This time, I'm the one groaning into her mouth.

When I feel her body relax a bit, I start to gently walk us back toward the bed. I feel the backs of her knees hit the mattress, and I part from the kiss briefly. "Lay back," I command softly.

Jesse looks up at me from hooded eyes. While her body isn't as tense now, she still looks unsure. I meant what I said earlier, that if she wanted to talk and not have sex, I'd be more than okay with that, too.

So I offer again. "We don't have to—"

"No." Jesse stops me. "I—" She licks her lips, hands still gripping my T-shirt in her fists as if she's afraid I'll disappear. "Can I be honest?"

My stomach drops, and for a brief second, I wonder if the reason she's hesitant and nervous is because she's a virgin. It wouldn't matter to me, but I'd rethink this moment heavily. Every woman deserves a first time that's perfect and with someone more significant than a man she just met.

I tuck a strand of her wavy hair behind her ear. "Of course you can."

She flattens her hands against my pecs and collects her thoughts before she looks back into my eyes again, her hazel depths full of emotions I can't place. "I don't normally do this."

My chin dips in a nod. "'This being sex?"

She blinks at me, her eyes widening before she shakes her head from side to side. "No, I, um... God, this is embarrassing. I've had sex just never gone home with someone like this."

"You mean someone you just met?"

She nods. "One-night stands aren't usually something that I do."

My chest tightens. I know why she thinks this is a one-night stand. If I didn't feel the way I do about her, I wouldn't have batted an eye at her assumption because I would have expected it to be the same thing, especially since I'm only visiting Madison for the weekend.

But that's obviously not how I'm thinking about her or tonight. I am, however, smart enough to know telling her she doesn't have to be nervous because she's the woman I'm going to marry is the wrong move.

You say something like that during your wedding vows, not after you just met a person. Otherwise, you just sound like a creep, maybe a stalker. Both of which I'm not. I'm simply a man who sees a woman and feels like there could be more, much more, than a one-night stand. I just hope I can make Jesse feel the same by the time we part.

I school my features so she can't see my feelings and place my hands over hers. "You have nothing to be embarrassed about," I assure her. "We can take things slowly."

She stares at me as if she wants to tell me more. Instead, she licks her lips and glances at mine. I wait for her to make the next move, wanting her to make the choice to kiss me or tell me whatever else is on her mind.

"Do you have a condom?" The way she blurts it out then flushes is almost too adorable, and it has me grinning. I guess she doesn't want to take things slow.

"In my wallet," I answer.

In another surprising move, she slides her hand out from under mine and down to the back pocket of my jeans. Before she can pull it out, I place my hand over hers. She looks up at me with questions in her eyes.

"That part comes later. First, sit on the bed, and lie back."

"You don't have to do that."

"Do what, exactly?" I tease.

Her cheeks burn. "I don't know—whatever it was you were thinking."

She knows exactly what I was thinking, and it's cute she won't say it.

I lay a hard kiss on her mouth before I speak again. "Even if tonight is our only night together, foreplay is essential." I run my nose up her cheekbone until my lips are near her ear. I gently take the lobe, biting around the pearl stud she has decorating it. She gasps from the sensation, and I pull her hips into mine, grinding against her. "I want to taste you before I fuck you, Jesse girl. Say I can."

"If you insist."

Her smart response has me chuckling against her ear. She shivers, and before she can change her mind and try to convince me to simply fuck her, I gently start to lower her back until we're both lying on the bed.

I help her scoot up until her head rests against her pillows, her shoulder-length hair fanning against the gray material of her comforter. I wish it was brighter in here so I could study every part of her, but that's for another time. A time I hope I get.

With our eyes locked, I move my body up so I can kiss her. I taste her mouth for a time as her hands explore the muscles of my back. My fingers thread in her soft hair, and I wait until her body is a near puddle in my embrace before I lay open-mouthed kisses down her neck.

I run my tongue over her pulse, feeling the thrum of it speed up before I suck on the delicate skin. Jesse grips my biceps, her hips tilting up in search of friction as she moans. The vibrations tickle my tongue, and I suck harder on her throat, leaving a faint red mark before kissing down toward her clavicle. My lips touch smooth skin, then in another moment, the skin changes to something tacky.

Her moans stop, and her muscles tense under my attention. I open my eyes to see what looks like a bandage of some sort, and when I lock my gaze with Jesse, her eyes are wide, almost nervous. I'd been so caught up in her I hadn't noticed it before. To be fair, it blends in with her skin as if it's not even there.

"Injury?" I ask softly.

She traps her lower lip between her teeth, and after a long moment, she nods. "Just don't put a lot of pressure on it, and I'll be fine."

I nod, able to tell by her body language that's all the information she's willing to give. As softly as I can, I ghost a kiss over the bandage. She shivers from the action, and I smile softly before doing it again.

Once I've kissed it better, I continue down, landing kisses on her cleavage, sucking and tracing over the soft white stretch marks visible near the scooped collar.

One of Jesse's hands grabs onto my curls, gripping them until my scalp tingles. I hum in satisfaction, considering asking her to pull harder. I don't have to, though, because when I suck on the top of her left breast, she does it on her own. My cock twitches against the zipper of my jeans, and I lavish the skin of the other breast.

"Ash," she sighs. The sound of my name on her lips only adds fuel to my fire. I lick and taste every part of her skin available to me until I can no longer hold back from seeing more of her.

I kiss down the valley of her breasts, soon reaching the front tie of her dress. I turn my hooded eyes up to find hers, and she nods in permission. I make easy work of untying the knot, my mouth salivating as I pull the soft pink fabric open.

The body she has hidden beneath is as beautiful as the rest of her. Most of her plush belly is covered by a pair of high-waisted lacy pink underwear, and her tits are pushed together by a matching bra.

I lick my lips and land a kiss on the fabric above her sex, her body trembling at the action. "Cold?" I ask.

She shakes her head. I place my fingers near the band of her underwear, giving her one last out before I bury myself between her thighs. But her eyes are nearly closed, and her chest and belly move with her shortened breaths. She's incredibly beautiful, and I want her to know exactly how beautiful. When she doesn't stop me, I curl my fingers on the fabric and tug down as I tell her to lift up.

When her underwear is gone, thrown somewhere on the floor, I'm left with a sight I'll keep etched in my memory for eternity: dress pooled beneath her body, bra still on, her thick thighs and legs slightly parted. The light is just bright enough I can see the plump lips of her neatly trimmed pussy wet with her arousal. I'm sure if I were to study her underwear closer, I'd find a wet spot on it.

My dick makes himself known, pushing harder against my zipper to the point of pain. "Stunning," I murmur under my breath. Her chin dips at my praise, and I shift back on my knees so I can remove my shirt. Jesse watches my every movement, her hands now fisting the comforter. While I'm not ripped like a lot of men these days, I'm comfortable with my soft yet strong body, and I have no problem putting what some may call a "dad bod" on display for her.

Once my shirt has joined her underwear on the floor, I shift so my hands settle on her thighs. Her breathing picks up again, and I caress the soft skin before adding a bit of strength to part them. My mouth waters when I see her swollen clit peeking out, and I maneuver between her now open legs, using my thumb and forefinger to open her like a budding flower. The musky scent of her arousal fills my nose, and I'm a goner.

I blow on her clit, and she audibly gasps, her hips tilting up and giving me the perfect opportunity to feast on her. The flavor of her pussy floods my taste buds, and a sound akin to a growl erupts from my chest. I lick and suck, her moans making my dick more painful by the second. My hips thrust against the mattress for some relief as I swirl my tongue around her clit, gently scraping my teeth over the nerves until her body convulses from the onslaught of sensations.

"Ash. Oh my god, Asher," she cries.

With smiling eyes, I look up at her while keeping my mouth suctioned on her sex. Jesse's eyelids are closed, and her head is thrown back against the pillows. One second, her hand is at her side, and the next, it's gripping my hair as it did earlier. She holds me where she wants me, her pelvis undulating off the bed as if she's trying to ride my face.

I continue to do what she clearly likes, alternating between hard and light suction while finding her soaked entrance with two of my fingers. I gently dip them inside, her arousal hot and dripping onto the bed. For a fleeting moment, I wonder if she normally gets this aroused with her partners or if this is all for me. I allow myself to believe it's the latter.

Wanting to give her more, I slide my fingers inside her tight channel. It flutters around my fingers, and I groan. Not to sound cliché, but holy hell, she's fucking tight. My hips move on the bed again, and I know I need to make her come or things will be over far too quickly and my promise to murder her pussy will not come to fruition.

"Oh!" Jesse exclaims as I curl my fingers inside her, the tips brushing over the rough skin of her G-spot. "That feels—yes!" She cries as I suck her clit again at the same time my fingers thrust. The squelching noise of her arousal only amplifies how turned on I am, and I move my fingers faster.

"Come for me, Jesse. Gush all over my fingers."

Her head tilts back, her hips buck forward. My lips meet her swollen sex, and I suck and lick as her bra-covered chest arches off the bed and my name falls from her lips like a battle cry. I ride her through it, gently lapping at her clit and enjoying the way her inner walls squeeze my fingers in an erratic beat. Her hand releases from my hair, and she uses it to signal me to stop. "No more, I..."

I blow on her clit, and her hips buck. "Sensitive?"

She nods, skin flushed and a bead of sweat dripping from the crown of her head. I wear a sly smile as I kiss her inner thigh, my lips and tight-trimmed beard wet with her arousal.

I wipe it with my hand, brushing it off on my jeans. Before she can question it, I kiss up her body until my lips meet hers. She doesn't balk at the taste of herself on my lips, allowing our tongues to meet. Her willingness to get a little dirty only has me hotter for her.

When her hands seek my belt, I break apart from her lips and kiss the tip of her nose, unleashing a grin. "Now it's time for a condom."

Chapter Six

Jesse

I'VE BEEN EATEN OUT twice before, and I thought it was okay. A little wet, kind of awkward. Especially when I would stare down at my partner and see my stomach and the top of his head. I'd focus more on my body and less on the action. But what Ash just did to me...

If I didn't before, I now believe in God.

I didn't even care about the awkwardness of it all or think of my stomach. I was completely lost in every sensation, the things he did with his mouth. *Wow.*

Ash crawls back off the bed, and for a moment, a bit of awkwardness comes back. Should I get up and clean myself off? Get him a towel for his beard? I've never been this wet or turned on before, and I'm positive I'll have to burn the comforter once we're done.

I lift my head, but Ash stops me by holding his hand up. "Don't move."

My body stops at his command, as if this near stranger has complete and utter control over me. In a way, he does. My eyes meet his, and he smirks, placing his hands on his belt. The metal of it jingles as he pushes down his jeans, revealing a pair of light-blue briefs that accentuate the outline of his very hard dick.

I felt it while he ground against me, and I knew he had to be blessed, but I don't know if I'm prepared to see what he's hiding. I lick my lips as best I can, my mouth dry from the lack of hydration in my body that flooded out during his assault on my pussy. I rub my thighs together, and Ash's eyes track the movement.

"Take the rest of your clothes off for me."

I lift an eyebrow at him. "I thought you said not to move."

He chuckles from his chest and clucks his tongue. "I didn't want you to get up, but I do want you naked."

I match his smile, feeling more comfortable than I ever have during sex. I'd think it would be the opposite given the situation, but there's something about Asher and the way he looks at me, the way he speaks. I feel at ease.

I put my hands behind me and sit up on the bed, the wrap dress falling from my arms and pooling on the comforter as I do. Once I have it completely off, I throw the bunched material to the ground, and Ash hums in appreciation. His heated gaze travels over my body as he brings his fingers to the band of his underwear.

"Now the bra, Jesse girl. I've been dying to see those pretty tits."

Damn. This man has a dirty mouth. It's something I didn't expect to like, but I'm not complaining. It makes me feel...wanted.

"Your underwear first," I say.

Ash doesn't protest or ask me to go instead, he simply pushes down his briefs and kicks them off. His erection stands proud against his rounded stomach, and even in the faint light, I can see how swollen and red the head of it is.

And yep, I was correct in my assumption that he's been endowed by whatever dick god exists. I'd honestly be afraid of it if I didn't have a sex toy collection that would have my mother send me to confession if she ever found it. I may not have had many sexual partners, but I have had my fair share of silicone dicks.

Ash clears his throat, and when my eyes meet his, I expect him to say something cheeky about me staring at his cock or at least be wearing a shit-eating grin. Instead, he eyes my bra-covered chest and walks forward until his knees are touching the end of the mattress. He wraps his hand around his length, gently stroking it. I didn't think I'd find that hot, but I do. I really do.

"Do you need my help?" My eyes never leave his as I shake my head to answer his question. "Then show me all of you, Jesse."

His words strike me deep. I know he means my body, but they feel like a hell of a lot more. The recent memory of the way he kissed the bandage over my ICD scar floods my mind. He didn't know what the injury was or why the bandage was there, but he was so gentle and reverent when he kissed it, way more than a one-night stand should be—or at least my expectation of a one-night stand. It should be quick and fast, not this. Not depth and connection. Ash is not meant to see all of me. Which is one of the reasons I put the bandage over my new scar in the first place.

Emotion becomes thick in my throat, and I attempt to clear it. I don't need thoughts like that obscuring my objective for tonight. Jesse before she nearly died may have been all for the potential of more than one night, but not this Jesse. This Jesse is here to get fucked and feel good. From here on out, no more emotions. No more reverent kisses or his face between my thighs. I wanted to have a one-night stand, and that's what I'm going to have.

I reach behind my back and unclip my bra, not allowing myself to think about the way my large boobs drop free from the cups or how I've always felt my nipples were too large and darker than most. Instead, I focus on the way Ash is looking at me as if he wants to devour me.

When it's clear he'd stare at my boobs all night if I let him, I wave a hand in front of my body. Asher's eyes meet my face, and he licks his lips.

"Condom?" I remind him.

"Right." He picks his jeans up off the floor eagerly, his ass cheeks flexing as he bends. I bite my lip at the sight, fresh arousal pooling between my legs. A few seconds later, he crawls back on the bed, condom in hand. He uses his free hand to grab my bra and throws it somewhere on the floor with the rest of our clothes.

When his attention is back on me, he opens his mouth to say something. Even though we've only known each other for a few hours, I'm going to guess it would've been a compliment or something dirty, but I don't give him the chance to speak. With a bit of force, I grab the back of his neck and seal my lips over his. My tongue licks into his mouth, greedy for another taste of him.

He chuckles against my lips but doesn't complain. With another dueling kiss, he tugs me into his body so his hard cock presses into my belly, a bit of his pre-cum marking the skin.

When I'm thoroughly kissed, I find his hand and take the square packet from his fingers. He sees the question in my eyes and moves so I have space to do what I want. I open the packet and remove the condom. Injecting myself with bravery, I take his heavy shaft in my hand. He hisses, the hot flesh jumping in my palm.

I stroke him a few times, watching his eyes roll into the back of his head and his lips part in pleasure. It's sexy, and I think I'll remember that look forever.

With his dick straining in my hand, I roll the condom on and meet his eyes. His gaze is intense—pupils blown, lips in a tight line. It looks as if it's taking everything inside him not to pin me to the bed.

I lay down on the mattress in hopes he gets the message: That is exactly what I want. His heated gaze peruses my body, and a curse leaves his lips. If I was braver, I'd just tell him to fuck me, but I've never been one to direct or dominate during sex. It's something I want to get better at. It was even an item I had but scratched out on my bucket list: to dominate a man. I'm honestly surprised I even asked Ash to go home with me at the bar, but it felt right in the moment. And I'm glad I did, or this may not be happening right now.

"Jesse girl," he groans. "You're so beautiful it kills me." He reaches out a finger and gently pinches my nipple.

My clit pulses at the touch, and the urge to tell him how much I need him inside me gets stronger. I part my lips to finally say it, but in another instant, I'm being pinned to the mattress. I sigh in relief as Asher's lips devour mine before he's licking a path down my neck and chest until the nipple he pinched is being sucked into his mouth.

My hands fly to his hair, and he gently bites down then kisses the hurt better. He does that again and again until I nearly cry out for him to stop—then he switches to my other breast. He gives that one the same attention, playing with my nipple until I'm squirming and gripping his hair so tightly it must hurt.

"*Please*." I widen my thighs and tilt my hips up, once again hoping he'll get the message that I want his cock. His mouth is amazing, but I don't want to wait any longer.

Ash looks up from my chest with swollen lips. "Please, what?"

I thrust my hips up, putting pressure on the hot skin of his shaft. He curses from the friction, and I look down between our legs then to his eyes once more.

"You need to be fucked, huh?" He bites my lower lip, moving his hips so his cock drags through my wet sex. The sliding feel of it drives me nearly insane.

"Yes...please, I...I need it," I say. "I need you to fuck me." Pressure eases from my chest at finally saying what I want.

Ash kisses my nose, one of his hands moving between us so he can line himself up with my entrance. He dips the tip of his cock in, and my eyes widen at the stretch of it.

"Take a deep breath for me," he says.

I inhale at his command. The moment I exhale it out, he sheaths himself deep inside my pussy. The stretch is a lot, and I squeeze my eyes shut, my hands gripping his biceps. He's big enough that it burns for a moment, but not in a bad way. I almost forgot what real dick feels like—so much better than silicone.

"Jesse." He brushes his lips over mine. "Open your eyes."

I meet Asher's hooded gaze. His brow is furrowed, but not in concern. The look tells me he wants to fuck me into the mattress but is holding back. I gently dig my fingernails into his muscle, tilting my pelvis up so he moves deeper. His head drops to my shoulder, and he lays an open-mouthed kiss to the space where my neck and shoulder meet.

"You're so goddamn tight." He licks at my skin. "Wet." He lifts his head up, and more curls, damp with sweat, flop onto his forehead. "I didn't hurt you, did I?"

It's sweet he cares, but I don't want to answer. Saying anything outside of dirty talk while his dick is inside me feels like heading into non-hookup territory, at least for me. For all I know, Asher is this intense and caring with every woman he sleeps with. But I know if he acts sweet and we get into pleasantries, we will blur lines I don't want to blur. I need to not talk. I need to only feel good.

"Fuck me, Ash. Hard." The brazen command is foreign on my tongue, but I need him to screw me and take away my thoughts. I need to keep this what it is.

When he stares at me again, I feel like he's attempting to read my mind. I wonder briefly if I've read him wrong—maybe he's a man of dirty words and doesn't like to be rough. But that thought is quickly pushed from my mind when he abruptly pulls almost all the way out before he slams back into my cunt so hard my entire body shakes.

"Fuck!" Spots appear behind my eyes as I cry out.

"Too much?"

"No, no," I chant. "I like it."

My answer gives him the permission he needs, because the next thrust is just as hard. Then the next is rough enough I hear the slap of our skin and the sound of my wetness as he enters me. Every part of my body is on fire, and each stroke of his dick only fans the flame.

I grip Ash's hair, keeping his head near my neck. He sucks on my collarbone then shifts down so he can suck on my sensitive nipples one by one. Every kiss and thrust builds me up, and I feel the ghost of my orgasm building, but I still need more. I open my eyes and watch the way his back flexes with each thrust, how his arms and broad shoulders strain from bracing over me. It's like watching a porno that I'm starring in.

I tug on his hair, and he lifts his head from my chest. "If you keep doing that, I'm gonna come," he nearly growls, but there's a smirk teasing his lips.

"Do it."

He shakes his head at the same time he thrusts into me. My body nearly jackknifes off the bed, and he nips at my chin. "I want you to come first."

"Again?"

My question makes him chuckle. "Yes, again. I want to feel this sweet cunt choke my dick as I come."

My inner walls squeeze around him at the suggestion, effectively cutting off Ash's commentary. His lips greedily find mine, and he continues to thrust, changing his speed to short and fast. The shift in movement brings me closer to the edge, but I still need that tiny push over.

Before I can maneuver my hand between us to touch my clit, Ash changes positions. He shifts back so he's kneeling and pulls me toward him, my knees now in the crooks of his arms and ankles near his shoulders. I groan, the tip of his dick nearly hitting my cervix given how I'm folded.

"This okay?" he asks.

I nod vigorously, glad I'm flexible to a certain extent. Once he's got a good rhythm, the sound of our coupling gets louder. His gaze zeros in on my chest, his eyes watching my boobs shift and move from his motions.

"Like I said, fucking"—*thrust*—"stunning." He drops forward, and his fingers find my clit.

"Yes!" I moan. "I—"

"Come, Jesse. I'm right there with you."

He gently pinches the sensitive nerves, and the missing piece to my orgasm clicks into place. Even if I wanted to stop it, I couldn't. I think I black out as I come, my body jerking from the force of pleasure coursing through me.

I faintly hear Ash praising me, or maybe he's swearing. His forceful thrusts turn softer and shallower, and before I know it, he's lowering my legs, and the heavy weight of his body presses against mine. He kisses me, and I open my mouth for him automatically, still floating between reality and pleasureland.

Asher pulls away, and I feel his fingers brush over my cheek. "You alive, Jesse called Jesse?"

A laugh bubbles from my lips, and I open my eyes to meet his amused ones. "I think so. You're alive, right?"

"Barely," he teases. "Though I won't lie. I would happily die buried inside you." My cheeks burn, and he chuckles lightly before kissing me again. "I'm going to go get rid of the condom and get a rag to clean you up. Where's your bathroom?"

"The door to the right of mine," I answer sleepily.

"Do I need to worry about flashing a roommate?"

I shake my head. "No, we're alone."

With a parting kiss on my forehead, he gently eases out of me before standing. I watch him walk off, his naked body coated with a sheen of sweat and cute ass flexing as he walks. As if he knows I'm staring, he pauses after he opens the door and winks at me over his shoulder.

Once he's gone, I close my eyes. The sounds of him using the restroom penetrate the thin walls of my room. My mind attempts to overthink what transpired between us, but I'm coming down from the endorphins of the evening, and I'm exhausted, so my brain stops working.

My breath evens out, and my body feels heavy. I remind myself I need to stay awake, that a stranger is in my home, and he's supposed to leave. But I feel myself sinking closer and closer to sleep until the last thing I remember is feeling the bed dip and a warm washcloth on my thigh.

Chapter Seven

Jesse

I WAKE UP TO the sound of birds chirping outside my window and a delicious throb between my legs. I groan as I stretch, my body feeling as if it ran a marathon last night. That's when I remember all of it: Kate, meeting Miranda and Gina, dancing...

Incredibly hot sex with Asher.

I sit up in bed, wincing when the sudden movement makes me dizzy. I didn't drink that much last night, but all the dancing and sex gave me a different type of hangover. My body hasn't had this much exertion in a while, and now I'm paying the price.

Once I have my bearings, I look down and realize I was tucked in. More cobwebs clear, and I remember that Ash had gone to the bathroom. I faintly recall the feeling of him cleaning me before I passed out.

Even though he's not here, embarrassment flushes my cheeks. I let him clean me and fell asleep. Dead asleep, apparently, which is unlike me. I usually wake up at the slightest noise. And I definitely am not the type of person to fall asleep with a stranger in my home.

Speaking of a stranger in my home—I look around the room and see Asher's clothes are gone. I glance at the pillow next to me, and by the imprint left on it, he must have laid down for a while, maybe even slept. I lay my hand on it to discover it's gone cold, and I don't see a note anywhere, either.

Despite me hoping for this outcome, I feel disappointment heavy in my chest. I rub my sternum as if that will clear the feeling away and look at the clock on the wall. It's almost eight, so I decide to get up since I know I won't be able to fall back asleep.

I pull back the covers, my body still naked. When my eyes catch a small bruise forming above my right breast, my thoughts stray to Ash again—and the fact he left without a goodbye.

I know it's what I wanted, and I should be jumping for joy I checked off my first item. Yet that feeling of disappointment in my stomach remains. In a way, it's kind of funny. I made it clear to him he was a one-night stand, and now that he's acted accordingly, I feel upset.

"Get it together, Jesse," I tell myself. This is good, more than good. I got it done and got not one but two orgasms out of the deal. What's more, Asher was an all-around nice guy who did, in fact, only murder my pussy. I force a smile on my face and bask in the afterglow of my accomplishment before the sudden need to pee makes itself known.

I climb out of bed and grab a pair of clean underwear, sleep shorts, and the old T-shirt I usually sleep in and head to the bathroom. Melissa's bedroom door is open, and she's not here.

I knew she was at Jordan's last night, and I don't expect her to be around this early in the morning. Lately, she's been sleeping at her fiancé's place, slowly moving her stuff into his condo except her bed, her dresser, some clothes, and a few odds and ends for when she sleeps here.

The open door is a reminder that I need to decide if I'm going to get another roommate when she officially moves out in about two months or turn the second bedroom into an office and hope my new admin job at a dental office works out for longer than the three-month trial period. I rub my face as I go into the bathroom. I can think about that later. I need a shower and coffee.

I flip on the light and go straight to the shower to warm up the water. Once it's turned on, I hang my clothes on the back of the bathroom door. I pee, then I wash my hands and grab a clean washcloth from under the sink. But when I step in front of the mirror and finally look up, my heart stops in my chest, because I realize what I have taped to the top right corner.

My bucket list.

Nobody ever comes in here except for me and Melissa, sometimes Kate. My parents and brother live up north in Door County, and my sister lives in Arizona, but I'm usually the one to visit. My mom and brother came down to help me after I got my implant, but I hadn't written the bucket list yet. Melissa and Kate are the only ones who know about it. Until now.

I blink at the list. Of course I had to write "Jesse's Change of Pace Bucket List" at the top. What kind of moron am I? I nibble my lip as I stare at it, my stomach churning at the realization Ash probably saw it. The steam from the shower fills up the room, and I wonder if that's why he left while I was sleeping. Or maybe he didn't see it?

That notion goes out the window when my eyes focus on the list and I read the first item.

Jesse's Change of Pace Bucket List

-∿-∿-∿-

☑ A one-night stand (It's okay to enter your slut era, Jesse. Remember, you don't have to be thin to get dicked down good! Xoxo, your best friend) P.S. If you want to make this more than a one-night stand text or call me at 555-831-3363. I'm in town for a few more days.
X, Asher called Ash

I read his note over and over again as a mix of emotions runs through me. It feels good he wants to see me again. Which I think is natural, because who doesn't want to be wanted? Then there's the disappointment I feel because he doesn't live here mixed with relief that this will remain a one-night stand. I'm also glad he's not angry about being an item on my bucket list. I thought he might feel used if he knew, but considering his note, I gather that's not the case. Another relief.

I step into the shower, my thoughts tumbling around in my mind like a hamster on a wheel, and wash away any leftover evidence of my night with Asher. His touch, his smell, the salt on my skin from dancing. I also peel off the silicone bandage and wash my incision that looks angrier than usual. It's healed but still red and sensitive. I press around the area, feeling the hard plastic implant under the muscle that's now part of my body forever.

The muscle around it is a little sore, and my left arm hurts a bit from all the dancing and acrobatics I performed with Ash. Nothing to worry about, it's simply a constant reminder of how my life has changed in the last few years and what I'm coming to realize is the reality of living with a foreign object in my body.

Once I'm showered, dried, and dressed, I pop out of the bathroom and am met by a flustered Melissa, who scares the shit out of me.

"Jesus, Melissa, are you trying to give me a heart attack?" I exhale, my hand over my fast-beating heart.

She huffs and wags her finger at me. "Not a funny joke."

"If I can't joke about it, I'd go crazy. You have to admit, it's a little funny."

She rolls her brown eyes and tucks a piece of curly caramel-colored hair behind her ear. "It's not, but whatever makes you feel good. Now come on, I brought coffee and gluten-free donuts. I came to make sure you weren't murdered since you didn't text last night after you went home with a rando."

"Where did you find gluten-free donuts?" I ask as she tugs me down the short hallway and into the kitchen area where we have a small dining table.

"You want to know where I got the donuts from instead of responding with 'Thank you for being concerned about me, Melissa'?" she chirps as she sits.

I follow suit and grin at her. "Thank you for being concerned about me, Melissa." I blow her an air kiss. "Now where did you find gluten-free donuts?"

She shakes her head and slides me a coffee. I notice right away that it's a half-caff peppermint latte made with oat milk, both adjustments I made to help with my ever-changing body since my heart attacks. The oat milk is more of a preference for my stomach, though I'm not completely dairy-free. And the half-caff is to help stop the ventricular tachycardia I deal with from flaring up. The ICD implant I got plus medications tend to keep it in check, but I don't need the added stimulant to make it worse.

The gluten intolerance is something that reared its ugly head recently. Who knows if it's related to Kawasaki disease and its effect on my system or if my body just decided to throw another curveball; nevertheless, it hurts my stomach and makes my joints hurt if I eat it. Fun times.

"My soon-to-be mother-in-law shipped them in from some fancy bakery in Chicago," Melissa answers. "She said there's a place in Madison now that offers them, but she read the reviews, and they sucked."

I take a sip of the coffee and sigh from the minty sweet yet bitter flavor. "And why are you giving me your soon-to-be mother-in-law's donuts?"

Melissa laughs. "I had her bring in a bunch of gluten-free stuff for you and my cousin, Mariah, for the engagement party tonight. She got some little cupcakes and cookies, too. The donuts were something I asked her to get if they had them since I know you miss them."

My heart warms at the care and sweetness of my friend. We've only known each other for two-and-a-half years. She became my roommate once she moved here from Michigan for a nursing job at the hospital nearby. In the time we've known each other, she's easily become one of my best friends. She's been with me through all my heart attacks, taking care of me when my family couldn't, driving me to appointments and even to the emergency room when I had my first attack.

If she'd come into my life after my health scares, there is no doubt in my mind I would have pushed her away for reasons similar to why I'm being so strict about my bucket list. But Melissa? She snuck in before the walls were put up. Not only is she one of my best friends, but she's also like a second sister to me.

"Thanks, that was really nice of you," I say.

"I didn't want you to suffer and not be able to eat anything."

"I really do appreciate it." I take another sip of my latte while Melissa smiles and opens the box of delicious-looking treats. She hands me a napkin, then we both take out a confection. I select the chocolate glazed while she grabs the vanilla with sprinkles.

After several bites, I can see that Melissa's dying to hear all the details about last night—it's written all over her face. I have no issue telling her everything, but it's fun to make her squirm.

Eventually, she can't handle it and cracks. "For the love of god, at least tell me if it was good!"

I swallow the last of my donut and wipe my mouth. "Define good?"

"Jesse! Don't play coy or whatever. I need the details before my head explodes."

"Alright, alright. It was...more than good."

"Oh no, don't tell me your one-night stand was the best sex of your life?"

"I won't tell you then."

She throws up her hands. "Was his dick at least average?"

Against my better judgment, I think of the way his cock stretched me, how it felt as he thrust inside me. I shift in my chair, which doesn't go unnoticed by Melissa.

"Oh my god, are you sore?!" The sheepish look on my face clues her in. "Dammit." Melissa groans. "Of course this would happen with a one-night stand. Life is unfair!"

She's so serious in her disappointment, I can't help but laugh. "It is what it is. At least it was good, right? Did you want it to be bad?"

She leans back in her chair, dusting crumbs off her hands. Her massive diamond engagement ring hits the morning light coming through the dining room window, flinging rainbows across the room.

"No, I'm glad you got dicked down good. You deserve it after the shit couple of years you've had. There's just a part of me that wishes you'd have gotten his number or something. Then you could have gotten dicked down several times."

I think of Asher's number written on the bucket list I now have tucked in my pocket but keep my face neutral as Melissa continues.

"Although the times I've kept seeing men I planned to only sleep with once usually led to situationships that had me in tears by the end of them. One-hundred-percent do not recommend. You remember Rob."

I cringe. "Of course I remember that asshole. He led you on for months before you met Jordan."

Melissa shivers dramatically as if she's trying to rid herself of the memories. "Anyway, back to you. How do you feel? Is it everything you'd hoped for? You don't look as refreshed and perky as I would have expected. Did he not get you off?"

I take a sip of my latte and smirk over the top of the lid. "No, he got me off..." I grin wider. "...twice."

She sighs and curses the one-night stand gods before she diverts her attention back to me. "So what gives? You should be on cloud nine."

"I'm tired is all."

Melissa stares at me, eyes narrowed. "I can buy that, but something else is going on in that head of yours. Tell me, or I'll eat all the gluten-free desserts before the party."

I gasp in fake offense. "You wouldn't dare."

Her lips tip up at the corners. "Okay, I wouldn't. But tell me, or I'll torture it out of you by singing 'Ninety-Nine Bottles of Beer on the Wall' until you give in." I bark out a laugh. "I'm serious—I'll do it."

I play with the cardboard sleeve around my latte. "I know you are. It's just... Honestly, I'm a little embarrassed."

"About?"

I move the holder up and down until I finally decide to spill. "He was a lot more than I expected him to be. He was kind, funny, and he pursued me in a way I've never been pursued before." Melissa stays quiet, letting me speak. I think about what I'm going to say next before I talk again. "You know, I thought I'd get tipsy, lose some inhibitions, meet a guy, have sex, and then he'd leave and that would be it. I thought the sex would make me feel empowered."

"And it didn't?"

I shrug. "No—well, yes, it did." I think of how I got to the point of telling Ash to fuck me and nearly blush. "But now I'm feeling a little confused is all. I didn't expect or want to feel this many emotions."

Melissa scoots her chair closer to mine and places her hand over the one still fiddling with the coffee sleeve. I look into her brown eyes, ones that nearly remind me of Asher's.

"Did you catch feelings?"

I huff out a breath. "No, I don't think so. I just expected to wake up and feel like a new woman. But when I woke up and saw he was gone, for a moment, I felt disappointed. I'm not supposed to feel disappointed over a one-night stand being a one-night stand."

"Jesse, those are natural feelings, especially if he's a good guy. I know how hard it is to find them. And I'd like to mention, you're not the first person to wake up after a good night of sex and feel things. Like I said, that's how many a situationship is born. Don't beat yourself up about it."

I look down at the table. When I don't speak, Melissa pokes my hand. "Are you leaving something out?" she asks.

"Do you remember where I taped my bucket list?"

She looks at me funny, sitting back in her chair. "Yeah, what does that have to do with anything?"

"I woke up this morning, and when I went to the bathroom, I saw that he'd crossed out my one-night stand item."

Melissa makes an *aww* sound. "That's kind of sweet."

She's right, it is sweet. "I thought he'd be upset and feel used, but he left his phone number." I pause as Melissa stares at me. "And a note."

She leans forward. "He did? What did it say?" It's hard to miss the excitement in her voice, which nearly makes me laugh.

"He responded to your little note about entering my slut era, said that if I wanted to make it more than a one-night stand, I should call him."

"Okay, ignore everything I said about situationships. I like this guy. I think you should call him."

"It's supposed to be a one-night stand, remember?"

"Yes, we established that. But you just said you were disappointed that he wasn't here this morning. And you said he was unlike anyone you've ever met."

"I did..."

"I know you're set on your bucket list. But what if—*what if*..."

"What if?" I ask when she pauses for too long.

"What if you stumbled upon a man who is boyfriend material? He could be your person, Jesse!"

My thoughts from last night pop back into my mind. How the old version of Jesse, the one Melissa knew briefly, would have loved the idea that Ash could be more than one night. She would have really loved Melissa's suggestion that he could be "my person."

Before I almost died, I believed in fairytales. Some may have even called me a romantic. But I lost that version of myself in the hospital. Maybe it was staring at the cold ceiling of the operating room wondering if that was the last thing I'd ever see. Or when I felt the left side of my body go numb and fear like ice rush through my veins.

Regardless of when it happened, I'm not that woman any longer. I won't allow myself to be. Instead, I'm looking for experiences. Living life to the fullest and crossing off my bucket list. And while I haven't told Melissa all this, I have told her I'm not looking for a relationship right now. I just left off the "never" part.

"It was a one-night stand," I reiterate like a broken record.

"I know. And you know I'm in full support of whatever you want. But sometimes life works in mysterious ways. You know I wasn't looking for Jordan when he came along so soon after Rob. Sometimes you find the thing you're looking for when you're not looking for it. Or in this case, the person."

"I get what you're saying. But I have things I want to do, places I want to see. He's not my person."

Melissa's happy features deflate, her eyes focused and lips tight. She stares at me the way she does when she wants to say something but thinks it will piss me off.

"What is it?" I ask.

She pauses and folds her hands on the table in front of her. "I know you're hesitant to say you caught feelings, but given everything we talked about, I'm going to say you have, at least enough for us to have this discussion right now. If there wasn't even a small part of you that wanted to see him again, you would have told me you had a good night and that's that. But I'm starting to wonder if you're only hesitant because you're afraid to get close to someone new, especially since you're so focused on just crossing off bucket-list items."

I curse Melissa's attentiveness to my emotions and feelings. It reminds me of Ash and how attuned he was to me last night. So much so I called him a mind reader.

I attempt to keep my face clear of emotions, not wanting to get into this right now. Or ever. "I'm not afraid. I just want to have fun, you know? We talked about this before."

"I know, I know. Just think about it, okay? I'd hate for you to miss out on something good. I mean, who knows? Maybe I'm wrong. But I think you should call the guy and see where it goes. Or at least get another two orgasms out of it."

I smile softly. "I get what you're saying, and I appreciate you looking out for me. But I think it's better to keep it as is. And did I mention he's not from here?"

"What?!" she exclaims. "Jesus, Jesse, you could've led with that!"

I laugh despite myself. "Sorry."

"Okay, now I really think you should just call him—"

"Nope, I'm going to end this discussion. I'll reiterate again that it was a one-night stand. Instead of calling him back, maybe I should start planning out my next one. I'm sure it'll get easier the more I do it."

Melissa raises her eyebrows. "Ooh, you have a taste for it now, huh?"

"You're the one who said to not be afraid of my slut era."

"True, but I should've added that if you find your person, you can be a slut for them instead."

I shake my head. "You're nuts sometimes, you know that?"

Melissa only smirks and stands up, coming to hug me from behind. She presses the side of her head against mine and says, "If you're so insistent about one-night stands, I can introduce you to my brother tonight. Maybe you can have an engagement party hookup to forget this other guy fast."

I awkwardly look up at her. She doesn't bring up her brother much in conversation. When she does, it's usually an off-handed comment about some funny text he sent. Nevertheless, I find it weird she's trying to get us together.

"Are you seriously offering to let me sleep with your brother?" I ask.

She stops hugging me and moves back so I can see her better. "What? He's nice, good-looking, and I can vouch for him."

"I thought you said he travels around in a RV or something."

"Exactly. I hardly ever see him. This is the first time he's visiting me here in Madison since I moved from Michigan. That means, if you hook up, you only have to see him at my wedding." She waggles her eyebrows.

"You *are* nuts."

"As long as you don't tell me the details, you're good."

"Thanks for the offer, but I'm not going to have sex with your brother after I just had sex last night."

Melissa pats me on the head. "You wanted a slut era, Jesse. Don't be shy!"

"Like I said, nuts."

"I'm fine with that title. But speaking of nuts, today is nuts. I gotta get going. I need to meet my parents and Jordan's to set up later, but before then, I'm getting a blowout and my nails done."

"Busy day."

"You sure you don't want to get your nails done or anything? I'll pay for it."

I shake my head. "No, I think I'm going to do some research and figure out if I can afford to cross any more items off my list before my job starts. I saw there are some good deals on flights to Wyoming so I can go to Yellowstone. You know how much I've been wanting to see Old Faithful and the Hot Springs. Then I want to see if I can manage a flight to Maine from there for the sunrise."

"Okay, if you're sure."

"Positive. I'll see you at the restaurant at six."

"Sounds good. If we find some time, we can bitch about Kate leaving you last night for the bartender. I knew I should have gone with."

At the mention of Kate, my stomach sours. I'd forgotten about her and how embarrassing last night was before I met Ash.

I clear my throat. "It all ended up working out."

"Sounds like." Melissa grins and kisses my cheek. After we say our goodbyes and I hear the door lock behind her, I lean back in my chair and pull out the bucket list from my pocket. I stare at Ash's number, my conversation with Melissa fresh in my mind.

For a second, "old Jesse" comes out, and texting him sounds like a good idea, but then I think better of it.

"It was a one-night stand, Jesse," I remind myself. "Leave it at that, and don't complicate it. Your heart has already been through enough."

My eyes scan down the list, and I read my bucket list to myself sans item one:

☐ Get a tattoo
☐ Watch the sunrise at Cadillac Mountain in Maine
☐ Say yes to something you want to say no to
☐ Take a dance class
☐ Ride a motorcycle
☐ Crash a wedding
☐ Swim naked in the ocean
☐ See Old Faithful at Yellowstone
☐ Swim in a hot spring
☐ Find a decent gluten-free pizza
☐ Visit at least four new states
☐ ~~Dominate a man~~ (Why did you scratch this one out, Jesse? Xoxo, your best friend)

I smile to myself at the last one until an image of Asher on his knees in front of me springs to my mind. I stand from the table and shake my head. Yep, I think it's good I already had that one crossed out. Thankfully, sex isn't involved in any of my other items.

I fold my list and put it back in my pocket, taking my morning meds before heading to my room to get out my laptop. I think I'll make good on what I told Melissa and start planning how I'm going to cross the rest of my items off.

The admin job I'm starting in a month makes the time I have very limited. I've also got a small budget until I start getting biweekly checks coming in. I'll be using some of my savings from my last job—that I had to quit due to my health issues—to pay for any items that require travel or money. I know I won't be able to do everything in a month, but hopefully I can make a good dent.

At least I already have one crossed off.

Chapter Eight

Asher

"Seriously, man? Why does your shit stink so bad?"

My chubby white, gray, and black-striped cat, GusGus, looks at me with judgy eyes as if I'm the one who shit the most heinous-smelling poop known to man and animal. It's criminal he looks so dang cute, though, because I can't be mad at him.

He meows then goes off to lay back on "his" blankets on the couch, kneading them and turning around three times before he finds a comfortable position to snooze in for the morning and probably the rest of the day.

"You're living the life, cat."

After I've finished cleaning out GusGus's litter box and spritzed some air freshener, I head to my small kitchen area and grab a cold breakfast burrito from the fridge. I've been living in this old Winnebago Chieftain from 1990 on and off for nearly two years now. While I do have a small gas stove to cook on, I've never been much of a chef nor do I have the mental bandwidth to cook most days.

I pop the burrito in the microwave and then pour myself a cup of coffee that I brewed earlier and watch the burrito spin around.

My eyes catch my reflection, and I stare at myself. Ever since I left Jesse's apartment as the sun rose, I've debated going back. The only thing that stopped me was that it would be weird to show up on her doorstep after I made the choice to leave, especially if she hasn't woken up yet.

The microwave beeps, and I pull out my burrito. I wrap it up in a paper towel as I look out the kitchen window. It's a nice morning, so I decide to eat near the lake. It's not too hot yet, but it's the last few days of July, and it's only going to get hotter and more humid as the day goes on.

I slip on my shoes and make sure I have my keys and phone before scratching a sleeping GusGus on the head. He meows at me, annoyed I woke him. I chuckle and head out.

The warm wind ruffles through my hair as I walk down the short path to the water. The park I'm staying at while I'm here for the week isn't that large, and it's full of families who are just starting to wake up for the day. Mostly, I see dads outside cooking sausages on the grill. I wave to a few of them and take a bite of my bean, egg, and cheese burrito. I groan when the center part is still cold. I could go back and heat it up for another thirty seconds but decide to live with it.

I take a second bite and make my way down the public dock. Lake Mendota isn't a large lake, but from where I am, I get a nice view of the state capitol and the green shoreline dotted with homes. It's my first time in Wisconsin, but so far, it's nice. I grew up in Michigan, which has similar vibes. In a lot of ways, this feels like being home again. It settles a small part of me that randomly gets homesick, even though I haven't lived in one spot for two years—and I haven't lived in Michigan for even longer than that.

My phone pings, and hope sparks in my chest that it might be Jesse. When I take it out of my back pocket and see it's an email notification from work, my chest deflates. It's only nine in the morning, so logically I know she could still be asleep, especially after how she passed out last night. I'm still bummed, though.

A smile plays on my lips as I think of our time together. After we had sex, I'd gone to the restroom to clean up and get a washrag for her. That's when I saw the bucket list taped to the vanity mirror. "Jesse's Change of Pace Bucket List" to be exact. The title was clever and ignited several questions in my mind. Like: What made her start a bucket list? I know it's not uncommon for people to have them, but what made her do it? Did it have something to do with the injury she was covering?

I also can't forget the first item: a one-night stand.

It was easy for me to put the pieces together that our night checked off that box. It made me question why she chose to put that on her list, though, and why it was important to her. I'll admit I felt a twinge of heartbreak in my chest at the confirmation of what she thought and expected me to be, but I understood it. I also can't deny I'm glad she chose me over some other guy—like that annoying bartender.

My thoughts drift back to the moment I returned to her room. I wanted to talk to her about us, to see where she stood and if there was a chance she'd be open to more than just one night. The chemistry between us was undeniable, and I like her—a lot. I was hoping to find out that my worry of her sticking to her one-night-only rule was just that: me worrying.

Sure, there's the small complication that I don't live here and am scheduled to leave for London in a month to help implement some software I developed at a hospital, but those plans can change. I'd happily throw caution to the wind to turn our one-night stand into something more.

Then I found her already asleep. Not wanting to wake her, I cleaned her up, tucked her in, and waited to see if she'd open her eyes. Before I knew it, I fell asleep beside her, the heat of her body and the comfort of her bed lulling me into dreamland. When the early morning sun woke me up, I found Jesse still dead to the world. I got up, went back to the bathroom to stare at her bucket list, and started a heated debate with myself.

I found myself wondering if she had stayed awake last night, would she have asked me to leave? Or did she feel the same connection I felt and would've asked me to stay for breakfast and round two? Or she could have felt awkward about the whole thing and hoped I'd leave on my own. It's clear she was after a one-night stand, and part of me wanted to give that to her.

She taped her list to her bathroom mirror. You don't do something like that unless it's important to you and you want to be reminded of it every day.

After I stared at the list for what felt like hours, an idea came to my mind. It was a risk, but it was a risk I felt I had to take. I crept back into her room and found a pen on her desk before going back to the bathroom. I left a note and my number, giving her the choice to do what she wanted. Because even though I knew I wanted her—that despite our lack of knowing each other, she fit with me—it felt like the right thing to do. The least creepy thing. I just had to believe she would text me or that our paths would cross again.

I polish off my burrito and walk down to the small beach. I toe off my shoes and stick my feet in the water. It's not too cold, and the connection with nature is a reminder of why I enjoy having a Winnebago instead of an apartment or a big house. I like being able to wake up in different places throughout the year, and I enjoy the freedom to walk out of my door and see something like this.

My thoughts wander to Jesse's bucket list. Some of them are things I've done, like seeing Old Faithful at Yellowstone and swimming naked in the ocean. Several oceans, to be exact. But a lot of them I haven't done, and I can't help but imagine doing them with her and seeing her smile every time she got to check something off her list.

By the time I'm done daydreaming like it's my job, an hour has passed, and a few families have come down to the water with blankets and picnic baskets. When my phone goes off, another spark lights inside my chest but is quickly doused when I see it's my sister. Not that I don't want to talk with her, but she's not the woman I was hoping would call me.

I hit accept and bring the phone to my ear. "Hey, little sis."

"Hey, big bro, what's up?"

"Nothing much, what's up with you?"

"Oh, you know, the big engagement party is tonight."

"You mean, you're out avoiding Mom in her party-planning mode?"

She chuckles. "When I left this morning, she was still trying to decide if her and Dad's outfits should match or not."

"Sounds like Mom."

"Anyway, just wanted to check in and make sure you got to town okay."

"Yeah, got in yesterday afternoon. I'm staying at Mendota County Park."

"Nice! You bring my nephew, too?"

"Of course. Though I'm not bringing him to the party." I can practically hear her pouting through the phone and laugh. "You need to get your own cat."

"I told you: Jordan is allergic."

"Right, right."

"Anyway, I'm waiting to get my nails done, but I wanted to tell you that my roommate is going to be at the party tonight. I want to introduce you."

"You trying to set me up with your roommate, Mellie?" I chuckle.

"Ugh. You know I hate when you call me that." I can practically see her frowning through the phone. "But yeah, I am," she continues. "She's a great woman."

While I'm sure Melissa isn't lying, it makes my stomach knot to think of meeting another woman after the night Jesse and I shared. "I'm not really looking right now," I say.

"Why?"

I pause. "It's complicated."

"Are you seeing someone?"

I want to say yes, but I don't know if Jesse will ever text or call me. For all I know, she's skeeved out by my note. Or worse, I read everything wrong last night and I was too forward or she didn't enjoy herself. Even though my rational brain knows that's not true, because I'd argue I fucked her into sleep.

"No," I finally answer, even though it kills me to do so. "I'm not."

Melissa giggles manically through the phone. "Okay, then. You can at least meet her. No harm in that."

"Mellie—"

"Oh! I've got to go. Nail time."

She rushes out a goodbye, and I exhale a long sigh before checking my messages. Sadly, there are still no missed calls or texts from Jesse, but I do have another work email. Duty calls. At least work can distract me from looking at my phone every two seconds. Maybe by tonight, Jesse will have contacted me. I can only hope.

Chapter Nine
Jesse

I HATE PARTIES. ACTUALLY, I think I hate all social gatherings. Or maybe it's just that I hate all social gatherings where someone I know isn't glued to my side at all times.

I wouldn't exactly call myself an introvert, as proven by hanging out with Miranda and Gina last night and dancing. But I'm not an extrovert, either. I'm a person who is fine being alone and likes my alone time, but I also like doing things. After last night, I see it's not so bad venturing out of my comfort zone. I can also be very chatty once I feel comfortable and after I get to know someone.

I worry sometimes that I talk too much, but I can't stand uncomfortable silences. That's why I always have a solid playlist ready when I'm traveling with someone—if we're not talking, at least the music fills the space.

"I'll take a gin and tonic please," I tell the bartender when it's finally my turn in line. The older man nods and gets to work making it while I look around the space.

Melissa's family rented out a nice venue downtown called The Stallion Inn. It's an old building from the 1950s, and it's super swanky. Everything is decorated in black and white. There are also lots of statues of white horses placed around the space.

Her family rented out the entire upper floor for the evening. It's packed with friends and family of both her and Jordan, meaning I don't know anyone. She warned me ahead of time that she didn't invite Kate, since they aren't close friends, and the only friends she's made in Madison besides me are coworkers at the hospital where she works. Of course I know Jordan, and I like him a lot, but we're not exactly besties.

The beautiful couple is currently talking to Melissa's cousins who came in from Michigan. Melissa told me to follow her around if I got uncomfortable, but I'm not going to hang on her like a lost puppy. My plan is to fill myself with alcohol and gluten-free desserts. Maybe if I get tipsy and hopped up on sugar, it will make conversing with strangers easier.

"Here you are."

The bartender slides me my drink, and I put a tip in the jar since it's an open bar—something you need at every Wisconsin party, or people will riot. Melissa may not be from here, but Jordan is. Jordan and I told her it was a must-have at any parties they throw but especially the wedding. Trust me, you don't come between Wisconsinites and their free alcohol at weddings.

I step away from the bar in search of a place to stand. There are some dining tables, but most of them are taken by older members of their family, and there are several standing tables around the perimeter for mingling. I see one open and make my way to it, setting my glass down after taking a long drink. When the awkwardness of doing nothing in the busy room gets to me, I give in and pull out my phone to pretend I'm texting someone but instead look at flights to Yellowstone and Maine.

My plan to spend the afternoon mapping out my bucket list fell to the wayside. I couldn't stop thinking about my conversation with Melissa. Despite my desire to keep things a one-night stand with Ash, I started wondering if I could sleep with him again and walk away. He would be leaving town, after all.

It led to me staring at my phone for hours on end, nearly texting him. It didn't help that I could still feel the ghost of his lips on my skin and the ache of him between my thighs. Maybe Melissa is right. Not about him being my person but about seeing him again. It would be stupid to not want to experience his amazing bedroom skills again, right? What if my next hookup is like my ex and isn't good with his mouth or they don't make me come like he could?

I take another sip of my drink, feeling the gin burn down my throat and help loosen my stiff muscles. I could change my list to a two-night stand. Or maybe he'd be open to me trying that last item I'd scratched out on my list? It *did* feel good to tell him what I wanted last night...

Feeling braver with the alcohol coursing through my system, I open up the text message I'd written to Ash but never sent.

ME:

> Hey, it's Jesse called Jesse.

A simple text, not complicated. Yes, I could make this work. A two-night stand. Or crossing that last item off if I can get myself to do it. This way, there would still be no attachment or possibility of a situationship since he's leaving.

My finger hovers over the send button, but before I can, a message pops up from Kate. I'd texted her earlier to ask if she was alive since she never texted to tell me she got home safe last night. If I hadn't seen her social media post of her at the farmers market this afternoon, I would've been concerned.

I close my unsent message to Ash for the millionth time today and open Kate's.

KATE:

> Hey! Sorry, today got away from me. I'm alive.

ME:

> Good to hear.

KATE:

> Did you end up meeting someone after I left?

My desire to tell her no is strong. The more I thought about what she did last night, the more upset I got. She was really going to try to pawn the bartender off on me. It made me feel like she didn't think anyone would want to hook up with me, something Kate knew I already struggled with prior to last night. Hence Melissa's note about being thin on my bucket list.

My entire life, I've been fat. And since my heart attacks, I've focused more on learning to love myself and be proud of my body for being strong and helping me survive.

But the trauma from a lifetime of living in a bigger body in a society that tells you it's wrong doesn't go away overnight. I'm not used to men calling me stunning in bars or wanting to hook up with me. So the fact Kate was going to pass Luke off on me as if I was a charity case made me angry. Really angry. Nobody should be treated like that—especially not by someone who claims to care about you.

KATE:

> It's okay if you went home. Luke was a decent lay, if you want me to text him for you. I bet he'd be game.

If it was possible to explode into flames, I probably would. I reread the text multiple times, wondering if I read it right. Every time I read it, I get more pissed. I take the drink in front of me and practically inhale it, the urge to text Ash stronger than it's been all day. I don't need pity fucks or my friend's help to have someone want to be with me. Ash was—is—proof of that.

I open my unsent message and place my thumb over it, but I'm stopped again from sending it when a body crashes into me from behind. My stomach hits the standing table, and it wobbles back and forth, nearly sending my empty glass of ice with a lime wedge to the ground. I manage to catch the glass, but my phone falls and hits the ground—thankfully face up so the screen doesn't crack.

"Oh shit, I'm so sorry."

The warmth of the male voice makes the hair on my arms stand up. A man with familiar brown curls bends down to grab my phone, and when he stands and hands it to me, I'm not sure who's more stunned: Asher or me.

"Jesse?" he asks, disbelief making his voice crack.

My lower abs contract, and my mouth falls open. I'm sure I look like a fish out of water. The man I was about to text is standing in front of me, as if I manifested him straight from my thoughts. His gaze travels down my body, and the crooked smile from yesterday appears on his lips as he takes me in. I'm wearing a dress in a similar style to yesterday's in emerald green, except this one zips in the back and the neckline is slightly more conservative. I didn't want to flash all my goods to Melissa's family.

"Are you alright?" he asks, grin turning to a furrowed brow and concerned frown. "I hope I didn't hit you too hard. I wasn't paying attention."

I blink at him, still not quite believing he's here. I close my mouth and swallow, my fingers flexing around my phone nervously over seeing him again. "I'm fine, just..."

"...shocked to see me?" he finishes.

I nod in answer as he sticks his hands in the pockets of his dark-brown slacks, my eyes taking time to study his form. He looks handsome in his dress clothes. The chocolate-colored sport coat and caramel-colored undershirt make his brown eyes stand out. If I could swim in them, I would. They're like pools of rich melted chocolate or espresso.

"I'm shocked, too," he says, "but I can't say I'm mad about it. Can I tell you a secret?"

My eyes fall from his gaze to his perfect lips, lips that did wicked things to me last night. Lips I've been dreaming of all day.

I nod again, unable to find my words. He takes a step forward so no one around can hear. "I've been checking my phone nonstop hoping to see a text from you. That's why I ran into you. Talk about fate."

My heart beats faster, the thumping more pronounced to the point I can literally feel each time the muscle contracts and expands. *Boom. Boom. Boom.* The doctor told me it can be a rare side effect from the ICD implant, that it's my heart contracting around the wire inside of it. I'm still getting used to it, and my hand automatically flies to my chest.

Ash's eyes drop to follow the motion, and I see the moment he spots the scar I didn't cover up tonight. I didn't notice till after I got here that I forgot to put concealer on it, and I didn't wear one of the bandages, either.

Thankfully, I haven't talked to many people since arriving so nobody has stared at it or asked me questions. But I can already see curiosity sparking in Asher's eyes, which is exactly why I usually cover it. I wonder if he's thinking about the moment he kissed it, though.

Because I'm thinking about it now, too.

His eyes flick to mine, and we gaze at each other. I should say something, tell him I was just about to text him, too. That maybe it is fate, even if I try not to believe in romantic notions like that anymore.

When he smiles again, this time wider, puzzle pieces I didn't know were missing lock into place, and I nearly gasp. Brown eyes, curly brown hair, only in town for a few days. Good-looking, nice—

"Oh good, I see you met my brother."

My eyes grow wide from the sound of Melissa's voice at the same time Ash's do. I turn to meet the excited smile of my best friend and nearly laugh at how crazy this is.

"I was hoping you'd find him; I wanted to introduce you," she adds with a smirk, one that looks so similar to Asher's I feel like an idiot for not putting it all together sooner.

I fucked Melissa's brother. And I told her all about it.

Chapter Ten

Asher

OUT OF ALL THE people in the world, the woman I've been obsessing over for just shy of twenty-four hours is my little sister's friend. And now that I think of it, she's probably the roommate Melissa's mentioned on our sporadic phone calls. I have a vague memory of a J name, and I'm going to assume it's Jesse.

Damn. The universe has a funny way of doing things, but I can't say I'm not here for it.

I consider my next move. Jesse looks shocked and embarrassed, but I, on the other hand, am struggling not to smile. My sister and I have never been weird about dating each other's friends because we both know we're good people. Have I pulled the big brother card a time or two on guys I thought weren't good for her? Yes. But she dated a friend of mine when she was in college, and she's tried to set me up with her friends a few times. It's not a big deal because we'd rather have people we like in our family than assholes.

I bite the inside of my cheek, clearly getting ahead of myself like I have been since the moment I laid eyes on her. Jesse hasn't texted me today, and I don't know if she was ever going to. I knew I was going to have to let her go if that was the case, even if it felt like a punch to the gut to think that way. But now, here we are. I ran into her at my sister's engagement party of all places.

"Everyone okay?" Melissa asks.

I turn my attention from Jesse to my sister. She looks confused, and rightly so. We've been standing here staring after her introductions and not saying a word. I shift my eyes back to Jesse and gesture to her with my hand, wanting her to take the lead. I'm not shy—I'd tell my sister Jesse and I already met—but I'm not sure if she's comfortable with it.

Jesse shifts on her feet until she's looking Melissa in the eye. "Ash and I already met."

"I gathered that." She laughs.

"No, Melissa." Jesse takes a breath. "We met last night."

There's a pause as Melissa's smile falters, her eyes tracking back and forth as her brain processes the information. Then she's laughing, a boisterous laugh that catches the eye of several of our distant relatives I never see and don't remember the names of.

"And how did you meet last night?" she eggs on her friend.

Jesse flushes the shade of rose that is now my favorite color and tucks a strand of her curled hair behind her ear. "Don't make me say it."

Her answer tells me everything I need to know: She spoke with my sister about our night together. Which, ew. I know my sister; she likes details, information. Lots of information. It's what makes her a good nurse. If Jesse did tell her, I know for a fact she asked her to paint a vivid picture. *Very* vivid.

Melissa frowns, then, before long, her face screws up. "Wait—he's—oh god." She makes a gagging noise that draws more attention to us. I rub the back of my neck as a great aunt walks by and asks Melissa if she's okay.

She waves her off, and then Melissa is tugging both Jesse and I by the hands toward a pair of French doors. The warm summer air hits me, a drastic change from the air conditioning we were just in. My hands feel clammy now, but I'm glad we're safely out of earshot of family members.

Once the doors are closed, Melissa turns to us, hands on her hips.

"I didn't know," Jesse blurts out.

"Oh, I'm not mad, you should know that after our talk earlier. Remember what I said?"

Melissa and Jesse share one of those silent conversations only women can have with each other that I'm not even going to attempt to interpret before Melissa turns her focus on me.

"I just—oh god." Melissa screws up her face. "I need to burn some things from my memory, but now I need different kinds of details. Like how did you two not figure it out?"

"We weren't exactly asking each other our family history," I say.

That makes Melissa gag again. "You know what? I don't need to know."

"You asked." I shrug.

She slugs me in the arm like she's done since we were kids. I wince and rub the smarting muscle. I'm about to ask her why she did that when she looks at Jesse. "Are you okay?" she asks her.

My focus turns to the woman in question, and I see she's still flushed. I watch as Melissa's eyes track to the scar below Jesse's left clavicle. I'd noticed it a few minutes ago when I'd run into her, the memory of kissing the bandage covering it last night coming to mind. I've seen scars like that before, but my mind can't place exactly what it is or what kind of injury would cause it. Broken collarbone, maybe? But that doesn't seem right.

"Yeah, fine. Processing everything. It's all a little weird. He's your brother," Jesse reiterates.

"It is, isn't it?" Melissa asks. "But while it may be weird—and this will sound weird when I say it—I'm glad it was my brother."

Jesse flushes harder, and by the embarrassment on her face, I think she'd prefer that I wasn't standing here for this conversation. "I'm gonna let you two talk. I'll go bother Jordan for a bit and find you both later."

Jesse eyes me gratefully, and Melissa nods. "We'll find you later," my sister says. "If people ask where I am, distract them with your singing skills."

"I can't sing."

"Exactly."

My chest shakes with laughter at my sister's comments before I smile again at Jesse, a promise that I'm not leaving here until we talk again.

Chapter Eleven

Jesse

"WHAT A TURN OF events," Melissa says. "I think I need a drink."

"I need ten."

We both break out into laughter, though hers is joyful and mine is more nervous.

"But seriously, I can't believe you slept with my brother!"

"Small world?" I shrug, still not believing it myself. "I totally forgot your brother's name was Asher. You don't bring him up often, and when you do, it's usually 'big brother' or some variation."

"It's okay. I told you to sleep with him earlier, remember? He's a good guy. And like I said, it's weird to say, but I'm glad last night was him. Better than some asshole."

"You're right; it is weird for you to say."

She chuckles. "Well, even if I'm glad it was him, I still need to burn my brain. I could have gone my entire life and the afterlife without knowing the details."

"You wanted them."

"Yeah, before I knew it was my brother."

I cringe. "If I could take them back, I would."

Melissa walks to the balcony's stone railing, looking out at the fountain in the small courtyard below. I follow her, leaning on the railing next to her.

"Did you end up texting him after I left?" she asks.

I run my hands along the cool stone. "I didn't." I pause, turning to her. She's beautiful with her hair perfectly curly and her sparkly white cocktail dress hugging her curves. "But I was going to."

"You were?"

I nod. "I know I said I wouldn't, but I got to thinking about what you told me. I was going to make it a two-night stand. But Ash ran into me before I could send the text."

"Okay. That should be a good thing, but you're frowning." She points to my mouth where my lips are, in fact, turned down.

"That's because he's your brother. I know you said it's not weird, but it is. Especially since he said he's leaving town in a few days. I don't want you to think it'll be more than what it is."

"I won't think that. Have whatever fun you want, Jesse. Just don't tell me the details again."

I chuckle. "You're one of a kind. I don't think a lot of people would be fine hearing any of this."

"I'm not most people. I love you, and I love my brother. And if you end up getting married, we'd be sisters."

I stare blankly at her. "I just said I didn't want you to think it'll be more than a fling, and now you're planning our future?"

"I can't help it," she whines. "I'm a hopeless romantic, remember? I thought you were, too, at one point."

Not wanting to get into her uncomfortably accurate observation, I place my hands on her shoulders. "I'm not going to sleep with, date, or marry your brother, okay?"

"But maybe you'll change your mind."

Her tone is so hopeful, I can't be annoyed or frustrated with her. "Let's not talk about this anymore. I doubt anything is going to happen between us now, anyway."

"But—"

"It's for the best. You should get back to your party. I'm sure people are missing you."

She groans. "My feet hurt, and I've had to tell the story of how Jordan and I met a million times."

"It's a funny story, and it's your engagement party. Not to mention, not many people can say they met their husband by puking on his shoes."

"I had bad sushi the night before I met him."

"A totally valid reason to puke on someone's shoes."

She smiles and looks through the doors to the party. I follow her gaze to see Asher speaking with Jordan. They're laughing about something, and I'm happy my friend's fiancé very obviously gets along with her brother.

I watch them for another moment until my eyes gravitate to only Ash. I admire him again in his brown suit. He really is handsome, exactly the type of guy I used to imagine myself with. Big, broad, someone who could throw me around, even at my size.

"Ahem."

My attention snaps back to Melissa and her loud throat clearing. The smug look on her face makes me blush, but I roll my eyes at her. "Don't get that look on your face. I stand by my earlier statement. I think it's best if nothing happens. He's your brother, and he's leaving soon. It's a sign to keep what we had a one-night stand and not complicate things."

While I say the words, I'm not sure I believe them. But in the end, I do think it's the right thing to do. I have my bucket-list items to check off, and I'm not going to delay them or screw them up.

Yes, it's better this way. For everyone.

"Or it's a sign to give him a shot?" Melissa tries.

"Melissa," I chide. "I know you're already planning our wedding in your head, but push those thoughts out of your mind right now."

Melissa opens her mouth, but I put my hand over her lips. "No, no. Let's move on." I lift my hand.

She groans. "Fine. Let's go back inside before my mom comes looking for me."

I grab her hand and squeeze it. "You look hot, by the way."

"Oh, this old thing?" she jokes, running her hands down her dress.

We both giggle, and I open the doors so I can tug her through and back into the party. Jordan spots us, waving us over to him and Ash. I try to ignore the way Asher's eyes follow me as we approach, his intense brown irises tracking my every movement. Thankfully, he doesn't focus on my scar; instead, his eyes land on my face, and he licks his lips.

My stomach flips, and yet again, I find myself wishing I was Jesse before my life changed. When I was living under the guise of being perfectly normal and didn't have the burden of wondering if every breath I take could be my last. The romantic version that imagined a Prince Charming, a man like Asher. Someone who liked me just as I am: plump body, tall stature, and all.

If I had met him before my heart attacks, I would have wanted him to want more. *I* would have wanted more. Or at least, I hope I would've.

"Hey, baby," Jordan greets Melissa. She folds into his side with ease as I stand next to Ash, my hands awkwardly at my sides. Damn, I wish this dress had pockets. "And hello again, Jesse," Jordan adds.

"Hello again." I smile as Melissa places her hand on his chest, showing off her massive diamond ring. Jordan is an anesthesiologist at the hospital where Melissa works and spared no expense for that baby. He's a great guy and super cute—tall and lanky with a square jaw, dark hair, and glasses. He and Melissa look like they were made for each other.

"What were you guys talking about?" Melissa asks.

"Ash was telling me about his travels around the US."

"Ah yes, my brother, the nomad. Where were you before this?"

Asher grips a cocktail he must have gotten before we came in and looks from me to his sister. "I was out in California—Joshua Tree, to be exact. Spent a couple of weeks floating around campsites while I got some work done."

"What are you working on now?" Jordan asks.

"I have a project I've been doing for a hospital in London. I had a lot of virtual meetings and development sessions, so it was easy to be in one place for a while because of the long days."

"You go to London next month to help them install, right?" Melissa asks.

My curiosity spikes at that. I knew her brother lived in his RV and traveled around the US, but I don't know what his job was or why he prefers living the way he does.

Asher's gaze flashes to mine, and it's almost as if he's hesitant to answer the question. After another second, he nods. "Yeah, I'll be there for two months."

My heart shouldn't sink at the information; I have no reason or rhyme for it to. I find myself repeating that what we had is nothing more than what it was. Even if we did want more, he's leaving. And not just to another city in the US but literally over an ocean.

"I don't know how you do it, man," Jordan remarks. "Living in an RV, traveling to other countries. Sounds difficult, a little lonely. I couldn't go that long without seeing my friends and family."

"Ash likes his work, and he likes to be alone. He travels with his little furry son, GusGus," Melissa says.

"You have a dog?" I ask. Maybe that's why he left this morning before I woke up.

He shakes his head. "A cat."

My lips turn up as I imagine Asher with a cat. I've always wanted to get one but never did. Before I left my last admin job at a local plumbing company to take care of my health, I worked long hours, banking overtime to put in savings. Then everything with my heart happened, and I wasn't going to get an animal during all that.

"I still can't believe you adopted a cat." Melissa laughs. "You hate cats."

Ash sips his drink with a smile. "It may be cheesy, but he chose me."

I can't help but smile because it *is* cheesy. Ash's eyes find mine, and for a moment, we stare at each other before Melissa breaks in with a loud, "*Awww.*"

"It's true," he adds.

"My brother, the cat daddy. Never thought I'd see the day."

The label makes Asher screw up his nose, and the rest of us laugh.

"And how have you been feeling, Jesse?" Jordan asks.

The question coupled with my name makes me freeze. My eyes dart from Jordan to Melissa, who looks apologetic, then to Ash. His forehead is wrinkled in curiosity, and I know I'm not going to be rude and not answer Jordan. He's been here for me right alongside Melissa, especially since he works in medicine, too. He even recommended the current cardiologist I'm seeing.

"Good. Everything looks good."

"Great to hear. The implant incision is healing nicely."

I swear everyone's eyes zoom in on my scar as he says it, and my cheeks burn hot. This is exactly why I like to cover it up. Maybe when it heals, I'll be more comfortable, and it should fade a lot over the years.

"Thanks," I say eventually.

There's a pause in the conversation, and I feel Asher's gaze hard on me. I know he's wondering what Jordan's talking about, and I decide to throw him a bone. I may not want the attention on me, and I know I don't owe him anything, but I hate when I feel like the odd man out in a conversation. "I have a heart condition caused by Kawasaki disease. It's something you get as a kid, but if it's not caught or treated quickly enough, it can cause heart complications in the future."

"What kind of complications?" Asher asks, tone serious now.

"I've had two heart attacks, and I received an ICD implant about two months ago due to life-threatening arrhythmia."

Melissa reaches for my hand and squeezes it. "Jesse here is a survivor. A fucking badass."

I flush at her praise and drop her hand. "It is what it is."

"You're too humble."

"No kidding," Jordan adds.

I brush them off with a smile, knowing if they continue, I'll get emotional. "I'm fine now, feeling good. My meds are finally working to keep my v-tach episodes down, and now things can go back to normal. I can finally live a little."

"Oh, yeah! How's the bucket list coming along? Melissa mentioned you were trying to plan some travel before your new job starts," Jordan chirps happily.

The mention of the bucket list has me blushing to high hell. Asher's attentive gaze is on me, but I can't bring myself to look at him. Not only does he know why I have the scar now, but he also is—was—a bucket-list item.

Melissa grabs my hand again, and I meet her eyes. She's apologetic, but she has nothing to be sorry for. I knew she told Jordan about the list—not about the sexual stuff but that I had one. I don't expect her to keep things from him. It's also a well-known fact that Jordan has no filter and often brings up things he shouldn't.

At the silence, Jordan looks around the group and scratches his chin. "Did I say something I wasn't supposed to?"

I shake my head and find my voice, not wanting him to feel bad. "No, you're fine. The list is coming along. Hoping to get to Yellowstone, and if I can get a good flight deal, Maine before the end of the month."

"Maine is a beautiful place," Ash's deep voice adds. "Have you ever been?"

I shake my head, still feeling embarrassed over the last five minutes of conversation. "I haven't been to a lot of places. Just Minnesota, Illinois, and Arizona."

"Seriously?" Jordan asks.

"My family didn't travel much."

"Maybe you should be a nomad with Ash for a bit before that new job of yours starts. Driving is easier than flying these days," Jordan says it like a joke, but I see the moment Melissa's face lights up like fireworks on the Fourth of July. She kisses Jordan's cheek and bounces on her toes.

"You're a genius, babe."

Jordan smiles. "Um, thanks?"

"He was kidding," I add quickly.

"It's a good idea."

My head snaps to Asher's, and I stare slack-mouthed at him. His brown eyes are pools of several different emotions. Curiosity, maybe, mixed with concern and a sparkle of excitement. Is he really considering this?

My stomach flips, and Melissa grabs my bicep. "Honestly, I don't know why I didn't think of it. Ash's RV is big enough!"

"No, I can't—"

"It's plenty big," Ash interjects. "Probably too big. I have my bedroom, and there's another room with a twin bed."

Melissa claps. "It's perfect."

I shake my head. "You have your own life, places you want to go and work you need to do. I'm not going to intrude like that."

Ash's features are serious as he says, "You won't be. I don't mind going anywhere you want. I just need to be back before I fly to London at the beginning of September."

"See!" Melissa says. "It *is* perfect. You start your job at the same time!"

I go to speak right as Jordan's mom comes over and interrupts. "Honey, we need you and Melissa for some pictures."

Jordan groans but agrees, taking Melissa's hand and kissing her knuckles. Before they can leave, my friend turns to me and locks our eyes together. "Talk to Asher, and please consider it. It seems too much like fate."

The mention of fate again has my heart pounding, but I press my lips together and nod. I'm not saying it to Melissa now, but there's no way I'm going to consider it. It would be insane to do what she's suggesting.

Once they're both gone, I stand awkwardly next to Asher.

"Want to go somewhere and talk?" he asks. There's a gentle smile on his face as he swirls his drink around in his glass. When I don't immediately answer, he continues, "Or we can stay here. Or I can walk away."

I appreciate that there's no pressure in his tone, so I agree to talk. There's no harm in speaking with him even if I'm going to say no. Besides, it would be nice to connect about everything that's gone down between us without strangers around.

"Let's go outside," I say.

His gentle smile turns to the lopsided one I came to know last night. I can't help but mirror his smile. He downs the last of his drink and sets the empty glass on the table, motioning for me to walk ahead of him.

I turn toward the balcony, but before I can take more than a couple of steps, I feel his hand on my lower back. I shiver when his breath whispers against my hair. "Let's go down to the courtyard; we can walk and talk."

I turn my head, the action bringing my face close to his. Words leave me, so I simply nod, not trusting my voice.

Ash maneuvers us through the crowd, his hand warm against my back. I won't say it out loud, but I like the way it feels. It's comforting and the support I need at this moment. A lot has happened in the span of twenty-four hours, and to be honest, I'm exhausted, both mentally and physically. I just haven't let myself completely feel it.

The walk down the steps to the courtyard is quiet. Ash doesn't try to speak, and neither do I, yet his hand never moves from my back.

Once we're away from partygoers, it's like I can breathe again. I suck air into my lungs, and Ash drops back, putting both his hands into his slacks as we start a slow walk around the perimeter, following a path surrounded by various flowers and lit with twinkling lights. The fountain's water splashing echoes in the quietness, and when I look at Asher, he's watching me with that lopsided grin of his tugging at his lips.

I want to say something, fill the space of silence as I usually do, but I hold it in until we've taken a lap. "I really am fine," I eventually say, "if you're wondering."

"I thought your name was Jesse," he teases, taking me back to our conversation last night.

A small laugh escapes me, and some of the tension that built upstairs eases. "You know what I mean."

He cocks his head so he can study me as we continue to walk. "I was hoping, after the night we shared together, you'd be more than just *fine*."

My heart rate picks up, and he smirks. He knows I was referring to my health but chose not to make it about that. I appreciate that more than he knows. All I've done for the past couple of years is talk about my heart, my condition, how I am. I don't want to talk about it anymore.

"Are you just fine?" he asks.

My pulse flutters even faster now. "More than fine."

His easy steps turn into more of a swagger. "Good to hear. On a scale of one to ten, ten being the best, what would you rate it?"

I bark a laugh. "The sex?"

"The sex, me...both."

I glance around, glad there's still nobody in the courtyard to hear this conversation. "I'm not going to answer that!"

He runs a hand through his brown tresses. "I know what I would rate us." He stops near a bench, and I stop with him, his body turning to face mine.

"I don't know if—"

"An eleven." He grins. "Actually, twenty."

I laugh again. "You said one through ten."

"I changed the rules."

I sit on the bench and cross my legs, looking up at him. "Do you do that often?"

He drops down next to me, spreading his arms over the back of the bench so his fingers could brush the tips of my hair if he wanted. "I've been known to do that, yes."

I think about the little I know of Ash and the time I spent with him. His nomad lifestyle, his forwardness, his note on my bucket list. Rule-breaking would be in line with his personality, which is the opposite of me.

"Makes sense," I say.

"How so?"

"Take my bucket list, for instance," I echo my thoughts. "The comment you left—you suggested changing the item on my list."

He chuckles, the sound low and warm. "That's true. But to be fair, I had good reason to." He pauses to meet my eyes. "Maybe it's selfish, but I wanted to see you again."

His gaze is nearly too intense, but I manage to hold it. "I guess you got your wish."

Ash smiles softly, and I swear I feel the ghost of his finger brushing the ends of my hair before he pulls his arms down and places his hands on his knees. "I guess I did."

There's a pause of silence, and I drop my eyes to look at my hands. This could be an opportunity to tell him I wanted to see him again, too, that I was texting him when he bumped into me. But I've made up my mind for real this time. And we need to talk about the conversation upstairs.

"Your offer to travel with you was very generous," I say, "but I think it's for the best that we part ways after tonight."

He frowns. "Why do you say that?"

Because you're my best friend's brother, because we slept together, because I can't let myself fall for you. It's not part of my new plan! my brain screams.

I play with the silver ring I have on my finger and sigh quietly. "We're practically strangers, Ash. People don't just get in a stranger's RV and go on a road trip with them for a month."

"Sure they do; happens all the time."

"Yeah, in murder documentaries!"

"This is the second time you've brought up being murdered. I'm getting concerned."

His smile is back, and it makes my heart skip a beat. "Yeah, well, I'm a woman. We have to be concerned about these things."

Ash takes my hand from my thigh and squeezes it. All my focus is now on him and the way my hand feels in his, the way his mouth opens as he speaks. "I'm not going to murder you. You're my sister's friend."

"If I wasn't, you'd murder me?"

Ash groans. "I'm not going to murder you, and I haven't murdered anyone else."

"Just pussies?"

"Not real ones but yours, yes."

I was already hot, and now I've begun to sweat. "You're impossible."

"You're hilarious."

I tug my hand back and tuck a strand of hair behind my ear. "Okay, take out the murder equation, and it's still a bad idea."

"Why?"

"Because we've slept together."

"People who sleep together travel in RVs together, too. Happens all the time."

I throw up my hands, but the laugh that comes from my chest is loud and happy. "You really are impossible."

"Not impossible, possible."

"God," I say under my breath. "If I were to go, we wouldn't be sleeping together."

"So you're saying 'if'?"

"I didn't—"

"You did." He grins. "You said 'if.' Next, you say 'when.'"

"Ash." I groan. "It's not a good idea."

"It is."

"I don't know how you can think that. This is your life, your home."

"Will you hear me out for a minute at least? I want to plead my case."

"Are you a lawyer now?"

"No, I'm a tech nerd."

I stare at him and realize how much sense that makes. I may not know him well, but he's smart, quick thinking. Definitely a hot nerd. No wonder I like him—I've always had a thing for hot nerds.

"Did you glitch for a second?" he asks.

I smile despite myself. "Fine. Plead your case—you have one minute."

"Why am I on a timer?"

I grin wider. "I don't know; it sounded cool. And now the clock's ticking, Asher called Ash. Plead your case."

He chuffs a laugh from his chest, and I consider taking out my phone to clock him but decide against it. He genuinely looks stressed by the idea of having a time limit.

"Okay, fine." He rubs the back of his neck. "The bucket list obviously is important to you, and while I don't like that my future brother-in-law spilled your medical history in front of me like that—that's gotta be a HIPAA violation or something—"

"He's not my doctor."

Asher nearly rolls his eyes and shushes me, the action making me bite back a laugh.

"Anyway, I don't know all you've been through, but from what I heard, it's a lot. I can put together the reasons for your bucket list, and I want to help you cross them off."

"So you want to help me because you pity me?"

He sits straighter, and his face morphs into that of anger and fear. "What? No! I could never, Jesse. Never."

When I take a breath and genuinely see the worry on his face, I see I've snapped about that a little too easily. Ash didn't do anything to deserve that comment. He's been nothing but kind. I guess Jordan bringing up my health annoyed me more than I thought.

"Sorry, I—that was a big assumption."

He takes my hand again and squeezes. "Don't apologize—I should reword that. When I saw your list in the bathroom, I didn't know why you put it together. And while I apologize for invading your privacy and reading it, I thought it was really cool."

"You did?"

He nods. "A lot of people go through life with a bucket list, yet they will never write it down or even try to cross them off if they do. Maybe what they want is too scary or too far out of reach for them to even consider it a possibility. But you're being brave. You're taking action. I admire that quality in people, and I admire you."

I fight back the heat that rises in my body. "It's not that big of a deal."

"It is, though. It really is. And maybe I'm selfish in this as well, but I want to help you. It sounds fun. I'm glad Jordan thought of it, because it really is perfect. He also mentioned something about a new job starting soon?"

"Yeah, in September," I say, a warm feeling developing in my stomach. He was paying close enough attention to remember that detail.

"Then we can make a plan and knock out as many as we can before then."

"And what about your plans?"

"I didn't have any for this month. I thought about going to Michigan for a bit to spend more time with my parents, but I can do that when I get back from London. All you have to do is tell me where you want to go, Jesse, and we'll go there."

"This all seems too easy."

"Why can't it be?"

I look down at our hands, still linked, and squeeze until he follows my gaze. We both stare at our interlocked fingers before I speak. "Like it or not, Ash, we have a history now. That complicates things."

He lets out a long breath. "Then we won't be anything more than friends." I look up into his eyes and see he's being serious. He keeps going. "There's no denying I'm attracted to you, and my note on your bucket list said all you need to know about if I would make our one-night stand more than that. But I like you, Jesse, and I want you to be comfortable. I'm taking your list seriously, and I'm taking you seriously."

"That plea was longer than a minute."

His crooked smile appears. "You didn't stop me."

"No, I didn't." I turn my attention back to our hands again, and when I look up, he's still watching me, waiting for me to speak again. "You really think we can do this?"

"I do."

"And you're fine with us just being friends?"

He doesn't hesitate before he dips his chin, and for a brief moment, I feel that earlier disappointment. Even if us being friends is what I want—or at least what I tell myself I have to want—it truly feels like the closing of a book.

"That means no sex," I reiterate. His lip quirks at the corner as if he knows I'm saying it to convince myself more than him.

"What kind of bucket-list helper would I be if I slept with you again and ruined your first bucket-list item?"

I remove my hand from his, immediately missing the weight of it, and rub my palm over my forehead. "We're not going to call you the bucket-list helper."

He grins wider now, to the point it overtakes his whole face.

"What's that look for?" I ask.

"Does that mean you agree?"

I blow a breath, my lips flapping comically. "I feel like you're going to show up at my apartment in your RV and drag me with you no matter what I say."

He laughs. "It's possible."

I look away so I can think about it for another minute. This is a big decision, something I should probably sleep on. But since my first heart attack, I've become less and less able to stop myself from making quick decisions. A side-effect of almost dying twice, I guess. Or at least that's what I tell myself when I say the next words.

"Okay, let's do it."

His features light up, eyes joyful. My body buzzes from the excitement I feel radiating off him, and I find myself smiling wide, too. Even if I feel like I might throw up.

"You're serious?" he asks.

"Don't ask me that, or I may change my mind." He mimes zipping his lips and throwing away the key. My shoulders shake, and I rub my now sweaty hands on my thighs. "Just promise me one thing?"

"Anything for you, Jesse called Jesse."

My heart skips a beat, and I wet my lips. "That we cross some items off your bucket list, too."

His smile warms. "I don't have one."

"Bullshit."

He holds up his hands. "I'm not bullshitting you. But I'll make one, and we can cross some off mine, too." There's a twinkle in his eye when he says it, and I wonder if maybe I'll come to regret my request at some point.

He stands a moment later. "Leaving?" I ask.

"Yep, I have a lot of cleaning to do."

I press my lips together to try not to laugh at how serious he looks. "This is your sister's engagement party."

He shrugs. "I did my rounds. She won't even notice I'm gone."

"She'll notice."

"I'll say goodbye to her, don't worry."

Ash offers me his hand to stand from the bench, and I shake my head. "I'm going to sit out here for a bit longer."

"You sure? Do you want me to stay?"

The desire to tell him yes is strong, but I shake my head. "I'm good. You go do whatever you need to do."

Ash puts his hands into his pockets, looking down at me for a moment before he finally nods. "Text me tomorrow, and we'll figure out a time to connect about logistics and details."

Excitement and anxiety of the unknown fills my chest, but a smile pulls at my lips nonetheless. "Okay, I will."

"Good." He exhales. "Talk to you later."

"Talk to you later."

Asher turns toward the doors, but before he gets too far, he stops and looks at me over his shoulder. "Oh, and Jesse?"

"Yes?"

"I hope you like cats with an attitude." Ash smirks.

I chuckle. "I do."

Ash walks through the door with my answer hanging in the air.

Chapter Twelve

Jesse

I YAWN AS I stand next to Melissa. I'm not exactly a late riser, but it's seven in the morning, and I haven't gotten much sleep these past couple of days with all the planning for my sudden road trip with Asher. But despite my tiredness, I'm both excited and nervous.

"Are you sure you have everything you need?" Melissa asks.

I look at the two bags and my backpack sitting on the floor next to the door of my apartment. "Yeah, it should be plenty."

"If I was going, I would end up taking over half of Asher's RV with my stuff."

"The RV's name is Winnie," Asher interjects as he walks to us from our apartment hallway, wiping his wet hands on his jeans after using the bathroom.

"What?" Melissa asks.

"The RV, her name is Winnie. And let's be honest, you'd fill the entire bedroom and the dinette area. Maybe more."

"Whatever," Melissa says. "Let's talk about why you named your RV Winnie." She smirks.

"I'm going to assume it's because it's a Winnebago?" I state the obvious.

Ash stands next to me and shakes his head. "It's a Winnebago Chieftain to be exact, and you'd think that would be the obvious answer, but no. That's not why."

Melissa crosses her arms over her chest. "Oh my god, Asher. Please tell me it's not because of your weird crush on Winnie from 'The Wonder Years.' You used to watch Nick At Nite obsessively when you were a kid."

"That crush wasn't weird, but no. That's not it, either."

I watch the sibling interaction with amusement before I snap my fingers. "Winnie the Pooh."

Ash's eyes widen at me as Melissa lets out a peel of high-pitched laughter. "That can't be it!"

When Ash doesn't answer, Melissa's eyes bug out of her head. "You named your RV after Winnie the Pooh?"

He shrugs. "Yeah, so what? If you remember, that was another favorite of mine."

She lets out another bark of laughter. "You're such a softie, Ash."

"Nothing wrong with that," I add.

Ash's smiling eyes meet mine. "Thank you, Jesse. Winnie the Pooh is iconic. And it also works because, yes, the RV is a Winnebago. And I also had a crush on Winnie from 'The Wonder Years.'"

"The truth comes out!" Melissa says.

"I wasn't lying about Pooh."

I look between the bantering siblings. It's nice to see they have a fun relationship. "I think it's a good name no matter why you did it," I say.

"Thank you, Jesse. I think so, too." Ash and I stare at each other for a moment—probably too long—before Melissa claps her hands together. I jump at the loud noise and turn to see her looking between the two of us with a silly grin on her face.

I've told her a million times in the last couple of days that nothing further is going to happen between me and her brother, especially since we're going to be in close quarters, yet she refuses to believe it. But I still hold firm to the plan Ash and I now have in place, one that involves a lot of driving and no sex.

We're going to check off bucket-list items and be back here in twenty days. That way, we both have time to get ready for our jobs. We have a lot of places to squeeze in, but we have a solid plan, and Ash is determined to check off my entire list—something I didn't think would happen so soon, let alone in twenty days.

"Okay, do you have your medications?" Melissa asks.

"Yes, Mom."

"Hey! You know it's the nurse in me."

"I know." I step forward, my back to Ash, so I can place my hands on Melissa's shoulders. "And I know you worry. But if I need anything, there are pharmacies on the road. I'm going to be fine."

"I know you are, and I trust my brother to take care of you if anything goes wrong."

"Scout's honor," Ash says. I turn my head and see he's holding up three fingers dutifully. Makes me wonder if he actually was a Boy Scout. I wouldn't be surprised if he was.

I give my attention back to Melissa, and she looks down at the scar that's covered by my T-shirt then into my eyes. "Do you have all your medical cards on your person in case the defibrillator is activated and you need to call your doctors?"

I shake her a bit. "Yes, but I'm not going to get shocked. At least, I hope not. My meds are working, and I'm at a low risk for that to take place. I'm good. Really."

The back of my neck prickles under Asher's stare. Despite the fact that we got together with Melissa the other morning to map out our trip, I haven't told him more about the effects of Kawasaki disease on my body or my implant.

I know I need to have that discussion with him since we're traveling together for a long period of time. He deserves to know so he can be prepared on the off chance something does happen. But I haven't wanted to yet. For a short period of time, I wanted to pretend that I was just a normal person getting ready for a road trip—nothing more, nothing less. I guess that's over now.

"Alright." Melissa half-smiles. "I'm so glad you agreed to do this. I can't wait to see the pictures. Be sure to get one in front of Old Faithful when it goes off!"

My smile lights up. "You followed my new social media account, right?" I drop my hands from her shoulders and pull my phone from my back pocket to open my profile.

"Yep, did this morning."

I look down and see that I have only her and Jordan as followers so far. Not that I expected more; I haven't posted anything yet.

"New social?"

Melissa looks up at Ash's question, and I shift so I can see Ash again. "Um, yeah. I decided to document the trip." I hold up my phone, and he takes it from me, studying the account.

"'Change of Pace,'" he reads aloud, "'a photo and video blog. Hi, I'm Jesse. Kawasaki disease Survivor & ICD (Implantable Cardioverter Defibrillator) Club Member. Follow along as I find my new pace in life.'"

I glance down at my tennis shoe sheepishly. I know I shouldn't feel embarrassed showing Asher the account; he was going to find out, anyway. It would be kind of hard to hide the fact I was documenting everything while we travel.

"This is great," he says.

I look back up to see his lips in a gentle smile and his gaze soft. "You don't think it's silly?"

"Why would I?"

I shrug, wondering why I asked that question. Ever since I did a Google search for Asher Jamison the night I got home from the engagement party, I've been a little in awe of him. I was right that he's smart and nerdy—more like smart, nerdy, and rich, especially after selling two tech companies. From what I was able to find, it seems like he works for fun, not because he has to. I'm still trying to figure out why he lives in an RV—and a vintage one at that.

"I...um, well..." I fumble.

"It's not silly, it's epic," Melissa says, saving me from whatever embarrassment I was about to walk into. "Maybe if it gets a shitload of followers, you can monetize it. Then you won't have to do boring admin work anymore. I know how much you hate being at a desk all day."

"That would be a massive long shot."

"I can help you," Asher says.

"Hell yeah," Melissa adds. "You know all this kind of stuff, Ash."

"Not social media exactly, but I'm good with numbers, data, algorithms. I bet, after some trial and error, we can figure out how to make this blow up." He hands my phone back to me, and when I grab it, our fingers brush.

I ignore the zing from his touch and pull back my hand. "You're already helping me with my bucket list and letting me invade your space." I hold up my phone. "This is just for fun."

"We'll have some downtime, and I like puzzles and figuring things out. If you want the help, then it's yours."

Melissa moves so she's between us, threading her arms around our waists and tugging the three of us together in a hug. "Oh, this is so great! The dream team."

Asher laughs. "You wanna come, Sis?"

"Hell no. Like I said, I'd bring too much stuff. You also know I don't like nature."

It's true; Melissa is not really an outdoorsy woman. Not that I have been much of one in the past, either, but I'm more willing to give it a shot than she would be.

"I hate to break this party up, but we should load up and get on the road if we want to get to South Dakota by tonight."

I agree, knowing he's right. If all goes according to plan, we'll be at a campground outside of Yellowstone in two days. Melissa turns to Ash and looks him dead in the eye, pointing her finger into his chest. "You take care of my best friend, yeah?"

"Cross my heart."

"Hope to die?" she asks.

"Stick a needle in my eye."

They both dissolve into brother-sister laughter before she hugs him. "Keep in touch, and let's not make it so long between visits."

"I'll do my best. But I'll see you when I bring Jesse home then again for your wedding."

"Don't remind me." Asher playfully glares at her, and she giggles. "Not about seeing you, but that I'm planning a wedding that's going to take place in two months. Sorry about making you come back from London for that so soon after you leave."

"I wouldn't miss it. Though you could move it to next year."

"I'm not dealing with building a house and a wedding at the same time. No, thanks."

After they chat for another minute about the house Melissa and Jordan are building next year, Ash declares we should get going again. I take the handle of one of my rolling suitcases, but when I reach for my backpack, I'm thwarted by Ash.

"I got it." He slings it over his shoulder and takes my larger suitcase by the handle.

"I can take my backpack."

"Already carrying it," he volleys.

I want to roll my eyes, but secretly, my stomach heats from the gesture. He opens the front door, and the hot summer air wafts inside. I'm glad I put my hair up in a ponytail. It's too muggy to wear it down.

Once we're out on the sidewalk, I stare wide-eyed at Winnie the Winnebago—or should I say Winnie the Pooh? It's a lot bigger and nicer than I expected, at least on the outside. Can't speak for the inside since I haven't seen it yet. The RV definitely has that vintage look with its long boxy frame painted in weathered cream with faded maroon stripes stretching along its sides and the famous W logo. The motorhome isn't flashy by any means, but it looks like Asher takes care of it.

Continuing to stare at it, I have a moment of "What the hell am I doing?" This RV is where I'm going to be living for the next twenty days. With Asher. My one-night stand, Asher. My best friend's brother, Asher.

"If you need a hotel at any point, tell Ash. I'm sure he'll get some rooms. Or one room," Melissa says in my ear quietly while Asher opens the storage area of the RV. It's a good distance away, so he can't hear what she said.

I turn to her and click my tongue. "That's not going to happen."

Her smile quirks, and she turns my body so I'm facing her, hands gripping my biceps. "I'm only going to say this once." She lowers her voice and puts her lips to my ear. "If you do come to a point where you want to cross this line you put up with Ash, cross the line. This is your road trip, your bucket list, your time to have fun. Don't give yourself all these rules and guides to follow. Be spontaneous and live, Jesse. You deserve it."

Her declaration sinks in, and the bridge of my nose stings. I know she's right. The bucket list's entire purpose is to do things I've never done, to break myself out of my comfort zone. But the situation with Ash is different. I'm not going to let myself cross into dangerous territory.

I swallow down the emotion building in my throat and blink before my eyes can become glassy. "Thanks, Melissa. I love you."

She waves me off as if what she said is no big deal. "I love you, too. I'll be following you the whole time." She winks.

"Um, that's creepy."

"On your social media, you doofus."

"I know, I know." I smile.

"Do you want me to put the backpack under here, or do you want it with you?" Ash calls over to us.

"With me," I answer then gesture to the suitcase I have next to me. "I'll bring this with me, too." The one I have has clothes I'll need for the first part of our journey, which includes a trip to Yellowstone to see Old Faithful, a stop at the Hot Springs, then a trip to the Oregon Coast. I can grab stuff from the one he put down below as needed.

"Great," he yells back before closing the door.

Even though I feel like we've all said goodbye a million times now, Ash and I both hug Melissa one more time. She watches me like a proud mom sending her child off to kindergarten while Ash opens the RV door for me.

"Have fun, kids!" she cries for good measure.

Ash chuckles, and I make my way up the steps into my new home for the next twenty days. Here goes nothing.

Chapter Thirteen

Asher

I TURN TO CLOSE the door of my home, my eyes meeting my sister's one last time as I do. She mouths "be careful" and winks at me. I screw up my nose, and she throws her head back and laughs. I cut off her cackles by securing the door but smile nonetheless as I walk over to Jesse, her backpack still slung over my shoulder.

Her back is to me as she looks around, and I find my heart pounding in my chest as she inspects everything with her eyes. From this vantage point, she can see the front of Winnie with the driver and passenger seats as well as the living area she's standing in and the kitchen/dinette area. It feels surreal having her here, especially since after our first night together, I was simply hoping she'd text me. Now she's here, and we're going to be sharing the same space, the same air, for nearly a month.

I find myself wanting to sink to my knees and send a prayer to every god, goddess, deity, and spiritual being known to mankind that this is now my life. I know it's temporary, but I want to make this special for her. If we end up as more by the end of it, I'll do more than pray in thanks, I'll devote my life to whomever made it possible.

I shut my eyes and inhale quietly. I promised myself I wouldn't be weird. I told her we would just be friends during this, that there would be no sex. I plan on keeping that promise unless she decides otherwise, which means I have to keep my fantasies of any future plans and calling her Mrs. Jamison one day in check for now. Even if it's difficult.

"Welcome home," I blurt out.

She turns to meet my gaze, folding her hands in front of her. "Thanks."

With her facing me now, I can see her brow is pinched and her smile is hardly a smile at all. She's also wringing her hands. "You're nervous," I say.

She blows a loud breath between her lips and laughs awkwardly. "Sorry, it has nothing to do with you. This is just—I can't believe this is happening."

I want to say the same, but instead, I take a step forward and set her backpack on the floor. "It's happening, and you have nothing to be nervous about. We're two friends going on a road trip to check off each other's bucket-list items, remember?"

"I do." She nods. "However, I don't remember you showing me your bucket list."

I place my hands in my pockets and grin. "I told you, it's a surprise. We're going to cross the first one off today, actually."

Jesse eyes me suspiciously. "I still don't think that's fair, considering you've seen mine."

"True. But in my defense, you showed me the version that's not complete."

"I don't know what you mean."

"I seem to remember a certain scratched-out item."

Jesse's cheeks and the skin of her neck flush a bright pink. "I don't know what you're talking about."

"Sure, you don't." I chuckle. There's no way I'm forgetting the item she crossed off and my sister left commentary on.

- Dominate a man

My dick twitches, and I shove that idea way back in my mind. I'm an asshole for bringing it up, but I want my items to be a surprise. What's more, I wanted to see her reaction when I brought it up, see if that's still a possibility for her. Because I'd be a more-than-willing participant. Sex wouldn't even have to be involved.

But that discussion can come much later. We're going to start with the easy items first.

Jesse opens her mouth again, but instead of words, she lets out a little gasp. My eyes draw down to the source of the perfectly-timed distraction: my cat, GusGus.

"Well, aren't you the cutest cat ever?" Jesse coos as she squats down to pet him.

"He prefers handsome."

She looks up at me as Gus headbutts her hand before walking circles around her legs. "Did he tell you that?"

"Yep."

"You have conversations with him often?"

"Hey, at least it's not a volleyball with a face on it I drew with my own blood."

She snorts and puts her attention back on my cat. I watch the sweet interaction and feel instant jealousy crawl around inside my gut as she scratches under his chin and calls him every cute name under the sun. Great, now I'm jealous of my cat. I need to get it together, stat.

"Want a tour?" I ask.

Jesse grins, her smile now happy and her shoulders eased of tension. Damn, GusGus is good. Maybe I should get him classified as one of those emotional support animals and get him a little vest.

"Yeah, that would be great," she replies.

With a final stroke to my cat's head, she stands to her full height, and I motion around the place. "This is a thirty-five-foot tag action model. As you can see, it's pretty spacious, and I renovated a lot of the inside, including new furniture and appliances."

"It's a lot bigger than I expected."

"It was a bitch to learn how to drive and park. That was the biggest issue for me in the beginning, but once I got the hang of it, it became second nature."

She frowns. "Are you sure you want to do all this driving? I told you when we planned the trip that I'm happy to cut down the list. It's a lot of places for twenty days, and—"

I hold up my hand to stop her from spiraling. "I told you, I don't mind driving. We have a solid plan that includes a good amount of stops to allow me to rest."

"You're really sure?"

"Positive. It's going to be fun. Especially when you see all the places I plan to take you from my list."

Jesse playfully glares at me, but all I do is chuckle. "This is the living area," I say, pointing to the two denim-blue reclining chairs with a small table between and a matching couch. "This couch pulls out into a bed if needed, but you'll be staying in the back room."

She nods, and I continue.

"Then we have the full kitchen with a refrigerator. It's got a gas stove and a small pantry as well as a microwave." I pull open the fridge door to reveal it's fully stocked, which is abnormal for me. "I did a grocery run yesterday. I hope you don't mind, but I asked Melissa what you like, and she mentioned you're gluten free and prefer oat milk. I got a bunch of gluten-free wraps, crackers, and even some cookies for you. Help yourself to whatever you want."

When she doesn't say anything, I close the fridge to find her stunned. And if I'm reading her correctly, she's about to cry. "Jesse, did I do something? If you don't like something, I—"

"No." She shakes her head, eyes blinking rapidly. "This is all great, more than great. Tell me how much I owe you."

Melissa warned me she'd try to keep everything even keel when it came to spending. I know it's not a secret I have money, and I'm fairly certain Jesse knows my business history given a small comment she made about an article she read. I didn't get a chance to ask her about it, because she changed the subject. In the end, if Jesse wants to pay for things and demands it, of course I will let her. But hell if I'll let her reimburse me for gluten-free snacks, something that shouldn't cost so goddamn much in the first place.

"No need to pay me back. But if you want, you can buy me a snack at my first bucket-list item," I say.

"Your bucket-list item involves snacks?"

"Sure, I love snacks."

She groans at my non-answer as I gesture for her to keep moving. She falls in step behind me as I show her the closet space where she can hang her clothes and put her shoes. I show her the bathroom next, which has a nice-sized shower I renovated and a standard toilet and sink, then we enter my bedroom. GusGus has already made himself into a little furball at the foot of the bed, and his purrs fill the air.

"This is my room," I say, patting Gus gently. He flops over so I can scratch his belly, and Jesse giggles. The giggle is such a sweet and melodic sound, and it doesn't help the inappropriate thoughts now swirling around in my brain at her being in my room with me, so near my bed.

My gaze travels from the navy-blue comforter with matching pillows to her soft and curvy body clad in a simple pair of green cotton shorts and a solid cream-colored T-shirt. The smile on her face is so innocent looking, I highly doubt she's thinking about me between her legs while gripping the sheets in the exact way she did the other night.

I look away from her and focus on Gus to collect myself again. "The cat sleeps in here with me most nights, but if you leave your door cracked, he may come visit you."

She hums at my commentary, and I walk us through to the next room, the last room in the RV. "This is where you'll be staying."

Jesse walks in and looks around. Her eyes go from the twin bed with a forest-green comforter to the desk with various items on it, including my laptop, then back to the bed. She does this several times before she speaks. "I can't sleep here."

"What? Why?" I ask. "Is it because of the layout? I know it's kind of annoying to have to walk through my room to get to the rest of the RV, but it gives you the most privacy."

"Oh." Her jaw ticks. "I didn't think of that."

"Sorry, I guess I should have said something."

She shakes her head. "No, it's okay."

"Then what's wrong?"

"This is your office."

"I think I mentioned that it was an office, too, didn't I?"

"I don't remember you saying that. Ash, I can't take over your entire space. I know you said you work for yourself, and you have a lot of free time, but I don't want to get in the way if you have things you need to do. I can sleep on the pullout!"

I take a step toward her and gently lay a hand on her shoulder. "Calm down, Jesse called Jesse."

The silly inside joke of ours seems to ease her. "Sorry, I just hate that I'm going to screw up your life."

"That's a big leap." I chuckle. "Trust me, you aren't. Far from it. I'd go so far as to argue you are improving on it. It can be lonely on the road, and if you haven't noticed, Winnie is big. It's nice I finally get to share her with someone."

Her pretty hazel pools stare into mine as if she's searching for a lie. Finally, she dips her chin. "If you're really sure."

"More than sure. Now, no more of that. That's the last time I want to hear you question if I'm sure, okay? If I didn't want you here, I wouldn't have said yes in the first place. Now, come on, let's get you settled."

I glance at my watch and see the time. We got an early start this morning, so it's only nearing seven-thirty. Which reminds me...I could go for a coffee or ten before we get this show on the road.

"Do you like dark roast?" I ask her as we make our way back toward the kitchen area.

"Is there any other kind of coffee?"

Warmth blooms in my stomach, and I grin. "No, there isn't." I reach into the fridge to grab two cans of cold brew made with the dark French roast I like. Once she has one in hand, I tell her to sit anywhere she likes—or if she wants, she can join me up front in the passenger seat.

To my delight, she chooses the passenger seat, buckling herself in and putting her coffee in a cup holder. I place my own can on the counter and observe her for a moment. She pulls out her phone, giving me time to memorize every detail of her, down to the different variations of brown in her dark hair and the way her eyes crinkle at the corners when she smiles at something.

Yes, I could very much get used to Jesse in my space. More than used to it. I just hope I don't end up getting my heart broken in the process.

Chapter Fourteen

Jesse

"I CAN'T BELIEVE YOU listen to cassettes," I say as we drive down the interstate, the sounds of The Beatles playing through the speakers. We've been driving for the last six-ish hours, and so far, it's not been awkward like I thought it might be. Asher and I have fallen into an easy back and forth chat, only stopping twice so far for gas and bathroom breaks and once for some lunch. A Subway sandwich for him and salad for me—god, I miss bread.

"I could've installed USB docks but decided against it. I renovated a lot of Winnie but wanted to keep some of its 1990s charm. The cassette tapes remind me of road trips with my dad when I was a kid in our old Woody Wagon."

The term Woody Wagon sparks memories of me in the back seat of my parents' minivan with my older sister. "Oh gosh, those cars were the source of a lot of bruises shared between my sister and I."

"Bruises?" Asher asks.

I nod. "I think it's a Wisconsin thing? Or maybe my sister and I made it up. But we'd hit each other when we'd see one. Same thing with VW Bugs."

"Slug bugs I've heard of, but not the Woody Wagons." He chuckles. "So you have a sister? Does she live in Madison?"

I shake my head. "She lives in Arizona with her husband and her dogs."

"Do you visit often?"

"I try to go once a year, but the last couple of years, I haven't gone." I expect Asher to ask me why, seeing as I gave him the perfect in to talk about my heart condition, but all he does is nod.

A moment later, he says, "I like visiting Arizona when it's cooler. The summers are way too hot."

"I'm the same way! I love sitting in her hot tub, but you can't do that when the air is already boiling you alive."

"Facts," Asher agrees as a familiar song comes through the speakers. I think it's The Beach Boys. "I love this song," he says, turning up the volume before placing his hand on his leg, tapping along to the beat. Something I've noticed he does a lot—even when there isn't music.

"Do you get your cassettes online?" I ask.

"Sometimes. I get a lot at record stores and flea markets."

I study Asher's profile: his well-trimmed beard, round jaw, curly hair that looks perfectly styled. Just when I think I may have him figured out, he surprises me again. I should've known he likes old music and flea markets, yet I never would've guessed. He's extremely different from Melissa, who hates camping and the outdoors and isn't afraid to buy and wear clothes that cost an arm and a leg.

No words pass between us for a few long moments, and I look out at the scenery passing us by. The rolling hills and plains of South Dakota meet my gaze before we pass an exit that would take us back to Minnesota.

My mind drifts to Kate as it had while driving through the state to get here. One of the few times I visited Minnesota was to visit her. She and another one of our high school friends attended a private college outside Minneapolis. My fingers itch to take out my phone and let her know that I've left town, but I still feel sour over everything that happened at the bar and her text the following day.

"You okay?" Ash asks.

His comment clues me in to my sour and scrunched features. "Yeah, I'm fine." I attempt to relax my face, but I'm still semi-frowning.

"Fine always equals not fine. Spill it, Jesse."

I pick at the hem of my cotton shorts, debating how to phrase this or if I should tell him at all.

"You don't have to say if you don't want to," he assures me a moment later. "But I figure we're going to be in close quarters for the next month. And we're friends, right?"

Friends. For better or worse, that's what I said we had to be.

I take a sip of the water I have in a cup holder beside me and glance out at the scenery again. "Do you remember the woman with me at the bar the other night?"

I turn my gaze to Asher again, and he's notably gripping the large steering wheel tighter. "I remember. She left with that asshole bartender."

I think of how annoyed he looked while trying to get his drink, and my lips tug at the corners. "That's the one. She was there that night to be my wingwoman—or at least she was supposed to be. She ended up leaving with Luke the bartender."

Ash nods. "Yeah, they left shortly after you walked off. I didn't get my drink until another bartender came and switched with him."

I fold my hands in my lap. "Want to know the reason I walked away?" He nods, so I soldier on. "My friend started flirting with him, and he made it clear that he'd hook up with her if she wanted. Then she got the brilliant idea to try to get him to sleep with me instead."

"You're serious?"

I feel validated that Ash didn't try to ask why that bothered me and seems equally annoyed at my friend's behavior. "Dead serious. I walked away because I wasn't going to be that guy's pity lay, you know?"

Ash doesn't answer me, but it's obvious he's angry by the way his knuckles have now turned white on the wheel and his lips are in a hard line.

"Sorry, was that too much?" I ask when he still hasn't said something a moment later.

"No." He exhales. "No, I'm just pissed for you. Friends shouldn't treat friends like that." His grip lessens on the wheel, and he turns his head to look at me for a brief moment. "For the record, you'd be nobody's pity lay. Any man should be fucking lucky and honored to get to be with you. I know I was."

His words are sweet, but years of never being chosen by men, a mediocre ex, and a few bad dates on top of feeling like people pity me for my condition sit deep in every fiber of my body. So it's hard for me to believe him, even if he made me feel good when we were together. Better than good.

I push the thoughts away and manage a small smile in thanks. "At the end of the day, I probably shouldn't have been so angry, but then she offered him up to me again right before I bumped into you at the engagement party via text. Said he was quote 'a decent lay if you want to try again with him. I bet he'd be game.'"

"Wow," Asher breathes.

"My thoughts exactly."

"Please tell me you told her off."

I shrug. "Maybe I should've, but I've ignored her since then. I didn't tell her about you. I also didn't tell her about this trip. I feel bad, but I keep waffling on what to say to her about the situation or if I should say anything at all. I know she thought she was helping me." I take a breath before admitting, "I also hate confrontation."

Asher is quiet again, but a cool rage simmers across his usually friendly features. "I have an idea," he says. "You can say no if you want."

I sink further into the blue chair that's more like a recliner than a normal passenger seat in a vehicle. "Okay, what is it?"

"Take out your phone."

I stare at him, confused for a second, but then I do as he asks. I hold it up so he can see it. "Now what?"

"Now we check off an item from your bucket list."

I wrack my brain for an item that would include using my phone, but I come up empty. "I don't understand," I say.

"Tell me if I'm wrong, but given everything you just told me, would texting your friend and telling her how you feel be something you would normally say no to doing?"

Realization hits me, and I can't help but think that not only is Ash very attentive, he's clever. "I don't know, Ash. Maybe I should just let it go. It's probably better that way."

"See, you just said no."

"Technically, I said 'I don't know.'"

"Semantics," he says.

I manage a chuckle and stare at the screen of my phone. He's right—normally, I would not do this. Even when I wanted to at the party the other night, I didn't.

"Look, Jesse," Ash adds. "You don't have to. But what she said, her words, they hurt you. I'm going to take a guess that this isn't the first time she's said hurtful things to you, either."

"You'd guess right," I say. Kate and I have been friends for years, and if there's one thing this current situation proves, it's that she's blunt and makes statements that come off as personal digs. I've probably shed more tears over her commentary than over anything my mom has ever said—which is saying something, since my mom is the queen of passive-aggressive comments that make me cry.

Come to think of it, Kate and my mom have a lot in common, especially their tendency to remark on my appearance or the choices I've made. It's always about things I wish they'd just leave alone.

"Text her how you feel." Ash's voice interrupts my thoughts. "What's the worst that could happen?"

I chuff. "Kate has a short fuse when she feels threatened. So I suppose the worst thing that could happen is she gets angry and doesn't speak to me again."

"And how does that feel?"

I think on it for a moment, imagining a life without a friend I've had since I was fifteen years old. I know we have a lot of memories together, and I do love her, but if she's not willing to even hear me out without getting angry or listen to my feelings, then why does she deserve to be in my life?

"It feels..." I pause. "It feels like maybe I should text her how I feel."

"Maybe?" he gently pushes.

I chuckle softly before I inhale a breath and exhale it out. I came on this trip to check off my bucket-list items, and I want to be brave. Now is the time to do that for myself. With another breath, I muster up the courage I felt dancing the other night, remembering how it felt to tell Asher what I wanted.

"Okay, I'm going to text her."

"Hell yeah!" Asher cheers happily. The sound of it makes me smile.

I open a text to Kate and start typing. Once I've gotten out everything I want to say, I feel as if I'm going to throw up. I send the message before I lose my nerve.

"Did you do it?" Ash asks after I've sat here for a minute.

"I did. She hasn't read it yet, but she may be at work."

He hums. "Well, I think you should turn off your phone."

I stare at the side of his smiling profile. "Why's that?"

"You sent the message, which means you've crossed off the item on your bucket list." He turns his face quickly and waggles his eyebrows. I laugh at the action, and it eases some of the nausea in my stomach.

"But why does that mean I should turn my phone off?"

"Because you sent it. No need to stare at your phone and work yourself up over her response. You can deal with it later."

Ash pauses to turn on his blinker. "Besides, now we're going to check off the first item on my bucket list."

I cock my head curiously and look out the window to see a big sign. "Seriously?"

He turns into the parking lot and smiles wider. "Seriously."

Once we're parked, he kills the engine and gestures out the windshield to a massive building in front of us. However, it's not just any building; it's a palace. And not just any palace but one with turrets shaped like stalks of corn.

A cackle slips from my lips, and I turn off my phone. His eyes meet mine again, and he looks like a kid about to go into a candy store.

"Welcome to The Corn Palace, Jesse. Let's get corny."

Chapter Fifteen

Asher

"ONE OF YOUR BUCKET-LIST items is visiting The World's Only Corn Palace?" Jesse asks, balking.

I nod happily. "I like corn."

"I mean, I do, too. But I've never even heard of this place."

"Then clearly you are not a fan of corn like you say."

"I said that I liked corn, not that I was a fan of it."

"Same difference," I chirp. Jesse shakes her head and smiles. The smile eases some of the anger I've been feeling for her since she told me about her situation with her friend. I'm very happy to see her more relaxed and glad this stop timed perfectly with her sending her text. We needed to get some fresh air. Or at least I did.

"Where even are we?" Jesse asks.

"The Palace of Corn."

She playfully rolls her eyes. "I mean what city, smarty pants."

"Ohhh, I see now. We're in Mitchell, South Dakota. We'll stay at a campground another hour from here for tonight, but first: corn."

"Alright. And your cat will be okay?"

"Yep. He's used to staying in Winnie alone. He likes it."

"It doesn't get too hot?"

My chest smarts at her concern for my cat. "I have an app on my phone that tells me if the space gets too hot. He'll be fine."

"Okay, let's go."

I pump my fist then check Gus's food and water before we exit the RV. The Corn Palace looms ahead of us, and I want to snort with laughter. I told Jesse this is on my bucket list, but truth be told, I didn't know this place existed until I googled it after we mapped out our trip. I will admit, though, this place looks awesome. I mean, who doesn't love corn?

"Is the art on the building made of corn?"

"It is!" We stop before we walk inside to check out the murals on the sides of the Palace. "They change out the art every year. It's made of corn, wheat, and straw. It's a way to showcase artists and draw tourists in."

Jesse crosses her arms over her chest. "How do you know all that?"

"I told you, I like corn."

She laughs. "You read it online before we came, didn't you?"

"May-be," I sing-song.

Jesse snorts as she walks to the front door, and I pick up speed so I can open the door for her. She thanks me with a slight tinge of pink on her cheeks that has my pulse quickening. Once we're inside, Jesse inhales at the same time I do.

"It smells like popcorn in here!" She bursts out laughing.

"I didn't expect that."

"Didn't read it online?"

I grin. "No, I must have missed that detail. But I do know that it's a popular attraction and local venue. They host entertainment nights and events. I think you can even get married here."

"Interesting," Jesse replies. "I'd probably just want to eat popcorn all night if I came here for an event."

"Facts," I agree.

We stand in the middle of the very large foyer and look around. There's travel and entertainment brochures lining the walls and a woman standing at a tall table to help tourists. She's in front of one of several pillars that's tiled in yellows, browns, and whites to look like corn. It's silly yet impressive.

When my gaze finds Jesse again, she's looking at a sign. "Want to do the free tour?" Her eyes sparkle with the question, and any trace of the woman who was afraid to text her friend is gone now.

"You don't think this is stupid?" I ask.

Her face turns serious, and she shakes her head. "It's something you want to do, which means it's not stupid."

My stomach flips at her sentiment. "But do *you* want to do it?"

"Hell yeah, I do! We can't not tour The Corn Palace at The Corn Palace. That's got to be cor-iminal or something."

I expel a loud belly laugh at her attempt at a pun, and so help me, if I wasn't already falling in love with her, I would be now.

"Let's go on that tour then," I say.

"Let's."

Jesse bites into her ear of corn, butter getting all over her lips as she chews. I bite the inside of my cheek to keep from laughing and hand her a napkin.

"Here."

She dips her chin and nibbles her lower lip, transferring the ear of corn to one hand so she can take the napkins with the other. "Thanks. This corn is good but messy. You want to try?"

When she holds it out to me like it's the most natural thing in the world to do, I'm not going to say no. "Sure."

I think she expects me to take the corn from her like a normal person would, but I lean forward and let her keep holding it.

My lips wrap around the ear while keeping eye contact with her. Jesse's gaze doesn't leave mine, and she licks her lips as I take a sweet and salty bite. The moment my teeth break into the kernels, some corn juice sprays out, and I pull back with a curse, making the experience way less sexy than it was in my head.

Jesse laughs. Hard. I swallow my bite, and soon, I'm laughing, too. I can't help it when her giggles are so contagious. "That was messy," I comment as I reach for a napkin.

"Good, though, right?"

"It is. Now, you need to try some chocolate-covered toasted corn kernels." I hold out the pouch to her.

"I know what both a toasted corn kernel and chocolate tastes like. I can imagine what a chocolate-covered one tastes like."

"That may be true, but you've never actually had one." I wiggle the pouch, shaking the treats around.

"Fine." She reaches into the bag with a clean hand to grab one and pops it into her mouth. I hear the crunch of the kernel as she bites down followed by a sweet-sounding moan. The intimate noise goes straight to my dick, and I remind myself that A, we're in a city-run establishment with families around, and B, I can't think of Jesse like that because she only wants us to be friends.

I sit up a little straighter. "They're addictive, right?" I pull the snack toward me and take another few, popping them into my mouth. An easy silence passes between us as we sit in the outdoor picnic area with other tourists and families and continue to eat our food. There are two kids running around the tables playing tag.

I observe Jesse with interest as she watches them goof around with a softness in her eyes. "Do you want kids?" I ask before I can truly think the question through.

Her eyes snap to mine, and she swallows the bite of corn she was eating. She sits straighter on the bench and places the half-eaten corn down.

"I'm sorry," I say. "That was personal. I shouldn't—"

"No." She smiles. "It's okay. It caught me off guard is all."

"Sorry," I apologize again. "Sometimes my mouth runs away with me."

"Please don't apologize. Your mouth is part of your charm."

"Oh?" I ask. "You don't say."

Realizing what she's said, Jesse's eyes turn down, and she tucks a piece of hair behind her ear. "I meant you say what's on your mind."

"My family always says I don't have a filter, which is partially true. Sometimes my mouth can get me in trouble, especially if I'm overstimulated or tired."

Her eyes bore into mine as if she wants to ask me more about what I said, but she nods instead. The kids playing tag run by again, their giggles making us both smile.

"The answer to your question is complicated," she says.

My focus returns to Jesse. Her features are heavier if not somber. By the change in her demeanor, I think I know where this answer is going to go. It's probably related to her heart condition.

I'll admit, I've been curious about it since Jordan opened his big mouth at the party, but I haven't asked her any questions. It was clear to me that she doesn't necessarily like talking about it, so I didn't want to force anything. Now I feel even worse for asking such an invasive question.

She opens a bottle of water and takes a sip. When she's done, she watches the kids play for another moment.

I shift in my seat. "Jesse, you don't have to answer. It was a question I asked to make conversation."

She shakes her head, taking another sip of water before meeting my eyes. "I've been meaning to have this conversation with you, so in a way, I'm glad you brought it up."

Confusion pinches my brow, and she snorts.

"Oh gosh, no. Sorry. Not about having kids." She laughs to herself. "What I mean is, I've been wanting to talk to you about what's going on with me health-wise."

"You don't—"

"I do," she interrupts. "You should have all my medical information in case something happens while we're on this trip."

Anxiety bubbles and pops in my stomach at the idea of something happening to Jesse. She's so young, vibrant, and the thought of anything but good things happening to her makes me feel ill...which I suppose is exactly why she hasn't talked to me about it. I know I wouldn't want to spill my health information to just anyone, especially people I haven't known long. Being treated differently is never fun, and it's something I have experience with, too.

I take a sip of my own water and fold my hands in front of me on the table, giving her my full attention. "Okay, I'm all ears."

Jesse laughs, and now I'm really confused. She was serious a moment ago, and now she's snort laughing. It's adorable, but I have no idea why she's doing it.

She wipes her eye from where it started to water. "Sorry, the unintentional pun was too good."

I'm all ears. I look down at her ear of corn and laugh. "Damn, now I'm sad I didn't intentionally come up with that one," I say.

"It's okay, I needed a laugh. It also should be mentioned I've been known to laugh when something serious or scary happens. It's gotten me in trouble on more than a few occasions."

The image of Jesse laughing at a funeral or something equally as inappropriate fills my mind and makes me smile. I can totally see her doing that.

"Okay." She takes a breath. "First, I want to preface everything I'm about to say with I'm fine. Not fake fine but actually fine. I should have told you before, but I got clearance from my cardiologist to be on the trip. I can do everything on my list. The only thing I can't participate in is something like bungee jumping. Hope that's not on your list?"

"No bungee jumping," I say.

"Cool."

She nods, then she lifts her wrist to reveal an Apple watch with a purple band I'd noticed earlier. She points to a silver thing attached to it and holds it out to me so I can see. "This has my emergency details on it."

She drops her hand and picks up her purse.

"In here, I also have a medical card with my doctor's number on it in case my heart is shocked by my ICD implant and nitro tabs I can take if I'm feeling like I'm having a heart attack." She takes a moment to pull out a little glass vile from one of the side pouches and holds it up to me.

"In case I can't get to them, you can grab them for me. I put one under my tongue and let it dissolve if I'm feeling symptoms of an attack, which are usually left arm pain, shoulder pain, jaw pain, clamminess, and shortness of breath, but I'll tell you if that ends up being the case. If I'm shocked, I hear I'll pass out and then come to, but nine-one-one should be called if I remain unconscious."

Jesse pauses to study me. I must look like I need reassurance because she smiles, her eyes soft. "But none of this should happen, Ash. It's all hypotheticals. My ICD implant has been tested and works, all my meds are doing their job, and my heart tests have been great. My body is functioning as normally as it can."

She starts to set her purse down, but then she stops and pulls out a tube of something. "I'm also on a lot of blood thinners. If I get a bad cut or anything, I'll bleed a lot more than usual. This powder helps create a clot. Hopefully we won't need it, either, but it's here. I've also got another tube in my backpack if we need more." Once she's done, she puts it back in her bag and looks up at me.

I try my hardest to keep my emotions about the reality of the information she's told me from showing on my face, but it's difficult. I'm not going to lie and say it's not scary for me to hear. I dare anyone to find a person who doesn't think it's scary. I'd thought that, eventually, when Jesse told me about her health condition, it would be easier to take in. But I don't think anything could have prepared me to hear what she's saying. Even after I looked up Kawasaki disease online the other night.

It was a quick search, one that only made me respect Jesse more for what she'd been through. I didn't know her whole story, but I know a person has to be strong to deal with what she has going on. I feel that even more now, and she's only told me about her medical needs and possibilities.

Jesse shifts in her seat and tucks a strand of hair behind her ear. "If you want to turn around and go home, I understand."

My stomach goes sour with panic at the idea of this trip ending before it's even truly begun. "What? Why?"

"That was a lot to hear. And I realize now that I've spoken it out loud, it was a lot of information to dump on you at The Corn Palace. We should've had this discussion when we were mapping out the trip instead of after we were already on it."

While she's right, I would've preferred it for no other reason than so I was more prepared. I would've stocked the first aid kit with the powder and more bandages for heavy bleeding. I would have made sure she knew that I had her back and was ready to take care of her if, god forbid, something were to happen. Instead, I feel like a schmuck. And Jesse feels like I don't want her here.

"I'm not turning back, Jesse. We planned an epic trip, and we're only one stop in."

She stares into my eyes as if she's searching for a lie. I have the urge to reach across the table and grab her hand, to make sure she knows I'm telling the truth, but I don't.

"You're sure?" she asks. "You looked like you might throw up for a minute there."

Guilt eats at my stomach, and I think of what to say to best reassure her, but I still want to be honest. "I'm not going to lie and say that everything you told me doesn't affect me, because it does." Her face falls, and this time, I do reach across the table, placing my hand over hers and squeezing. "Only because the idea of something happening to you is scary, Jesse. But I'm glad I know how to help you if you need it."

"The chances of something happening aren't likely. Maybe a cut, but nothing that would require the clot agent unless the cut is pretty deep," she adds.

"Got it: Keep super sharp knives away from you."

She rolls her eyes. "I know how to use a knife."

"Thank god." I smile softly. "But in all seriousness, I'm glad you told me. Thank you for being honest. If you're okay with it, could you write the information down? I don't want to forget it in the slim chance that something does happen."

I reluctantly pull back my hand, already missing the warmth of her skin against mine. With the distraction of her touch gone, I start to think of where we can stop and get more of that powder and bandages, maybe pick up a pulse oximeter for her fingertip just in case. But I don't want her to feel weird if I do that.

"Sure, I can write it down." She looks at her hands before her eyes flutter back to mine. "But can you promise me something?"

"Anything."

"Now that you have that information, please don't treat me differently. Yes, I've had two heart attacks. Yes, I have an ICD. I know all that, and I don't need to be reminded. I promise I'll tell you if I feel like anything is off. I don't want to be hovered over or my decisions questioned. I want to enjoy this trip without feeling like I'm being supervised. It's a big reason I was hesitant to bring up anything in the first place."

My mind attempts to catch up with everything she's saying, but I'm focused on the fact that Jesse is as positive and happy as she is. I've met people who've been through and faced a lot less who would not be in the mental state she is right now or be on a trip like this, crossing off bucket-list items. I truly am in awe of her, and I hope at some point over the next month, she opens up to me more about what she's overcome, because I want to know everything about her.

"Ash?"

I look her in the eye when I say my next words. "I won't treat you differently."

"Really?"

"If you ask me to do something, I'm going to do my best to do it." I pause. "Can I ask you for a promise in return?"

"I think that's only fair."

"I know you said you would, but please be honest with me if you're feeling bad or you can't do something. I'm not you, and I'm not going to assume anything. That means I'm trusting you to tell me if there is anything wrong."

"I promise," she says without hesitation. "Thank you."

I dip my chin in a nod. "And thank you."

Jesse picks up her corn, and I pick up my chocolate-covered corn kernels. We eat in silence for another minute, both of us lost in thought. When my eyes lift to Jesse's a minute later, she's not looking at me. Instead, she's watching the kids run around again. This time, they have ears of corn in their hands, and their mom is yelling at them.

Jesse looks stunning, nearly finished corn cob in one hand and her shoulder-length dark hair blowing in the gentle breeze with the sun glowing around her. I pull out my phone from my pocket and snap a shot. When she hears the noise of the camera, her head turns to see what it was.

"Did you take my picture?"

I nod, looking down at it. It's beautiful, soft, and natural. It screams Jesse. I hold it out so she can see it, and her eyes study it for a long moment. She doesn't say anything, but after a time, she looks up at me, an emotion in her eyes I can't read.

"Why did you take it?" she asks.

I pull my phone back and snap a few more of the surrounding area. "You need pictures for your social media account. Can't forget The Corn Palace. Stop number one!"

I put my phone down, and when I look back at her, I swear I see disappointment in her features, but she replaces it with a smile. Did she want me to have a candid picture of her on my phone? Hope lights in my chest, and I consider telling her the truth. I did take it for me—the social media account was a last-second cover up, even if her needing pictures for her profile is true.

"Thanks," she says, putting her corn down. "I nearly forgot since I don't have my phone." Now her face does sour, and I know what she's thinking before she speaks. "Do you think Kate's texted back?"

"Maybe." I throw a corn kernel at Jesse, and it hits her straight between the eyes. She looks shocked before she glares at me.

"You hit me with corn."

"Looks like."

She picks up the kernel that landed on the table and launches it back at me. It soars past my head and nearly hits a kid running by. She gasps, and I let out a laugh.

"Maybe you should put 'get better aim' on your bucket list."

Jesse scoffs, but her face is all smiles again, which was exactly my goal. "Rude!" she exclaims.

I chuckle. "You ready, sharpshooter? We should hit the road and set up camp for the night."

She wipes her hands on a napkin and nods. We stand and throw away our items before walking back through the building to get to Winnie. When we exit the front, I stop her and snap a picture of the Palace then get a selfie of us with some of the corn art in the background. Once I've gotten clearance with Jesse that she likes the picture, she gently knocks me on the shoulder.

"Was The Corn Palace everything you wanted it to be?" she asks.

My memory of our afternoon together plays through my mind like a movie. The tour we took, laughing together at silly corn puns, the fact that everything smelled like buttery popcorn. Watching Jesse look at the murals with wide eyes and amazed smiles then learning more about her and understanding her better. I'd argue this has been one of the best days of my life, not including the night we met. The best part is this is only our first stop. We're only getting started.

"It was more," I answer.

Chapter Sixteen

Jesse

WE'RE NEARING THE CAMPSITE in South Dakota for the evening, and I have yet to turn my phone back on. I also realize that I never did answer Asher's question about children. Instead, I'd spiraled into a well of information that I should have told him before I even stepped foot onto the RV.

When we'd gotten together to map out the trip, I'd had the words about my health on the tip of my tongue. I was going to lay everything out to him before we even planned the first stop.

Then he'd come prepared to our meeting, and Melissa joined us. He'd already known great places to land for RV-friendly camping and had his secret bucket list mapped out. I didn't want to ruin the day by talking about my heart or anything. But now that I've spoken to him, I see I had nothing to worry about.

"Okay, here we are," Ash says.

I look out the window as we turn into our park for the night. Since it's summer, the sky is still lit up, but the golden yellow-and-orange sun is dipping low in the sky. He drives down a road lined with campers, and the first thing I notice is that this place is packed with families. Some are grilling their evening meals, while others are roasting marshmallows by the fire.

A smile creeps at the corners of my mouth, and excitement sparks in my veins. My family was never one for camping. We'd gone twice when I was younger, three times if I count the retreat I did with the Girl Scouts. My mom was the troop leader for my sister's troop, and I got to tag along on the event. But everything was inside, so I'm not sure I could count that.

"Do you count RV sleeping as camping?" I ask.

He drives further down the road to bigger camping spots that will fit his large RV. "I mean...yes?"

I huff a laugh. "So that's a no, then?"

"Depends on who you ask. Some would call it glamping."

"Ah, yes, like *Troop Beverly Hills*. Minus the Beverly Hills Hotel, of course."

"Oh shit, I forgot about that movie. Melissa used to watch it all the time with our mom."

"Did you like it?"

"I mean, the main actress is a babe. So yes." I snicker, and he glances at me. "Come on, you have to admit I'm right."

I hold up my hands. "I didn't say she wasn't a babe. She is."

Asher looks satisfied with my answer as he pulls to a stop and kills Winnie's engine. "I'm going to get us set for the night. Why don't you make yourself at home? Then we can figure out dinner."

"Do you need help?" I ask. I don't want to sit around like a lump while he does all the work. "You've got another set of hands now, remember?"

Since we're parked, he turns his body toward mine, a smile shining on his face. "I've got it for tonight. But if you want to go back into my room and bring GusGus a treat and some snuggles, he'll fall in love with you. Later, I'll have you give him his wet food. He may never leave you alone after that."

I smile at the idea. I'd almost forgotten GusGus was here during the ride. I expected him to come up to the front, but Ash said he prefers to sleep during long rides and cuddle and play in the middle of the night while Asher's trying to sleep. He groused as he told me the story, but I could tell he wasn't really annoyed. It made me excited to hear how Gus came into his life. I have a feeling it's not a usual story given the way he talks about the cat.

"Are you sure?" I ask.

"Yep, trust me. You'll be doing me a favor. Maybe he'll wake you up in the middle of the night instead of me for cuddles and playtime."

"I'd be fine with that."

Ash chuffs. "I'll remind you of that when he wakes you up every night at three am for the entire trip." He unbuckles his seat belt and opens his door. "Treats are under the sink in the bag with the cat and fish on it."

"Got it," I reply.

He hops down from the RV while I unbuckle my belt. Instead of exiting through the passenger door, I turn my chair around to go to the kitchen. It's nice that the seats swivel, so if I want to go to the back during a long drive and use the bathroom, I can. And given how much water I drink, especially because some of my meds give me dry mouth, I've already done it a few times today.

With my chair turned, I stand up, hearing Asher say hello to whomever our neighbor is for the night before he shuts the door, closing me in with silence. The hum of the engine, Asher's friendly conversation, and the old music from the cassettes are no longer able to distract me.

My phone feels heavy in my back pocket, and the text from earlier comes back into my mind. I have no doubt Kate texted me back or tried to call me after I sent her the message calling her out for how she made me feel the other night. I should be brave and turn my phone back on, but I find myself wanting to wait until I've got some food other than corn in my stomach and Asher beside me.

That thought alone should have me asking him to turn the RV around and go back to Wisconsin, but it doesn't. In a way, I like it. He makes me feel safe and has since the moment we met, which is a good thing, even for people who have just decided to be friends.

Leaving my phone where it is for now, I make my way to the kitchen. I take in my new living quarters for a minute without Asher standing next to me or the RV bouncing down the road.

Winnie is nice and genuinely feels like a home on wheels. I know that's what it's meant to be, but it's funny seeing one in person, especially one that looks like it belongs in a '90s time capsule.

While Asher has done a lot to update it, including new furniture and appliances that are very modern, he's kept the interior look the same. The kitchen is the most obvious with its almost clunky-looking cabinets of dark-stained wood. I look down at the carpet and see that it's also new, yet he selected a dark brown you'd find in older homes from the '80s and '90s. In the kitchen, the floor looks to be made of wood, but I'd bet anything it's linoleum.

A loud meow draws me from my observations to GusGus, who's rubbing on my legs. I bend over and pat his head. "You hungry?"

His loud meow tells me yes.

"Alright, let's get you a treat, and then we can cuddle on the couch for a bit."

Another meow confirms this is a good idea. He's a very talkative cat.

Once I've given him a couple of little fish-shaped treats and he's hoovered them up, I move to the couch and expect him to follow, but he has a better idea. He runs toward Asher's room, and when he stops in the bathroom and meows very loudly a few more times, I follow him. He leads me into the decent-sized space and hops up onto the bed where there's a pile of blankets for him.

I sit down on the edge of the mattress and pet Gus's velvet fur. I become mesmerized by the white, gray, and black colors running through my fingers and delight in the way his soft purrs vibrate against my hand, almost tickling me. A soft smile washes over my face, and my eyes become heavy. The space back here is warm from the summer day, and I forgot how much long road trips take out of you.

The desire to curl up on Ash's bed with GusGus sprawled on my stomach, lulling me to sleep, makes my eyelids grow heavier. Doing that would be weird, though, so I fight the feeling of tiredness and give Gus all the attention he wants while I turn my focus to the walls of Asher's bedroom.

Much like the rest of Winnie, it's a mix of old and new. I run my free hand over the comforter and notice a few photos on the wall. One is of a waterfall, but another is of GusGus playing with a mouse toy, and what's funny is that the frame around it reads, "My Son." I wonder if Melissa gave that to him; it would align with her personality.

Another minute passes, and before too long, Ash is standing in the door with a half smile on his face as he watches me and his cat.

"See, I told you he'd love you forever."

"He's a sweet cat."

"You say that now. But like I said, just wait till late tonight."

I glance down at the cat and decide by simply looking at his sweet face, eyes closed in contentment and purrs loud enough we can hear them, that he does strike me as the kind of cat that would be trouble.

"Did you get everything set for the night?" I ask.

"I did. We can have dinner now. Or if you want to use the shower or anything, let me know."

I look at the bathroom next to his room, remembering I'm going to have to go through his bedroom every time I need to use it during the night, and press my lips together.

He sees the look on my face and rubs the back of his neck. "Sorry again about the bedroom/bathroom situation. Downsides of living in an RV."

"It's okay, but I was just thinking I'm going to feel bad every time I have to use it when you're asleep."

"Oh, please don't. If I'm asleep, I'm a deep sleeper. So don't worry about it."

One of my hands continues to stroke GusGus while the other tucks a strand of hair behind my ear. "But if it gets annoying, I can sleep in the living area. I really don't mind."

"Nonsense. I want you to have a real bed, not a pullout. If you want, you can take my room instead. I don't go to the bathroom that much in the middle of the night, and I—"

"No," I cut him off. "I'll be fine."

He searches my eyes then nods. "Okay, but let me know if you want to change."

"I'll be fine." I laugh softly. "Now, tell me what you're thinking for dinner."

He motions for me to stand, and I follow him into the kitchen to see pre-made burger patties laid out.

"Grilling?" I ask.

"I figure we can take advantage of the night. It's nice out, and our neighbors are an old, retired couple from Pennsylvania so they're already going inside for the night. Plus, our spot on the river gives us a good view of the sunset. By the way the sky is starting to look, I think it's going to be a nice show."

"Sounds perfect."

Chapter Seventeen

Asher

I SHOULD'VE HAD SOMEONE travel with me a long time ago. Scratch that. I wish I would've found *Jesse* years ago to bring her along with me.

She's made the last day more than enjoyable, and I find myself wanting the evening to drag out. I know that we have many more of them coming after tonight. Nineteen, to be exact—not like I'm counting or anything.

"Wow, you were right," Jesse calls from the riverbank a few feet away. "The sunset is incredible."

I want to be cheesy and look at her instead of at the sunset when I say my next words, but I keep my eyes on the sky while I flip Jesse's burger, which she requested to be cooked to a perfect medium. A woman after my own heart. "Wait till you see them over the ocean in Oregon. That coast has beautiful sunsets, some of the best I've seen."

She walks over from where she was standing near the top of the riverbank and looks down at the grill. "Where do you keep this?"

"In storage compartments under the RV. This one is nice. It's small enough and easy to store when I travel."

"Do you use the indoor kitchen often?"

"Honest answer?"

She grins. "Always."

"Sometimes. But mostly I buy frozen food or eat a lot of spaghetti and pre-packaged meals. I'm not that great of a cook."

She looks from me to the burgers then back to me. "Should I be worried?"

I snicker. "I can handle some burgers. And didn't you know that men are biologically programmed to be able to cook meat over fire?"

Now she's the one who snickers. "I must have missed that memo."

"It's true. Me man, this fire. I make meat over fire," I say in a deep, caveman-style voice.

"*Woooow.*" She draws out the word and whistles.

Her response only makes me lean into it more. "Now you sit. Me give you burger."

"You sound like Cookie Monster."

I wet my lips and put her burger with cheese on a plate then flip mine before doing the same. "You don't think I have a career in voice-over? Outside of the Cookie Monster, that is."

"Probably not."

I snap my fingers. "Dang it, I thought that could be my side hustle." I hold out her plate to her, and she takes it before walking to the small folding table I set up while she was inside. Sitting next to it are two oversized soft-backed folding chairs. On the table, we've got some burger fixings and two cans of raspberry-flavored sparkling water.

I take the rest of the patties off the grill. I purposely made extras that we can reheat tomorrow if we want. I join Jesse at the table, and she spreads mayo on top of her gluten-free bun but adds nothing else to it.

"No other toppings?" I ask.

"I'm a simple girl when it comes to toppings. Unless there are grilled onions and Thousand Island dressing."

"Noted for next time."

"You're an everything guy?" she asks as she watches me stack my burger with lettuce, raw onion, dill pickle, tomato, mustard, and mayo.

"That I am."

She looks up at me after she puts her bun on her burger. "That makes sense."

"It does?" I ask as we take seats next to each other, burgers in our laps and bodies facing the water so we can watch the remaining sunset.

"I may not know you that well, but you seem like a man who has the all-or-nothing mentality."

My interest piques. "How so?"

"You've done a lot in the time you've been on this planet, and you've made more money than I've ever seen in my lifetime, all because you were willing to do what you love and take risks. You live in an RV traveling around and doing whatever you want, when you want. And you invited a near stranger to live with you for almost a month. I don't know, it seems like you go all in."

My skin heats from her assessment, and I dip my chin. "Did you Google-search me, Jesse?"

I can see her skin flush even in the darkening light as the sun nearly sets completely. "I did."

She thinks I'm weirded out; I can see it all over her face. But I had suspected as much, and I'm not weirded out. I'm also not going to fault her for doing it. It inflates my ego hearing that she looked me up of her own volition, which means she was thinking about me like I was thinking about her in the time we were apart. Besides, I googled her, too. There wasn't much to be found besides a recently-updated LinkedIn profile and a Facebook page she never uses.

"Sorry, maybe that's not something you tell someone," she says.

"Don't be sorry, I think it's normal in this day and age. Did you find anything good?" I ask as I pick up my burger.

"Besides the fact you're a genius, not too much."

I chew and swallow a bit of my food. "A genius, huh?"

Jesse takes a sip of her drink. "That's what *Business Today Magazine* and all the other articles I found detailing your business ventures called you. Not everyone starts a business in high school."

"True, but some could argue you don't have to be smart for that just have no attention span and get hyper-fixated on and obsessed about things until you figure them out."

That makes her smile. "Geniuses come in all different forms."

I lift my burger in a toasting motion. "That's true. Though in my case, more ADHD managed with a daily stimulant."

Jesse pauses, eyes soft. "Thank you for telling me that. You didn't need to."

I swallow another bite. "I've known I had it since I was a kid, and mostly, I manage just fine. If I can't, I'll talk to my doctor, and we adjust my dose."

She nods, eyes still soft, and picks up her burger. I attempt to pretend I'm not watching as she bites into it, her pink lips making me think things I shouldn't. I take another bite of mine, too, so I don't seem like a creep with a mukbang fetish, and wait for her to chew and swallow.

"Verdict?" I ask.

"Maybe genius only applies to tech and not to the kitchen?"

I scoff and place my hand over my heart. "You wound me, Jesse called Jesse."

"I'm kidding! It's actually pretty good."

I use the hand over my chest to beat it like a caveman. "Like me said, man makes good food over fire!" She rolls her eyes, and my belly flips at her playfulness. "What else did the internet tell you about me?" I ask after she's swallowed another bite.

"Do you really want to know?"

"Sure. Unless you want to cut this conversation and play a game instead." Her face scrunches up, and I cock my head to the side in question. "Not a fan of games?"

She shakes her head. "From time to time, I guess. But I only like games like Family Feud or occasional trivia. Board games are my worst nightmare."

"Noted."

"You're a board game lover, aren't you?"

I think of the stash I have in a cupboard and rub the back of my neck. "Guilty."

She cringes. "Sorry."

"Why are you saying sorry?"

Jesse puts her burger down and stops to think for a second. "I don't know. Maybe it's because I feel bad that I don't like what you like."

"That's not true. I liked The Corn Palace—did *you* like The Corn Palace?"

"I did." She glances at me from beneath her dark eyelashes. "It was corny."

I laugh. "That it was." I place my burger down on my plate and sip my drink. When I focus back on my travel companion, I find her picking at her burger bun. "Jesse?"

Her gaze meets mine. "Yeah?"

"You don't have to like everything I like. Friends can be friends without having all shared interests. I don't care that you don't like board games; there are plenty of other games I think you'll enjoy."

She lifts an eyebrow. "Like what?"

"Twenty questions. But instead of guessing what a thing is with twenty questions, we play the version where we just ask each other twenty questions and answer."

"Is that really a game?"

"Yep. In a way, it's like trivia."

"But there's no winner for this game."

"You win by getting to know the other person."

"I googled you, remember?" she volleys, her hazel eyes shimmering with mirth.

"But did Google tell you that I have a sixth toe?"

She barks a laugh. "Liar."

"How do you know?"

Her skin flushes, and I know she's thinking of me naked. Can't say I'm mad about it.

"I didn't notice a sixth toe," she admits.

"Would you bet on it?"

She looks down at my sneakered feet then up to my eyes. "I would."

I cluck my tongue against the back of my teeth and slap my knees. "Fine, I don't have a sixth toe. But I do have a club thumb."

"What the hell is a club thumb?"

I hold out my two thumbs in front of me so she can see them. One thumb looks normal while the other looks like I stubbed it and it got squished. It's the same length as my other thumb but looks funny.

"It's a genetic mutation lots of people have. Back in the early 1900s, palm readers called them a Murderer's Thumb.'"

Jesse dips her chin as if she's embarrassed, and it takes me a second to think of why. Then I remember my words from the other night: *The only thing I'm going to murder is that pussy of yours.*

I run my fingers through my hair. "Anyway, kids used to make fun of it."

Jesse regains her bearings and groans. "Those kids are dumb."

"Facts." This time we both laugh, and the air around us eases.

Jesse takes another sip of her drink and picks her burger up, relaxing back in her chair. After she's had another bite, she gets my attention.

"I'll play twenty questions," she says, "but only if you agree to two things."

My smile brightens. "Anything."

"I go first."

"Alright, easy enough. And the second?"

"We break the questions up over our trip. That way, we always have something to talk about."

"I don't know, I think we'll still have lots to talk about regardless."

"You say that now, but I hate awkward silences. We're bound to run out of things to talk about over the course of twenty days."

I want to argue with her because I know that's not true. Not to mention, when I think back on our drive today, there were several times when we didn't speak. I wonder if she realizes that or if she simply didn't realize our silences didn't feel awkward. But she looks so serious right now, and for whatever reason, this means something to her, so I agree.

"Okay," I say. Jesse holds out her hand, but I don't shake on it yet. "Wait, I have one condition."

She pulls her hand back and crosses her arms over her chest, looking so serious I nearly laugh. "Go on," she says.

"If we ask a question to clarify a question, it doesn't count toward the twenty."

"Then we shouldn't even call it twenty questions."

"We can call it 'question game.' This way, we have more to talk about."

"What an original title. Again, I thought you were a genius," she quips.

"Damn, you're a ballbuster." I smile devilishly at her. "But I like it."

Jesse seems happy as she agrees. "Fine, question game it is."

"Does that mean we have a deal on this game thing?" I ask.

She holds out her hand once more. "We have a deal."

I place my hand in hers, relishing its warmth and how it feels so right in mine before I give it a firm shake.

"Now finish your dinner," I command. "We've got a long day of driving tomorrow. We can start our game then."

She sits up a little straighter in her chair and salutes me. "Yes, sir."

Chapter Eighteen

Jesse

It shouldn't feel weird that I'm showering in an RV, but it feels weird. Prior to now, I've never been in one, only seen them online and had one or two random fantasies of buying or renting a van and traveling across the country to check off my bucket list. But I never imagined being in one with a full-blown bathroom and shower. It really is like being in someone's home on wheels.

The water pressure is perfect, the shower is spacious enough that two people could fit—*we won't go there*—and the water is nice and hot. I honestly could spend a long time here enjoying the water sluicing down my back and the humid air against my skin.

But one of the downfalls of an RV is the limited water tank and hot water. Asher told me I could use all the hot water I wanted since he'd shower later, but I don't want to be rude. Not to mention, I'm excited to get a move on because today's nine-hour drive gets us outside of Yellowstone, which means tomorrow we see Old Faithful and the day after, the Hot Springs.

The thought has me speeding up my shower. Once I'm finished, I grab the fluffy white towel he provided and dry my body, wrapping my hair up so it doesn't drip water down my back, and swipe my hand across the mirror so I can see my face to moisturize and add a light amount of makeup. I stare at myself in the mirror, naked except for the towel on my head. My cheeks are pink and dewy from the shower, and my ICD scar looks redder than usual because of the heat.

I smile at myself and nearly let out a small laugh. I can't believe I'm here right now and that, by this time tomorrow, I'm going to be looking at Old Faithful. It truly is surreal, considering a few days ago, I was wondering what few things I could get done and hoping I could squeeze both Yellowstone and Maine off my list before next month.

Now I'm here. In Ash's bathroom. Making a cross-country road trip in twenty days.

Asher. I smile wider thinking of him. After we finished dinner last night, we packed up everything, and he showed me how to lock up Winnie before he had me feed GusGus. He wasn't lying when he said the cat would fall in love with me—I spent the night snuggled with the purring kitty. And just like Ash said, sometime around three am, I woke up to him biting my toes and wanting to play. Eventually I got him to go back to sleep, and I woke up at six to the smell of coffee.

Asher snorted when I told him what happened and said "I told you so" before handing me a hot cup of dark roast and giving me the details of our drive. After which he showed me how to use the shower.

Between the coffee and the hot shower, I feel refreshed and ready for the day. I apply my moisturizer, deodorant, a bit of mascara, and a light-pink lipstick before moving to grab my clothes—only to find there aren't any.

"Shit!" Panic wells in my gut, and I search around the small bathroom, hoping they will magically appear. I wrack my brain for where I left them, because I know I grabbed what I needed out of my bag before I came in here.

Then I remember. I had my makeup bag in one hand and my clothes in the other, but before I left my room, GusGus had demanded a head scratch, so I set them down on the bed to free my hand.

I curse again and look around the bathroom for another towel besides the one on my head. The only thing I find are a couple of hand towels. I crouch down to look in the cabinet under the sink, but there's only toilet paper, a first aid kit, and other random supplies, including tampons and condoms. For a second, I wonder if Asher got those tampons for me and the condoms for us, but I quickly scratch that from my brain.

We're a one-night stand. I'm sure those are for him if and when he needs them, and tampons...I shake my head. It doesn't matter if they were for someone else before me. If he did get them for this trip, then he's thoughtful. That's it. It would almost be a little embarrassing but kind of sweet.

What are you doing, Jesse? I push my thoughts away and stand. I need to think about more important things, like getting through Asher's room to mine without him seeing me naked. It shouldn't be a problem since he went to the kitchen area, if I remember correctly, and I didn't hear him walk into the bathroom while I was showering—which he would have to do to get to his bedroom.

I take my wet towel off my head and wrap it around my body—mostly around it—pinching the top part together. It's pretty worthless, because when I move, everything sort of hangs out. It makes me wish I would've brought oversized towels or a robe with me to avoid this. Maybe I can grab one at a Walmart or something the next time we get supplies.

Makeup bag in hand, I decide I'm going to make a run for it just in case. But hopefully I'm right about Asher's location and he won't know this ever happened.

I press my ear to the closed door to try to hear him, but it's quiet. I'm going to take that as a good sign and pray I get to my room without issue.

I push the door open leading to the bedrooms and bolt into Asher's room. I make it two steps before I'm tripping over something, and the loud meowing of GusGus rings through the air. A split second later, I hit a soft yet very solid wall. A squeak leaves my lips as I fall forward, my body bouncing. I think I'm going to fall to the floor, but strong arms lock around me to prevent it from happening.

It takes my brain a few seconds to catch up to what happened, and when it finally does, I look down to see Asher beneath me on the bed. He's looking up at me with wide surprised eyes and a slight grin teasing at the corners of his mouth. "If you wanted me back in bed, Jesse, all you had to do was ask. No need to use my cat as an inciting incident."

I blink at him, my brain still not fully online. He shouldn't be here; I thought he was in the front of the RV. I blink, then blink again.

Asher's brow pinches in concern. "Are you okay?" His arms squeeze gently, the heat of his skin searing against my bare back.

Bare back...

"Oh my god!" I pull away, and Asher immediately lets me go. "Oh my god," I exclaim again. I scramble off him, my entire body turning pink. I snatch my towel off the floor and hold it to myself.

"Jesse—"

"Oh my god," I repeat again. "I'm so sorry."

I faintly hear Asher apologizing, but I don't wait to listen. I practically run the short distance to my room, buck-ass naked with tits and belly jiggling, slamming the door behind me. Safe inside, I close my eyes and rest my back against the door to catch my breath. When I open my eyes, I'm faced with the culprit that tripped me: GusGus.

He sits on top of the mattress, large black eyes watching me, tail slowly moving back and forth like a snake across the comforter.

"You," I say as I take a step forward. "Did you do this on purpose?"

Gus meows, and I swear he's smiling. I expel a long breath and scratch under his chin. "You're a meddler, aren't you?"

He doesn't meow this time, but I think he smiles wider in agreement. Looking at him now, he has the same sly glint in his eye I've seen in Asher's. No wonder this is his cat—they have similar qualities.

After another pat to Gus's head, I grab my clothes from exactly where I thought I left them. I slip them on, the adrenaline of falling on top of Ash leaving my body, and now all I'm left with is embarrassment and a hint of something else. My skin still tingles from where he touched me, the ghost of his arms on my back like a brand. My skin becomes hot for a new reason now, and I curse Gus for tripping me and Asher for being in his damn room. I definitely need to get a robe.

I blow out a tense breath and get my hairbrush from my bag. There's a mirror on the back of the door, and I ignore staring into my eyes as I brush my hair. A minute later, I swipe through the last tangle, and a knock vibrates through the door. My heart skips a beat as heat rises up my neck. I consider diving back into bed and hiding there for the rest of the road trip, but that would be stupid. I have to face Asher, and it's better to do it now.

I give myself a silent pep talk in the mirror before opening the door. I expect Asher to be grinning or making silly comments to ease my embarrassment, but he doesn't. He looks serious and even a little embarrassed himself, a far cry from the man I left only ten minutes ago.

"I texted you, but you didn't answer."

I cross my hands over my chest, hairbrush still in hand. "My phone is still off."

"Oh." His brow furrows.

"You texted me?"

"Um, yeah. You've been in here awhile, and I was trying to give you space, but I wanted to check on you."

"It's been less than ten minutes." I laugh.

He rubs the back of his neck. "Really? It felt like an hour."

Another soft laugh spills from my lips. "It was not that long, but I'm okay."

"Good." He smiles softly. "I should've waited to go to my room till you were done."

"How did you even get to it?"

He points to the back door behind me that leads out of the RV.

"Oh, right."

"It was dumb and inconsiderate. I thought you'd be longer, so I went to change. I'm so used to being here alone, I honestly didn't think it through."

"It's fine."

He shakes his head. "It was dumb of me. I also should've warned you that GusGus likes to trip people. I'm still trying to figure out if it's intentional or not."

I look back at the cat, who is now sleeping innocently on my pillow. "I'm going with intentional."

Ash chuckles, and I meet his eyes again. He parts his lips to speak but closes them. Another second goes by before he holds out something I didn't see he had until now. A green robe.

"You can use this while you're here. I should've hung it in the bathroom before, but I forgot I had it."

I glance at the robe then into his warm eyes. "You don't want to use it?"

He shifts on his feet. "I actually just cut off the tags. Don't tell Melissa, though—it was my Christmas gift last year. Apparently it's expensive or something."

I take the offered item, the material soft and fuzzy beneath my fingers. From the looks of it, it's big enough that it will fit me. "I'll keep your secret."

He grins back at me. "Thanks."

We stand there staring at each other for a moment, and I find myself getting lost in the pools of his beautiful and unique eyes, layered with so many shades of brown—just like the curls of his hair. I noticed the different highlights within the tapered tresses while we were outside of The Corn Palace yesterday. It made me want to run my fingers through each strand.

"Well, um, I'm sorry again."

Asher's voice brings me back to reality, the one where we're just friends. My stupid—*no, smart*—doing.

"Don't worry about it."

He nods before rubbing his hands together. "Should we hit the road? I made you some peanut butter toast...on gluten-free bread of course."

"I hate peanut butter," I deadpan.

His eyes go wide, and his mouth drops open as if I ended the world. The look makes me snort, and I pat his shoulder in a friendly way. "Ash, I'm kidding."

He exhales a comical breath. "Oh, thank god. I love peanut butter. Maybe more than I love money."

I shake my head and laugh. Asher Jamison is one of the most interesting people I've ever met. I can't wait to learn more about him through our game. I just hope we don't have any more naked run-ins. Not only because it's embarrassing but also because I don't need to be reminded of how nice it feels to be in his arms.

"Come on," I say, laying the robe on the bed. "Let's go eat some peanut butter toast."

Chapter Nineteen

Asher

"ALRIGHT, LET'S PLAY."

Jesse rubs her hands together excitedly like this question game we "invented" is the best thing to ever happen to her—which tells me maybe she likes games more than she thinks. It makes me wonder if she's a competitive person who hasn't owned that part of herself yet.

"I've been trying to think of a good one since last night," she says.

"Have you?"

"Gotta make 'em good. They have to be so they have good subsequent questions."

Yeah, I definitely think she's competitive...and a perfectionist. I smile softly to myself while keeping my eyes on the road. We're only about an hour into our drive for today. We spent the first half hour deciding what cassette to listen to, but now that we've got a '90s mix playing, it's time to start our game.

"Okay, shoot. Let's hear it."

"What's something you could talk about for hours at length without getting bored?"

"Did you google that?" I chide.

Much like how her skin flushed when she ran into me naked earlier, it does so again. "And if I did? I thought we're making our rules. Which means Google is fair play."

I expel a short laugh. "Okay, you're right about that."

"Of course I'm right," she chirps. "But I didn't google it. My phone has been off. I got that from my brain."

I bank her phone still being off for later conversation and dip my head. "It's a very smart brain."

She giggles, and the sound warms me to my toes. "Okay, so answer it."

My hands grip the wheel at her commanding tone, and I shift in my seat. "Let me think for a second. Something I could talk about for hours at length without getting bored..." I repeat.

"Yep. Just say what comes to your mind first."

I nearly say "you," but like many of my inappropriate thoughts, that would be weird to say. I push that back and think of something deep and honest since she's told me so much about herself already.

"Mythology," I answer.

Her head turns, and I watch from my periphery as she studies me, gaze burning a hole into the side of my head. "That was not what I was expecting you to say."

"Did you think I'd say coding or something about business?"

She bites her lower lip. "Maybe."

I chuckle. "I mean, I could talk about coding and business at length, but it can be kind of boring—at least to talk about. Not when I'm actually doing it."

"Makes sense." She leans forward in her seat. "So what kind of mythology?"

"I am a fan of most, but I have the most knowledge of Norse."

"Okay, you surprised me again. I feel like most people say Greek."

"It's one of the more popular, and don't get me wrong, I love Greek mythology, too. But I saw a book on Thor when I was a kid and wanted to be him. And not comic book Thor—Thor with the round belly and solid arms. I've never been svelte or overly muscular. It was the first time I saw myself in any form of media, and I thought that was cool."

"That *is* cool," Jesse adds. "That was how I felt when I saw the movie *Hairspray*. I wanted to be Tracy Turnblad."

I'm not a big musical guy, but when I look at Jesse and see how her face has lit up by simply speaking about it, I think I should watch it. I want to know about the movie and the character that made her feel seen.

"Goes to show how important it is for kids to have themselves represented in the things they consume. I know that seeing Thor on that cover and learning about the mythology of him changed my life."

Jesse briefly pauses before speaking again. "If you're comfortable sharing, I'd love to know how."

I sit taller, wheel still gripped firmly in both hands. I have Winnie on cruise control, and even though we're driving down the open road with the South Dakota scenery on either side of us, I want to be alert while also answering Jesse's questions.

"A lot of people these days know Thor only from popular superhero movies," I begin. "And while that's a fun depiction, he was more than that. He's the son of Odin, the chief of the gods, and he himself is the god of thunder, storms, and strength."

"I definitely knew that part." She smiles.

"I'm sure you know, then, that he wields a powerful hammer. But a lot of people don't know it has a name: Mjölnir."

"Mjölnir," Jesse repeats, but it comes out sounding like *mall-near*.

I chuckle. "It's Mjölnir like *MYAWL-neer*."

She tries again and fails, laughing on her third try. "I'll leave that pronunciation up to you. What does it mean?"

"Now that's an interesting question. It's Old Norse, and there's been some heavy debate among scholars as to what it means. The dictionary says it means 'lightning,' which makes sense because of his powers. But there really isn't a direct answer. I personally like the theory that it means 'new snow' or 'white' based on the color of the thunderbolts when they strike the sky."

"You really do know your stuff."

"I am a genius nerd, after all."

"Yeah, yeah," Jesse teases. "Now finish telling me about Thor."

A jolt of a thrill courses through me, one that has me feeling like a kid again. I begin to tell her about how Thor protects both gods and humans from giants, Jötnar—another word Jesse can't pronounce—and how he's strong but sometimes hot-headed, embodying loyalty and bravery.

Answering her, seeing her smile and how she's getting as interested as I did when I started to learn about Thor, reminds me why I love mythology so much. It also helps me see how lost in work I've gotten the last few years. I've hardly had more than random fleeting thoughts about Thor or any Norse god in a long time.

"I can see why you like mythology so much—especially Thor."

"Really?"

"He's strong, loyal, brave, protective. We might've just met, but considering the little I knew of you before, all of the articles I've read, and the time we've spent together, you're all of those things."

"You think I'm strong?"

"Of course that's the one you pick to highlight out of everything!"

"I want to hear you confirm it." I go to say more, but Jesse leans over and slugs me in the arm.

"Woody Wagon!" she yells joyfully.

A laugh bursts from my lips, and I shake my head at her. That was a good diversion from her having to answer. I'm not sure if there was even a Woody Wagon driving by, but it was funny, nonetheless.

"Is that how Thor changed your life?" she asks.

"With Woody Wagons?"

She slugs me in the arm again, and I press my lips together to seal in laughter.

"Be serious," she says. "I really want to know."

I exhale a breath, bringing old memories to the surface. "I was teased a lot when I was a kid. I hit puberty before most of my classmates, so I shot up like a weed. But unlike most boys, I didn't shed the 'baby fat' along with my height, so I was tall, pimply, and chubby. Looking back on old pictures, I think I was cute, but that's not how people treated me."

"Kids can be mean," Jesse says, "and I bet you were cute."

"Were?" I smirk.

She rolls her eyes at me. "You're still cute. Now finish your answer."

I internally fist pump for getting the compliment but keep the success from my face before I answer. "Along with my looks, I struggled with my classes. Either I was completely engaged in the subject and learned everything there was to know very quickly, or I got bored and couldn't focus, often disrupting class by standing up or asking if I could use the bathroom to move around. I hadn't been diagnosed with ADHD yet, so my teachers just thought I was lazy or uncooperative. Some even thought I was stupid. One day, during lunch, a kid tripped me, sent my lunch flying all over the floor. Impulse control was a huge struggle for me, so I shoved him hard before I could stop myself and got suspended for a few days."

"Not going to lie, I'm glad you shoved that kid."

My heart thuds faster at her defense of little me's actions. "I have that same feeling, but my parents, not so much. But that was when they finally decided to take me in for testing. After my diagnosis, my mom brought me to the library while we waited for my medication to be filled at the pharmacy. That's when I stumbled upon the book with Thor on the cover, and the way he looked drew me in. And it was called. *Thor: God of Thunder, What You Don't Know.* I was hooked before I even read it."

"Do you still have it?"

"*Pfft*. What do you think?"

"That you probably have it in every edition."

"And a special hardcover I had made."

"Made?"

"Yep, hand-bound."

"You really are a nerd," she chirps.

"Yeah, yeah. You wanna hear the rest or not?" I tease.

She gestures for me to keep talking and adds, "Go on."

"That book was the first book I read cover to cover after I started taking my medication. I cried afterward because it was the first time my brain was quiet and I could focus without wanting to do a million other things at once."

"That's beautiful," she says.

"Not only did it show me I could do anything, but Thor also made me feel all those things you mentioned. Brave, strong, and confident. Then I got obsessed with mythology, with gods and goddesses. In my own way, I felt invincible. I stopped letting kids get to me and focused on school and showing people I wasn't dumb. Eventually, I took my first computer class. From there, I developed my first app that helps with brain focus. It plays soothing frequency music that creates positive brain states for focus, relaxation, and sleep. Anyone can use it, but it's helpful for those with ADHD."

"I did read about the app in an article, but hearing it from you is way better than Google."

My stomach warms, and I smile. "Did you catch what the app is called?"

"Something with a B," she answers.

"Bragi, which, in hindsight, sounds like bragging, but it's the Norse god of music. I couldn't name it anything else in my mind."

"I love that."

"Me, too. The company that bought it tried to change it, but I put in the sale contract that they couldn't."

"Smart."

"Names are important, Jesse called Jesse. Especially names given with meaning."

"I think my mom named me Jesse because it sounded cool and she was into gender-neutral names. She almost named me Blake."

I think on that name for a moment and shake my head. "Jesse suits you, and if it sounded cool to your mom, then it was given in meaning."

"That's a stretch!"

I smile. "Fine, then you should look up what it means on Google—that is your specialty," I tease. God, she's going to have at me when she finds out I googled her, too, but it's fun to tease her, and she doesn't seem to mind it.

Jesse laughs, only proving my point. "I can look later," she says. "I want to know more about Thor."

I think over my options. I've been blabbing for a while now and told her a story very few people know. It's nothing I have a problem sharing, but it's also not a story that comes up often. I want to know more about Jesse, and I want her to turn on her phone. She's been avoiding it since yesterday.

"I think it's my turn for a question. You can ask me more after I grill you," I say.

She groans. "Maybe we should establish solid rules."

"Nooo, we make the rules as we go along. Those are the rules."

She huffs but gives in. "Okay, ask. But since we're making up rules, I'm asking you more questions later, and they don't count."

"Deal."

"Deal," she echoes me.

"Why haven't you turned your phone on?" I ask.

From the side of my vision, I see her head flop back against the seat. "I had a feeling you were going to ask that. But as a reminder, you were the one who told me to turn it off in the first place."

I bite the inside of my cheek. "Okay, you're right there, I forgot about that. But I meant for a bit while we enjoyed the finery of The Corn Palace."

She sighs. "I know, it's just...."

"Sorry, is this too personal? I can ask something else."

She shakes her head. "Even if it was, you just spilled your guts."

"Hey," I say seriously. "This isn't tit for tat here."

She turns her head to me, and I glance at her for a second, doing all I can to convey my seriousness through my eyes.

"I mean that. We make the rules, remember? If you want to pass, you can. But clearly it's bothering you. Maybe talking about it will help."

I put my eyes back on the road, and she stares out the windshield along with me. While I do want to know the answer, I'm also never going to force her.

"I feel like we already talked about this yesterday," she says.

"You can say whatever you need to, Jesse; I don't mind if you repeat yourself. I understand texting your friend was big for you. It's okay to have feelings about it."

She's quiet for another minute, then she exhales a loud breath. "I guess I'm just scared of what she said. I know I shouldn't care about hurting her feelings, but I'm sure I did. We've been friends a long time, and the more I thought about it, the worse I felt that I texted instead of called. I know it's kind of stupid, and I shouldn't be such a chicken about it. I just hate confrontation, and I hate when people are upset with me."

"Let's back up." I have the itch to pull over so I can look her in the eye while we talk about this, but I know that would make her uncomfortable. I take a breath before I continue. "Why do you think your reaction is stupid?"

"Because normal people would just tell her how they feel and not turn off their phone to ignore reality. I'm too sensitive, I think."

"Are you too sensitive or just afraid of the consequences of standing up for yourself?"

Jesse pauses and rubs a hand over her face. "I...I've never thought of it that way."

"Standing up for yourself will generally come with a reaction from the other party because they're afraid, too. But you can't control how they react, and sometimes you have to say something that other people won't like. And may I add, I think being sensitive is a good trait—it means you care. It's better than the alternative, don't you think?"

"I don't know, sometimes I think not caring would be easier. It would lessen my anxiety." She tries to smile.

"Maybe, but then you wouldn't be you. I think caring, even too much sometimes, is a good trait. I'd argue that the world would be a better place if more people cared like you do. It also proves to me that you really do care about your friendship and you want Kate to respond in such a way that you can keep your relationship. I don't see anything wrong with that."

I catch Jesse wiping at her eye from the corner of my vision, and now I wish I had pulled over. I want to wipe her tears for her, take her into my arms and let her cry or do whatever she needs to do. Something tells me, with everything she's been through, she hasn't let herself feel the way she wants to. Especially if she's worried about being too sensitive and caring about what other people think of her.

"I don't know if I'd call that trait good," she says.

"Great," I retort. That earns me an honest smile, and I feel a little better at the sight. "Look, you can keep your phone off the whole trip if you want, but you wouldn't be able to do your blog/vlog thing."

"Shit," she says. "I keep forgetting about that."

I chuckle. "I could take pictures for you, but I think that would defeat the purpose of it being yours."

"Can't argue with you there."

There's another pause of silence, and this time, I'm the one to break it. "If it helps, pretend you're Thor. That's what I do when I need some extra bravery. And no, I'm not too old to do that—sometimes, we all need to pull some extra confidence from somewhere."

"WWTD," Jesse says.

"What Would Thor Do?"

"Send the hammer to take care of all his problems," she quips. I bark a laugh. "That's one way, I suppose, but if I may say something?"

"You may," she replies.

"You're already brave, Jesse. Like you said, we may not have known each other for long, but from everything you've told me, you are brave. You don't need to be Thor or anyone else. Just be you. Whatever Kate said, you can handle it. Just know that I'm not judging you, whatever you choose to do or however you respond."

Jesse taps her fingertips on her knees before her hand goes to her belt buckle and she turns to face me. "What are you doing?"

"Going to get my phone. Is that okay?"

"Yes, of course, just be careful."

Jesse smiles and unclips her belt. It doesn't take her long before she's back in the passenger seat and buckling herself back in. She closes her eyes and takes a few inhales and exhales.

"What are you doing?" I ask.

She opens one eye and grins cheekily. "Channeling Thor."

A wide smile covers my lips, and my "falling in love" barometer moves to "I'm in trouble" levels.

After another few breaths, she opens her eyes. "Okay, here goes nothing." She holds up her phone and turns the power on. We're quiet while it boots, the sounds of a Backstreet Boys song playing through the speakers. Not my usual choice of music, but that's the fun thing about the cassettes I got at a thrift store. A lot of times, I don't know what's on them, just the year or genre.

When her phone powers on, it starts pinging. I know the moment she gets Kate's notification because her body tenses strongly enough that I see it in my periphery.

"She texted and called," Jesse says.

"Did she leave a voicemail?"

"No, just the text." Jesse goes quiet, and a minute passes before she lets out a long exhale that's near a sigh.

"You good?" I ask.

"That was...anticlimactic." A moment later, she laughs, then she presses her head back into her seat. "I really built that up in my head. I know you said caring too much is a good trait, but maybe I can lighten up a bit."

I glance at her, happy to see a relieved smile on her face. I know I could still argue that point, but I let it go. "Good message?"

She hums. "She said she's sorry, that she wants to make it up to me. And that we should talk."

"You can go to the back and call her, if you want."

Jesse shakes her head. "I'll text her for now and call her later. I need to breathe for a moment so I can get my words together."

I give Jesse the space she needs, hearing her soft cycle of breaths joining the notes of music. Faintly, GusGus's collar jingles from somewhere in the kitchen. It reminds me I have to give him a treat later for creating the whole "Jesse falling into my arms naked" incident. Truly, he deserves all the treats for that. Hell, I'd rescue him again just for that moment.

"Ash," she says a minute later.

"Yeah?"

"Thanks."

"For what?"

"For helping me find my inner Thor."

My pulse quickens, and I meet her gaze. "Anytime, Jesse called Jesse. Now, look up what your name means."

Chapter Twenty
Jesse

"Holy shit." I blink, then blink again.

"Better than photos?" Asher asks from beside me.

"Better than my dreams." I stare wide-eyed at Old Faithful from behind the corded barrier, the water shooting nearly two-hundred feet in the air as it erupts from the large hole in its mineral-coated basin. The water droplets catch in the mid-afternoon sun, creating rainbows of light in reflections before falling back down again. It's summer, so there are a lot of people and kids around, but their *oohing* and *aahing* only add to this moment. It's a moment I'll never forget.

"Beautiful," Asher mutters from beside me. With the crowd, our shoulders are nearly touching. I turn my head and look at him. He's gazing at me, eyes sparkling. The intense way he's staring makes my cheeks flush, and I admit I kind of like it. It makes me feel like a schoolgirl being crushed on. But I shove that feeling aside, attributing his one-word statement to Old Faithful.

"Will you take a quick picture of me in front of it?" I ask. "Then I want one of us." He nods with a small smile and goes to take the phone from me.

"I'll snap one of you two!" an older woman interjects from next to me. "Get in there quick before it ends! We're lucky this is a longer eruption."

"Oh, thanks!" I hand her my phone, and before I can ask Asher how he wants to stand, he pulls me into his side with one of his arms snug around my shoulders. I tilt my chin up at him with a laugh, and at the same time, he looks into my eyes.

"So adorable!" the woman exclaims. "Smile now."

I flush from the praise, and Asher squeezes me before we face the camera. He leans down a second later so his lips are against my ear.

"Now, get one of you alone for social media," he says.

Asher steps to the side, and the woman snaps a couple of photos without even asking then hands it back once we're done. I say my thanks then give my attention to Old Faithful, who's still going, though the height of the water is lower now as the eruption begins to fade. It's incredible to see, and I can't wait to explore more of the park.

Ash steps back up next to me, his arm resting against mine once more, as we watch the final water bubble and peter out.

"Did y'all come here for your honeymoon?"

My head snaps to the woman who took our photo, and I think I turn as hot as the water inside Old Faithful. "No!" I say a little too loudly. "No, we're not—I mean, we're just friends," I stumble out.

"Oh, dear. Sorry, you two looked so in love."

My skin burns, and I thank god that I put some good deodorant on this morning because now I'm not only sweating due to the heat. My gaze drops from the woman back to Old Faithful, even though it's not erupting anymore.

"It's okay. We're really good friends," I say.

Since Asher's arm is touching mine, I can feel his body shaking with laughter. Glad he thinks this is amusing, because I'm mortified. Did we really look in love? That's impossible since we're only getting to know each other. Sure, we had sex, we're on a road trip together, and I fell on him naked, but we're friends. Just friends. And there's no way we looked in love—that lady clearly needs her eyes checked.

"I see," the woman chirps. "Are you here for long?"

I suck in a quiet breath and hope I don't look as red as I feel. "Today and tomorrow."

"Have you explored the park yet?"

"A little this morning," I say.

After our long drive yesterday, we got into an RV park that had what Asher calls a "full hookup." Despite it being a long day, he showed me how he gets Winnie set up at each campground, which includes plugging into electric, sewer, and freshwater lines. He showed me how he levels the RV so things don't fall out of cabinets and the fridge, too, and lastly, he turned on the propane tanks for hot water.

Once that was set, we ate leftover burgers and crashed for the evening to wake up early and take in the sights. We spent the morning exploring some of the park before we got to Old Faithful, making a stop at the gift shop where Ash bought a postcard to send to Melissa—which I thought was sweet of him.

"Well, enjoy," the woman adds. "If you have a chance, don't forget to check out the Hot Springs."

"That's on our list," Asher replies.

"Good," she chirps. "Good for loosening things up. Muscles, I mean."

I think my eyes bug out of my head, but Asher just laughs again. "Sounds great," he says.

"Oh, I see my family is ready to go." She points to a group not far from us. "Nice chatting."

The woman walks away, and I turn to Ash. His warm eyes, full of mirth, are highlighted in the summer sunlight, bringing out the varying shades of brown.

"She was..." Ash pauses to search for the right word.

"Bold?" I say.

"I was going to say friendly."

"That's one word."

Asher runs a hand through his curls. "Do you want to get more pictures, or are you ready to head to the Grand Prismatic Spring?"

I observe Old Faithful, the sleeping beast quiet once more. "I got some pictures before it started erupting, but I thought we could take that trail you mentioned."

"The Geyser Hill Loop Trail?" he asks.

"That one."

His lopsided grin appears. "Sounds good to me. Anything for God's Gift."

I shove him and roll my eyes. Ever since I googled what the name "Jesse" means and found out it means "gift" or "God's gift" in Hebrew, it's been Asher's favorite thing to call me.

"You'd better stop, or I'm going to start calling you One Who Lives by an Ash Tree or Ash Grove," I quip.

"I prefer the Hebrew meaning of my name."

"Of course you do."

"I mean, you seem pretty 'happy' and 'blessed' to be in my presence, God's Gift."

I roll my eyes again. "Didn't you say your mom named you after a TV show character she loved?"

Asher smirks. "She did. A very hot one."

I shake my head. "You're impossible, you know that?"

"You like it," he teases.

I press my lips together in an attempt to deny it, but he's right. I like his clever comebacks, his funny jokes, and the ease he has about him. He really is a happy person, and the meaning of his name does suit him. Not that I'd ever tell him that.

"Come on, let's get going, you goofus. Limited time, lots to do."

"Goofus?" I glare at him, and he holds up his hands in laughter. "Just never heard that one before. But it's unique; I like it."

I huff an incredulous laugh and wave him toward where I saw the trail started on the map. He falls in step beside me easily, his own chuckles meeting my ears as we start the loop.

"Did you know this trail is at the heart of one of the world's greatest concentration of geysers?" Ash asks a few minutes into our walk.

"I did not know that."

"I watched a retired couple's RV video on this trail last night before I fell asleep."

We stop in front of a geyser that's steaming, the white plumes flowing into the air like clouds. There are other people around, but this one isn't as busy as Old Faithful was.

"Did you really?"

He nods. "I wanted to be prepared."

I cock my head at him, and my mind races a million miles a minute. Did he want to be prepared because he wanted to make this day great? Or did he do it because he was worried about my heart condition and what I could handle?

The latter makes my gut churn. While Asher hasn't given me a reason to think he'd coddle me, and he said he wouldn't treat me differently, he may be doing it unintentionally. I hate that it does, but the comment leaves an icky feeling lurking inside me.

When I called my parents to tell them I'd be going on this trip, the first thing my mom told me to do was take it easy and stay prepared for anything. When I told her some of the stops, she said to make a list and consult my doctor—all the things I'd already done, things I didn't need to be told to do. I understand her worry, but after the last few years of being asked if I'm okay every two seconds and the anxiety my condition naturally causes me, anyway, I was hoping not to get that from Asher.

"Oh, give me your phone!" he exclaims.

I do as he asks, though my thoughts are still spiraling. He steps back from me and holds up my phone, but he must see my frown, because he puts it down.

"You okay?"

I nearly laugh. In wanting to not be asked if I'm okay, I created a situation where him asking me that question is totally valid. Not wanting to get into my own hang-ups now, or maybe ever, I push my thoughts back.

"I'm good." A light gust of wind blows by, sending the hair I've left down fluttering in the breeze.

Asher's cheeks lift in a smile from behind the phone, and he snaps a picture. He does that a few more times before he walks back and hands my phone to me.

"I bet those are going to be good; the lighting here is perfect. And that wind with the steam were paid actors."

I smile at his comment, holding my phone. "Thanks."

"You don't want to look at the pics?"

I shake my head. "I will later. We have lots to see and little time."

"Are you sure you're okay?"

"Why wouldn't I be?" I take my own photo of the geyser as it bubbles then start to walk down the path toward the next one.

Asher walks beside me. "You were really excited, then your energy shifted."

I turn to look at him and smirk. "Are you into yoga and meditation, too?"

"No, just vibes."

His comment eases some of the tension in my body, and a short laugh leaves my chest. "I'm just thinking is all."

"That can be dangerous."

"That it can."

"Want to talk about it?"

"Not really."

"That's fair."

I put my phone then my hands in the pockets of my shorts and look out at the steaming landscape. If there's one thing I'm learning about Asher, it's that he never makes anything feel forced. I appreciate that about him.

Deep down, I know I should tell him what I'm feeling and thinking, ask him what he meant by his comment instead of assuming. But for now, I want to enjoy Yellowstone.

"This is one I wanted to see," I say a few minutes later as we stop in front of a boiling spring. It's not very large, and it's shaped like a human heart. It's a deep, clear pool of icy-blue water, almost a teal at some angles. It's so pretty it nearly looks drawn on the ground, as if it isn't real.

"The Heart Spring," I say.

"Aptly named," Asher adds.

I stare at it for a long moment, watching the bubbling water. It's a cool juxtaposition: water that looks like ice yet is hot enough to burn you. From what I read, it's not always active, but today it is.

I don't know how long I observe the Heart Spring, but before long, I find my eyes beginning to water. It's almost too much standing here, feeling my heart beat while the water in the pool boils. The active liquid reminds me I'm alive, that I'm taking charge of my life. That I'm actually out in the world living and doing this.

The sound of Asher shifting beside me reminds me he's close and can probably see I'm near tears. If he notices, he doesn't say anything.

Another breeze passes through, and I push my hair behind my ear. I pull out my phone and adjust the lighting how I want it then snap several pictures. Instead of waiting to look at them, I open up my photos and stare at the spring I've captured both in my memories and now in digital film.

"This is going to be the first thing I post," I say.

I tip my chin up at Asher and hold my phone out so he can see it. It's only a picture of the Heart Spring, but the light is perfect, and I can see the bubbling of the water and tell it resembles a human heart.

"I think that's perfect," he says.

I put my phone back in my pocket then watch the spring again, my eyes getting lost in the icy-blue depths of it. "Have I told you why I wanted to come here?" I ask after a few minutes.

"You haven't."

I face him, and his gaze is soft as he waits for me to speak. "Coming here, seeing Old Faithful, this park. I liked the idea of witnessing something bigger than myself."

Ash nods. "Mother Nature has a way of reminding us how small we really are in the grand scheme of things."

"She certainly does." I look back out at the pool. "This place is reminding me that time is limited, that I want to see and do as much as I can before my time is up, you know?"

Asher frowns. "You have time, Jesse. You're not even thirty yet. At thirty-two, I'm the old man out of the two of us," he attempts to tease, but I can tell my comment is still troubling him.

I force a wide smile on my face and tug on his arm. "This is too heavy of a topic. Let's keep going, One Who Lives by an Ash Tree or Ash Grove."

My name-calling does exactly what I want it to, and he agrees. "Lead the way, God's Gift."

Chapter Twenty-One

Asher

Jesse's been different since we visited Old Faithful, and I can't figure out why.

We were fine before, laughing and joking. We still do both, and we've continued to ask each other questions and share things, but now it feels strained. Her smiles are more like an effort than instinct.

I've replayed and obsessed over our conversations again and again. She made that unsettling comment about her limited time on this planet, but nothing else stands out as the moment everything shifted. I'm hoping that changes after a dip in a hot spring.

I lay back against the couch in the living area, enjoying a moment to rest my feet after a long two days of walking and exploring. After we finished up the walk around the geysers yesterday, we took a cab to the Grand Prismatic Spring. The downside of having such a large RV like Winnie is not being able to maneuver places easily. If we'd had more time to plan, I would've gotten a car to hook up and bring along. I don't mind the cabs, but Jesse keeps trying to pay for them since this was her bucket-list item. Of course, I won't hear it.

This morning, we drove Winnie to the Mammoth Hot Springs and explored then made home for the night at a nearby campsite, one with hot spring pools we can swim in. After all the activity over the past couple of days, my sore body is ready for a soak.

I exhale and find myself drifting. But before I can fall asleep, my phone pings. With a groan, I pull it out and see an email notification from the company I'll be working with in London next month.

I've tried to ignore my work since we left Madison, but my emails are piling up. It's not unusual for me to go without answering them for days since I'm contracted and not full-time, but this time I've waited longer than usual. Add to that, I'm not the most organized person and never have been.

If I keep to a routine, it's easier. With the introduction of Jesse into my life, though, my routine has been thrown off. I'm utterly focused on her and our trip together. Not that I care—I'd let her ruin me and my life in any way she likes—but I know I'm going to have to face reality soon since I am being paid.

"Okay, I'm ready."

I startle, bolting up on the couch to the point I nearly fall off. Jesse covers her mouth to keep from laughing.

"Sorry, I thought you heard me coming."

I stare at her, my heart racing in my chest as I take her in. She's got her hair up in a high ponytail, but tendrils of her dark-brown locks frame her round face enhanced with a tiny bit of makeup—her go-to, I'm beginning to realize.

My favorite part about her look right now is the little T-shirt dress she's wearing. It's a forest-green color, one that makes the green in her hazel eyes stand out. The last time I saw her in a dress was at my sister's engagement party. This one isn't that fancy, just one of those cover-up style dresses a lot of women wear to the pool, but it's stunning on her nonetheless.

All the moisture leaves my mouth at the beautiful picture she makes, and it takes everything in me not to comment and make it awkward. We agreed to be friends, and honestly, do friends tell friends they look beautiful, hot, stunning? Maybe, but not in the way that I want to say it. Nor would they be imagining the swimwear that lies underneath said little green dress.

I swallow. "I was looking at a work email."

She smacks her forehead. "Oh my god, do you need to work? I didn't even think about that. You should've said something!"

I stand from the couch so we're facing each other. "A, don't hit yourself, and B, I make my own hours. Don't worry about it."

"If you need to stay back, I can go to the springs alone."

"Not a chance. I'm not missing a bucket-list item check-off. Speaking of which, if you haven't crossed them off yet, I was thinking we should have a ceremony where we do."

She looks at me funny, her smile perplexed. "A ceremony?"

"Yeah, like, we sit by the fire, have a drink, and do an official check-off of the ones we complete."

"Not sure that counts as a ceremony."

"We make the rules on this trip, remember?"

She smiles at that. "Speaking of, we still have our questions for today."

I rub my hands together. "I've got a good one."

She eyes me. "Should I be scared?"

"Maybe." I shrug. "Now let's go; our reservation is for sunset."

"Reservation?" she asks.

Whoops. Busted. "Don't be mad, but I may have called ahead and rented out the space for us."

"I'm trying to figure out why I'd be mad about that, but...I looked on the website, you can't do private rentals."

I consider my options carefully and figure it would be dumb to lie. "You can do private rentals, but you have to call and talk to the right person."

Jesse studies me. "You mean have the right amount of money?"

"Yes. Are you angry?"

She takes a moment but then shakes her head. "It makes me a little uncomfortable that you're spending your money on me, especially since I can't pay my half, at least I'm assuming I can't. How much was it?"

"It wasn't cheap, but I don't want you to pay. I know this was on your bucket list, but I wanted this, too. I want to enjoy the springs without other people around, and I thought it would be nice to have some relaxation and quiet after all the driving and exploring we've been doing."

Jesse studies me, and a small smile tugs at her lips. "I think I have a new bucket-list item."

I cock my head. "And what's that?"

"To be rent-out-a-hot-spring rich."

I bark a laugh. "It's possible, especially if we can get that social media page of yours going and monetizing. Make you a big-time influencer."

"I don't think I'll ever get that big. But thanks for reminding me I need to post for today."

"Bring your phone; we'll work on it while we soak."

"I thought you wanted to relax?"

"That is relaxing for me." What I really want to say is *being with you is relaxing*. But even though she's bantering with me, I still notice that spark before Yellowstone isn't in her eye.

"Alright, let me grab it, and then we'll go."

"Sounds perfect."

"Holy shit," Jesse exclaims.

"Holy shit is right." I stare out at the valley, the green and brown hillsides illuminated by a pink-and-orange sunset.

The large hot spring, which looks like a giant pool, is nestled between. There are lounge chairs around the edges for people to sunbathe during the day, and there's a smaller in-ground pool as well that looks like a hot tub. Jesse removes her dress to reveal her swimwear.

"I'm for sure putting 'rich enough to rent out a hot springs' on my bucket list," she says.

I chuckle and lift my shirt over my head, dropping it onto a chair near the edge of the pool as fast as possible, not wanting to miss a moment of Jesse in the green suit she's wearing. It's a two piece that shows the tiniest sliver of skin on her belly, but the top dips dangerously low, giving me a nice view of her perfect tits. And the back, which I'm staring at right now, hugs her ass perfectly. A round and lovely backside I never got time to appreciate our first time together.

"I know it sounds cliché, but if I can do it, so can you," I reply.

"Like it's that easy." Jesse turns to me as she drops her now-folded dress on a chair next to mine.

"I'll do some targeted research on how to grow your account fast. May not be as hard as you think with the right marketing."

Jesse doesn't say anything right away. Her eyes drop down to my chest then to my navy swim trunks before traveling back to my eyes. She tries to cover the way she blatantly checked me out by clearing her throat and looking away, but her cheeks match the color of the sky. It may be stupid of me, but hope blooms in my chest that my feelings aren't one-sided. I had wished that, during this trip, she'd be open to changing her mind, and maybe that's not as far off as I think.

Could that be why she's been acting funny? Between the naked run-in and the woman asking if we were on our honeymoon at Yellowstone, it's possible...

"If you say so," she interrupts my thoughts. "Shall we get in?"

"Sounds good." I point to the hot tub-looking pool. "This one is hotter than the big one. Which one do you want to do first?"

She looks at the two pools then points at the big one. "Swimming sounds nice. My body is a little sore from all the driving and walking."

"Yeah, my feet could use a massage." I waggle my eyebrows at her.

She gags. "I'm not touching your feet or anyone else's."

"No foot fetish then?"

"Absolutely not. Feet are nasty."

"No footsie then, either?"

"If you try to touch me with your foot, Asher, I'll punch you."

I laugh loudly as I follow her down the steps of the large pool that's illuminated by lights under the water. Not going to lie, I very carefully watch and enjoy the way her ass jiggles with each step. By the time I get into the water, I wish it was cold instead of warm.

"Oh wow, that feels nice." Jesse moans as she sinks into the water until it's up to her chest. "Too bad it smells like eggs."

"I think I've gotten used to it," I say, taking a large sniff of air. "Or my sense of smell is shot."

"I'm more used to it now than I was yesterday."

My lips turn up thinking of when we first arrived at Old Faithful. She took a large breath of air and promptly coughed, scrunching up her nose like a bunny.

"I keep telling my brain it smells good," I say.

"Are you trying to brainwash yourself, Ash?"

"Yep."

"You know what, that's smart. I tried to do that once with chocolate."

I cock my head in question as I drop down in the water beside her, nearly groaning from how good it feels on my sore muscles. "What do you mean?"

"I did one of those group weight loss things as a teen. The group leader told me to smell chocolate then take a bite of broccoli. I guess that's more trying to trick your brain than brainwashing. But I will say, that group felt a lot like brainwashing for other reasons. Once, that same group leader told a lady she could chew her favorite candy then spit it out."

"That is...fucking awful."

"I know, right?" Jesse laughs sadly to herself. "That's when I told my mom I wasn't going to go anymore. Want to know the truth, though?"

"Of course."

"I actually got kicked out."

We wade into the deepest part of the water. We can still stand, but it's just deep enough that the surface brushes against the tops of Jesse's shoulders.

"Kicked out?" I ask.

"Yeah, I told her that you still absorb calories from chewing, and it can cause stomach ulcers. So the 'spit and don't swallow' method won't work."

Despite how much I wish I could go back in time and throttle that group leader, I find myself gleefully smirking alongside Jesse. "You really called it the 'spit and don't swallow' method?"

"Yep. Then I finished off that lovely sentence by saying she was promoting eating disorders. They told me never to come back after that and refunded my mom for the rest of the month."

"I told you you're brave, Jesse. Seems you always have been. I think you were just too invested in the outcome with your friend, Kate, since you care about her. In this situation, you didn't care if you were kicked out. You wanted to be."

She swirls the surface of the water with her hand. "You're probably right. Though in this case, I'm not sure that's brave. Just calling out her bullshit."

"It *was* bullshit, but you called her dangerous behavior to others' attention. You may have even influenced other group members' decisions to leave the group because of what you said. God knows that group sounds like it was harmful."

"It was," she says. "I gained all the weight I lost back and then some. After that, I decided to try to love my body. I'm a Midwestern girl with meat on her bones, and I didn't want to starve myself or end up with an eating disorder like a lot of girls in my school. I'm not going to say that the journey has been easy or always successful, especially after everything that happened with my heart."

Her confession tumbles around in my brain, and I'm honored that she feels safe to tell me. She didn't have to share any of this, but she did.

"The commentary my sister wrote on your first bucket-list item makes more sense now." *Remember, you don't have to be thin to get dicked down good.*

She hums, a quiet smile on her face. She's probably thinking about how lewd that commentary was, even if it is good advice.

Jesse moves the water between us with her hand, watching it glide through her spread fingers. "I've let it be a hang-up with men before, and it stopped me from having a lot of experiences I could've had in college because I didn't feel desirable. I think that's why Kate attempting to pass Luke off to me hit me so hard. It brought me back to those moments when all my friends were getting picked up at bars in college and I was left with the creepy drunk guy who was twice my age and always just happened to be where I was."

I think of the Jesse I met at the bar in Madison. I would've never guessed what she's saying to be her truth. I watched her dance like nobody was watching. She was open and perfect in bed with me. There was some shyness in the beginning but nothing that led me to believe this was how she felt about herself. It only made me believe she was inexperienced.

I meet her eyes. "Maybe this is inappropriate to say, but college men are boys. They don't matter. You are desirable, Jesse, more than desirable. I have no doubt had we met before the bar, I would've beelined my way to you and done anything to get your number."

"I have a hard time believing that," she says quietly.

My gut tells me to move closer to her, to tuck the damp strand of hair behind her ear and cup her cheek. To look into her eyes and beg her to let me make her believe it so she truly knows what I'm saying is real.

But I know that's something she must believe for herself. There are no number of words I can say that will change that for her.

That doesn't mean I'm going to stop letting her know how desirable I find her. I'll just have to be more subtle and meaningful in my word choices. Because Jesse *is* desirable. The most desirable woman—person—I've ever met.

"Anyway, sorry. I didn't mean to take your comment down such a depressing path. I don't talk about that with anyone."

"It wasn't depressing, Jesse. I like when you get real with me."

She starts to swim in the water, and like a puppy, I follow. We go down to the end and back in a breaststroke before she speaks again.

"You're easy to talk to, Ash. I haven't found that with anyone but Melissa in a long time. And she's been so busy with her wedding, we don't get to talk like this anymore. It's been...nice."

"Just nice?"

She splashes a bit of mineral water on my face, and the taste of it is salty and strange on my lips.

"Always so quippy," she says.

"You like my quips."

She slaps water at me again, and when I try to splash her back, she swims away. Before she can get far, I grab her by the foot and drag her back. She yelps and tugs her leg back so I let it go, but she turns and throws water at me again. This time I'm ready, so I dowse her, enough that the water soaks her face and gets in her mouth. She makes a face at the taste, and then she wipes at her eyes and glares at me.

"You're so gonna get it!" There's a brief pause before she launches at me. Her arms go around my body, and I'm met with the sight of her wet cleavage before I go under. I close my nose and mouth. The warm water isn't like normal pool water—it feels softer, and because of the minerals, it has more buoyancy. I immediately start to pop back up from below and seize the opening to wrap my arms around Jesse's waist. My head breaks the surface, and I'm met with Jesse's peeling laughter and the splashing sounds of water.

"Don't you dare push me under!" She squeals, wriggling in my hold.

"You just pushed me under." I tighten my arms around her, enjoying way too much how her wet body feels sliding against mine.

"You splashed me!"

"You splashed me!" I counter.

Jesse stares me down as she shoves at my body, attempting to get out of my hold, but I'm stronger than her. My arms clamp harder around her until our heaving chests are pressed together, our mouths close enough I wouldn't have to do much to bridge the gap to kiss her.

"You really are a menace."

I lift an eyebrow at her. "You started it."

She giggles, and the sound does things to me that are not appropriate for people who are only friends or for this venue. While I haven't seen anyone except the woman who let us in, I know there are a few staff members lurking around. When I booked the hot spring, I did ask for them to keep their distance, but I know they're probably watching or near enough they could come see what position we're in at any time.

Regardless, time stills as I hold her. The sunset is finished now, the pink sky turned into dusk and the sun below the horizon. The in-ground lights of the pool illuminate us from below, and droplets of water hang like dewdrops on blades of grass from Jesse's dark lashes.

"Ash," Jesse nearly whispers.

My eyes lift to meet hers, but she's not looking into mine. She's staring at my lips. I lick them, my mouth gravitating toward hers as we soak in the warm water, water that makes me feel as if we're weightless.

If this were a different scenario, I would have closed the distance and kissed her already, done what I've been dreaming of doing since the moment I left her apartment. I want to taste her again, feel her tongue against mine and her fingers gripping my hair. But I hold myself back. Not only do I need her to make the first move with me again, I want her to. I want her to show me she wants me as much as I want her.

"Ash." The way she says my name so tenderly almost has me taking what I just thought back.

"What do you want, Jesse girl?" I whisper.

Her hands have found their way to my shoulders, and she digs her nails into my skin. Jesse worries her lower lip, and in her eyes, I see her thoughts move a mile a minute. I know without her words she's not going to ask me to kiss her nor is she going to kiss me.

Disappointment aches in my chest, and I gently let go of her waist. When her hands drop from my shoulders and she steps back, the warm water no longer feels warm.

"Want to try out the hotter pool?" she asks quietly.

"Yeah, that sounds good."

"We can ask our official questions for today. I want to know what you've drummed up."

Jesse smiles at me, and my disappointment diminishes a little. Even if I didn't get my kiss, I get to spend time with her. And that makes up for it.

I follow her to the hotter tub, and we spend the rest of the two hours I rented asking our questions. I find out her guilty pleasure is watching *The Real Housewives of New York*, every season, multiple times. We talk about reality TV for a while after that, and she decides to ask me the same question. I tell her how I like to eat pineapple on pizza, and she ribs me for it. Then we spend the rest of the time sharing weird food combinations until we're back inside Winnie saying our goodnights.

Now, lying in bed with GusGus curled at my feet, my mind keeps circling back to the moments before I let her swim away and the fact that I still don't know what's tearing her up inside. Maybe tomorrow will bring me closer to unraveling the mystery that is Jesse. I just hope she'll let her guard down and see how much I want her.

All of her.

Chapter Twenty-Two
Jesse

I PUT UP A wall between Asher and me, and I hate it.

We left Yellowstone two days ago and spent day five of our road trip driving to Twin Falls, Idaho, making a stop on Asher's second bucket-list item: The Idaho Potato Museum. I haven't stopped saying the slogan "Free Taters for Out-of-Staters" since then.

Today, day six, has been spent driving and listening to music, volleying questions back and forth that apparently "aren't official questions" in our question game. With that in mind, I asked him further questions about his love for mythology. When we weren't speaking about that, I've been posting on my social media account and asking Ash algorithm and random tech questions.

We've been on the road for five of our eight-and-a-half-hour drive to Florence, Oregon. We'll be staying for a few days, and Asher says another item on his bucket list is there.

I'm acting like everything is good. Ash, for all intents and purposes, seems fine, too, but I feel him holding back as well. My nagging thoughts from Yellowstone keep eating at me, especially after he picked up a package he'd had sent to a mail locker we stopped at yesterday. Inside were first aid items, including some of the blood clotting agents I mentioned to him on our first day.

I can't blame him for doing that, but it didn't help the thoughts that keep poking at me and making my insides feel itchy, ones that say he's treating me differently even if he doesn't mean to. Then there was that near kiss at the hot springs. It took everything in me not to give in like I wanted, especially since I was feeling vulnerable after dumping my guts—another thing I didn't intend to do. Not to the guy I can't stop thinking about and find insanely attractive.

I truly feel like I'm going crazy. I know I have to talk to him about that itchy feeling soon so I don't say something I don't mean. We're not even halfway through our trip, and I don't want to screw things up and make things more awkward than I feel like I already have. Even if everything on the outside seems normal between us.

"Jesse?"

I turn my head toward Asher, who's dutifully driving. It's another thing I feel bad about, though he claims he's fine and will let me know if we need to pull over. I'd offer to drive, but I don't feel comfortable driving such a giant home. His home.

"Yeah?" I ask.

"You okay?"

That damn question again. I turn my body to look at him. He has one hand on the wheel, the other tapping out a beat on his knee. "Yeah, I'm fine. Why do you ask?"

"I've said your name three times, and you didn't hear me."

My cheeks burn. "Oh, sorry. I was thinking."

"Dangerous," he says.

A small laugh puffs from my lips. "Yeah, tell me about it."

There's a pause of silence before he says, "I was asking if you want to stop and stretch for a bit. There's a rest stop coming up, and we can make some sandwiches."

"Yeah, of course. Do you need a nap or anything?"

He shakes his head. "No, I'm good. Though I could use some coffee and a foot rub."

I scrunch up my nose. "Yes to the first, no to the second."

"Okay, deal." He smiles.

Minutes later, we're pulling into a rest stop with bathrooms and a picnic area. Asher checks on GusGus once we're parked and gives him fresh food and water while I pull out stuff for sandwiches that we picked up at the store yesterday after the potato museum.

"Oh!" I say, reaching behind Asher to go into one of the snack cupboards. "We need to try the weird potato chip flavors we got."

"Ah, yes." He laughs. "What kind did you get again?"

I hold up the bag of cucumber and lime chips. "I'm excited."

"And I'm still confused by that flavor."

"Me, too, but when in Rome, right?"

Asher chuckles and assembles his sandwich alongside me. The kitchen counter space is small, but we've done this a few times now, and we work well in the small space with each other. I've learned he likes everything on everything, which I find fitting with his all-in personality, while I go for basic. I finish with the mayo and hand it to him, then he hands me the cheese packet.

Once we've finished up, he grabs sparkling water for me and iced coffee for himself. Gus meows at us as we're about to walk out of the RV, and Asher shakes his head at me as I walk back to the kitchen to give him a treat.

"He's got you wrapped around his chubby cat paw."

I pet Gus on the head and down his back. "Like he doesn't have you wrapped around both of his? Actually, all four."

Asher chuckles. "That's true. You know, we can bring him outside with us. I have a harness."

"Oh, you really are a cat daddy, aren't you?" As soon as the words are out of my mouth, I want to hit myself on the forehead for calling him daddy in any variation.

The crooked grin Ash is so good at tugs at his lips. "Like you said, he has me wrapped around his chubby paws."

Asher walks back to me and hands me the drinks he's holding then goes to the couch. I didn't realize it before, but there's a storage area under it. He pulls open a drawer and takes out a blue harness and a leash. Immediately, GusGus runs over to Ash and starts rubbing on his dad's legs. Asher secures the harness and clips the leash.

"Oh my god, that is adorable," I say.

"He loves playing in the grass and pouncing on bugs."

"Gross."

Asher looks up and laughs again. "Lots of toppings on burgers and sandwiches, the smell of sulfur, feet, and bugs. The four things Jesse called Jesse doesn't like."

My skin prickles at the idea he's keeping a log of facts on me, but I brush it aside. "That's not true. I also hate natural deodorant."

"I feel like there's a story there," Asher says as he walks toward where I'm now standing by the door.

"You'd be right. But not before we eat, please. And no more talking about bugs or feet."

"Noted."

Asher gestures for me to go first, and I open the door, hopping the short distance to the ground. The air is a bit cooler now that we're getting closer to the West Coast, and a gentle breeze ruffles my hair.

"Have I mentioned how nice it is not to smell rotten eggs anymore?" I ask as I inhale the fresh air that has a note of summer grass and pine trees.

"Maybe once or twice." Ash takes a seat at the picnic table, securing Gus's leash tightly around one of the wooden legs. I slide his food and drink over to him before sitting across the table. Once he's satisfied that Gus is good, we crack open our drinks and settle in, the distant hum of freeway traffic serving as our backdrop.

"I never asked how you got GusGus. I know he's a rescue, but that's it."

Ash swallows the bite of his sandwich and looks at Gus who's sunning himself in the grass and rolling around in it. "Two years ago, after I got Winnie and fixed her up, I took a little road trip down the East Coast. I stayed a night at a campground outside of Orlando. I must have left the door open and not been paying attention at some point, because about three hours into the trip to Key West the next day, I heard what sounded like a cat meowing."

I watch GusGus, who is now pouncing on the grass like a crazy cat. "He stowed away with you, huh?"

"That he did. I pulled up to the rest stop and searched the entire RV for him. Eventually, I found him hiding under my bed. I coaxed him out with some leftover chicken. He was covered in fleas, skinny, and in dire need of a bath. I had to clean and treat the entire Winnebago with flea spray after I got him cleaned up."

"Sounds like a great time," I tease.

"Oh, the best," he answers sarcastically.

I can picture Asher cleaning his Winnebago and grumbling about it the whole time. I admit it makes me smile more than it should. "I take it you tried to find his owner?"

He nods. "I figured he didn't have one by the shape he was in. I took him to a vet, and they couldn't find a microchip, and he wasn't wearing a collar. I looked up lost cats in the Orlando area, too, and nobody was looking for him."

"Poor guy."

Ash gives his attention to GusGus, and it's hard to miss the little smile on his lips. "Nothing poor about him now," he jokes.

"That's true; he's living the life."

"I didn't want him at first, so I tried to pawn him off on the vet."

"I remember Melissa saying you were a dog person."

"Never liked cats, never wanted one. I wanted a border collie."

I chuckle. "I can totally see that."

Asher runs his hand over his jaw and puffs his chest out a bit. "Right? Anyway, she said if I put him in a shelter, he'd probably be overlooked because he was not a kitten and would need extra time and care to get him healthy. Then he looked at me with those big ol' eyes, and I took him home with me."

"Now you're a cat man."

"Cat daddy." He winks.

"Oh god." I groan, picking up my sandwich. "I should never have brought that up again."

"I like it," Asher says. "Call me daddy anytime."

I search around for something to throw at him but come up empty-handed. He sees my dilemma, and his shoulders shake with laughter. When his amusement subsides, we fall into an easy silence while we eat our sandwiches. Halfway through, I pick up my bag of cucumber and lime chips. Asher does the same, reaching for his ketchup ones—a popular item in Canada.

I pop one of my chips in my mouth, and my eyes widen in surprise.

"Good or bad?" Asher asks.

"I can't decide." I take another chip and chew slowly so I can get a better taste. "It's salty with a little bit of the lime zestiness. But then...sweet."

"Interesting," Asher says before popping a ketchup chip into his mouth. After he chews, he holds out his bag to me. "Tastes like ketchup. Wanna try?"

"Sure, you want to try mine?"

Asher keeps his eyes on me, and they glint in the afternoon sunlight. "I always wanna try yours." He smiles.

I pick a chip out of my bag and throw it at him. He laughs and takes the fallen chip off the table before popping it into his mouth.

"I could've given you a clean one."

"Five-second rule," he says after he swallows. "And you're right. It's zesty *and* sweet. Now try mine."

I try to keep all things dirty out of my head, dirty things Asher so nicely put there, and take a chip from his bag. "Yep, it tastes like tomatoes."

"I think I'll stick with normal chips or sour cream and onion from now on."

"Me, too," I say, "but it's fun to try new things."

"Agreed. Speaking of new things, last night, I couldn't sleep. I was looking at your list, and I know you want to ride a motorcycle."

I nod. "Ever since I saw *Born to Ride* starring Uncle Jesse."

"From the TV show Full House?"

"Yep."

"I've never heard of that movie."

"Most people haven't. But I may have had a mild obsession with Uncle Jesse. He had my name and the same spelling."

"That's a fair obsession. Maybe we'll have to have a movie night. I need to see why you want to ride a motorcycle and put it on your bucket list."

"Maybe it's a dumb idea. It's one I'd only tell people if it happened afterward. Well, besides Melissa and now you."

"Why is that?"

My eyes travel to GusGus. He's no longer pouncing—now he's basking in the sun again. "Because they're dangerous." I pause for a moment and put my bag of chips down, wiping the crumbs off my hands. "I can hear my mom in my head: 'If you fall off, Jesse, it'll be worse for you. Think about your health.'"

Silence passes between us after I finish the impression of my mom. I know she means well, but I'm an adult and make my own decisions with my doctors.

"Jesse."

Ash leans forward on the table. My eyes meet his, and I see concern in them.

"Please don't let your next words be 'Maybe she's right.'"

The only way I can describe the look on his face now is one of disappointment. It makes my stomach sour, and my mouth waters as if the food I just ate is going to come up. I take a sip of my sparkling water to try to ease the feeling.

"I wasn't going to say that. I was going to ask if something is bothering you."

"Nothing's bothering me," I snipe, proving that something is wrong.

"Right. And monkeys can fly."

Leave it to Asher not to sugarcoat his thoughts. I think about saying something quippy back like he often does to me, but I manage to keep it in.

"Look, you don't have to tell me," he says. "But I must have said something when we were at Yellowstone because you've been a bit off since then, and I don't know how to fix it."

"Not everything is fixable, Ash."

He taps his fingers on the table. "I know that, but if I did something, please tell me. We still have a lot of time together on the road, and I don't want you to be miserable."

When I don't say anything, he continues.

"I know how much you hate awkward silences, after all. I'm trying to avoid that."

The corner of his lip turns up, and I can't help but mirror it. "You said something at Old Faithful. About being prepared."

I watch his mind try to rewind and remember what he said. "About the hike?"

I nod. "Are you being careful with me, Asher?"

His brow furrows. "Huh?"

"Did you look up easy hikes because you were worried about my heart and if I could handle it?"

Asher's mouth opens and closes, then he looks away toward Gus. What feels like an hour passes before he meets my eyes again, and I see the answer written on his face.

"I didn't mean to," he says. "I didn't even realize I did it."

My chest smarts, and I take in a shaky breath.

"I'm serious, Jesse, I never meant to—"

"I understand," I cut him off. "I guess it just brought me back to reality, you know? That no matter who I meet or what I do from now on, people will always treat me differently." My eyes start to sting. "Even when they don't want to."

"Jesse—"

"It's not your fault, Ash. Really. I think I'm just mourning the days when I didn't have to worry if a stupid hike was too much for me and when others didn't have that same worry." My stinging eyes turn watery, and a second later, Asher stands and sits next to me on the picnic bench. He reaches for my hand and sets it on the top of the table.

"For what it's worth, I really am sorry, so fucking sorry for breaking my promise to you. To be truthful, I thought I was being helpful and prepared verses treating you differently, but now that I'm thinking about it, I see how I was doing exactly that." He rubs his brow and continues. "And I picked up more of the blood-clotting powder without telling you I was going to do it. Fuck, I'm a dick. I really screwed up, didn't I?"

I shake my head. "I see now how silly it was to ask you for that promise."

"It wasn't—"

I hold up my hand to stop him. "It was. I *am* different. I do require some accommodations and forethought. I was being unrealistic; you weren't. You're not a dick for caring, and I know your heart is in the right place. I'm upset because of my own hang-ups. I should have told you sooner what was bothering me. I just...I hate feeling this way. Too sensitive sometimes, remember?"

"We went over this. You're not too sensitive. Your feelings are valid, and you're perfect just the way you are. I think I'd feel the same way if I was in your position. And in my own way, I can relate. Like I mentioned before, people treated me differently before I was diagnosed with my ADHD, and I hated it. They were always making me feel like an idiot or some impulsive kid. And in my adult life, when I have hard days, I've wondered why

I couldn't be normal. But then I remember I don't want to be like everyone else, and I don't care what people think of me. I like being me. So, truly, I'm sorry if I made you feel bad for who you are. I don't wish that feeling on anyone."

"Oh, Ash," I say, feeling like an ass for not thinking of that. Of him. I've been so caught up in my own thoughts and feelings. "I'm so sorry." I look into his eyes. "You didn't do anything wrong. I think...I think I overreacted."

He shakes his head. "You didn't."

I want to argue with him, tell him that I did, that I was selfish in a way. He was only being sweet and thoughtful. I see that more clearly now. But I know he won't hear it. His mind is made up.

I look down and wipe at the tears threatening to fall, silence blanketing us once more. When my chest feels heavy and the weight of not speaking becomes too much, I meet his gaze again. His brown eyes are soft and kind, and in the depths of them, I find no pity or anger.

"You know," I say quietly. "I think part of the reason I made the bucket list was to feel normal again. To do things that would make me..." My voice trails off.

Asher gently squeezes the top of my hand. "Make you what, Jesse?"

"Feel alive."

His Adam's apple bobs in his throat, and he pulls his hand away. "Can I hug you?"

The heaviness in my chest eases a bit. Asher's request may be an odd one, but it's not for him and his personality. I think he may need the hug more than me by the way his own eyes have turned glassy.

Before I can finish nodding my head, he's pulling me into his arms.

The position we're in is a little awkward, and my body is tense against his. He waits for me to settle then pulls me in tighter, resting his chin on my head.

He inhales a breath, and it reminds me of the first night we met and how he smelled me. The funny memory triggers my body to relax, and I can't deny it's nice to be in his arms. More than nice. A warmth spreads in my chest, overtaking the heaviness, and I exhale. God, it really does feel good to be held. Maybe we both needed this hug.

A gentle breeze ruffles my hair as Asher pulls back. His hands slide to my biceps, and our eyes meet. "I need you to know that you're right. I *do* care—I care about you, Jesse. I care about your safety, and I care about making sure nothing happens to you."

"Thank you," I say softly.

He releases my arms and drops his hands back to the table. "I'm going to make you a new promise. I'll preface it with I can't guarantee I won't do or say something wrong going forward, but I can guarantee that I'll never question your choices. I won't treat you like glass or put you in a bubble, I promise you that."

The urge to argue that he doesn't need to promise anything attempts to break free from my lips, but his features are so determined that I nod. "That means a lot to me. And it means a lot that you care that much, Ash. I hope you know I care about you, too."

His eyes light up, and his crooked smile returns. "Do you now?"

I bump his shoulder with mine. "Don't get excited. Friends, remember?"

Asher's eyes glint in the sun, and I can't help but think he looks like a sly fox—cunning and clever, with a plan behind his eyes. What that plan is, I don't know.

"Well..." He leans toward me so our heads are closer, similar to the other night in the hot spring. "If you ever change your mind on that front, I can promise you I won't treat you like glass, Jesse. Quite the opposite."

My skin sparks at the image his words have conjured. If his plan was to have me thinking about him fucking me into the mattress, it worked. My attention focuses on his smiling lips and his mischievous eyes. It takes everything in me to draw the "friend wall" back up and gently push him away.

I stab my finger into his chest. "Behave."

He chuffs. "Where's the fun in that?"

I remove my finger from his chest and point to his spot across the table. "Go be a good boy, and finish your sandwich."

"Yes, ma'am." He salutes.

I hold in a laugh as Asher gets up and goes back to his side of the table. When he sits, a curl from the top of his head drops over his forehead, and my hand itches to reach across the table and pull on it.

He takes a bite of his sandwich, still grinning while he chews. My chest shakes with laughter, and I pick up my own food. Leave it to Ash to turn our conversation around one-eighty. I'm no longer thinking about my health hang-ups. Instead, I'm thinking about our hookup, which I'm not sure is a good thing. But he's good—I'll give him that.

Maybe too good.

Chapter Twenty-Three

Asher

I'M TRYING VERY HARD to answer some work emails, but I'm finding it impossible to do when Jesse is sunbathing while working on her social media channel in front of me.

It's our second day in Florence, Oregon. We decided to hang around the state park we're staying at to relax, mostly because Jesse insisted she wanted to let me work and rest from driving.

I'd tried to deny that I needed to do both of those things, but my stiff body needed rest, and my near-bursting inbox did need my attention. But when I agreed to the idea, I didn't think I'd be staring at Jesse in a bathing suit while trying to do it. Sure, I could go inside. But where's the fun in that?

I write a response to the hospital's email about my travel arrangements for September. I want to tell them I'm not coming, but instead, I'm confirming my flights to London and the accommodations—because Jesse is still adamant about this "just friends" thing between us. That doesn't stop me from hoping we're on the verge of something more.

She thinks I don't see the way she looks at me when she assumes I'm not watching, but I see it. Oh, I see it. I notice every glance she sneaks my way, and I never miss a chance to steal a glance of my own. Like right now.

I peer over my laptop and smile as she takes selfies. She's lying on a portable lounge chair I brought out for her, wearing a similar suit to the one she had on at the hot springs. This one is a hot-pink color and shows a tiny bit more stomach than the green one did. My eyes rove over her body, taking in the thickness of her thighs, the softness of her belly, and the swell of her ample chest.

Jesse tucks some of her hair behind her ear and smiles, taking another photo. She's taken several, more than several, but every time she looks at one, she frowns. When she does it with this next one, I close my laptop and get up from my chair.

"Want me to take them for you?"

Jesse tilts her head up at me, meeting my gaze from behind a pair of wide-lensed tortoise-shell sunglasses. "You're supposed to be working," she says.

"I'm good for now. I can do the rest before bed tonight."

She sits up on the chair, automatically dropping her hands in front of her stomach as if I haven't ever seen it and holds her phone tightly in her hand.

"It's okay. Something I took is bound to be fine."

I hold out my hand and do the universal "gimme" motion. "Let me take some. The light is nice right now."

I don't know if that's true or not—I'm no photographer—but I do know she looks hot. I want to capture the pictures for her so she can share them with the world. So they can see how beautiful she is. So *she* can see how beautiful she is.

"Are you sure?" she asks.

"Positive. Now hand over the phone."

Jesse leans forward and holds out her phone to me. When I take it, I make sure our hands brush. I don't miss the way she shivers from the touch. I'm not ashamed to admit that these little moments when she shows her attraction to me confirms there's still hope for more between us. I just need to let Jesse be the one to cross that line again. Even if it gets harder the more time I spend with her.

"Okay, lie back on the chair, and do whatever feels comfortable."

"Are you my photographer and director now?" Jesse smirks.

"Yep. Should I have a cool name and accent? I do like a little role play." I waggle my eyebrows at her.

Her laugh rings out, swirling around our private campsite, one I booked on purpose so we didn't have other people near us. Not that I don't mind that sometimes, but I'm selfish and want Jesse all to myself as much as I can get her.

"What kind of accent?" she asks.

My brows stay lifted in shock that she's letting me play and not shutting down this silly idea. I clear my throat and smirk. "I can do French? *Voulez-vous coucher avec moi ce soir.*"

She laughs again. "Hmm, what about Italian?"

"Oh yes, *bellissima, bella,*" I kiss my fingers, and she laughs again. "Or German. *Guten tag, Fräulein. Das ist wunderbar.*"

"Are you reciting what you learned in high school foreign language classes?"

"Maybe..."

Jesse's body shakes, making the tops of her breasts jiggle. "I think Italian was the best one."

"Very good, *bella*. Now pose for me."

More comfortable and loose now, Jesse shifts and lays her upper body back against the chair then bends her knees, keeping her legs together but slightly tilting them.

"*Perfetto*. You make this man blush with how beautiful you are." I lay the Italian accent on thick so I sound like a sexy Italian man. Or at least what I think one sounds like.

Her skin matches the shade of her suit from my praise. I use it as motivation to keep going with the accent and compliments, wanting to see every section of her skin available to my eyes blush. "Put your arm up over your head." I wait for her to do it then kiss my fingers. "*Bellissima.*" I snap a few photos on her phone but don't look at them, wanting to keep the momentum.

Once I'm satisfied with that pose, I help her put the chair flat and have her lie on her stomach. It takes everything in me to keep my eyes off her ass when she flips over. Which is hard, considering her swimsuit is riding up, causing her round cheeks to peek out.

I clear my throat. "Bend your knees and cross your ankles then lean on your elbows." My accent sucks, but Jesse is still smiling, so I keep doing it. I snap a few more photos then look around the campsite. We're close to a freshwater lake and surrounded by green pine trees. Not far from here, there are sand dunes. I also remember seeing a gazebo down a short path we could easily access.

I drop the accent as I say the next part. "Want to snap some pictures around the area? I bet people on social media would go crazy for the dunes."

"You mean my five hundred followers?" She chuckles.

"Hey, the other day, you had zero. That's a great start."

She sits up on the lounge chair. "I suppose you're right. Though I wouldn't even have that many without your help."

"It's your content that people are interacting with. I'm just helping it get seen a bit more." Her lips part, and by the way her brow is furrowing, I know she wants to fight me on this. I hold out my hand before she can. "Come, *bella*," I say in the accent again. "Let's go get some more pictures."

Jesse lets out a dramatic sigh, but she's smiling as she gives me her hand. I help her to her feet and reluctantly drop her hand so she can slide on a pair of flip-flops and tie a matching sheer pink wrap around her waist. I would have preferred she left it off, but I'll admit, it's pretty. The way it hugs her hips and helps to show off her curves is nice. More than nice.

Before we can go, she grabs a bottle of sunscreen off the ground and puts a little on her finger, applying it to her implant scar. My body heats from head-to-toe. I'm beyond elated that she feels comfortable enough to do that in front of me. After our conversation at the rest stop—not to mention what she'd done when we first met—I'd have easily bet money she would have it covered up right now. But so far on this trip, I haven't seen her do it once. I wonder if she consciously knows she's not hiding it.

Jesse holds the sunscreen up to me, and I cock an eyebrow. "Want me to rub you down, Jesse girl?"

"You would love that, wouldn't you?"

"I'm not going to lie and say no." She giggles, and my heart squeezes in my chest at the perfect sound.

"I'm good for now," she says. "I did the rest of my body not long ago. I wanted to make sure my scar doesn't burn since the incision is still healing. But I thought you might want some since you're no longer in the shade."

"Ohhh, so are you offering to rub *me* down?"

Her chin dips to her chest as she eyes the T-shirt-and-shorts combo I'm wearing. "I think you can put lotion on your face and arms without my help."

I pout, making her giggle again, and she takes her phone from my hands, replacing it with the bottle. I quickly apply some sunscreen, and when I'm done, I take her phone back. "Let's go to the dunes first, then we'll make our way to the water," I say.

"Lead the way."

Chapter Twenty-Four

Asher

I'M CONVINCED THAT IF Jesse saw herself the way I do, she'd have a career as a model. Out in the open, with the chance of people walking by, it took her some time to get comfortable, but now, I don't even have to direct her or make jokes. She simply gets into positions, and I snap the pictures while making funny comments in my bad Italian accent. She's even gotten rid of her wrap for several photos.

Currently, I have her lying on the beach near the lake facing the water. I've taken photos of both her and the beautiful surroundings so people can get the full effect if she posts it on social media, which I hope she does. I hope she posts all of these on social media.

"Yes, yes," I chant in the accent. "Now drop your head back, shake out those beautiful locks."

If Jesse's cheeks weren't already tinged pink from all the activity we've been doing and the warm air, I would say she's blushing.

Despite that, she does as I ask, dropping her head back so her dark hair shakes and her chest pops forward. I have her take off her sunglasses and close her eyes, letting the bright sunlight make it seem as if there's a spotlight on her.

I wet my dry lips, speaking in my normal voice. "Watch out world, Jesse called Jesse is going to be the next *Sports Illustrated Swimsuit* model."

She shoots me an exasperated look. "You're ridiculous."

"Just calling it like I see it." Her hazel eyes remain on mine, like she's searching for the truth. My eyes flick down her body, and I make a show of checking her out.

Jesse averts her gaze to the water, turning a brighter pink. When she doesn't say anything else, her focus now on the rippling lake, I sense that our photoshoot is done for now. I put her phone in my shorts pocket for safekeeping and settle next to her.

"Ask me your question for today," she says a minute later. "Make it a good one. I'm in the mood to go deep."

By the smirk playing at the corner of her mouth, I know she said that last part on purpose. The tease. Not that I'm any better.

I shift so that my body is in the same position as hers, our knees bent and feet digging into the sand while we use our hands to prop us up. I consider my next question carefully, because I know it's not something she likes to be asked about. But she's given me permission to go deep, and I want to hear her story.

"Why did you write your bucket list?" I ask.

Our heads both turn at the same time to meet each other's stares. "You know why."

I nod. "I know what you told me at the rest stop. What you said makes sense, but I want to know the deep answer, Jesse girl. Why did you make it? Why are the things on it so important for you to check off?"

The corner of her lip twitches. "That's two questions."

My heart skips a beat from the playfulness in her tone. I'm glad I didn't upset her with the question. "It's a follow-up question, so it's part of the question."

"Okay, you're right."

"You don't have to answer."

"No, I want to. This question is not what I expected. I thought you'd ask me what a heart attack feels like or if I saw my life flash before my eyes or saw angels or something when it happened. That's what most people would ask me—*have* asked me."

"As you know, I'm not most people."

"True."

"I'm curious because other people I've met who have been through life-or-death experiences don't automatically make a bucket list, much less make it and take action to follow through on it."

Jesse nods in agreement. "Have you seen the movie *Last Holiday*?"

"The one where she thinks she's dying so she goes on her last vacation?"

"Yes! With Queen Latifah."

"My sister made me watch that."

"Funny you should say that, because I watched it with Melissa. Coincidentally before I had my first heart attack."

"Wow, talk about timing."

"I know, right? Anyway, when I was on the operating table having the clots removed—which you're awake for, by the way." She shivers but soldiers on. "That movie popped into my mind. I started thinking about how scared I've been my entire life to do anything outside of my comfort zone."

I try to push the image of Jesse lying on an operating table out of my mind, because the thought is nearly too much to take. I find myself wishing I could've been there with her, wishing I knew her then. I swallow the sad emotion down.

"What do you mean?" I ask.

"Melissa didn't tell you anything about me, huh?" She chuckles.

I shake my head. "It's not like Melissa and I had that much time to talk before you and I left. She mentioned her cool roommate from time to time when we talked, but she didn't divulge your life to me or anything about your health."

She smiles softly. "When you put it that way, it makes sense. I wouldn't be telling my siblings about my friends' lives, either, I guess."

My eyebrows shoot up. "Wait, you have more than one sibling?"

"I do. My sister is two years older than me, the one in Arizona. Then my brother is four years older than me. He and his husband live in Door County, where my parents are."

"Google did not tell me that," I quip.

Jesse's mouth drops open. "Wait, you googled me?"

"Maybe a little."

She scoffs but not in anger. "What did you find out?"

"Nothing much. I know you went to college at UW Madison, that you've had a couple of admin jobs. I also know you really love coffee and sunsets from the pictures you post on your personal social media."

She bumps my shoulder. "Well, not all of us can be rich geniuses."

"Maybe not. But not all of us are smart, brave, and stunningly beautiful."

She flushes. "Whatever. But I guess it's only fair since I googled you."

I chuckle and bump her shoulder back.

"But I'm curious," she adds. "Did you google anything about Kawasaki disease?"

I look out at the water and dip my chin. "A bit, but only because I'd never heard of it before. I was curious, but I didn't want to pressure you into speaking about it."

"I can understand that."

I turn my head back to meet her eyes. "You're not upset?"

She shakes her head. "I know I reacted badly to you wanting to be prepared for the hike and about the clotting agent, but I'm sorry if I made you feel like you can't ask me anything about it. You should be able to ask me. I just don't like when people treat me like a science experiment or like I'm someone to fix or to pity."

"And I never want you to feel that way."

"I know you don't," she says, "and I appreciate it. But you did the natural thing. Though now I get to tease you for googling me, too."

"All's fair in love and war."

She rolls her eyes. "Alright, Google Boy. Let's get back to the game. Do you want to know the rest of the answer to your questions or not?"

My chest shakes at my new nickname. "I do. Please proceed."

We both lay back in the sand, staring up at the fluffy white clouds against the bright blue sky that look so perfect, it's almost like a painting.

"I went to college because I wanted to make my parents proud. I hated school but felt like I had to go. I studied random things, getting a degree from the business school because I couldn't think of anything else to do. The entire time I was there, I dreamed of traveling, going to the places I saw my friends going to as kids that my parents couldn't afford to take us to like Yellowstone and the ocean. I even wanted to study abroad but didn't have the money. And if I'm telling the truth, I was scared to do it."

"That's normal I think, especially if you haven't traveled much."

"True, but for me, even when I was a kid, I was like that. I let people convince me that because I was in a larger body, I couldn't do things like taking dance classes, being on the swim team, trying out for plays, getting dates. I've let my fear of rejection, of being singled out or alone, get in the way of what I wanted to do so many times."

More items on her bucket list make sense now, especially the dance class one. One I plan to move up the list and remedy as soon as possible.

"And your heart attack changed that?"

"Yeah. I didn't necessarily see my life flash before my eyes. Instead, that movie came to mind. And I started to think, if I die right now, I'll die feeling like I haven't lived. And Ash..." Her voice nearly cracks. "What kind of life is that?"

Without thinking, I grab her hand. She doesn't pull away; instead, she squeezes my hand back. For a minute, neither of us say anything, just continue to watch the clouds. I know she asked me a question, but it was not for me to answer.

Eventually, she continues, but she doesn't remove her hand from mine. "When I found out I would have died had I not gone into the hospital and that I had undiagnosed Kawasaki disease as a child that caused the aneurysms in my heart, I really got to thinking I should make a list of all the things I've always wanted to do. But then I had my second heart attack, so I never got around to writing it down.

"After that, I lost my admin job at a local plumber because of all the time I had to take off. I was worried about cash flow and didn't want to blow through my savings. I needed it for rent. It wasn't until I got my ICD and hired at this new job that I finally made the list and decided to use a bit of my savings to knock some out this summer. Getting my implant, realizing that I really could just drop dead at any moment, made me want to do more with my life, to live like the character in the *Last Holiday*—not just wait until the time is right. It's why I called it my Change of Pace Bucket List. I had to change my pace along with my heart."

When she finishes speaking, I'm squeezing her hand tighter than when we started. She shared a lot of information in her answer, but one sentence stood out: "drop dead at any moment."

"Jesse," I say quietly. Her head turns, and our gazes meet as a breeze picks up off the water and gently ruffles our hair.

"Yeah?" she asks when I don't finish my sentence.

I swallow, trying to figure out my next words. "What you said, about dying at any moment. Is that—"

"True?" she interjects. I nod, and she squeezes my hand again. "I'm doing good. I wasn't lying to you before. It took awhile to figure out what meds work and don't work. With my blood thinners, I take meds that help slow down my heart to keep it from going into V-tach. But the reason I got the ICD and not just a pacemaker is because my doctors were worried about the amount of arrhythmia I was having every day. The pacemaker paces my heart if it goes too high or too low, but if it goes into an abnormal rhythm for too long, it can attempt to shock me back into a normal rhythm. If that fails, then yes, I could die. I could also die from a heart attack—the implant can't prevent that."

"And what's the likelihood of both?"

She shrugs. "Could never happen, or it could. I go in for regular testing every year—like stress tests and an echo. With the arrhythmia, the risk of getting shocked gets larger as I get older. Thankfully, the implant can send the readings to my doctor. They download them every few months to make sure the meds are still doing their job. So far, it's been good, but that could change. If so, I may need an ablation down the line, but I'm hoping that doesn't happen. To be honest, I'm not sure if I could handle another surgery, at least not anytime soon. I'm sick of hospitals and being poked and prodded."

"I can't imagine going through that. You're fucking strong, Jesse."

She shrugs. "What other choice do I have?"

"You could be miserable. You could be at home still thinking of doing the things you've been dreaming of. But you're not. You're here, you're doing it. And you're doing great."

"Right now."

"But you said your doctors will let you know if that changes?"

"They will."

I run my thumb over the tops of her knuckles and inhale a quiet breath to keep myself together. I feel bad that I'm the one drawing strength from her—she's been through so much. I'm in awe of her, and she doesn't even see how amazing she is.

"Did I scare you?" she asks.

"Truth?"

"Always."

"A little." I grip her hand so she can't pull away.

"I suppose it's not every day your travel companion tells you they could drop dead."

Her words, the way she says them so carelessly, make my chest ache. But I also understand why she does it. If I was her, I'd probably detach from the possibility, too—makes it easier to stomach.

"No, but you won't, Jesse."

"I could."

"But you won't."

Her lips turn up into a smirk. "What are you going to do, invent something to stop me from ever dying, Genius Boy?"

I tap my chin. "If I invented immortality, I'd be really fucking rich. But all that aside, I bet you a million dollars you'll outlive me. And we're both going to die old wrinkly people who start every sentence with 'What did you say?'"

She laughs. "I wouldn't waste your money."

"It wouldn't be wasting it."

She shakes her head. "Like I said, you're impossible."

"I'm right is what I am."

"If you say so."

"I do."

"Can I at least revise one thing then?" she asks.

I drop her hand and turn my body so I'm facing her. "What's that?"

"That we die at the same time."

I raise my eyebrow at her, her statement surprising me. "Are you planning on being at the same nursing home as me, Jesse girl?"

This time, there's no mistaking her flush. "I just don't like the idea of you dying."

"Really?"

"Of course not. I don't like the idea of anyone I care about dying."

I know she said she cared about me before, but this feels deeper. The flame of hope I have that she wants more with me burns brighter. "If you keep saying things like that, I'm going to start thinking you're falling in love with me."

Jesse groans and flicks some sand at me.

"You really want to start a sand fight with me? Remember the hot spring?" I tease.

Jesse's cheeks turn a deeper shade of pink before her eyes dart to my lips. I know she's thinking about our almost kiss now, just like I'm thinking about it. The air, while already hot, turns hotter, and before I know how it happened, our heads are close enough that I can feel her short breaths on my lips.

"How do we always end up like this?" Jesse says quietly, making no move to put distance between us.

She wets her lips, and I find myself wanting to say the reason we keep ending up like this is because she's mine. Because we're meant to be together. But I'm starting to see why Jesse may not be inclined to have more than a one-night stand with me. It has nothing to do with following the bucket list and everything to do with how she feels about herself and the insight she just gave me. I think she's afraid because she thinks she's on a timer, one that could run out at any moment.

I shift in the sand, and the curl that always flops from the top of my head brushes her forehead. "I think I have an idea," I whisper.

Her eyes move from my lips to my eyes. "You do?"

"Mmm." I reach a sand-covered hand up and trace my finger down her jaw. "We keep ending up like this because I'm irresistible. All the ladies love me."

The playful joke makes Jesse laugh and pull away. I immediately miss the warmth of her breath washing over me and the fruity smell of her sunscreen.

While I wish things were different, I knew I had to break the tension. I don't want to kiss Jesse again because we simply get lost in the moment. Knowing what I know now, I truly do want her to choose it, to kiss me not just because she's spilled her fears and truths. I want a kiss that means more than that.

I just hope she figures it out before our trip ends.

Chapter Twenty-Five

Jesse

I can't sleep. Asher is on my mind—he's always on my mind. I grab my phone from where it's charging off the floor and settle back in the twin bed. It's comfortable. Not as comfortable as my bed at home, but for being on the road, it's nice. Much better than the crap motels I would have stayed at if I had done some of my bucket-list items alone.

As I mentioned to Ash earlier, before I got hired for this new gig, I'd been jobless since I had to take so much time off. I'd had a good amount of savings from my prior job since it paid well and gave me health insurance, and with new money coming in soon, I would have been able to cross a few things off and still pay rent before I got my first paycheck. But thanks to my Bucket-List Helper, I've hardly spent any cash so far.

I'm still not sure how I feel about it, but Ash has money. And in one of my short check-up texts to Melissa, she told me to let her brother spend his money because he has a lot of it and nobody to spend it on. Again, not sure how I feel about it all, but at the same time, he's an adult, and he can spend it however he wants to. Right now, I'm trying to enjoy it and not think about it too much. I can figure it out later if I need to.

I open my phone to see it's after midnight, which means it's after two am in Wisconsin. While I've sort of adjusted to the time-zone change as we've made our way to Oregon over the last week, I should be dead tired. Especially after my day with Asher taking pictures in the sun. Instead, my mind is trapped in an endless wheel thinking about the man sleeping in the room next to mine.

Knowing I won't be able to sleep if I try again, I open my photos and decide I should make use of my time awake and post on social media. Ash didn't see, but while he was showering earlier tonight, I decided to make a video of me. I've been avoiding it, but after my talk with him on the beach, I felt compelled to get some of my story down on video.

I know social media enough to know that people want to connect with you at more than just a surface level. My profile is aptly named "A Change of Pace," but I haven't explained why the name has more than one meaning. Currently, my page is full of pictures, ones that have been getting a decent amount of likes and comments thanks to Asher's ability to understand all things tech. He's great with hashtags and SEO, things he's now taught me to do on my own.

I pull up the video and watch it one more time. My skin is tanned, and I see flecks of sand on my chest and arms from where we lay together and talked for far too long...*and almost kissed again*.

I shake the idea away and watch as I talk to the camera. It's a simple introduction—who I am, why I made the page, a brief rundown of Kawasaki disease, and why I have an ICD. I'm smiling in the video, but there's no missing my eyes are glassy.

After everything that's happened with my heart, I've tried to pretend that I'm still normal. I've avoided talking about my health, and I've hid my implant scar to avoid looks and questions. But in this video, the red line is prominent below my left clavicle, and as I watch, it comes to my attention that I haven't hidden it since I've been on this trip. It's a realization that makes my heart beat faster in my chest and my eyes burn.

The video finishes, and I tap to my profile, finding the video upload button before I can change my mind. I don't want to watch it again and again until I find a reason not to post it. Once it's queued to load and I've written a caption with keywords and hashtags, I click the button to choose a cover image. My photos open, and a picture pops up, making my breath catch in my throat.

The sun is bright, but so is my smile. I'm sitting on the lounge chair, and my head is tilted back in laughter, my hair brushing my upper back. Every part of me is on display since I wasn't wearing a wrap around my waist. The sun highlights every curve, dimple, and roll of my body wrapped in my two-piece hot-pink suit. A picture like this would've once been something I hated, but in this one, I look...

Beautiful.

The stinging in my eyes turns to tears. I set the cover with that image, hitting post before any sort of bad thoughts can enter my mind. I watch the video upload, gripping my phone in my hand as I blink away the wetness in my eyes. It's kind of funny, because up until last week, I hadn't taken any steps to actually live the change of pace I wanted for myself.

Yes, I'd gotten my new job. Yes, I had made the bucket list. But I hadn't truly started to do what I had set out to do. Now here I am, traveling more than a lot of people do in their lives—including myself, up until now.

I notice the video has been uploaded and switch over to my notes app. My bucket list is pinned to Asher's fridge—his idea—but the digital version makes it easier to track my progress. He had suggested some kind of fire ceremony to mark each accomplishment, but our nights have been all about eating, showering, and crashing after our busy days. Now that I think about it, I haven't checked off a single thing since our one-night stand.

Staring at the screen, I smile at how much we've already done: a one-night stand, seeing Old Faithful at Yellowstone, swimming in a hot spring, visiting at least four new states, saying yes to something I wanted to say no to. As I check off the items, a wave of pride and happiness swells in my chest. It's finally sinking in—I'm really doing this.

I wipe away a tear that's managed to escape and look at the remaining list sans the one I scratched out on the paper version:

Jesse's Change of Pace Bucket List

- ☒ A one-night stand
- ☐ Get a tattoo
- ☐ Watch the sunrise at Cadillac Mountain in Maine
- ☒ Say yes to something you want to say no to
- ☐ Take a dance class
- ☐ Ride a motorcycle
- ☐ Crash a wedding
- ☐ Swim naked in the ocean
- ☒ See Old Faithful at Yellowstone
- ☒ Swim in a hot spring
- ☐ Find a decent gluten-free pizza
- ☒ Visit at least four new states

Ash said he has a surprise for me tomorrow, and I wonder which of these he's going to help me check off. Or maybe it pertains to his mysterious bucket list? Maybe he's found the largest saltwater clam. My stomach flips as I visualize him with his curly hair—single curl plopped on his forehead—and lopsided smile as he stands next to a massive clam. It would totally be something he would do.

I flip from my bucket list to my photos again. I skip past the million he took of me while he did his horrible Italian accent and go back to the ones we took at Yellowstone. When I get to Old Faithful, my scroll stops on the photo the woman snapped of us. The one who thought we were on our honeymoon. I'm looking into his eyes, and he's smiling at me. The geyser shoots up behind us, offering a picture-perfect background.

I zoom in closer on our faces, recognizing this is the kind of thing you do when you're crushing hard on someone. But I can't find it in myself to stop. I admire Asher's face, his curly brown hair and well-trimmed beard. He's looking at me like I've hung the moon, and seeing us like this, frozen in time—it's doing something to my insides.

My words from earlier echo and bang around in my mind. *How do we always end up like this?*

His answer to my question made me laugh. Ash is always making me laugh, more than anyone I've ever met. Not only that, he makes me feel safe.

I regard the photo once more, this time focusing on my face, on the way I'm looking at him. My features are soft, my smile is bright, and you'd never guess by looking at me that I was at Yellowstone to see Old Faithful. You'd think Asher was a phenomenon of Mother Nature given the way my eyes are beaming, showing how much I'm in awe of him.

My fingers trace the side of his face, and my brain switches from innocent thoughts to dirty ones. I can almost feel Asher's breath on my lips, feel the way his arms held me in the hot spring. Those thoughts morph into the ones from our night together—the one that started everything.

The way his tongue wickedly brought me to orgasm, how his dick moved inside me, the way his soft hair felt between my fingers and his beard scratched my thighs. My clit throbs, and I rub my legs together to try to suppress it, but all it does is make it worse.

I don't have to touch myself to know that thoughts of him have made me embarrassingly wet. My cheeks heat from the fact that I hardly had to think of him at all to get turned on.

I'd be lying if I hadn't had these thoughts and reactions to said dirty thoughts before now. The night after the hot spring near kiss, I'd almost touched myself. I would have, too, had GusGus not decided to jump up on my bed and interrupted me. Not to mention, the door to my bedroom is kept slightly ajar so the cat can come in if he wants, meaning Ash could potentially hear me or see me if he was creeping. Not that he would ever do that.

Needless to say, I kept my hands above my waist, tossing and turning with thoughts of him and the same ache between my legs.

I turn my phone off and stare at my cracked bedroom door that I can barely see in the darkness. Gus is not in my room tonight, meaning he's either with Ash or in the living room area on the couch. I imagine Asher sleeping soundly, his mouth slightly parted and curls messy. I've learned that he sleeps shirtless and in athletic shorts, and I can vividly see his naked chest with a smattering of dark hair in my mind's eye. I'd also be lying if I said I haven't imagined running my fingers through it as he fucked me senseless again.

I grow wetter, probably soaking my underwear, which means I'll have to get up and change them, anyway. I suppose I *could* touch myself—it's not like I can't be quiet. Add to that, Asher is sleeping. If I really listen hard, I can hear his soft snores. On the nights I've had to use the bathroom, he's either been wide awake due to insomnia he struggles with because of his ADHD and the stimulant he takes or dead asleep like he told me he'd be, meaning he won't wake up now unless he has some sort of sixth sense about masturbation happening in his RV. The stupid thought nearly makes me laugh.

I shift on my bed and part my legs, deciding that I need the release. It will help ease some of the sexual tension between Asher and me. And maybe if I do, we'll end up with less near kisses and long stares.

This is also a way to not ruin my bucket list or sleep with him and make the feelings for him I've been trying to deny stronger.

Decision made, I gently run my hand over my breasts, squeezing one of them through the fabric of my pajama shirt. I bite my lip at the sensation, imagining it's Ash teasing them instead of me.

Images of him play like a movie behind my eyelids as I slide my hand lower until it's beneath the elastic of my shorts. My thoughts turn from him toying with my breast to a new scenario, one where he walks in on me and catches me in the act. I bet he would slyly grin and pull up the desk chair to watch.

Ash is one-hundred-percent the type of man who would give me instructions. Who would maybe even pull out his cock and masturbate along with me. So many lewd thoughts tumble in my mind, and I bite my lip harder to keep from crying out as my hand touches my wet and swollen clit. My hips lift off the bed as I play with myself, knowing that I will not last long. I'm too wound up, too needy.

My brain switches to Ash back on the bed with me. Now his hand grips me around my throat and gently squeezes as his lips come to my ear. Then his low, rumbling voice starts whispering words of praise to me. He tells me how stunning I am, how much he wants to fuck me after I come.

I circle my clit faster and faster, the phantom sensation of Asher's grip on my neck and his hot commands in my ear.

My mouth parts as I feel myself near release. I imagine Asher gripping my neck harder, his lips sealing over mine as I come, and I cry out his name, my body convulsing from the strength of my orgasm. For a moment, I feel like I'm floating, hovering among the stars and clouds. I allow myself to bask in the sensations, my fingers still on my pulsing bundle of nerves and muscles twitching in its aftershocks.

When I'm finally able to breathe, my body relaxes on the bed, but then movement coming from the other room forces me to freeze. My heart pounds in my chest as I realize I cried out. Not just cried out—I cried out *Asher's name*. And not quietly.

I close my eyes, my breath nearly nonexistent as I hear Ash move in his room. His steps seem to come closer to the door then stop. It's too dark for me to notice if he's by the door, but I keep my eyes clamped shut like a child pretending to sleep.

For seconds, I wait, wondering if he'll open the door to check on me. But then a moment later, his steps move away, and I hear the sound of the bathroom door closing. I get up and find my backpack, taking out wet wipes I keep in there for emergencies. I clean my hand off then change my underwear as fast as I can. Before I hear the toilet flushing, I'm already back in bed with my eyes closed as I attempt to calm myself and quiet my breath.

The noise of his bed shifting and his throat clearing are the only things that make me finally relax. When I'm wrapped in silence once again, I flip over and stare up at the ceiling, my heart still pounding in my chest, which makes me feel the wires of my implant inside its chambers.

I place my hand over my heart and will myself to calm down. Maybe he didn't hear the cry. Or if he did, he didn't know what woke him.

I rub a hand over my face and nearly smack my forehead. I can't believe I did that. I got myself off to a man I told myself I can't have while he was literally in the other room. A bashful smile plays at my lips, and the post-release feeling of my orgasm hits, making me tired.

As I slowly start to fade into dreamland, I wonder if Ash has gotten himself off to me, too. I push that dirty thought away and allow sleep to take me.

I hope tomorrow isn't awkward.

Chapter Twenty-Six

Asher

JESSE STARES UP AT the bed and breakfast with a lighthouse visible on the cliffs in the distance. "You're something else, you know that?" she says.

We'll be staying the night in a historic cottage that was once the lightkeeper's home. The charming Queen Anne-style building with white siding and a burnt reddish-orange roof has only six rooms—I'm still shocked that I managed to snag two rooms on such short notice. It also happens to be in the vicinity of two more things on Jesse's bucket list, which I have yet to divulge.

"Didn't I tell you I have a thing for lighthouses? It's why I put it on my bucket list."

"Okay, color me intrigued. Adding that to the question bank for later."

I smile crookedly at her, and for what seems like the millionth time today, she flushes. Not the normal flush that always seems to color her cheeks, but the kind of flush she gets when she's extremely embarrassed.

This morning, when she woke up and came out dressed and ready for coffee, she nearly turned into a tomato. I asked her if she was okay, and she said she was just hot from her shower, which was total bullshit. It made me wonder if she had a sex dream about me. I know I had one about her. It was so vivid that I woke up with a hard-on when dream-Jesse called my name in the most beautiful cry.

I clear my throat, hoping I'm not blushing like her now. "Sounds good. Want to go inside and get our rooms? I think if we stand out here and stare any longer, people might call the cops on us for loitering."

Jesse hoists her overnight bag on her shoulder and nods as she follows me toward the cottage. I open the gate of the white fencing, letting her go first. I enjoy seeing her take in the scenery. The pathway to the porch is lined with various wildflowers, and I see a daisy that's become uprooted so I bend down to pick it up off the ground. Before Jesse can take the final steps to head in, I stop her.

She turns around, and I hold out the flower. "For you."

Her hazel eyes drop to the daisy in my hand, and that deep blush returns again. I lift up my hand and tuck the flower behind her ear, my fingers brushing the shell of it. I don't miss the way she shivers at my touch before I pull away to see the full picture she makes. The contrast of the white-and-yellow flower against her tanned skin and dark hair is stunning. I want to get out my phone and capture the memory of her but use my mental memory instead, burning it into my brain so I can never forget it.

Jesse reaches up to secure the flower better. "Th-thanks," she stammers.

"You're welcome. You should wear flowers in your hair more often. It suits you."

Her lips turn up in a bashful smile, and she dips her chin to acknowledge my comment. Once she turns to walk up the stairs, a smile of my own warms my cheeks. I told myself I'd do everything in my power to make sure Jesse always knows how beautiful she is, and I mentally pat myself on my back for being successful in my motives. Because not only did she smile, she also didn't make a comment trying to reverse my compliment or deny it. It's a change from the Jesse before our trip started.

With my shoulders back and spirits high, I trail her up the steps and into the lobby of the B&B. She stands at the dark-stained wood desk, and when I'm next to her, I ring the small golden bell.

"This place is cool," Jesse says as she looks around.

"It is, isn't it?" I'd looked at the pictures online, but in person, it's even better. While it's not the fanciest place, it's decorated as if it's someone's home. The wood-floored room we're in is painted a seafoam green with white crown molding, and historical photos hang on the walls. Many photos feature the lighthouse we could see on the cliffs and people I assume used to care for it—or maybe the current owners' relatives.

A second later, a frazzled older woman walks into the room, her bright ginger hair windswept and cheeks red from exertion. "Hello there, sorry to keep you waiting. We have a wedding happening later today, and it's been a crazy morning! Are you checking in or here for a tour?"

"Checking in," I say. "I called the other day, Asher Jamison."

"Oh yes, yes. I remember speaking with you. I'm Missy Branson, the owner." She flips open her reservation book. Old school—I like it.

"I have you in the Lightkeeper's room, one of the best in the entire place. You'll both love it."

I feel Jesse stiffen beside me, and my brow pinches. "I booked two rooms."

Missy frowns then looks down at the book, flipping the pages back and forth before looking up at me apologetically. "Oh, shoot. I'm so sorry! It looks like my son must've put a couple here for the wedding in the second room."

"Do you have any other available?" Jesse asks.

"I'm sorry, we don't. Just the one."

Okay, maybe I don't like old school...or do I?

I look at Jesse, and she's not frowning, but she *is* staring at me for what I'd like to do next.

"What size bed is it again?" I ask.

"A king. I'm afraid that's all we have, too."

"Do you have a cot?"

"Afraid not," she says apologetically.

"It's okay, Ash," Jesse interjects. "You stay in the room. I'll stay in the RV with Gus."

I shake my head then look at Missy. "Will you give us a minute?"

"Sure thing, just ring the bell when you want me to come back. I'm so sorry again." Missy walks off, leaving me and Jesse alone.

"It's really fine," Jesse starts right away. "This is your bucket-list item. I can go back to the campground later. Then GusGus won't be alone."

"The whole point of booking this place was for us to experience it together. I'm not sending you back to the campground, and you know Gus is fine. He's got plenty to eat and drink, and I have the cameras on to check on him. I'm sure he'd be upset if you interrupted his alone time."

Jesse laughs. "He would not."

"Oh yes, he would. He loves to poop and stink up the place when I'm gone overnight. That way, when we get back, we have to air it out while he silently laughs at us. Trust me when I say he's looking forward to it."

"Ash! Seriously?"

"You've smelled it. You know my cat. I'm telling the truth."

Jesse sighs, but she's still smiling. "Okay, maybe, but there's only one bed."

"I can share."

She places her hands on her hips. "I don't know if it's a good idea."

I step forward so I'm closer to her. "If it makes you uncomfortable, we'll both go back to the RV and just spend the day exploring. But I had planned to give you this room—it has a view of the lighthouse at night and a claw-foot tub. We have a full day here, so it's easier if we stay. I'm happy to sleep on the floor or a couch if there's one."

"You paid for the room!"

I shrug. "That's neither here nor there."

Jesse sighs and looks around the place. I know this may not be an item that was on her bucket list, but I know she likes it here. I can see it written all over her face. She wants to stay, and I'd bet money that she wants to stay in the room with me but is having a hard time letting herself admit that.

"Let's at least look at the room, yeah? We can always decide later," I suggest.

Her gaze turns to mine, and she nods. "Okay."

"Really?" I smile.

"Really." She smiles back.

Excitement zips through my veins, and I ring the bell to get Missy back before Jesse changes her mind. I mean, she still could, but I don't think she will. Especially when she sees the room. The pictures looked awesome, and I have no doubt it will be better in person.

"Did you decide then?" Missy asks.

"Yeah, we'll take the room."

"Oh, good. The bed is comfortable to share."

"Is there a couch?" Jesse asks.

"Oh yes, there is. It might be a tight squeeze since you're both so tall. That's why I didn't mention it before."

"See," I tell Jesse, "it's all good." She playfully shakes her head at me. "We will definitely take it, Missy."

"Just fill out this information, and I'll give you a key." Missy hands me a paper form to fill everything out, including my credit card info, while she tells Jesse more about the house.

"This home was built in 1892, and the lighthouse you saw on the cliffs cast its first beam of light in 1884. With its age, you can imagine the place has some quirks. Your door sometimes gets stuck, but just jiggle the handle a few times, and it works. And if you hear some creaks in the night, it's just the house settling...or maybe a ghost."

I give my attention to the two women just as Missy winks at Jesse.

"Ghosts?" Jesse asks with a swallow.

"We're unsure. Are you a believer?" Missy responds as she takes the clipboard from me and checks it over.

"Um, I don't know."

The red-headed woman grins and puts the clipboard down to grab a set of keys with a blue motel keychain on it. "Don't worry, dear—if there are any, they're friendly."

I take the keys from Missy as Jesse faces me, her eyes wide. Shit, is she really afraid?

"Just go up the stairs to the right, then your room is to the left and all the way down the hall at the end. If you need anything, I'll be in and out until about six. If you'd like to tour the lighthouse this afternoon, you can walk down the path you might've seen coming in. It's about a ten-to-fifteen-minute walk that takes you by the beach then up to the lighthouse. Breakfast tomorrow morning is served at eight-thirty. Anything else I can do for you?"

"It said online there's private access to the beach?"

"Yes, the wedding is being held on a section of it this evening. But if you're looking for more privacy"—she near smirks at me—"you'll get it once they clear out for the reception near the lighthouse."

"Thanks."

"Enjoy your stay, you two. And don't worry about the ghosts. They tend to stay away when two people are in the room." Missy winks discreetly at me and leaves.

Did Missy just help me out with Jesse? Am I that obvious?

"Okay, well, now if I stay here, you can't leave," Jesse says.

I meet her gaze and find her face is pale. "Are you really scared?"

"I hate ghosts. I hate anything scary, really. So if watching a horror movie was on your bucket list, you can do that one on your own."

I cough a laugh. "That's not on my list. And I swear, there was nothing online about this place being haunted."

She shivers. "Let's not talk about it anymore."

I step next to Jesse and throw my arm around her. "I'll protect you, don't worry."

Jesse rolls her eyes then points at my lips. "Shut it."

My chest shakes with laughter, and I drop my arm so we can walk to the stairs. From what I can see, the rest of the home is much like the downstairs. Old pictures line the walls, except instead of seafoam green, the hallway is painted pink. When we reach our room, I unlock the door, and sure enough, it sticks. I wiggle it a few times before it swings open. I let Jesse go in first and follow her, closing and locking the door behind us.

"Wow," she exclaims. She walks to the window overlooking the cliffs, dropping her bag near the foot of the king bed covered in a blue comforter that matches the walls.

Jesse's head turns to see the lighthouse in the distance off to the right, and I walk up next to her. The view is incredible, and I'm glad Missy's son gave the other room to the couple instead of this one. Not only can we see the lighthouse, but the ocean is vast from this viewpoint. I could watch the lapis-blue water splash onto the shore and surrounding cliffs for hours and never get sick of it.

"I can't believe I'm seeing the ocean."

Her words register in my brain, and I look at her stunned face. For a second, I forgot this is Jesse's first time seeing the ocean. She told me her family never went to the coasts, always opting for cheaper vacations to nearby Wisconsin lakes or family waterparks in the Wisconsin Dells.

"It's incredible, right?"

"It goes on forever," she says. "I can't wait to put my feet in it."

"We could go now if you want, but I was thinking we could go down after we crash the wedding and skinny dip."

Her head snaps to mine. "What?"

"You had "crash a wedding" on your list, or did you scratch it out like that last item?"

She playfully bumps my shoulder. "I didn't scratch the wedding one off, you menace."

I hum. "Good. I also have one other thing planned for this afternoon, but we have to take a ride to a place about fifteen minutes from here to do it."

She looks at me skeptically. "What is it?"

"A dance class."

Her eyes widen like saucers. "How did you plan all of this? Is this magic you have or something?"

"No magic. I found the B&B while looking for beaches with private access."

"I thought you said you have a thing for lighthouses?"

"That was just a bonus." She raises her eyebrow. "Okay, fine. You got me. I do like lighthouses, but it's not exactly a bucket-list item I planned. Once I saw this place and read the history, I added it, but I don't have a lighthouse collection or anything."

She chuckles. "I'll accept that. But how did you know about the wedding?"

"I didn't."

"So you're saying that was pure luck."

"The universe works in mysterious ways. Maybe it's because you're God's Gift."

She groans. "I thought we were past that name."

"Seems fitting for the moment," I chirp.

"And the dance class?"

"When I was googling what was in the area and the studio popped up, I thought it was meant to be. Seems like it was, since we can test out our new dance moves at the wedding reception." I give a little boogie move, and she giggles.

"You really want to do all this with me?"

"What else am I going to do, hang out here with all the ghosts?"

She shivers and makes a gagging sound. "Please don't remind me."

I bump her shoulder this time. "Don't worry, she said if there's two people, they stay away."

Jesse rolls her eyes. "Yeah, I'm sure that's how ghosts work. Did you pay her to say that?"

I snort. "Nope, I would never."

"Suuuuuure."

"Okay, maybe that's something I'd do, but I didn't." I turn Jesse so she's facing me, my hands gripping her upper arms. "I meant what I said. If this makes you uncomfortable, we don't have to stay here. We can go and interrupt GusGus's poop extravaganza."

She screws up her nose. "Gross."

"That's what I'm saying."

A sincere smile plays at her lips, and she nods. "We can stay here. With all your plans, it really does make sense."

I cheer with happiness on the inside. This little excursion is turning out better than anything I could've planned. Of course, I will be a gentleman and sleep on the couch or the floor if she wants, but I like being near her. And after the last week together, I've gotten used to sleeping in a room next to her at the very least. I wouldn't want her or I to go back to the RV while one of us stays here. And I don't want her to miss the opportunity to stay at a place like this—even if there are ghosts.

"Perfect," I say before looking at my watch. "We've got a couple of hours till the dance class. Want to go snoop around the property and try to make friends with the wedding party so we don't look like creepers when we crash later?"

Jesse exhales and nods. "Sounds like a plan."

Chapter Twenty-Seven

Jesse

"Okay, I have a confession to make," Ash says.

I look over from where I'm standing near the bed and nearly start drooling. He's wearing the same suit he wore to Melissa's engagement party, except he's holding a matching brown tie in his hand. He looks, for lack of a better word, hot. Especially since he hasn't buttoned the coat yet and he's not wearing shoes. I like the more casual look, and it doesn't help the blush I've been trying and failing to conceal all day while being around him.

From the second I first saw him this morning, he hasn't given any indication he heard me coming last night with his name on my lips. But it still doesn't make me any less embarrassed. And with the way he looks now mixed with the phantom feeling of his arms around me during our dance class together a mere two hours ago, all I can think is dirty thoughts.

Before he came out of the bathroom, I was imagining him laying me flat on the bed and putting his hands on me instead of my own. Now I'm imagining his suit on the floor next to him while he kneels and the tie he's holding secured around his wrists while I—

Ash clears his throat, and I look into his eyes. I lick my lips and plaster a smile on my face, knowing my cheeks are definitely red. "What's your confession?" I ask.

He smirks. "I've never tied my own tie."

I scoff. "You're lying."

"I'm not." He takes another step forward and holds it out to me. "Do you know how?"

"I did it for my ex a few times, but it might take me a second to figure it out. Haven't had to in a long time."

I swear Asher's face sours at the mention of my ex, but a second later, he's smiling. "Still, I'm sure you'll do it better than me."

I take the tie from his hands and have him stand up straight, looping the fabric around his neck so it lays flat.

"How do you not know how to tie your own tie? I thought you were a millionaire or something."

He chuckles. "I have my servants do it for me."

"Ha ha," I deadpan as I cross the wide end of the tie over the narrow end.

"Truthfully, it's one of those things that requires concentration, the kind that overstimulates me, and I get frustrated. I find having someone else do it or just not wearing one is easier."

"That makes sense."

Ash goes silent after that, but I can sense his eyes on me as I work. Because it's been awhile since I've done this, it takes me a second to fully remember all the steps. Eventually, it clicks, and I bring the wide end under the narrow end before wrapping it around the front. After a couple more steps, I get the knot right and slide it up to his collar.

"There, all done." I meet his warm gaze, and without thinking, I smooth my hands down his shirt. The fabric feels starchy under my fingers, but the heat of his skin seeps through my palms and warms me.

"Jesse-approved?" he asks, his voice huskier than it was a moment ago.

I remove my hands and nod, stepping back to give us some space and take in the full picture. "Jesse-approved. You look nice."

"Just nice?"

I laugh. "Alright, you look more than nice. You look very handsome. The bridesmaids at the wedding won't be able to keep their hands off you."

He scrunches up his nose. "You're my date."

I stare into Asher's eyes and am struck by the sincerity I see in them. I know I shouldn't be surprised—he hasn't tried to hide that he's still interested in me—but despite my little self-pleasure session last night and all the daydreams I've had today, I still am trying to stick to my guns.

"If you wanted to hook up with one of them tonight, I wouldn't fault you." As soon as the sentence leaves my mouth, I feel bile rise in my throat. I shouldn't have said that. It's the last thing I want, but it's also not fair to lead him on. He should be able to have fun if he wants to and not wait on me, even if the very idea of it makes me want to cry.

Asher stares at me, unblinking, and I feel terrible. We spent the afternoon dancing and laughing together. We touched more today than we have the entire time we've known each other. Even when the dance instructor asked if we wanted to change partners to get more experience, we stayed together. I stepped on his toes several times when we got to the more complicated dances, and at one point, he joked about having to get a bubble to dance with me, but he never switched partners. And I was glad for it. I liked being held by him. It was one of the most fun things I've ever done. It reminded me of the first time we met, dancing in the bar in front of all those people.

Ugh, my thoughts are all jumbled. One minute, I want him, and the next, I'm pushing him away. It isn't fair to him. And now, given the way he's looking at me, his smile gone and eyes lackluster, I know I've hurt his feelings. I debate whether or not I should say something. My mouth opens and closes several times, but no sound ever comes out.

After what feels like an hour of us staring at each other, Asher takes a step forward so we're close enough to feel each other's body heat.

"Jesse," he says. His voice is firm and commanding, and he nearly sounds like a different person. "I want you to hear me when I say this."

He pauses again, his brown eyes penetrating mine with the intensity he always seems to give me and only me.

"You're my date. I'm crashing this wedding for you because I want to. I dressed in this suit for you because I saw the way you looked at me while I was wearing it for my sister's party."

"Ash—"

"Please. *Please*, let me finish."

My shoulders fill with tension, but I nod.

"You asked me yesterday why we keep ending up in positions like this." He looks down at my lips, and I automatically dart my tongue out to wet them. He sucks in a shallow breath. "I don't want to hook up with a bridesmaid. I want to go to this wedding with you. I want to spend time with you. If you don't want that, then I'll go back to the RV and let you have this room tonight. You can go to the wedding—"

"No." I shake my head vehemently. "That's not what I want." I exhale and turn my face to the ground. My temple pounds, and my stomach hurts.

"Then tell me, Jesse girl. What do you want?"

I lift my gaze to his and feel my heart and mind pulled in different directions. My heart wants to fling myself at him. Lay my lips on his, push him back on the bed, and skip the wedding. But my mind tells me that all of this is a bad idea. We have things left to do on the trip, and he's leaving for London soon. I can no longer have the fairytale.

I also know that crashing the wedding with him will only make my heart want him more. So I settle for a compromise, or at least what will satisfy both in some way. I'll go to the wedding, but there will be no longing glances or funny business. We are going as friends.

"I want to crash a wedding with you, Ash." I smile softly at him. "I want to show off our dance moves and make fools of ourselves in front of complete strangers. I—"

Ash shifts on his feet. "You...?"

I want to be held by you. Kissed by you.

"I'm sorry for what I said. It was stupid."

Asher's gaze flicks over my face, and though he tries to hide it, I can see the disappointment in his eyes. He told me he wanted me, and I avoided answering. But I'm still trying to reinforce the last of the bricks in my crumbling wall that will keep me from falling hard for him. Because if they collapse, I don't know if I'll be able to build the wall back up—and for both my heart's and mind's sake, I need to keep those bricks where they are.

"Please," I say. "Can you forgive me?"

Ash takes a step back, and while it's what I want, I can't deny it hurts. "There's nothing to forgive." He slides his hand down the tie and studies it before looking back at me, his crooked grin on his face again, though I've seen it enough to tell that it's not a true one. He's putting it on for me, to make things easier. "It looks good. Thank you."

"You're welcome," I nearly whisper.

"Now, are you going to wear that, or are you going to put on that dress you got earlier? I like this ensemble, but something tells me you'll stick out."

I look down at my T-shirt and shorts then back up at Ash. "You were hogging the bathroom. I was waiting." I attempt to tease him.

It works, because the mood in the room lightens a bit, and his smile turns more genuine. "Are you saying I take a long time to get ready?"

"If the shoe fits, Cinderella."

He huffs a laugh. "You're funny."

"I try."

Ash glances at his watch then back to me. "It's nearing seven. We should head down in about twenty minutes if we want to hit the cocktail hour that my third cousin, James, told us about."

At the mention of James, I laugh. When Ash and I went down to check out the grounds earlier, we ran into some of the wedding party as we went to explore the lighthouse. I got to find out just how good Asher Jamison is at schmoozing people and getting information out of them. It was impressive to watch, and I felt like I got a good glimpse of the kind of businessman he is and why he's so successful.

Within ten minutes of talking to James, Ash had convinced the guy that he was related to him and I was his date for the wedding. After he got over his moment of confusion, James readily agreed with Asher that it's easy to forget third cousins, especially when you haven't seen them in ten years.

Once James was convinced he knew Asher and just forgot about him, he proceeded to spill every piece of information we needed to know, including the bride's and groom's names, what time the cocktail hour started, and how annoyed he was his sister had the wedding here since the closest hotel was twenty minutes away and down a winding road, which he hated because he got motion sickness.

Honestly, I didn't pay attention to a lot of what he was saying because Asher had his arm around me the entire time, turning my brain into mush by playing the role of my boyfriend. At one point, he even kissed my forehead. Talk about swoon.

I clear that thought before I get in trouble again and point to the bathroom. "I'll go get ready then." Asher nods at me, and I walk past him, grabbing the dress I found earlier at a thrift store that I'd hung in the closet near the bed.

Since I didn't know we'd be crashing a wedding today, I hadn't brought anything wedding-worthy in my overnight bag. Ash offered to get us a ride back to the RV, but after the dance class, I saw the store and was surprised and elated to find they had a plus-size section. I was even more surprised when I found a perfect boho-style maxi dress in a pale yellow that had three-quarter-length sleeves made of a lacy material and looked good on my tall, round form.

I didn't ask Ash what he'd thought, opting to surprise him. A notion I'm questioning now, since I shouldn't want to surprise or look good for a man I'm attempting to *not* have feelings for. One I stupidly told to sleep with a bridesmaid.

God, I suck at this.

With dress and makeup bag in hand, I go into the bathroom and put on some makeup. I use the curling iron the bathroom was stocked with to add some nice waves to my shoulder-length hair. Once I've deemed myself good, I stare at my scar in the mirror.

As I noticed last night, I haven't been covering it up. But we're crashing a wedding, and the last thing I want is questions from strangers, even if Ash is the one pretending to be related to the groom. I don't need people who don't know me or Ash being concerned for my well-being.

I apply a layer of foundation and put setting spray on it followed by another layer and powder then more setting spray. After I'm satisfied, I put on a pair of fake diamond studs before slipping into the dress.

It's nothing extravagant, not that I expected a dress for twenty bucks to be. But it looks good on me, flowing over my curves. The V-neck shows off just the right amount of cleavage and covers nearly all my makeup-covered scar.

Satisfied, I exit the bathroom twenty minutes later to find Asher staring out the window, looking at the sun beginning to set over the Oregon coastline.

"I'm ready," I say as I slip on a pair of low heels I also found at the thrift store. When I look up from my feet, Asher has turned around, and his eyes are zeroed in on me.

"Wow, you look..." He trails off.

When he doesn't make a move to finish the sentence, I frown. "Is it bad? I know it's not the best wedding attire."

"No, you look..." He takes several steps toward me until he's close enough to grab my hand. Without warning, he spins me like he learned to do in the dance class. The movement catches me off guard, and I giggle as I nearly fall into his arms. When our eyes meet again, he's gazing at me, the intensity from before back in his eyes.

"I look like what?"

He swallows, Adam's apple bobbing in his throat. "Like the sun."

My skin prickles, and he pushes me back out again so he can get a better look. "I can't wait to show off our moves on the dance floor. Everyone will be looking at you."

"On second thought, maybe we should skip the wedding," I say.

Ash tuts and drops my hand. "Absolutely fucking not. We're crossing off that bucket-list item. And we're going to have fun doing it."

"I really look okay?"

"You look beautiful. Like God's Gift."

I snort and flick his chest before holding out my elbow to him. "Let's go, One Who Lives by an Ash Tree or Ash Grove. Before I lose my nerve."

He joins in my laughter, looping his elbow through mine. I can't help but notice he doesn't try to take the lead. He lets me guide us, his arm comfortably tucked in mine all the way to the cocktail hour.

Chapter Twenty-Eight

Asher

THE BOISTEROUS WEDDING RECEPTION buzzes inside a large white tent adorned with lilies and twinkling lights. Meanwhile, I stand at the bar, lost in my thoughts as the celebration goes on around me.

I nearly screwed everything up in the room. I'm worried I was too forward with my words or got too emotional. But when she suggested I could sleep with a bridesmaid, I nearly lost it. I kind of did. I'm glad we recovered from it, because even though I'm frustrated, the last thing I want to do is fall into her trap of attempting to push me away. Especially when every time we're near each other, her actions are the opposite of what she says she wants.

Not only have her cheeks been turning pink around me more than usual today, she refused to be anyone else's partner at our dance class. I also didn't want to dance with anyone else, but that was a given.

What really convinces me that she wants something more between us, though, is her pretend girlfriend act—it's absolutely flawless. She's not just holding my hand or letting me wrap my arm around her waist. She gazes at me lovingly, fixes my tie when it's askew, and even fed me a bite of cake when nobody was watching. She's so good at the act, even I'm having a hard time remembering we're not dating.

You'd never guess she was nervous to crash this wedding. The Jesse with me here is the Jesse I met at the bar, the one who danced like no one was watching, the one who asked me to go home with her. And it's not only me she's got eating out of her hand—she's got the entire wedding party, including the father of the bride, too. She spent twenty minutes talking to him about cheese. Yes, cheese. When he learned she was from Wisconsin, he said he was a UW Madison alumni. Then they got on the topic of cheese curds. The only reason they stopped talking about them was because his wife wanted to dance.

Jesse is on the dance floor now. I can see her from my spot at the bar, dancing with two kids. I sip a glass of whiskey and water as I watch her. Her skin is dewy with sweat from the summer air, the breeze from the ocean doing nothing to cool her down. She's been dancing too much and laughing too hard under the bright lights of the fancy dance floor that was set up. Not that I'm complaining—I wasn't lying when I said she looks like the sun.

With the flowing yellow dress twirling around her as she dances and the bright smile on her face, she's shining. So brightly, it nearly blinds me. Maybe it's stupid, but ideas and dreams start to flourish in my mind. I allow myself to wonder what kind of wedding Jesse and I would have. If it would be like this, small and intimate, or something big and extravagant. Maybe she'd want to go to Vegas and get married by an Elvis impersonator. I could totally see us doing that.

One of the kids, a little girl, steps up on Jesse's toes. She can't be more than four or five and is wearing a cute poofy pink dress. The image of them dancing together only makes more thoughts I shouldn't be having run rampant. My memories drift back to our time at The Corn Palace. Jesse never did answer if she wanted kids. With everything I know now, my thought that her hesitation to answer had to do with her heart makes even more sense.

I feel like an idiot for asking her that question to begin with—it's a deeply personal question. Had she asked me, I think my answer would be whatever she wanted. I'd love to have a family with her or keep our family just us and GusGus. All I know is that I want to be the earth to her sun.

My chest aches, and I take another sip of my whiskey, stopping myself from downing the whole thing. I don't want to get drunk, not when I'm still planning to take Jesse to the ocean later to check off another item. I'm curious how that will go, but I'm trying not to think too much about it. Or the fact that we'll both be naked.

"You're not related to this family, are you?"

The hair on the back of my neck rises as I turn to the owner of the deep voice. My eyes land on the groom, Matt, whose eyebrow is up in question. He's similar in height to me, but the guy looks like he eats a dozen eggs for breakfast and rescues kittens on the weekend—like a blond Superman. I'm strong, but he could probably knock me out if he wanted.

"What makes you say that?"

"My wife and I were talking, and she said she did a family tree project with her niece, that little girl right there"—he points at the girl dancing with Jesse—"earlier this year. Said she'd remember a guy named Asher, if that's even your real name."

"That's my name."

"But you're not related to my wife." I notice how this is the second time he's said *my wife*. And he's grinning like a lovesick fool every time he says it. It's sickeningly sweet, but I totally understand it. I'd be the same way if this were my wedding to Jesse.

"If I say I'm not, will you kick us out?"

"Depends."

"On?"

"On if you're a creep or just having some fun crashing."

"Not a creep."

"Right. Well, this booze was expensive," he says, eyeing my glass.

"I have money." I start to reach in my back pocket, and Matt laughs.

"Nah, man, I was just yanking your chain. It's all good. It's kind of a fun memory to say we had wedding crashers, and my wife likes your girl. I think everyone here does."

"She's easy to like."

"You been together long?"

My eyes find Jesse, who's now dancing with the little boy who looks to be the same age as the girl. "We're actually not together."

"You're shitting me!"

"No, I'm not," I say almost sadly. "We're on a road trip together—long story."

He eyes me like he's working something out in his head. Then a moment later, he claps my shoulder roughly. "I've been in the friend zone, man. With my wife, actually."

"Really?" I take another sip of my drink.

"We grew up together. I lived across the street from her my whole life. Our moms are friends."

"When did you start dating?"

"Not until two years ago, when we both turned thirty."

"No shit? That long?"

He chuckles. "I pined after her like a lovesick pup for ages. Watched her date asshole after asshole. She almost married one."

I think about being in his position but with Jesse. It makes me ill. Not to be dramatic or anything, but if I had to live through what this guy did, I think I'd die.

"What changed?" I ask.

"I knew she was meant to be mine from the moment I could understand what that meant. So I waited for her to see me. It was hard, and there were moments I nearly gave up. But I was patient, and one day, we went out and got sloshed. I laid my heart out for her to squash, but she agreed to a date. Two years later, here we are."

"Sounds...hard."

"But worth it. It's part of our story, and I'd do it again if it meant I ended up here." His eyes find his bride, who's dancing with her dad. The love in his eyes as he watches her is so clear and true, it's enough to make a person who doesn't believe in love change their mind.

My heart throbs in my chest, and I focus on Jesse, who's looking at me. She sends me a gentle wave then motions for me to come to the dance floor. When I turn back to my new friend, he's smiling at me with his pearly white—and very straight—teeth.

"What?" I say.

"You look at her like I look at my wife."

I swallow down another gulp of my drink. "Funny story, we just met over a week ago."

"Well, damn. You got it bad, my man."

"You have no idea."

His hand smacks my shoulder. "I feel your pain. But something tells me you won't have to wait as long as I did." He slaps me on the shoulder again. "Nice meeting you, Asher. And good luck." He turns to leave but then stops. "And enjoy the free booze. Just don't drink it all." He winks.

I watch him leave before giving my full attention back to Jesse. Instead of politely asking me to join her on the dance floor, she gestures toward the kids with her head and mouths "Save me."

Holding back a laugh, I set my drink on the bar and head toward the floor lit up by string lights with a DJ in front of it. The soft glow of the light only makes Jesse stand out even more. I'd be remiss if I didn't notice that some of the single groomsmen have been eyeing her all night.

"May I cut in?"

The kids turn, and the little girl stares up at me with wide green eyes before her cheeks turn pink. The boy with her pouts and goes to argue, but then the music changes to a slow song. Before I can beg him to let me have Jesse, they run off the floor, laughing.

"Thanks," she says as I take her hand. When my right hand lands on her lower back, she grimaces. "Sorry, I'm sweaty. It's hotter than I expected it to be."

"I'm not afraid of a little sweat." She screws up her nose, but I mean it. I pull her closer so our bodies are nearly touching and smile at her. "You really are putting those dance lessons to good use."

"This is our first time testing out a slow dance, though."

"Need I remind you we have danced before?" I pick up my left hand and signal I want to turn her. Her chin dips, and I ease her gently under my arm before pulling her back into me.

She's smiling timidly now, and I know she's remembering that night like I am. It was a different kind of dancing, the kind I wouldn't do at a wedding in front of children and people I don't know. It has me wishing we were in private so I could spin her around and pull her backside against me.

"I know," she says, her tone wistful.

The slow song continues, and I lead her around the floor. At one point, my eyes flick down and notice for the first time tonight she's covered her scar again. The urge to use my thumb to take off the makeup is strong. It's part of Jesse, a sign of how strong she is, and I like seeing it.

She notices where I'm looking, and I nearly blush at being caught. I didn't mean to stare that long.

"I didn't want the party guests to ask any questions since we don't know them. Otherwise, I would have left it."

"You would've?" I ask, not moving my gaze from hers.

She nods, her hand flexing against mine. "I think I'm starting to get more comfortable with it. I even posted a video to my social media account last night. I haven't checked to see if anyone watched it."

"About your implant?" I say as I move us across the floor, avoiding other guests.

"Yeah, among other things. We talked the other day about social media and what makes it successful."

"I remember." I smile.

"Connection, sincerity. I figured it was time to tell my story, why I named my channel Change of Pace. I don't know if anyone will care, but—"

"They'll care," I assure her. "You'll have to play it for me later."

She bites her lip and, after a second, dips her chin. "Okay."

My mouth tips into a smile, and she exhales, her shoulders relaxing. We sway to the music, and I turn her out again, pulling her body closer to mine when she returns to me. Jesse doesn't try to pull away; instead, she sinks into my arms.

With her against me, the reception around us fades. I don't know if it's because she's tired or it's a choice she's making to fit with our act, but she rests her head on my shoulder.

The action puts my nose close to the crown of her head, and I breathe her in. Much like the first night we met, her scent is intoxicating—sweet and floral with a hint of salt from her constant dancing.

Her head tips back so she's looking at me. "Did you just smell me?"

I smirk. "Maybe."

Jesse laughs, and the sound is better than any sound in the world. I'd fight anyone on that. Her head rests back on my shoulder, and I do everything I can to memorize this moment. My left hand grips hers a little tighter, and my fingers gently press into her low back.

I inhale her again but softer this time, relishing the warmth of her pliant body. I close my eyes, and when I open them, I make eye contact with the groom, who's holding his wife and leading her across the floor. He makes a show of looking at Jesse then back to me before winking.

A ball of anxiety forms in my stomach, and I hold Jesse closer, my fingers gripping her hand tighter and my hand on her back flexing to keep her near. The action makes Jesse pull her head back so she's looking into my eyes again.

"Are you okay?" she asks.

I swallow the thickness I feel in my throat and manage a smile. "Yeah. Just enjoying the moment."

Something flashes through her eyes, and her pink tongue darts out to wet her lips as it has so many times before.

"Here we are again," she nearly whispers.

"So it would seem."

I wait for her to pull back or for my senses to fully come to me so I'll step away and give her the distance she's been saying she wants, but I can't move. Our dancing slows to near non-existent steps. From a distance, we probably look as if we're standing in place.

After another moment that seems like hours, Jesse's lips part, and her head tilts. My heart beats loudly in my ears, and my breath halts in my chest.

Her gaze is locked on my lips, and I don't blink, worried that if I look away, the moment will be broken. In the background, I think I hear a voice or maybe voices chanting for us to kiss. I don't know if it's Matt or the entire group of guests—all I know is that Jesse hasn't pulled away. There's a playful smile on her lips as her lashes flutter like butterfly wings.

"They want us to kiss," she says.

The sound of the people on the dance floor chanting becomes clearer in my ears, and I have no doubt my new friend was the one who started it because I hear him cheering the loudest.

"Sounds like they do." I faintly smile.

Kiss! Kiss! Kiss! The small crowd of cheers grows louder now.

"We probably should." She licks her lips again.

"We don't want to disappoint them."

"No, we don't want that," she says.

My heart halts in my chest as I wait for her to close the distance. My fingers twitch on her body, and I do everything in my power to wait for her.

Kiss! Kiss! Kiss!

My gaze lingers on her lips, and for a moment, I forget how to breathe. My eyes fall shut, and before I can reopen them, Jesse's lips find mine. It's only then that my heart remembers to beat.

Chapter Twenty-Nine

Jesse

I'M KISSING ASHER AGAIN. Not only am I kissing him, I'm kissing him in front of strangers. Ones who think we're dating and that he's their third cousin they somehow forgot. What is my life?

His lips are tentative against mine, not commanding like they were the first time we kissed. For an instant, I think it's because of the situation we're in or he's still upset about my comment earlier, but when I part my lips and our tongues meet, he unleashes. He lets go of my hand, sliding it to join his other hand on my low back, pulling me into him so I can't even tell where he ends and I begin.

The party around us disappears, and I'm swept up in the lips I keep dreaming about. In the lips I've imagined finding mine again since the moment they last parted. Part of my brain is telling me to stop, trying to remind me of why I told myself this was a bad idea, why I kept resisting. But I push it away, too wrapped up in the sensations he brings to my body, in how I can taste whiskey on his tongue.

"Okay, you kissed!" a man yells.

"Get a room!" a female voice adds.

I pull my lips from his, my body flaming from head to toe. Ash rests his forehead against mine, and I open my eyes to meet his. His brown pools are shining with laughter, and when I lift my head, the groom, Matt, is dancing past with his wife, Jessica.

He smacks Asher on the back, and I let out a small embarrassed laugh.

I cock my head at Asher. "Want to get out of here?"

The sparkle in his eyes turns to heat. "Yeah?"

The question I asked strikes me, and I know they are the words I spoke to him at the bar when we first met. I stare into his warm eyes, dilated from our kisses. His skin is flushed, too, and I can see the hope in his expression. His hands are still weighted on my low back, and I want to feel them drift further down.

I think back to the night of Melissa's engagement party, how I was going to text him, take him up on the offer to see each other again. Things are more complicated now, but I was already holding on by a thread, and the kiss we just shared broke it. So what if we have some fun together again? We're both adults. It doesn't have to mean more than what it is: two people having sex. People do it all the time without it leading to a fairytale ending—one I yet again remind myself I can't have.

"Yeah," I answer.

Ash takes my hand, and instead of tugging me from the floor as I expected him to, he kisses my knuckles. The skin he kissed tingles, and before I can respond, he pulls me into his side so we're facing the dancing bride and groom.

"You both leaving?" Matt stops their dance and tugs Jessica into his side, facing Asher like he's an old friend.

"Yeah, man, congratulations." They shake hands, and I say goodbye to Jessica. She hugs me and thanks me for coming, and then I shake Matt's hand.

"Feel free to crash any of our parties in the future," Matt says. "You both are a blast."

My stomach drops, and my eyes bug out of my head, making the couple laugh. Asher squeezing my shoulders makes me look at him.

"I hadn't had a chance to tell you we'd been found out," he says.

"Oh god," I mutter. "I'm so sorry."

"Don't be!" Jessica laughs. "Matt and I think it's fun. We plan to do it now, too. Thanks for the idea."

"You're welcome?"

The couple laughs again, and we say our final goodbyes. Jessica tells me to friend her on social media, and she'll send me some pictures once she gets them back from the photographer. After that, it takes us what seems like ages to leave as we say goodbye to the people we became friends with, including Jessica's dad. The whole time, Asher holds my hand in his, and I make no move to pull it away, enjoying its steady warmth.

Once we've made it out, we come to the part of the sandy path that forks. We stop in front of a sign showing one way to the beach and another back to the B&B. The noise from the reception has faded to a low hum of music and laughter, and the wind blows from the ocean to cast my hair across my face. I use my free hand to tuck some of the strands behind my ear and look at Asher.

"Still up for that dip?" he asks.

The faint light lining the pathway illuminates his features enough for me to see his focused gaze. After the kiss we shared, I had forgotten about the next item he planned to check off my list tonight.

"We don't have any towels."

Ash grins. "Where's your sense of adventure, Jesse girl?"

Jesse girl. I love when he calls me that. "Honesty, I'm more concerned about you ruining your suit."

"Fuck the suit." I let out a bark of laughter, and he squeezes my hand.

"It'll probably be cold."

He reaches his free hand up and tucks a strand of hair from my face. "I'll keep you warm."

A shudder runs through my body as he uses his finger to trace my jaw. "Will you?"

"If that's what you want."

"It's what I want," I say.

His finger traces my lip before he suddenly drops his hand, tugging me toward the ocean. I laugh at the sudden jerk, nearly tripping on my feet. He holds me steady, and then we're taking off toward the water. Ash holds me in his grip the entire trip down the steps to the beach, making sure I don't fall in the low light.

When we reach the water, the beach is no longer lit by the light of the steps. Now it's only the moon and the stars highlighting the waves crashing on the sand and the light from the lighthouse on the cliffs that adds its own eerie glow. I shiver from the breeze, the heat of the reception lights and all my dancing leaving my body.

Ash drops my hand, and I turn to see him unbuttoning his suit. My eyes meet his face, which has been transformed by his crooked grin. He chucks his jacket on the beach then pulls the tails of his shirt from his slacks.

"Are you just going to stand there and watch?" he asks.

"I'm waiting for you to get more clothes off. I only have the dress, my bra, and underwear on."

If I could see the full color of Ash's eyes, I imagine they would be darker now. Even with the lack of light, I can see the way his arms flex as he grips the end of his shirt tighter.

When it's completely free from his slacks, he reaches for the buttons, slowly undoing them. It's torture, and when I study his face, I think he's doing it on purpose. I use the moment to take off my shoes before standing upright again, watching as Ash shrugs his shirt off. He lets the fabric join his jacket and tie in the sand before he toes off his shoes and socks.

"Now you're wearing more than me," he says, gesturing to his pants. "I only have one item left."

"Did you go commando?"

"Maybe."

"You did not."

"I did."

My eyes fall to the front of his pants, the breeze making the fabric pull tight against the bulge I can see there. My nipples harden, and I lick my lips. Despite the cool breeze and the goosebumps forming on my skin, I feel hot again.

"If you want me to turn around, I can," Ash says after a moment.

My gaze flicks back to his, and I shake my head. When I wrote "skinny dip in the ocean" on my bucket list, I didn't think anyone would be with me, much less a man I once slept with and can't get out of my mind.

A part of me feels as if I should have him turn around, but I don't want him to. I know Ash finds me beautiful, and I feel comfortable around him, especially after our photoshoot and our dance lessons today. He's never given me any reason to be ashamed of my body. Maybe I would have had him turn around before we met, but not now.

"You can watch." My answer carries on the breeze.

His eyes don't shift from me as I start to bunch the material of my yellow dress, mimicking the slowness he used to unbutton his shirt. His lips part as I pull the fabric up and over my head. I hold it in my hands for a moment, eyes meeting his again. Ash softly smiles, a smile that feels like it's only for me.

His hands reach for his belt, and he unbuckles it then unzips his fly. When he drops his pants to the ground and steps out of them, I see he wasn't lying. He's completely naked underneath, nothing hiding his arousal. His gaze shows he's not ashamed of his desire. Far from it—he stands confidently with his shoulders back, not making a move to hide himself.

Using his boldness, I slide off the pair of white high-waisted underwear I have on and kick them near my dress. I don't meet his eyes before my bra has joined them, and I hear his breath suck in. He hesitates for a beat before he takes a step toward me as if I'm a deer that will bolt at any moment, which I suppose I deserve. I've not exactly given him any reason to think I won't change my mind and go back to the room. And I'd be lying if I said there wasn't a part of my brain still telling me this is a bad idea.

When we're close enough I can see the familiar intensity within his eyes, he stops and holds out his hand. I take it, the strength of his grip familiar now. He brings his free hand up to my cheek and holds the side of my face as if I'm something to be cherished.

"You're beautiful," he mutters.

"So are you, Cinderella."

His hand stays splayed on my cheek as he laughs. "What do you say we get in before I turn into a pumpkin?"

A smile plays on my lips. "Good thing we have time before midnight."

With a smile matching mine, he drops his hand, using his fingers to leave a trail of fire down my neck then over my clavicle until his fingertips gently ghost over one of my hardened nipples. I suck in air through my teeth, arousal pooling between my thighs from his attention.

"Or if you want, I can carry you in."

My pulse quickens. "Oh please, you can't do that!"

Before I know what's happening, I'm being hoisted up. I let out a squeal, my breasts now pressed against his chest. The quick motion leaves me no choice but to wrap my arms around his neck and legs around his waist to hold on.

"Ash! Oh my god. Asher! You're going to throw out your back."

A deep chuckle rumbles against my body, and then we're moving. "I've got you, Jesse girl."

My wide-eyed gaze meets his amused one as he takes a step. The distraction of his naked body pressed against mine and the surprise at being picked up for the first time since I was a child stops me from realizing we're entering the water before it's too late.

Cold water from the waves splashes against my ass, and I grip Asher like a kid afraid to go into the deep end of the pool for the first time. "Asher!" I squeal.

"You wanted to skinny dip in the ocean!" He nearly cackles.

"Maybe I—"

My words are cut off as he walks us in, the chilly water touching my back and making me cry out. "Oh my god, it's fucking freezing!"

"The Pacific Ocean in this area is usually between fifty-six and fifty-nine degrees in the summer."

"Oh my god." My muscles seize from the cold, and I shiver. "Why didn't you tell me that?"

"When you said it would be cold, I figured you knew." He takes us further in until the waves are at our chests. I cling to him as tightly as I can, nearly forgetting we're naked as I savor his body warmth and the safety I feel in his arms.

"Just breathe through it—you will get used to it," he says over the lapping of the water.

I inhale a long breath and blow it out, doing that a few more times until my jaw unclenches and my body acclimates to the water. When my muscles begin to ease, I go to speak. A bit of saltwater splashes in my mouth, and I screw up my nose and nearly gag. "Oh, that's salty. Even more than the hot spring."

"I keep forgetting you've never been in an ocean before," he replies, face twitching like he's attempting not to laugh.

He turns so he's facing the shore, and I can look out at the midnight waves, the flash of the lighthouse and moonbeams illuminating the water. It really does go on forever. I have to admit it's a little frightening, not knowing what's out there.

The water laps at my chest and arms, and I inhale the smell of salt and sea. It's a different smell than the lakes I grew up with that were more earthy and sometimes fishy.

"Being here feels surreal," I say. "We'll have to come back in the morning so I can see it in the daylight. I bet the beach is even more beautiful."

He hums, and I turn my head from the ocean back to Asher. He's staring at me, droplets of water clinging to his beard. "Thank you," he says.

I tilt my head to the side. "For what?"

"For letting me be a part of this."

"Skinny dipping?" I tease.

"All of it." His tone is serious, and I pause.

I could reply with "you're welcome." I could say I couldn't have done any of this without him, but I don't want to use my words. So instead, I unclasp one hand from behind his neck and drag it up so I can thread my fingers through his hair. At the same time, I grip my legs tighter around his waist. While his dick isn't hard like it was before we entered the cold water, I can still feel it between the apex of my thighs.

His chest stops moving, breath caught in his throat. I tilt my head so my mouth hovers over his. His hands on my ass squeeze the flesh, but he doesn't seek my lips like I expect him to. He waits for me to take the lead, something he's done more than once tonight. With my lips wet from the ocean, I don't wait another moment to dive in.

Our mouths connect for the second time tonight, the pads of his fingers digging into the skin where he's holding me, bringing our bodies closer together—something I didn't think was possible. My hard nipples press into his chest, and I open my mouth without hesitation. There's no audience this time. Even if someone did come down to the beach right now and see us, I wouldn't care. I'm too absorbed in Ash.

Our tongues collide like the waves on the shore. He whimpers into my mouth, and the sound does something to me, rewiring my brain. The images of him that I conjured earlier with his tie around his wrists and him at my feet moves to the forefront of my mind. I can feel my arousal leak from me, washing away into the water. I grind against Ash and dig both of my hands into his hair.

The water reaches higher on my back as he moves us a bit further from shore. I gasp, and he uses the shock of the chilly water to delve into my mouth as if he's consuming me. He breaks the kiss, and I tilt my head to the side as he kisses the corner of my mouth and the skin under my ear.

"I'm going to set you down," he says against my neck. The flavor must be salty, but he doesn't care. "I need my hands."

"Okay." My feet touch the sand, the cool grains squishing beneath my feet. For a brief second, I feel insurmountable joy inside me. My first time in the ocean. But the thought exits as Asher's fingers reach between my legs while his other hand grips my outer thigh.

"Keep holding on to me," he commands.

I gasp again and take hold of his wet shoulders, his fingers finding my clit and the other hand hitching my leg over his hip. He holds me there to give him better access.

"Tell me if this is too much," he says, lips brushing the skin of my neck.

"More."

My demand is simple, and Ash follows my direction. I grip him harder, pulling him closer to me as I bite the skin between his neck and shoulder when he pinches my clit. A larger wave crashes against my back, rocking us. Our bodies get closer yet, and Ash circles his fingers faster then slower. The motion is methodical, like the waves yet unpredictable.

"Ash," I groan. "Kiss me." I lift my head, and his crooked smile meets mine.

"Demanding tonight," he says as he nips at my lips.

"I need more."

"Greedy, too. But I like you this way." He kisses me, and since I'm the one with free hands, I grip his hair again. Tight.

His low cry bleeds into my mouth, and our tongues explore. Asher's fingers do as I requested, going harder before dipping slightly inside me. I gasp, and he swallows it, doing it again until

I feel my orgasm cresting like a wave. My release is coming on too soon—but at the same time, not fast enough.

I kiss Ash deeper, harder, rubbing my nipples over his chest and feeling more sensations than I've ever felt in my life all at once. Joy of being here, Asher's touch, the cool water, the tiny grains of salt and sand on our skin, the breeze of the night air, and lust. It's all so much, I think I may burst.

"Ash." I whimper against his lips. "Ash, I think—"

He bites my lower lip, his fingers pressing down on my clit. I drop my head back to his shoulder and bite down as I come, my body jerking against his. He holds me as my orgasm washes through my body. The sensation tingles through every finger and toe, all the way to the top of my head.

Ash sucks on my pulse point, his fingers still pressing on my clit and his other hand gripping so hard I wonder if there will be a small bruise in its wake. Moments after, when I feel I can finally speak, I pull back so I'm staring into his hooded moonlit eyes. His hand leaves my clit to rest on my hip, while his other softly cups my cheek after releasing my thigh.

"Hi," he murmurs.

"Hi."

He tucks a strand of wet hair behind my ear and softly smiles. "I think I may have to call you Rán from now on."

"Rán?" I try to mimic how he said it.

He nods. "Norse goddess of the sea. One of the most powerful goddesses, I might add."

"Does she lead sailors to their deaths?"

"Not in the way a siren would, though she and her husband create all the sea storms. So you could say they may be the cause of the death of sailors."

My heart thuds in my chest. "You think I'm that powerful, huh?"

He grips my chin with his thumb and forefinger. "You have no idea."

My eyes dart to his lips, and I lean into his touch, fully prepared to kiss him, when something brushes past my leg. A squeal leaves me, and I'm moving so quickly out of Ash's arms, he nearly falls and goes underwater.

"Jesse?" Asher cries.

"Something touched my leg! Get out!"

"Jesse!" Ash calls again, but I keep going.

When I'm about thigh deep, the cool breeze hitting my naked skin and making me shiver, Asher catches up to me and grabs my hand. He whirls me to him, and the look of amusement on his face can be seen even in darkness.

"Why are you smiling?" I cry. "We almost got eaten by a shark!" He chuckles, and I glare at him. "Don't laugh!"

In his free hand, he holds up a long plant. "It was seaweed."

Heat crawls up my neck, combatting the cold I felt before. "Oops."

Asher chuckles again and drops the weed, pulling me to him so our bodies are melted together. "You ran so fast, I thought you'd run all the way back to the B&B naked. I liked the view, though."

I press my face into his shoulder and pinch his nipple.

"Ouch!"

"You deserve that."

"On second thought, maybe Rán isn't the best nickname for you."

I pinch his nipple again, and he yelps. "Deserved that, too."

I lift my head, and before I can meet his eyes, my body is spinning away from his. A loud smack resounds in the air, and my ass smarts. I'm turned back around before I can respond, and then his lips are on mine, swallowing my surprise. The whole thing is disorienting, and by the time Asher is grinning at me again, I'm blinking wide-eyed at him.

"Did you just spank me?" I ask.

"Yep."

I pull away from him and place my hands on my hips. His eyes travel down my curves, and it's then I remember we're standing in thigh-deep water, completely naked. Add that to the list of things I never thought I'd do. It's also further proof of how comfortable I am with Ash. I just let him get me off in the ocean for god's sakes, where anyone from the reception could walk down.

The natural bashfulness one would feel in this situation sets in, and I move to cover myself. Ash steps forward and grabs my wrists. "Don't."

"Anyone could come down."

"Then let's go back to the room. I'm not ready for this night to be over."

I grip Asher's hands. I'm not ready for this night to be over, either, but I need to talk to him about what all this—what we just did—means for us and what he expects from this...from us. I'm still battling with my head and my heart, but there will be time for that later. For now, I want to enjoy tonight and worry about everything else tomorrow.

"Let's go back to the room," I say.

Chapter Thirty

Jesse

ASHER PUSHES OPEN THE door to our room, and we nearly stumble in, our lips connected. He hasn't stopped touching and kissing me the entire way here.

The second the door closes, he pushes me back toward the bed. I stop him by grabbing his half-buttoned shirt, still wet from being used as a towel.

"We should shower so we don't get sand everywhere."

He nips at my earlobe, his hot breath sending shivers up my spine. "It did say on the website it was big enough for two."

"It did not." I laugh.

"It did."

I chuckle as he grabs my hand, flipping on the light as we enter the bathroom. The shower *is* big enough for two, and the arousal that's been constant between my legs grows even stronger.

"I think I'm adding shower sex to my bucket list," I say.

Asher maneuvers me back so my ass is pressed against the sink. His hips meld to mine, and he grinds his erection against the wet fabric of my dress.

"I like the way you think. I'm adding it to mine, too." He seeks my lips again, opening his mouth so our tongues duel. I bring my hands up to clutch his hair, and he allows me to dominate the kiss, relaxing into my hold. When I pull back, his eyes are wicked, just like the grin on his face.

"Do you have a condom?" He nods. "Go get it. I'll start the shower."

He smiles wider and plants a short kiss on my lips. "Yes, ma'am!"

I laugh as he walks from the bathroom with the eagerness only a man about to get laid can have. I turn on the shower to heat the water before I strip my wet and sandy clothes from my body. I catch my reflection in the mirror and turn to face it.

There was a time when I hated looking in the mirror for prolonged periods of time. It's still not my favorite thing to do, but even I can admit I look happy. There's a smile on my face that always seems to be there when Ash is around, and even though my hair is wild and I'm covered in salt and sand, it doesn't detract from how I feel right now: beautiful. Wanted.

"Fuck me, Jesse girl." Ash walks up behind me, and I see the square packet in his hand and that he's ditched his clothes once more.

He puts the condom on the sink, placing his chin on my shoulder and wrapping his arms around my middle. I relax back into him as if I've done it a million times before. The part of my brain that wants to tell me doing this with him shouldn't be this easy—that I shouldn't be crossing this line at all—tries to come back online, but I shove it away.

His hand strokes my hip, and we stare at our reflection in the mirror. "Stunning." He kisses my shoulder then my neck. "I can't wait to fuck you again."

I press my ass back into his length, the heat of it nearly making me moan. I bite my lip and stare into his eyes through the mirror. "Then what are you waiting for?"

He grins and trails his hand up my waist and over my breast until his fingers brush along the scar that's now free of makeup, having not survived the ocean water. "Stunning," he whispers.

I fight back the sudden urge to cry and spin around so we're facing each other. If I let myself feel too much, let him burrow deeper into my heart than he's already managed to do, I'll have a harder time when we talk about what this means. But he's got to know this is only for the trip. We've never made plans otherwise. He's leaving for London soon, after all, and I'm starting my new job.

I press his lips to mine and kiss him hard, taking the lead again. When his kisses have pushed any further thoughts from my mind, I pull back, taking the condom off the sink. He doesn't need me to tell him what to do next. With my hand in his, he opens the frosted shower door. After he checks the water temp, he walks in, tugging me in after him.

The hot water pounds down as I enter the square shower stall, and Asher closes the door behind us. The space is big enough for two people, but that doesn't mean it isn't a tight fit. Our bodies have only a few inches between them, and every time one of us moves, our skin touches somewhere.

He looks down at me as the water cascades over my hair, and I blink it away from my eyes. "Hello again."

"Hi."

His hand reaches up and pushes some of my wet locks from my face before cupping my cheek. Our lips meet once again, and the water splashes over us both, washing away the sand. I clutch the foil packet and decide I don't want more foreplay or to take it slow. I want to feel him inside me again.

With my free hand, I trail my fingers over Asher's soft stomach until I reach his pubic bone. I gently use my nails to scratch the sensitive skin, enjoying the way he groans into my mouth and his muscles tense. I trail further down until my palm meets his cock. When I wrap my fingers around his warm shaft, his kisses stop.

"That feels good." He nibbles my lower lip.

I stroke him, enjoying the heat of him in my hand. My lower stomach clenches at the memory of how full I felt the first time we were together.

"I want to make you feel even better," I say. The motions of my hand grow stronger, and his head drops to my shoulder.

When I brush my thumb over the swollen tip, he twitches against me.

"Shit, Jesse girl. If you do much more of that, I'll come down the drain."

I ease the pressure and lighten the strokes of my hand. "We don't want that, do we?"

"No." He palms my breasts. "We don't." He rolls my nipples between his fingers, and my head tosses back so the water rushes down my neck and chest. After another bout of playing, he places his hands on my waist, and I look into his eyes.

"Put the condom on me," he says.

I smile at his request and open the packet. He studies me, the water coming down around us, our skin now flushed with the heat of the shower. He hisses as I take his hard length in my palm, pumping him twice more before I roll the latex down. As soon as it's in place, he takes me by my biceps and moves us, spinning me so my chest is pressed against the cool tile wall and he's plastered to my back.

"Is this okay?" he asks.

I feel his dick digging into my ass and the scrape of his nipples against my back. I've never been taken from behind like this, and if he were to reach down and touch between my legs, he'd find me leaking with arousal.

"Fuck me, Ash. Please." There's no hesitation in my voice like our first time together. I know what I want.

He rests one hand next to my head, and I feel the tip of him at my entrance. When he pushes in, my forehead drops to the wall. "Oh my god."

"Shit, Jesse," he groans. "I missed your perfect cunt."

His filthy words have me shoving my ass back, sheathing his cock fully inside me. His hands reach up to press against the wall on either side of my head, and he pauses to catch his breath before he retracts his hips and thrusts all the way back in. We both groan at the sensation of being joined together, and I reach one of my hands up to join his, interlocking our fingers. Now we're connected in every way possible.

"Jesse," he moans. "Fuck."

"Harder," I tell him. "I want to feel everything."

He drops his head to my shoulder, and the sounds of his grunts fill the space, mixing with my cries. In and out he goes until I feel my orgasm barreling toward me like a freight train. My pussy clenches around him, and Ash moves his free hand, wrapping it around my front. His fingers find my clit, and he circles around and around, adding just the right amount of pressure.

"God, your fingers feel so much better than my own."

Asher thrusts again. "You touching yourself while thinking of me, Jesse?

If my skin wasn't already pink, it would be now. He thrusts hard again, and I cry out a curse. "Oh fuck. Yes!"

"When?"

"Last night."

"That why you've been so shy around me today?" He thrusts again, the sound of our skin smacking resounding around us.

"Jesus!" I cry. "Yes!"

"God, that's hot." He thrusts yet again. My inner walls clamp around him, and he tenses against my back. "I'm going to come, Jesse. Fuck, you feel so good." He sucks the skin of my shoulder, and my blood pounds in my ears.

"I'm right there with you," I whimper. "Faster, please."

Ash pistons his hips, the sound of his skin hitting mine probably loud enough to wake our neighbors. Then he pinches my clit, and stars erupt behind my eyes as Ash grunts his release along with me, his thrusts getting choppier as he empties into the condom.

When he can't move any longer, he stills against my back, his forehead resting on my shoulder and our fingers still locked together. We take a minute to catch our breath before he places a kiss on my skin and eases out of me.

"Definitely a good idea," I say, near breathless.

He turns me to face him. "Which part?"

"Adding that to the bucket list."

Ash blinks at me through the steam, water clinging to his skin and lashes. For a moment, I think he looks sad or disappointed, but then he pastes a smile on his lips. "Let's get you clean, Jesse girl. Don't want any sand in the bed."

Chapter Thirty-One

Asher

I WAKE UP TO a sudden movement on the bed and a gasp. It's early morning, and the room is lit by a dull glow of light. I turn my head to find Jesse clutching the sheet to her bare chest and looking around the room.

"Jesse?" I ask groggily. "What is it?"

She gasps again and stares at me. "You scared me."

I blink away the sleep from my eyes and sit up, placing a hand on her back. "What's wrong?"

Her fingers grip the sheet. "Don't laugh."

"Okay...what is it?"

"I swear I heard the sink in the bathroom turn on and off."

I push down the laughter I feel bubbling in my chest and run my hand along the smooth skin of her back. "Do you want me to go check?"

"What if the ghost is still in there?"

Now I do chuckle. "I think I'll be fine."

I pull the sheets off my body without waiting for a response. Jesse's eyes track my naked form as I walk around the front of the bed and over to the bathroom. The wood floor is cool against my feet, and when I reach the bathroom, I check the sink. The faucet is off, and the basin is dry. I let out a breath, glad I don't have to tell her it may have been a ghost.

I walk back in the room to find Jesse still clutching the sheet to her chest and her eyes wide as she stares at me.

"The sink is dry. No ghosts."

She lets out a visible sigh of relief, and I make my way back to her, diving onto the bed so she bounces. Once I'm under the covers, I pull her into me, and she lets out a squeak.

"Breathe, Jesse girl. No ghosts. Plus, I'm here. Missy said they won't come when two people are in the room."

Jesse puffs out a breath, blowing a lock of hair that had fallen in her face. "Sorry I scared you," she says. "I really thought I heard the sink turn on."

"It's okay. Though I think I should be rewarded for being so brave."

"Do you now?"

"Between that and saving you from the seaweed last night, yep."

Jesse laughs. "Shower sex wasn't good enough?"

I quickly roll over and pin her to the bed. Her naked body is warm and soft under me, and my dick that was half-hard already gets harder. "Sex with you is always good enough."

Her gaze flutters to my lips and back to my eyes. I lean down and seal my mouth over hers, my length dragging over the lips of her pussy that are surprisingly wet.

I pull back from her and kiss my way to her neck and chest, sucking a nipple into my mouth. She cries out, hand gripping my hair. I look up at her, releasing her nipple with a pop. "Sensitive?"

She nods, so I lay a gentle kiss on it. I continue to lick and suck down her stomach, but she stops me before I can go further by tugging on my hair again. I lift my gaze, thinking I'll meet a heated stare, but instead, she looks nervous.

"What is it?" I ask.

"I want to try something," she replies tentatively.

My stomach flips, and it doesn't take a genius to figure out what she wants to try. "Oh?" I ask.

Her grip on my hair tightens, and she pulls me up so I'm propped above her again.

"I—god, I shouldn't be so scared to do this, but I am," she says.

"Do what?" I smirk.

She looks at me expectantly. "You know what."

"Do I?"

She huffs a breath, her fingers twitching against my scalp. "I had an idea last night when I saw your tie." My cock jumps against Jesse's stomach, and her eyes widen before a lazy smile moves across her face. "You like that idea, don't you?"

"I like anything when it comes to you," I reply.

Jesse's cheeks turn pink. "You really would be fine with it? Not being in control?"

"I don't need to be in control. In fact, I think I've let you take the lead many times." She wets her lips, and I watch the movement, all the blood rushing from my brain to my dick. "I trust you, Jesse."

Jesse brings one of her hands to hold my chin. Her body gently shifts under mine, and I'm reminded of how wet she is as our hips move against each other. My head dips down, and I wait for her to kiss me, but it never comes. Before I know what's happening, she lets go of me and does her best to pull away while still beneath me.

"What's wrong?" I ask.

"I think we should talk."

My cheek twitches. "It's okay to be nervous over something you haven't done."

Jesse lightly pushes on my chest, and despite not wanting to, I roll off of her. She turns on her side, and I follow suit, lying down beside her. When she maneuvers back a bit, it doesn't take a genius to see she's putting physical distance between us. My stomach sours as she shuts her eyes before opening them a few moments later.

"You're right, I am nervous," she says quietly. "But Ash, I need to make sure that before we do anything else, you agree what happened between us last night and anything going forward is just..." She closes her eyes again and clenches her jaw. When her lashes open, there's a visible pain in her irises as she says, "...casual."

The lust coursing through me dispels from my body as if it's been magicked away. When Jesse kissed me at the wedding, instead of airing on the side of optimism, I should've known it didn't mean what I had hoped. Not only that, but I should've also known it was what she was thinking. And truthfully, I *did* know.

Before we got in the shower, she brought up the bucket list. She even made clear afterward she was glad she mentally added "shower sex" to it. Add to that, there was no point during our trip she expressed she would want anything more than casual with me if we were to cross a line again, only her stolen glances at me and our almost kisses. But there were never any words to confirm her feelings.

I flip gently onto my back and stare up at the blue-painted ceiling. A hole in my gut is growing by the minute. Jesse is still watching me, and I don't think either of us are breathing.

Part of me wants to say fuck it, wants to tell her I'll let her do anything she wants to me for the rest of the trip. But after the time we've spent together and what we've shared, I don't think I can. I thought I could give her whatever she wants, but not this.

"Ash," she whispers. "You know I hate awkward silences."

I force a sad smile to my lips as I turn my head toward her. I search her eyes, the hazel irises that seem to have branded themselves into my soul. "I'll admit," I say, "there was a voice inside me that thought when you kissed me at the wedding last night, that maybe..."

"Maybe what?" Her brow is pinched, and I flip myself so I can fully face her.

"That maybe you'd be open to being more than casual."

"Asher, I—I don't. I'm sorry, I—"

"It's okay," I stop her. "You don't have to try to explain. It's my own fault for getting my hopes up. I should've kept my promise to be your Bucket-List Helper. This is the second promise I've broken to you, and I'm sorry I failed."

Jesse sits up, gripping the sheet to her chest and looking down at me. "No. You haven't failed. You haven't done anything I didn't want. I'm the one who kissed you last night. I'm the one who failed. I should've talked with you before we did anything. And…" She thinks about her next words before she speaks them, her fingers flexing against the sheet in her hands. "Please understand. I like you, Asher. I really do, but…"

"…we can't be more," I finish for her. I sit up so we're on the same level. The tension between us grows tight, so thick you'd have to saw it in half, but I push through. "If I use one of my questions to ask you why you can't, will you answer it right now?"

Jesse worries her lower lip, looking down at the wrinkled comforter. I know without her saying it that she won't.

"I'm sorry, Asher," she answers softly.

I want to tell her to stop calling me Asher. I like it better when she calls me Ash. Asher feels as if she's trying to put distance between us, distance I don't want, despite her rejection. "Don't be, really."

She shakes her head. "Fuck, I feel awful. I've never done anything like this, and I got in my head about it."

"You mean shower sex? I know," I tease to lighten the mood.

"That. But you know you were my first one-night stand. Before that, I hadn't had many sexual experiences. This casual thing, doing spontaneous stuff, it's not me. I don't know how to do it right."

I want to say she's doing it right, that I'm the one who has feelings. Or at least I'm the only one who's truly willing to acknowledge them. "But it's who you want to be?" I ask.

She sighs, still gripping the sheet to her chest. "I think so." She groans. "I don't know. All I know is I can't go back to the way I was living before. That's not what I want. I don't want to be boring. I don't want to sit at a desk job and waste my life away—I want to live like it's my last holiday."

The irony of what she's saying is not lost on me. I want to tell her that maybe what she wants is what we've been building together in such a short amount of time: someone to support and love her. Someone she trusts who she can have an intimate connection with, one who will never judge her and show her that her life is way more than just a collection of items to check off. It's also interesting that she's mentioning a desk job, since she hasn't brought it up much in the time we've been together.

I ignore the sharp pain I feel in my chest at her continued rejection of me and softly smile. "Well, the good news is you're doing it. You're living. More than most people."

"I am, but I'm sorry if I hurt you in the process. It was wrong of me to cross that line last night and hope you'd be on the same page. I—"

"Stop, Jesse. I get it, okay? We're on this trip for a reason.'"

Her eyes close, and when she opens them, they're a little sad, but I also see happiness in them. "A trip I wouldn't be doing without you."

I wave her off. "You would've. You would've found a way."

"Maybe. But I wouldn't be here in this B&B. I wouldn't have gotten to experience the hot springs the way we did. The wedding was special, and the dance classes, sex—" She flushes. "All of it so far has been because of you. So thank you, Asher."

"I like it when you call me Ash better," I admit.

Jesse studies me from beneath her lashes, and my heart quickens in my chest. "Thank you, *Ash*," she repeats.

"Like I said, no thanks needed."

Jesse picks invisible pieces of lint off the bed. "If you want to end the trip early, I'd understand."

"Why the hell would we do that?" I ask.

Her eyes snap back to mine. "I just don't want this to be awkward between us."

"It'll only be that way if we make it that way. We're still friends, aren't we?" The word "friends" makes me sick, and I don't miss the way Jesse's face falls slightly, igniting a bit of hope in my chest that maybe she'll still see that we could be more than casual. Even if it makes me a fool for thinking it.

"Of course we are," she says.

"Plus, we have a lot of work to do."

"Work for what?"

"Given all your new social media followers, maybe you won't have to go back to a desk job."

She sits straighter on the bed. "What are you talking about?"

I grin crookedly at her. "I was going to tell you when you woke up."

"Tell me what?"

I reach over to the nightstand next to the bed and unplug my phone. Then I settle back against the pillows and open Jesse's social media, pointing to her new follower count. Her mouth drops open, and had she not been near the middle of the bed, I think she would've fallen off the mattress to the floor.

"Does that say two-hundred thousand?" she asks.

"It does."

She grabs my phone and blinks down at it. "Ash, my video has over five million views."

"I know."

"Oh my god." She exhales. "Oh my god!"

I place my hand on her shoulder. "Don't panic, this is a good thing. A really good thing."

"But how?!"

"Who really knows how to explain these things? The algorithm was in your favor, and your video was emotional, and you spoke to people. Just look at some of the comments."

Jesse scrolls while still clutching the sheet to her chest. After a few minutes, she looks up at me with tears in her eyes. "What does this even mean now?"

"That we can try to start monetizing. I have to do some research, but I think we can start reaching out to brands that make sense for you. But you should make more content, see if you can get the same engagement. That way, we have analytics to give companies, and we can get money out of them."

"I can't believe you know so much about this."

"Genius, remember." I tap the side of my head. "But in all seriousness, I did research, too. A lot of this is new to me, and when I want to know something, I get a bit obsessive about it. Like mythology."

She smiles softly. "Another thing I have to thank you for."

"Being obsessive?" I tease.

That makes her laugh. "You know what I mean."

"Nah. You can thank Google for that advice."

Jesse grins and hands me my phone back. "I should get dressed."

"Me, too."

"I'm sorry again—"

"No, no more sorrys. We're good, Jesse called Jesse. Let's use the next part of the trip to see if we can't get you out of your desk job. Hell, maybe you can even buy a Winnie of your own."

"Maybe a van."

I'm both sad and happy at the idea of her traveling without me. While I'd want to be there with her, I also like that it's something she'd even consider. I could definitely see her in a van.

"Those are easier to manage, and then you don't have to get a car to hitch up if you need to drive around at locations," I say.

She smiles. "That is very true. Now close your eyes, I need to get up."

"But I've seen it all," I pout.

She laughs, but to my surprise, she climbs out of bed and starts collecting her clothes buck naked. I rest back on the headboard and fold my hands behind my head, holding up my phone. "Want me to take a picture for your page? I bet it would get a lot of views."

Jesse chucks my shirt at my face, and by the time I get it off, I hear the door to the bathroom closing. I chuckle to myself then stare at the bathroom door. While I'm glad we can joke and laugh, the ache in my chest at her rejection of me hasn't gone away. I hear the shower turn on, and I pick up my phone. It's still open to her video. After she fell asleep last night, I couldn't sleep, so I went and watched it. Several times, to be exact. But I let it play again.

"Hi, my name is Jesse, and I'm a Kawasaki disease survivor. And no, it has nothing to do with the motorcycle brand." She pauses to smile, and I smile along with her. *"We think I got sick with KD when I was four, but we can't be sure. Since it went undiagnosed, it caused inflammation in my body, specifically my heart. Two years ago, at twenty-six, I had a heart attack. That's when they found I had aneurysms in my heart caused by the rare disease. So rare, in fact, that a child's chance of getting it in North America is one-percent. Lucky me!"*

She chuckles sadly, and my chest smarts.

"Despite being treated, I had another heart attack last year, and two months ago, I got an ICD implant to treat the ventricular tachycardia caused by the scar tissue in my heart from the attacks. I made this page to share my story with you and to let you know it's never too late to have a change of pace. To live every moment like it's your last."

I look at the woman on the phone then to the bathroom door. I don't have to use one of my questions to know why she doesn't want to be more than casual with me. The writing is on the wall.

But despite her rejection, there's that pesky hope in my chest that I can't squash. One that, despite everything, thinks she will still change her mind about us. That she'll tell me why we can't be more so I can help her see that she's wrong.

Everyone is on a ticking clock. Not a living thing on this planet can escape the fact that, one day, their time will be up. I want her to know she doesn't have to keep living like everything is temporary.

My eyes flick over her sun-kissed face on the video, and I exhale a long breath, thinking of how Matt waited for his bride for decades. Not days, *decades*. My insides twist, and I place my phone on my chest.

I truly don't know if Jesse will ever allow herself out of the rules and constraints she's made, if she'll ever stop checking off a list and allow herself to live like she wants. But thinking of Matt's resilience, of his willingness to wait for Jessica, I know I can't give up. Even if my logical side tells me I should.

Maybe it's stupid, and I'll probably get my heart broken, but I have ten more days with Jesse. Ten more days I'm not going to waste.

Chapter Thirty-Two

Asher

"How's the famous woman this morning?" I ask Jesse as I walk into Winnie's kitchen area, freshly showered. We're at a campground in Nebraska, and today we're making our way to Indiana before we head to Maine.

She's downing a few pills from her pill box, reminding me I have to take my med, too. I walk to where she's standing and grab my bottle, taking a pill out.

"I'm not famous," she says after she finishes swallowing.

"I don't know. I saw the video you posted yesterday. You added another five-thousand followers in a day with that one. Nice keywords, by the way."

She smirks at me. "Learned from the best."

I shoot funny finger guns at her. "You're a fast learner. It's all you, Jessie girl." I put my pill on my tongue and wink at her then grab a bottle of water from the fridge to wash it down. When I close it, Jesse's bucket list is staring me in the face, reminding me of what I'm resigned to: friend and Bucket-List Helper. At least for now.

I pull it down and show it to her. "We need to check off the new items. Still disappointed we didn't do a fire ceremony for the other ones." I fake-pout.

She chuckles. "It's not a ceremony if you're just sitting by a fire crossing off items on a list. Besides, I still haven't seen yours."

I erase the pout off my face. "Okay, fine. But we should check off the rest we've done."

"I did cross them out on the copy I have in my notes app."

"Wait, wait. You have a second version?"

She dips her chin sheepishly. "Sometimes I like to look at it, see if I want to add anything. Makes it easier to also have a digital version."

I lean my hip on the counter. "Are you hiding new items from me, Jesse girl?"

I wiggle my eyebrows, and she snorts. "No. It's all there. On both versions."

I look down at the list and see she added "have shower sex" unabashedly, showing me how much her confidence has grown in such a short time.

"Are you ever going to show me yours?" she asks.

"I've already shown you mine." I wink.

"Ash!" she chides. "Be serious."

I grin through a laugh. "I'll show you my list in due time. But I gotta keep them a surprise."

"Like Carhenge yesterday?"

"Hey! That was fun. Now you can say you've seen a tribute to Stonehenge made from cars. You even got a keychain."

"That's true. It *was* fun." Jesse moves to the couch, plopping down next to GusGus and giving his head a scratch. He only lets her pet him for a few seconds before he jumps down and walks off, making Jesse pout.

"I think he's still mad at us for leaving him overnight."

"Probably. It may have been a couple of nights ago, but he can hold grudges."

She sighs as I sit down next to her. Her bucket list is still in my hand, and I have a pen I grabbed from a junk drawer.

"Okay, I know you did this electronically, but we should check the rest we've done off. This is the OG list," I say. "I also need to see you check them off as your Bucket-List Helper."

She smiles. "Sure, let's do it." I try to hand her the list, but she shakes her head. "You do it."

"You sure?"

"Yeah, you've been such a big part of this. It's practically your list now, too. Especially since you won't show me your real one."

"Alright." I lay the list on my knee. "Do we need to check off one-night stand twice?" I tease. "Or is that being blacked out since we kind of fucked it up...pun intended."

Jesse looks into my eyes and shakes her head. "I decided it counts. It was what it was when we did it. It stays. We make the rules, remember?"

My lips tug up at the corner of my mouth, and I move down the rest of the list, crossing off the items we did in Oregon: *take a dance class, crash a wedding, swim naked in the ocean, shower sex*. Looking at all the finished items, I feel a sense of pride.

"We've done a lot! But we still have a few to go." I point to the items *get a tattoo, watch the sunrise at Cadillac Mountain in Maine, find a decent gluten-free pizza*. "Have you thought more about the tattoo?"

"Actually, while you were showering, I found a place we could stop on our drive today that takes walk-ins. What I want won't take long. You game?"

"You want me to get a tattoo?"

She laughs. "That's not what I meant, but you can if you want."

I tap my chin playfully. "I do have a few ideas."

"It better not be my name on your ass."

I scoff. "You wound me, Jesse girl. That was my plan." She slaps my shoulder, and I chuckle. "But I am game."

"Let me guess, you're not going to tell me what you're going to get."

"Nope. You?"

"Not if you aren't."

"Let's show each other after."

"Deal."

"Deal," I reply.

"I'm still in shock you found a place with the best gluten-free pizza right by the tattoo place. It was like fate. I really do believe you have magic or something."

I put my hands in my pockets as we walk back to Winnie, stationed in the back of the parking lot. "Look, all I did was Google. I was shocked myself. Even more shocked that the pizza was bucket-list worthy."

She smiles along with me. "I guess I should be thanking the Google gods. I'd drive here just for that pizza."

"I'm glad I found it then." I put my hands in a praying position. "And thanks, Missouri, for having great gluten-free dough."

Jesse shakes her head at me as I open the door to the RV, letting her get in first. Once we're both in and the door is locked, she turns to me.

"Are you sure you're good enough to drive the rest of the way to the campground in Indiana tonight?"

"Yeah, I'm good. But I want to see your tattoo first."

"We're supposed to leave the bandage on for twenty-four hours. Not to mention, it's under my shirt."

"I don't mind."

She snorts. "Of course you don't."

"Did you take a picture?" I ask.

"I did."

"I've got one of mine—let's send them at the same time."

"Eager, are you?"

I nod. Mostly I want to show her mine. I want to see her reaction when I tell her what it is.

"Okay, fine. Let's do it." Jesse pulls out her phone, and I do the same. When we both have our tattoos queued up, we count to three and hit send.

The text Jesse sent pops up on my phone, and I open it. When I see what it is, I smile. The spot she chose is under her left breast, and it's a tattoo of a heartbeat.

"Is this your actual heartbeat?" I look up at her to find her wide-eyed, tears threatening to fall from her eyes. "Jesse?"

She looks up, and I see her visibly swallow. "You got the Norse rune for 'heart' over your heart?"

Shockwaves move through my body. "How did you know that's what it is?"

"I may have looked it up. I almost got the same thing."

"What?"

Jesse looks at the picture on her phone and then back to me. "In case I haven't told you enough, this trip has meant a lot to me. Hearing you talk about Thor, all the Norse gods, and mythology, I looked up a symbol for heart and nearly got it. But I thought it would be—" She looks down at her feet.

"Would be what?" I ask, taking a step closer to her.

She clears her throat. "Too much."

That hope I felt the other night, despite our agreement to be friends, flares like a lighthouse on the Oregon cliffs. I know she didn't get the tattoo, but the fact that she thought about it means something. She was going to get a memory of me that would have been forever. It's the exact reason I got mine. Not only to commemorate this trip but also to honor her—her heart. To have a piece of her with me, always.

"For the record," I say. "It wouldn't have been too much."

Jesse's eyes land on my lips like they have so many times before. My pulse thrums, and I consider what to do. It's been two nights and three days since we left Oregon, which means I have a week left for her to see she can still have me beyond casual. My hand itches to cup her cheek, to lean forward and press my lips to hers.

"I guess there's always my next tattoo," she says.

Warmth blooms in my chest, and the hope burns brighter. "That's true."

"And you're right, it's my heartbeat. I asked for a copy at my last EKG."

My eyes drop to her shirt automatically where I know the tattoo lies before Jesse clears her throat. "Eyes up here, buddy."

A crooked grin takes over my face. "Where's the fun in that?"

She snorts and puts her phone in her pocket. "Come on, let's hit the road. I still have a question to ask you."

"Ooh, can't wait. Tell me it's a good one."

"I want to know more about this job in London."

"Boring," I groan. But really, I'm teasing her because the last thing I want to do is think about London. I'd rather she ask me a question that gets me closer to her, closer to her asking me not to go or if she can come with me. It's not as if she's excited about her desk job.

She chuckles. "Fine, I'll ask you about the erotica collection I found in your desk."

Jesse thinks I'm going to be embarrassed, but I'm not. "Now that's more like it."

"Perv." She laughs.

"More like cliterature connoisseur. I like to know what women like."

"Did you just say 'cliterature'?"

"I did."

"Oh my god, forget I asked. Now let's go, we've got lots of road to cover."

I salute and follow her to the front of Winnie. "Yes, ma'am."

Chapter Thirty-Three
Jesse

"I STILL CAN'T BELIEVE you had the world's tallest filing cabinet on your bucket list," I tell Ash as we sit around the campfire he's built for us. We're staying in a campground in Maine, our last official stop before we head back to Wisconsin, back to reality.

"If I remember correctly, when you saw it, you said: 'Holy shit, that's really cool.'"

"I did not."

"I have it on video. You should post it to your bazillion new followers."

"I do not have a bazillion. But I did get another few thousand after the video I posted yesterday."

"The one where you talked about your scar?"

"Yeah." I tuck a strand of hair behind my ear. "A lot of people said they could relate to how I feel about it. How at first it was hard to look at but now I'm starting to love it and what it represents."

"Hell yeah!" Ash puts his hand up for an air five since he's too far away. Even though I find him ridiculous, I smile and air-five him back.

"Now enough about that. Back to the filing cabinet. I will admit it was cool—but I'm still judging you over the world's largest ball of paint in Indiana. That should not even be a roadside attraction."

"Wait, wait, wait. You said that was cool, too!"

I sit up in my chair. "I did not say that! I said it looks like one nut of a ball sac."

Ash sips his drink. "I know you did. I just wanted to hear you say 'one nut of a ball sac' again."

I grab a marshmallow from the bag sitting on my lap and throw it at him. It hits him in the arm, and he scoffs.

"I already know you like me, Jesse called Jesse. You don't have to flirt with me by being violent."

My cheeks heat, and I throw another marshmallow at him. With reflexes like a cat, he snatches it out of the air and pops it into his mouth.

"Thanks," he mumbles around it. "Delicious."

I shake my head at him and lean back in my chair. I should be grateful he's still teasing and flirting with me like he was before, that he hasn't changed since that morning at the B&B or after I found out he got a Norse rune heart tattoo. But I'd be lying if I said I didn't wish he was more reserved—and that things had become a bit more awkward between us.

At least then I could pretend it's easy for me to be this new version of myself, the one who is fine with writing off what we had as a casual fling that's over now.

Even if at night I lie awake wishing he was beside me, fighting and losing a battle of touching myself while imagining all the things we could do together. How I could kiss the tattoo on his heart while he traces his finger over mine. Though now, when I pleasure myself, I've learned to cover my mouth and keep quiet.

I inwardly curse Ash for being flirty and change the subject, not wanting to think about my sleepless nights while he's sitting right in front of me. I pick up the stick I have propped against my chair and pluck a marshmallow from the bag, putting it on the end so I can roast it. "I know I asked you more about your job on our drive here, but I realized I've never asked you one of my subsequent questions. Mind if I ask it now?"

Ash picks up his own stick and makes the gimme motion toward the bag of marshmallows. I chuck him one, and he easily catches it. "Shoot, Jesse girl."

My heart flutters as I put the stick in the fire. "Winnie, traveling across the country, not seeing family that often...why did you choose it?"

He jabs his own stick in the fire. "I like traveling, seeing new things, doing whatever I want. I like to be mobile and not stuck in one place."

The way he says it sounds practiced. It's an easy answer to a presumably easy question. But after traveling with him, getting to know him, and the way he's made it clear that if I said yes, we could be more than what we are, it makes me think that's not true.

"Did you always know that?" I ask.

He nods. "I have a love-hate relationship with routines. They're good sometimes, for work and business, but I hate them in my day-to-day life. Once I had my ADHD med figured out, I excelled in classes and learning but also hated how boring they were. I hated going to school and doing the same thing every day. Everyone thinks I graduated early because I'm smart, but I wanted to get out as fast as I could. It's one of the reasons I started working on my first app—to keep me busy."

"When did you get the idea to travel in an RV?"

"My aunt and uncle live in a park in Nevada. He used to sell mobile homes and travel across the country to conventions. As a kid, he'd tell me all his stories and show me all the pictures of places they'd visit. I liked the idea and always knew that, once I was done with school, it was something I wanted to do."

"That's cool."

"He helped me find Winnie. He wanted me to get something fancy and new, but I thought it would be fun to fix her up. I was okay with some quirks. I've also thought about selling her recently, so I'm glad I didn't get something new and pricey that may be harder to sell."

"Sell her?" My eyes snap to him.

"Yeah, you never know what could happen in life." He meets my gaze, his eyes focused and intense. "I could change my mind about traveling. Maybe I'll want to settle down in the Midwest and travel for fun. Rent a car, fly back and forth. Be in one place yet still be spontaneous."

My stomach tightens at the implication. He's looking at me as if I'm what happened. As if I could be the one to change his mind. I also didn't miss how he said he'd settle down in the Midwest.

"Do you want a family?" I don't know why I ask it. I shouldn't want to know. Yet, a part of me does. He asked me back at The Corn Palace, but neither of us ended up answering.

He pauses before he asks, "A family? Of course. But if you mean non-fur-baby children?" I nod. "It would depend on what my partner wants," he finishes.

My eyes stay on his, a thousand thoughts running through my mind. Does he want children, or is he saying that because he doesn't know what I want?

I should tell him I don't want kids in case he's wondering, but I don't want to get into the why: how I could have them, but I don't want to risk the stress on my body. How I'm not sure I'd want to give up my free time to raise them.

I should say something, if for no other reason than to push any idea of him and I away further. Not only for him but for me.

"You're on fire."

I blink. "What?"

"Your marshmallow is on fire." He smirks. It's then I realize he has his out of the fire, and mine is in full flame.

"Shit!" I pull out my stick and blow on the flaming confection. When the fire is out, it's burnt to a crisp.

Ash chuckles and holds out his stick. The marshmallow on the end is a perfect golden brown. "Take mine."

"It's yours."

"And now it's yours."

I shake my head. "Eat it. Then show me how you got it perfectly golden brown on every side."

He laughs again and pulls off the treat, popping it in his mouth before scooting closer to me so our chairs are as close as they can be. I pull out two more marshmallows after I discard my burnt one in the fire, and we both pop one onto each of our sticks.

"The trick is to find embers, not direct flame. Direct flame equals flaming marshmallow," he says.

"Got it."

I focus on the fire and find the embers. I stick it near the glowing chips, and Ash touches my arm, making my skin prickle.

"Keep it at least six inches away from the embers. Not too close, not too far."

"Six inches. The perfect length."

Ash barks a loud laugh. "That was a good one."

I smirk. "I can be clever."

"That I know," he says. "Now rotate it, like a rotisserie chicken. Wait for it to get golden brown on the outside and puffy. Then it's good."

The whole process takes a couple of minutes, but it works. I smile brightly when I pull back the perfect marshmallow. "A genius, even at marshmallow roasting."

He snickers. "I try."

We eat our marshmallows, and even though I do it right again with my second one, Ash doesn't move his chair. I revel in his nearness yet hate it at the same time.

After I've had my fill, I decide to ease the silence. "Do you get lonely traveling all the time?"

Ash sets his stick down and stares into the fire. "Sure, I think that's only natural. But I have GusGus. My work."

The sullen tone of his voice and the way he doesn't look at me makes me think maybe he's been lonelier than he is letting on. Or maybe he hasn't realized how lonely he's been.

"Do you go to bars often for company while on the road?" I ask.

Asher's head snaps to mine, and I think my heart stops in my chest.

"You mean to pick up women?" There's no tone in his voice that tells me how he feels about my question—his is a simple and straightforward question. But the lack of tone makes me wonder if I've made him mad, like when I was dumb and told him he could hook up with a bridesmaid. Apparently, this new version of me has foot-in-mouth syndrome.

"Sorry," I backtrack. "That was a personal question. I don't know why I asked." I *do* know why I asked, though, because I want to know if what we did was something he does often.

"We've been asking each other personal questions," he answers. "But I'm curious if you really want to know."

The answer sours my stomach because it alludes to his answer. "Maybe not."

Asher and I stare at each other, and I wonder what he's trying to see. Then the corner of his lip twitches as he fights not to smile and loses.

"Why are you smiling?"

"Because you care."

His words roll around in my mind, and all my alarm bells go off. Here we are, talking about feelings. Getting too close to one another. Sitting too close to one another. *Again*. Even after I attempted to draw a line in Oregon and again after the tattoos.

I could have easily kissed him then. I also could have easily gone into his room at night and asked him for more, but I've kept myself at bay because I respect him and don't want to lead him on more than I feel I already have. Even if it was accidental.

Asher turns his upper body, the side of his face cast in the fiery glow, eyes more fervent than I've ever seen them. "I need to know why you care about me picking up women at bars, Jesse," he says.

"I don't care, I—"

"Please don't lie."

"I'm not lying."

"I know you don't think that, but you are. There's a reason you asked the question you did. I want to hear you say why."

"Why are you pressing this?" My jaw clenches.

"I know I said I could be your friend. And Jesse, I'm trying. I want to be, but—but being around you, having you in my space...I know you feel what's between us. You even said with your own words you like me, and I know it's not just because we slept together. We have something here that's more than just *like*, don't we?"

"Ash, I..." I pick at my jeans. "I don't know what to say."

"You can be honest and tell me how you truly feel. I won't be mad if I'm reading you wrong, but I can't deny my feelings anymore, and I need you to be truthful with me. At least then I can try to deal with the aftermath."

The aftermath. I turn from bubbling frustration at him to angry at myself that I thought we could sleep with each other, go on a road trip together, then sleep with each other again and just walk away from that with one or both of us unscathed. Especially since before my heart failed me two years ago, all I wanted was to live in a fairytale—until I didn't any longer.

"Just tell me, Jesse. Why do you care about me going to bars for company?"

After a long moment, one in which I don't answer, he releases a sigh. He shifts and starts to get out of his chair. I should be glad he's stopping the conversation, but instead, I panic.

"Are you leaving?" I ask.

"I'm going to answer some emails that came from the office in London. When you're finished out here, let me know, and I'll take care of the fire."

"Wait," I plead. "Okay, wait."

He stops, still in his chair, his body turning to mine again.

"I can't answer that question," I breathe out.

"Why, Jesse?"

"Because." I gather courage. "I'm trying not to care. I don't want to care."

His eyes bore into mine. "Tell me why you don't want to care?"

"Asher. You told me you were fine being friends."

"I know I did. I am, but you keep making me think otherwise. You pull away, but then you ask me questions about family and get jealous over past hookups. We almost kissed again the other day—"

"I didn't! And I'm not jealous!"

He chuckles disbelievingly. "If that's what you need to tell yourself."

"I don't know what to say to you...I don't know what you want me to say."

"I want you to be honest. Tell me why you don't want to care?"

"Because!" I yell, standing from my chair to look down at him. "Because I could die, okay? I could *die*. Do you really want to be involved with someone who could just fall over dead?!"

"Jesse," he says quietly.

Even in the firelight, I can see the sadness, the pity in his eyes. Exactly what I never wanted to see from him. It's why I wasn't even honest with Melissa or Kate or anyone about why the one-night stand was on my bucket list. Why I've started to envision this new life for myself, one that's more like the life Ash has—of spontaneous travel and bar hookups—one it sounds like he may not even want anymore.

"Don't—" I say. "Don't pity me."

Ash stands to meet me. "I'm not pitying you."

"You are, though. You feel bad for the poor girl who's afraid of her own damn body. Afraid that one day, it might fail her. And you know what's worse? You're right to."

"Stop telling me how I see you. Stop telling me what I feel."

"I'm telling you because I see it. I see it in your eyes right now."

"You're seeing it because that's what you want to see. You want an excuse to run from how you feel for me."

"And how do I feel for you?" I challenge.

"I know you care. I know you care enough to wonder about other women. You asked why we keep ending up like this."

His eyes drop to my lips, and it's then I see we've gravitated toward one another, even in frustration and anger.

"It's because we're not just friends, Jesse. No matter how much you want to say we are."

"You can't want me, Ash. You can't."

"You're only saying that because you're afraid."

"I am afraid!" I cry. "I am." Tears fill my eyes. "What if we start dating and you change your entire life for me, and then I die?"

"That's a risk for everyone, Jesse girl. Life isn't guaranteed for any of us."

"Maybe so, but my heart could stop. I could enter a non-responsive state if I'm not revived in time. Death is a reality more for me than it is for you. And you don't deserve to have someone defective. You deserve someone whole."

"Jesse." He takes my biceps in his hands, holding me firm. "You're not defective. How could you think that?"

"Because it's true. It's my reality."

A tear drops down my cheek and then another. Asher's hands grip my arms hard, as if he's afraid I'll disappear if he lets go. And maybe I will.

"I will never deny that what you've been through is more than most people will ever have to deal with in their entire lives. But you are not defective. You're strong, capable, talented. You may be healing, but you're not defective. Far from it. If you don't believe me, ask the people who follow you now. Ask my sister, who adores and admires you. You had something awful happen to you, and now you've turned that into something amazing."

"I hear what you're saying, but it doesn't change the fact that what I say is true. I will not allow you to fall for me only to be left alone."

Asher stares into my eyes, and I see his are glassy with tears, too. A moment later, he drops his forehead to mine. I close my eyes, breathing in his scent mixed with the smell of smoke and fire.

"Too late," he whispers. My heart skips, and Asher lifts his chin and presses a kiss to my forehead. "I'm going to go inside. Let me know when you're done out here."

"Ash—"

"It's okay," he says. "I'll be okay."

He pulls back and walks toward Winnie. With each step he takes, my heart breaks. Once he's safely inside, I watch the light turn on through the blinds of the living area window, seeing slivers of Ash through the panels. He runs his fingers through his hair and rubs his face before walking toward his bedroom.

With him out of sight, the tears come freely. I sink back into my chair, my gaze fixed on the flames flickering in front of me. My voice barely a whisper, I speak to Asher as if he can hear me.

"I think it's too late for me, too."

Chapter Thirty-Four

Asher

I LIE IN BED, staring at the ceiling, while the faint sounds of Jesse moving around in the bathroom drift to me. It's only four in the morning, and we're both up before the birds, ready to check off two of the last items on Jesse's bucket list: see the sunrise at Cadillac Mountain in Maine, the first place you can see the sun rise in the United States, and the other item she doesn't know about yet.

GusGus jumps up on the bed and onto my chest, staring down at me with wide eyes. "You smell like tuna." He meows but continues to look at me. "I'm not giving you more till later." I expect him to run off, but instead, he plops down on my chest.

I stroke his soft fur, and his purrs melt into me, easing the tension that's been there since last night. I hardly slept, Jesse's confession tumbling around in my mind. I had guessed that her biggest hangup when it came to me had something to do with her heart, but to hear her say it was a whole different ball game.

All night, I tried to put myself in her shoes, and I do get it. I get why she's afraid, why she wouldn't want to be a burden on a partner or even friends, for that matter. But the only thing that keeps looping in my mind is that she cares. That if she didn't feel the way she does, she'd give us a chance.

"What do you think, GusGus?" His dark eyes peer into mine, cute little head cocked to the side. "Don't give up?" He meows, and I chuckle, scratching behind his ear. The world is silent for a minute until the soft sound of Jesse humming floats through my closed door. I haven't heard her hum before, but the soothing melody has my eyes closing.

From the moment I met Jesse, I've been imagining a future with her. I did say I would marry her, and in my dreams, I still do. It's one of the many reasons I haven't let the hope of us die. And now, after her questions last night where she asked me if I want a family and what I want for the future, that future with her is even more vivid.

I'd wake up in the morning to her wrapped in my arms or the sounds of her humming. We'd drink our coffee outside or maybe in bed. We'd see the sun rise and set in every state. We'd watch GusGus play in the grass, and I'd help her take photos for her social media page and get so many brand deals and partnerships she wouldn't know what to do with herself.

I could still work if I wanted, and we could travel together overseas with Gus in tow. Or I could be her assistant and help her soar, make sure she never needs to go back to a desk job again. Not that she would, anyway, if she was with me, but I know she'd want to work.

I'm also more than happy to say screw London and find them a replacement—it's not like I need the money. And while I enjoy what I do, I do it because it's something different, something to occupy my brain space.

Jesse is right, I do get lonely on the road. But I wouldn't need the jobs or the distractions with Jesse. We could carve our own path, make our own rules. Have a fun and spontaneous life together.

Meow.

My eyes refocus, and I look into the judgmental gaze of my cat. "I'm going overboard, aren't I?" He meows again, and I sigh. "You're right. But I can't help it—I think I lov—"

Knock. Knock. Knock.

At the sound, Gus jumps off the bed and heads to the door. I sit up and rub my tired eyes, mentally telling myself to get it together. I may as well grab my notebook and start writing "Mr. Jesse" on everything.

"Ash? Did you fall back asleep?" Jesse calls through the door.

"No, sorry, coming!" I open the door, and she's smiling at me, a tight smile I don't like at all.

"You ready to go?" she asks.

"Yeah," I say, quickly scanning her outfit. "But grab a jacket."

"It's cooler but not bad outside, I checked. And I've got this long-sleeved hoodie on."

She does, but it's one of those lightweight track-style ones. "Trust me, grab a jacket."

Jesse's about to argue with me when the unmistakable sound of motorcycles pull up to our campsite, probably waking up any camper in our vicinity. Oops.

Her tight smile softens, and her eyes light up. "You didn't?"

"I did. I hired them to drive us to and from the park."

"Google really does find you everything, huh?"

I smirk, secretly wondering if Google can tell me how to win a skittish woman's heart—and not just with flowers, gluten-free pizza, and motorcycle rides.

Jesse steps forward, and for a split second, I think she's going to kiss me. She does, but her lips land on my cheek. Warmth blooms in the hole in my chest as her eyes meet mine. "Thank you, Ash. You really are magic."

Heat crawls up my neck, and that hope in my chest still flickers despite myself. "You're welcome," I say quietly.

Her eyes flutter to my mouth and back to meet my gaze. The puff of warm air from her breath skitters across my lips, and my lower abs tighten. We stand like that for who knows how long, until the rev of an engine makes her step back.

"We shouldn't keep them waiting," she says.

I nod in agreement, and she spins away from me, walking toward the door while calling back, "If one of the motorcycles is red, I call dibs."

Jesse rubs my back as we hike the short distance up Cadillac Mountain from the public parking area, where the bikers dropped us off.

"Are you sure you're alright?" she asks through a stifled giggle.

"I'm fine," I mumble. "But I think I'll walk back."

Jesse snickers, and I playfully glare at her. I want to be mad at her for laughing at me, but she looks so goddamn happy. Even with the sky only beginning to light up, she's ecstatic with her wide eyes and rosy cheeks. I, on the other hand, still smell the musky cologne of burly biker Dave clinging to my clothes, and my stomach feels sick. Who knew riding a motorcycle was so fucking terrifying?

"You can't walk back; it's too far, and Dave would miss you. You sure got close to him on that ride—maybe your nickname should be koala bear."

"Shut up," I groan, which only makes her laugh harder.

"But seriously, thank you." She links elbows with me and squeezes. "I didn't think I'd get to cross that one off, and you delivered."

My entire body comes alive from her touch. Even though I know it's meant to be friendly, that stupid hope flares from the flicker it dimmed to back up to a flame. It makes clinging to Dave while he drove us here like a maniac worth it.

"You're welcome. Couldn't leave an item unchecked." Granted, there's still one item, the item she crossed out before doing. But I know I can't make that come true for her—she has to be the one to decide that, because even though I'd give my body over to her with no strings attached, I don't know if I could handle the aftermath. Or if she could, either.

Jesse squeezes my arm again like she knows what I'm thinking as we crest to the top of the mountain.

"There are a lot of people," she says.

"Sadly, I couldn't close a public park down during tourist season." *Though I did try.*

Jesse chuckles, pulling her arm from mine, much to my displeasure. "It's okay, I like it. It's like the pictures I've been looking at since I was a kid. Now I'm in one."

"You never told me how this became a bucket-list item."

She smiles as she remembers. "I did a project in fourth grade and was assigned to Maine. We had to write to the tourism office and get brochures sent. One of them was about this place, and I thought it would be so cool to see the first place the sun rises in the US."

"And you remembered it all this time. I love that."

She dips her chin. "Sometimes things stick with you. It also helps that I love sunrises and sunsets in general."

I nod, knowing that information about her already. "Do you want to go sit at the front or stand here?" I ask as I look out at all the people.

"Front," she says.

We maneuver our way through the throng, and I check my watch. The clouds are lit from the sun's impending rise, and I can feel the excitement of the people and families in the air.

Once we find a seat on a cold stone between a group of friends and a couple, Jesse relaxes, looking out at the sky. "It's beautiful here."

"It is," I say, looking at her. The mountain is beautiful. We have a panoramic view of Maine's coastline, forested hills, and the Atlantic Ocean. With the sky lighting up, we can see the harbor below with boats docked along the shore.

But she's more beautiful, and I want to tell her that. I open my mouth to express what I'm feeling, even though I shouldn't, but I'm interrupted by Jesse's gasp.

I shift my gaze to where I should be looking and see that deep blues and oranges have begun to light up the sky. Everyone around us has gone quiet, and I take a second to pull out my phone. I don't want Jesse to miss a moment of her dream to see this, so I'll capture the memory for her. She doesn't notice me taking pictures, or if she does, she doesn't say anything.

Another minute goes by, and the crowd oohs and aahs as the top of the sun rises. Jesse grips my arm. "There it is," she whispers.

My eyes move from her hand to the view again. The sun continues to rise as the minutes tick by, turning the sky a pink-and-yellow color. It casts a glow over the entire area, lighting up Jesse's features and hazel-green eyes that have become glassy.

I place my hand over hers on my arm, and she takes in a small breath. When her eyes meet mine, she smiles softly. "It's even better in person," she says.

"It's beautiful." *You're beautiful*.

My hand lingers over hers as we sit together, watching the sun climb higher until the vibrant colors dissolve into the daylight. We stay until the crowd disperses, leaving only Jesse and me in the quiet stillness of the early morning.

She turns her head, our arms touching and fingers interlocked. "Kiss me," she says, her voice a gentle whisper.

My eyes flick to her slightly parted lips and back to her hazel pools. I search them for any sign that things have changed since last night, that this is more than just another moment where we can't stay away from each other. That it's more than another item to check off her bucket list.

My heart pounds in my chest, and blood whooshes in my ears. "Will it change anything between us?" I ask.

Jesse's jaw ticks, and her gaze shifts from mine to the ground. She doesn't need to say no; she said it with her action. I drop my hand from hers and pull back.

"I'm sorry, I shouldn't have asked," she says weakly. "I know it's not fair." A single tear tracks down Jesse's cheek. My fingers itch to brush it away, but I keep my hand at my side.

"You're right; it isn't fair," I reply.

Her mouth opens to speak, but nothing comes out. A light gust of wind blows hair across her face, and when she tucks it back, I decide it's now or never. I don't know what about the action triggers me, but I need to lay my heart out here and now. Completely. This may be my only chance.

"Can I say something?" I voice.

"Of course, you know you always can."

I run my clammy palms over the coarse fabric of my jeans. "From the moment I saw you at the bar, I was a goner. Had we not gone home together that night, I would've gotten your number. I would have asked you out and taken you to dinner every night if you'd have let me. When it was time for me to go to London, I would've obsessively texted you until you asked my sister if I was a stalker. Better yet, I would have postponed or cancelled my trip to get to know you better."

Jesse stares at me as if I have two heads. "You would've?"

"When I said I fell for you, Jesse, I meant it. Sadly for me, I fell fucking headfirst into a no-diving zone." She cringes at the metaphor, and I pick up her hand. "It's not your fault. It was my choice. I knew from the moment I saw your bucket list on your bathroom mirror what I was to you. But I hoped by leaving my message you would text or I could somehow find you again, that it would be easy to change your mind. Then we came on this trip, you made your rules, and I thought maybe if you felt even a fraction for me what I feel for you that things would be different. And Jesse, I think they still could be."

Jesse stares at my hand, forehead pinched and eyes watery again. "This is a lot," she whispers.

"I know, I can be a lot—"

"No, no, Ash. You're perfect the way you are. I just—" Jesse pulls her hand back and stares out at the water. When I'm about to ask her if she's okay, she speaks, not looking at me. "When I was little, I used to dream of being saved by a prince. I used to dream of marrying one and having lots of little children running around in our big castle. As I got older, I was overlooked, told I wasn't attractive, that I was too big for men to like me."

"But I still wished and dreamed a prince would come and love me for who I am. I was wishing that up until my health scares. Getting the implant finally made me see that fairytales aren't for me. Who would want a princess who may not be able to give their prince a fairytale ending, you know? So I changed what I wanted. I made my bucket list and wrote down a one-night stand."

She took a breath. "I said it was because I wanted to own my body, to be someone different, and while that's true, it wasn't completely why. I was protecting myself with the item and the rules around it, protecting my heart and potentially someone else's." She turns her head to me. "Then you come along. You come along and make me believe in the fairytale I so desperately wanted. But I don't get to have those, Asher. I don't get to have a happy ending."

"Jesse." Her name leaves my lips in a pained exhale. "You can't believe that."

"I do. I told you last night, I'm not cursing you with me."

My already cracked heart shatters. "You wouldn't be a curse. You're a gift."

Her cheek twitches from the reference, but there are no smiles between us.

"Look at me, Jesse girl." Our eyes meet, and I take her hand, running my thumb over her knuckles. "You said you wanted to live like you were dying, but you're not dying. You're living. Please, live with me."

Another tear drops down her cheek. I reach up a free hand to wipe it away, but she beats me to it, severing our connection. And with that simple move, I know my answer.

"I can't, Ash. I'm so sorry."

"Jesse—"

She stands and dusts off the back of her pants. "I'm going to go for a walk. I'll meet you back here in a bit."

I make a move to stand, but she stops me by holding out her hand. "Please, I need some time alone. I don't want to be chased."

Her words stomp on the pieces of my heart, and despite not wanting to, I listen, watching her walk away.

Chapter Thirty-Five
Jesse

ONE MONTH & FIVE DAYS LATER

"I DID IT, I quit my job!" I exclaim as I enter Melissa's bedroom. She's picking up the last of her things, having them moved to where she'll be living with Jordan after their wedding in five days. At least until their new home is done next year.

"Look at you, quitting a desk job after one month to be her own boss." Melissa claps her hands and walks over to hug me. "Did you do something else, too?"

"Not yet." I pull back.

"Why? The lease is up on this apartment soon. You could buy the van and go be the amazing influencer you are."

I smile at her faith in me. "Buying a van is a big decision."

Melissa hooks her fingers over her belt, brown eyes staring at me almost the same way Ash does—did. Intense, as if she's trying to read my mind. "Big decision? Or like you're closing a door on something else? Or should I say some*one* else?"

I groan. "Not this again."

"Just saying." She shrugs nonchalantly, as if me dating her brother wouldn't be a big deal in the slightest. To her, it wouldn't. It would be the best thing ever.

"I've told you a million times—Ash and I are just friends. I'm not going to be traveling with him again."

Melissa walks over to her bare mattress and sits down, picking invisible lint off her jeans. "Not that you could, anyway. He's selling Winnie."

My stomach feels as if a knife has been driven into it, and my eyes widen. "What?"

"Yeah, he's got some buyers to meet with while he's here for the wedding. He didn't tell you?"

I think of the last text Ash sent me. It had nothing to do with Winnie. It was simply him congratulating me for quitting my job so soon. A simple text between people who parted a life-altering road trip as "friends."

"It's not like we talk to each other all the time," I say, fingers subtly playing with the new bracelet on my wrist, one I bought for myself.

Melissa crosses her arms over her chest. "Yeah, right."

"We don't," I counter. "We're friends."

"If you say so."

"I say so. If we were more than friends, wouldn't he have told me he's selling Winnie?" Even saying that makes me want to hurl. It shouldn't. I have no claim to Winnie, even if she now holds some of my best memories.

Melissa sighs sadly. "It was a last-minute thing. He thinks he's going to stay in London longer, says GusGus likes British mice. Something about them having an extra bite."

I debate whether to laugh or cry on top of feeling sick to my stomach. He didn't give me those details. But I guess I don't deserve to know, nor should I. After the heart-to-heart Asher and I had on the mountain in Maine, our relationship changed. The drive home to Wisconsin was reserved, full of awkward silences I realized we'd never had until then.

After we got back, we didn't speak for over a week. I was training for my job, and he went to London. Every night, I would hold my phone and think of texting him, and every night, I didn't, too chicken to reach out, wondering if he even wanted to hear from me. He did say he wanted to stay in touch, but I'd hurt him. I made things weird.

Then one Friday night, he texted me. It was a picture of GusGus catching his first mouse in London. He made a joke about how he must like them because they eat sharper cheese.

I laughed and nearly cried when I read it. I'd felt a hole in my heart since he left, one only he could fill. Then he texted, and everything felt right again. It was a feeling I didn't fully allow myself to feel or analyze. I just let myself be happy we were talking.

Slowly, over the last three weeks, it's felt like we're really friends. He even continued to support my Change of Pace channel, looking over my first brand-deal contract and helping me negotiate more money. Honestly, he's a better friend than I deserve, and I'm grateful for him. But I won't lie and say our continued texting hasn't made me question if I made the right decision regarding our relationship. Even if my brain knows I did.

"You okay?" Melissa asks.

I meet her curious yet concerned gaze and walk over to sit next to her on the bed. "Gus does like the British mice," I answer, unsure of what else to say. Melissa doesn't respond, and in the silence, my thoughts drift back to her news about Asher.

He wants to sell Winnie. He may stay longer in London. Given our friendship and everything we've shared, I really am curious as to why he didn't tell me.

Was he afraid I'd be upset? I mean, I am. Even if I have no right to be. He did mention during one of our question sessions that he recently thought of selling Winnie and settling in the Midwest. But I thought that was a way for him to see where things stood between us. But if he's thinking of staying in London...

"You look awfully sad about this information. You're acting like you're togeth—"

"Don't say anymore." I stop her. "I'll repeat: We are just friends. Apparently not that great of friends since he didn't tell me about Winnie or staying in London, though."

Melissa wraps her arm around my shoulders and pulls me into her side. "What happened between you two on your trip?"

"I told you: We had a great time, crossed off the entire bucket list." *Except that last one*.

"Yes, you told me that part. But I know something must have happened beyond that. You've both been different. Asher texts me more than he ever has in his life. It's odd."

"Shouldn't that be a good thing?" I ask.

"It is, but it's just weird. And you." She squeezes me. "I love this confidence you've found and how much you've grown into yourself. The woman who left wouldn't have quit her job so soon, even with the money you've got coming in with brand deals. You've also been wearing tighter clothes, showing off your curves. And those videos you post are so honest and open. Your confidence is fucking hot."

I flush. "Um, thanks?"

Melissa smiles gently. "But another thing that's changed is you stare at your phone like you're waiting for it to go off. When it does, and it's Ash, your entire face lights up. If it's not him, you look like someone stole your dog."

"I don't have a dog."

Melissa throws up her hands. "See, I don't buy that nothing except 'bucket list helping' happened on that trip. You even get smart with me like my brother does."

I groan. "Can we please talk about something else? Like your wedding happening soon?"

"No. Nope. We've talked enough about that. I want to know why you're in love with Asher but he's been living in London and you're here thinking about buying a van and traveling without him while he's thinking about selling his RV!"

"I'm not in love with him," I counter.

"Yeah, and I'm not in love with Jordan."

I gasp. "You're not? I should tell him before he gets stuck with you."

Melissa smacks my arm. "See, smarty pants."

I sigh. "You're not going to let this go, are you?"

"I figure I'll wear you down eventually."

"You could ask Ash."

"I tried, but he won't tell me. Says it's your story to tell."

My chest warms at his thoughtfulness, the care he still has for me. "Sounds like him," I say.

"Hmm, so are you going to tell me? Or do I have to torture it out of you by playing Jonas Brothers at my wedding all night?"

I gasp. "The horror! You know One Direction is the superior boy band."

"You wish," she chirps. "Now, spill, or I'll do it, I swear!"

I have no doubt Melissa would. "If I tell you, you have to promise not to throw up."

It takes a second for Melissa to realize what I'm saying, then she smiles. "You slept together again?!"

"We did."

She gasps. "Can I say *yay* and *ew* simultaneously?"

I laugh. "Yes."

"Yay-ew!" she says oddly.

I shake my head. "Are you sure you want to hear the rest? It might take awhile."

"I've got nothing but time, baby."

I know that's not true. She's got family arriving in town for the wedding, but I lay it all out for her, anyway. Minus the "ew" details.

"Okay, that's a lot," Melissa says. We've left the bedroom and are now sitting at the dining room table with a glass of white wine in our hands. It's only eleven in the morning, but we both thought the conversation needed a bit of wine.

"Tell me about it," I say, taking a sip.

"Are you okay?"

I play with the stem of my glass, my silver bracelet catching light from the morning sun and reflecting into my eye. A fresh wave of emotion makes the bridge of my nose sting, and I swallow. "Honestly, I don't know."

"I can understand why you didn't want to spill about what happened between you and Ash on your trip. But what I don't understand is why you didn't tell me you felt this way about getting into a relationship...about your life."

I rub my fingers over the bracelet, feeling the cool silver and the custom etching I had put on the band beneath my fingers. "I guess it's because it makes people uncomfortable to talk about death. To hear the reality of what could happen to me one day."

"I hear what you're saying, and I understand. But you don't have to feel those feelings alone, you know? I'm here for you. I don't ever want you to think you can't talk to me. Especially about heavy stuff like this."

I reach out for her hand across the table and grip it. "I know, thank you. I guess I was even afraid to say it out loud because it would be real, and I didn't want people to pity me. I want to live my life and feel good about it when my number comes up."

"And do you feel good about it?"

Her question stops me in my tracks, and I pull my hand away. "Of course I do. I don't have a desk job anymore. I'm doing things my own way. I have money in my checking account, and I've done everything on my bucket list. What's not to feel good about?"

"So if you were to die right now, you wouldn't regret anything?"

"No." I look at my friend, her curly hair and brown eyes so much like Asher's. "I mean, I don't think so."

"No? Or no, you don't think so?"

"Do you have regrets?" I volley back, not wanting to answer her question.

Melissa steeples her fingers. "I've thought about this. I don't have any."

"Seriously?"

She nods affirmatively. "If I were to die tomorrow, I wouldn't have regrets. I lived how I wanted to live, I made my choices, I got to meet the love of my life. I hope I don't die tomorrow because I'd like to marry Jordan, but everything I've done, said, and did has led me to today. And I'm happy. Really happy." Her smile glows, and I swear there's light shining through her pores. She *is* happy.

"Not one regret?" I repeat. But it sounds almost like a question I'm asking myself.

Melissa's bright smile turns softer. "It's okay if you have regrets, Jesse. Unless that isn't what you want."

"I—I didn't think I had any. I don't want to have any. The whole point of the bucket list was so that I wouldn't."

"So it's not just a 'no' or a 'think,' it's a 'yes,' you do have regrets? Or should I say 'a' regret?" She asks with a hope in her voice that nearly makes me smile.

My gaze drops to the bracelet on my wrist again. I bought it after I received my first brand-deal payout. It's etched with *WWTD*, the mantra I've had on repeat in my mind since the road trip, when things felt hard.

My pulse slows, and memories of Asher fill my mind. His lopsided smile. His floppy curl on his forehead. Him cuddling with GusGus. His strong arms wrapped around me. The way he always made me feel comfortable and safe. Happy. Beautiful. How when he left, it felt like a hole was in my heart.

My thoughts shift, and I imagine never having any new memories of him again. How it would be to have that hole grow as time goes on with only friendly texts to fill it. It feels...like death. And while I could never and would never regret anything where Ash is concerned, would I regret following my head instead of my heart?

"Fuck." I put my face in my hands, and Melissa scoots closer so she can rub my back.

"Living your life isn't just about checking off items on a list and calling it a day. Living your life is doing what makes your heart happy, what makes your soul happy. If everything were to end right here, right now, would you regret at least not trying a relationship with Asher?"

I let out an exhausted breath and meet Melissa's gaze. All the fears I had about letting myself be with Ash rush to the surface alongside all the good feelings he's given me.

"I've been trying this last month to move on," I say. "I keep telling myself it's for the best. But, Melissa...what if I become a burden to him? What if he regrets me?" My voice breaks.

She pauses before she speaks. "Think of it this way: If things were the opposite, would you consider Ash a burden?"

"Of course not!"

Melissa sets her hand on my shoulder and squeezes. "Then why would you be?"

I puff out a breath, her words hitting me like a freight train. "I have no answer."

"Jesse, let the people who love you care about you. You're not a burden. You never will be. Please don't let your fear of dying stop you from living."

"The irony." I groan. "And you sound like Ash."

"I'll take that as a compliment; he is very smart."

I chuckle softly and pull Melissa into a hug. "I have some thinking to do."

"What is there to think about?" she counters.

I throw up my hands as a last defense. "I spent the entire road trip pushing him away, and this last month, I've attempted to keep my feelings in check. I can't just change my mind."

"And why not? It sounds like you want to. You wouldn't be keeping your feelings in check if you didn't have the feelings to begin with. Stop thinking so hard!"

"It's not that easy."

"Or it is," she counters.

"Melissa..."

"Can I give you a word of advice?"

"You'll tell me, anyway," I tease.

She chuckles. "True. But if you love him, if you want to make a move, do it soon. I think the only reason he's thinking of staying in London and selling Winnie is because he misses you. He'll never admit it, but I know him. He's an all-in type of man, so if he goes all in in London, I don't know when he'll come back. If you want to be with him, Jesse, you have to tell him. And soon."

"He'd never stay in London forever. He loves to travel," I say quickly.

Melissa shrugs. "He can travel Europe."

My heart nearly stops at the idea of Asher doing what she's saying. If he stays in London...

The bridge of my nose stings again, and I think of Winnie being sold. Of him being in London with GusGus. Of me not being with them. I look down at my bracelet and mentally say the familiar mantra: *What Would Thor Do?*

I know what he would do, and it wouldn't be living a life of fear.

The final bricks of the weak wall I'd built to keep Ash out falls, and I embrace how I felt for him since the moment I met him—not only happiness but rightness. Asher is right for me, the person I always dreamed of finding. The person I've spent so much time pushing away when I didn't need to.

My heart beats as fast as hummingbird wings, and I know what I need to do to make this right, to show him how I feel for him—how I think I've always felt for him.

I slam my hands on the table, scaring Melissa. "I have an idea!"

"What is it?"

"I'll tell you soon, but I'm going to need your help."

"Please tell me this involves you doing some romantic gesture to win my brother over."

"Yes."

"Thank you, lord baby Jesus. I'm so in!"

I laugh. "Good. Then let's get started."

Chapter Thirty-Six

Asher

BEING BACK IN WISCONSIN is both nice and painful. I've never called this state home, but with everything that happened, I'll forever associate it with Jesse. And with that comes a feeling of home, one I shouldn't have, especially considering we parted from our road trip as friends. Friends who now text more than I've ever texted anyone in my life.

Is it stupid of me to continue a relationship with a woman I'm head over heels for? Probably. But despite what went down in Maine, I couldn't completely walk away. I tried. I really did. But my stubborn heart won out. It took me approximately a week and four days before I caved, using a picture of GusGus as an excuse.

I kept thinking about Matt and his bride, Jessica, how he waited for her until she was ready. I know I could be waiting forever, but every time we text or one of those texts turns a little flirty, I have hope I was right. That Jesse is and will always be mine.

My phone goes off, and I pull it out, expecting to see Jesse's name. Instead, I see my sister's. I pick it up with a smile on my face.

"Hey, Bridezilla. Something go wrong?"

"Ha ha. I'm the opposite of a bridezilla. I'm a bridechilla."

I chuckle and stand to check my suit in my hotel room mirror, ready to grab my shoes if she needs me. "I can be at your room in a few minutes if you need something."

"Nope, all good here. But I do need you to go down to the parking lot."

"What? Why? Don't I need to be at your wedding in"—I check my watch—"an hour?"

"I have a buyer for Winnie who could only meet now. They want to see her."

Confusion flares in my brain. "A buyer for Winnie?"

"Yeah, since you're thinking of staying in London longer. You're selling her."

"Did you fall and hit your head or something? I never said I was doing that."

"I don't know, that's what I thought you said." I can hear a smile in her voice, but I don't understand what's going on.

"I said I was thinking of selling her eventually. And I never said I was staying in London. I said maybe a few days longer since I had to come here for your wedding and so I could see some sights after I'm done."

"Well, I heard you're selling Winnie and moving to London. Maybe travel Europe."

I let out a long sigh. While I told Jesse I was thinking about selling Winnie on our trip, I said that because I was trying to gauge her, see where her head was at. Because if she wanted to, I would sell Winnie, get a home and settle down, travel for fun and to be spontaneous. But I'd do that if it was a decision we made together. I wouldn't sell her just because—especially since it's full of memories now. Memories I want to cling to for as long as possible.

"You can text the guy and tell him I'm not selling. At least not right now."

"I don't have time—wedding to get to. Just go down there, and tell him to eff off."

"I also have your wedding to get to."

"You're wasting minutes. Just go! See you soon."

Melissa hangs up, and I'm left with a knot in my gut and a lot of confusion. I quickly check my appearance since I won't have time to come back to the room; I'm wearing a black suit that needs a tie. I silently curse and grab it, pocketing my wallet and keycard. Hopefully I can ask someone to help me before the ceremony.

It takes me only a couple of minutes to reach the parking lot where I have Winnie parked. I only got a hotel room because of the wedding, deciding to use it for the bathroom and showering.

I check my watch again. My sister is crazy for doing this—and so close to the time of her wedding. But I shouldn't be surprised; Melissa has always been spontaneous and done questionable things. I guess it runs in our DNA.

I exhale a breath as I lift my head, preparing to tell the man who wants to buy Winnie that she's not for sale. But my next breath catches in my chest, and I stop in my tracks.

Standing in front of me is not who I was expecting. It's Jesse. Her dark-brown hair is curled to perfection, and her body that was made to be worshiped is wrapped in a glittering burgundy dress that reaches the ground. She's stunning.

"You're not a man," I blurt out.

Jesse laughs softly and takes a step toward me. "Nope."

My eyes track down her body again, taking in the dress that's cut in what I can only describe as a modern Nordic style with long sleeves that have been slit to show her arms and a scooped neckline. Across her waist lies a thin, rope-style belt being held together by a round golden clip.

When I meet her eyes, they're soft, and she's worrying her lip. I want to tell her how stunning she looks, but instead I ask, "What are you doing out here?"

"You can't sell Winnie."

"Jesse, I—"

She takes a step toward me. "You can't sell Winnie. You can't sell her, and please don't move to London. I know GusGus likes the mice there, but he'll be okay. You can't sell Winnie," she says, nearly breathless.

My heart pounds in my chest, and I try to contain a smile threatening to overcome me. I love that she was concerned about GusGus.

I wet my lips, not missing the way she tracks the movement. "Why can't I sell her?"

Jesse plays with a silver bracelet on her wrist, seeming to take strength from it before she speaks. "Because I don't want you to."

I take a careful step toward her, the small distance between us growing smaller now until there are only inches between us.

"And why don't you want me to?"

Jesse grips her wrist. "Because I care."

The shattered pieces of my heart start to glue themselves back together at her words. The flicker of hope in my chest, the one I've clung to since I met her, begins to flare. "About?"

"About you. About Gus...about us. Please, Ash. Don't sell our memories."

Our memories.

"I wasn't planning on selling Winnie. Or moving to London."

The confusion I felt minutes ago riddles Jesse's face. "But Melissa said—" Then Jesse laughs, a loud cackle that comes from her chest. "That meddler. Did you know she was doing this?"

I shake my head. "I was as confused as you up until now."

Jesse shakes her head, another soft laugh spilling from her. "Okay, wow, this is embarrassing." Her chin tips down, and I see the flush of her cheeks rise.

"So you didn't mean what you said then?"

Jesse looks up and shakes her head. "No, I did mean it. I—god, Ash. I was so scared when she told me you were thinking about staying in London. If you weren't here for the wedding, I would've bought a ticket and flown there."

"But you wouldn't have come after me if it wasn't for Melissa's meddling?"

Jesse's gaze drops down to the tie in my hand. Without a word, she takes it from me and loops it around my neck. Her body is close enough that I can smell her perfume and the scent of whatever product keeps her curled waves in place. The light of the late afternoon sun glints on the silver band on her wrist, and I see there's an engraving on it: *WWTD*.

My eyes meet hers, and she's smiling softly. "I got the bracelet a couple of weeks ago. Used my first brand payout to buy it." Jesse finishes knotting my tie but doesn't step back. Instead, she places her hands over the lapels of my suit jacket.

"*What Would Thor Do*?" I ask quietly.

She nods. "Every time in the last month, when something was hard or something I normally wouldn't do comes along, I'd think of you and ask *What Would Thor Do*?"

"Did it help?"

She nods. "Melissa telling me you were selling Winnie and moving to London may have given me the final push to be here, but if I'm being honest, I was looking at tickets to London weeks ago."

"You were?"

"I've been lying to myself. To you. To everyone, really. I told myself you were a fairytale I couldn't have, that you were out of my reach, but I've been putting you out of reach. I've been trying to convince myself it was better that way, but in doing so, I not only hurt myself—I hurt you. And I'm sorry. I'm so sorry for hurting you."

"I understand why you did."

"I know, and I love you for that. But I was wrong. I was wrong to push you away. You were right when you said I was living like I was dying, but I'm not dying. I am alive, and I've never felt more alive in my life. Especially when I'm with you."

My brain is attempting to compute everything she's saying, but I'm stuck on the part where she said she loved me.

I swallow, the muscles in my throat tense. "Are you saying you want to give us a try?"

Her smile is soft, and her fingers grip the lapels of my jacket like she's afraid if she lets go, I'll disappear. "I'm saying I want to live with you, Ash. If you'll have me."

"You're serious?"

"Dead serious." I glare at her, and she laughs gently. "I don't want to live my life like a checklist. I just want to live it."

"With me?"

Her smile turns brighter. "With you...and GusGus. Even if that's in London."

The hope in my chest burns bright, turning into the reality I've dreamed of for two months now. "I wasn't moving to London," I assure her. "And I don't blame you; Gus is cute. I'm sure he'll be sad he missed this."

"Missed what?"

"The first time his Cat Daddy told his Cat Mommy he loves her."

Jesse's entire chest and cheeks turn a deep pink. I wrap my arms around her waist and press her warm body into mine.

"A little soon for all that, don't you think?" she asks. "We have a lot to figure out. I feel like I have so much to make up for. And you've only known me for—"

My lips ghost over hers, effectively cutting her sentence off. I don't need her to make up for anything, because I understand her reasons. I only care that she's here and she wants me.

I also don't need to point out that she's already said she loved me. I know she'll say it soon enough.

"Ask me to kiss you again, Jesse."

She looks into my eyes, and I see hers are glassy. "Will you kiss me, Ash?"

"Yes." My lips seal over hers, and her mouth molds to mine. My hand drifts down her back, pulling her further into me until I don't know where she ends and I begin. She tastes like minty toothpaste and something sweet, like a peppermint candy. Like a home I never want to leave.

I tangle our tongues, and she moans into my mouth. I drop my hand lower, ghosting the area of her low back, getting lost in her.

Before I can cup her ass, the loud sound of clapping has us pulling apart. "Oy! Are you going to come watch me get married or not?"

Jesse and I both turn to see my sister in her wedding gown and full glam, looking as beautiful as ever, with a wide smile on her face.

"We'll be there in a minute!" I yell.

"We could change this into a double ceremony if you both want!" Melissa calls back.

I look down at Jesse, who's smiling wide, her head on my shoulder and her hand lying where the heart rune has been tattooed.

"Wanna get hitched?" I ask her.

"Not today, but maybe another day." She grins.

I turn my gaze back to my sister and shake my head. "This day is all yours, Sis. But pencil in the same time next year."

Melissa smiles bright. "Will do! See you at the wedding. You, too, future sister-in-law."

I give my attention to Jesse, who's as bright as a ripe tomato on the vine.

"Too much?" I ask.

Jesse pulls me down until our lips are touching. The kiss is brief, but she puts an intensity into it I've never felt before. "You're never too much, Asher called Ash. I think you're just right."

My gaze penetrates her hazel eyes, bright and full of life. "Just think?"

Her mouth spreads into a playful smile. "You *are* just right. And you're just right for me. I'm sorry it took me so long to say it."

I drop my lips to hers and kiss her with everything I have. I tease her and taste her, my hand cupping her cheek, feeling the soft curls of her hair brushing my knuckles. When I pull back, she reaches up to tug the curl flopped down above my eyes.

I kiss her forehead and grip her hand in mine. "Wanna skip the wedding? We could check that last item off your bucket list?"

Jesse's head falls back, and she laughs. "We're not skipping your sister's wedding. And I told you, no more lists. I want to live."

"Okay, but what if I told you it's on *my* bucket list?"

"Really?"

I reach into my back pocket, pull out a folded piece of paper, and hand it to her. "Want to look?"

"You carry it with you?"

I brush my finger along the silver bracelet on her wrist. "I was holding on to a piece of you hoping one day I could show you."

Jesse's eyes turn glassy again, and I watch her face as she unfolds the paper and stares at the single item.

"That's not on here."

I smile softly. "There's only ever been that one."

Jesse looks at the paper and traces her finger over my one item on page.

Ash's Bucket List

☐ Follow your heart

I open the jacket of my suit and hand her the ballpoint pen inside it. "Check it off for me?"

Her eyes dart to the paper then to me before she softly takes it. I watch with bated breath as she checks it off, a tear tracking down her cheek when she hands the pen back to me. When I go to take the paper, she holds it to her chest.

"I'm keeping it."

"We could burn it in a fire ceremony."

She shakes her head. "Absolutely not. It's mine now."

A lopsided grin plays at my lips, and I brush the tears away from her cheeks before kissing her softly.

"It's always been yours." I hold out my arm, and she links her elbow with mine. "Now let's go crash a wedding."

"We're invited to this one."

"Doesn't mean we can't cause some chaos. Get Melissa back for meddling."

Jesse laughs and hip-checks me. "*What Would Thor Do?*"

"We could change it to *What Would Loki Do?* for the night. He *is* the god of mischief, among other things."

"No, we can't do that."

"Okay, fine." I sigh. "No mischief. For now."

"We always have tomorrow," Jesse sing-songs.

Tomorrow. "And the next day. And the next. And the day after that, Jesse girl."

Jesse grips my elbow and nods. "Yes, we do."

Is it too early to tell her I knew I'd marry her from the moment I saw her? Maybe.

But I will...soon.

Epilogue

JESSE

One Month Later

"DID YOU GO WITH the pink one?" Kate asks through the phone. I run my hands down the little lingerie number she helped me pick out last week. It's a corset top that hugs my waist and makes my boobs look bigger than they already are.

"Yeah. I'm going to save the green one for a different night. Maybe his birthday."

"I solidly agree with that choice. The pink screams feminine yet domineering. Are you feeling ready to tap into that inner goddess?"

I snicker through the phone, happy I have someone to talk to about this.

Kate and I were strained for a little bit after my text to her about how her actions and words affect me at times. But we've been working on our friendship and being more honest. We've known each other since we were teens, and the friendship was worth another chance. Especially since she never tried to make me feel bad for calling her out.

It's also nice to be able to talk to someone about the sexier elements of my relationship with Ash, because I'm not going to talk to Melissa about sex with her brother. Nope.

"I'm ready. I've been ready," I say.

"I'm surprised you didn't go with him to London."

"He's been busy trying to get everything done at the hospital so he could come back without having to extend. He didn't want me to have to sit around. I offered, but we decided to go back to explore Europe together next year. I also had to fly to the Boundary Waters to do that brand deal with that plus-size outdoor clothing company the other week."

"Oh, yeah. I forgot to mention how hot those pictures were. I saw them on your page. I can't believe you have over five-hundred-thousand followers now."

"Me, neither. I didn't think people would find me that interesting."

"You're the most interesting person I know, Jesse. Own your newfound influencer status. The people love you! And so do I."

I flush even though she can't see me. "Well, thanks. I'm trying."

I hear the sound of a car pulling up outside. We have Winnie parked at a cute little Wisconsin state park with a full hookup near a lake. The best part is it's the middle of the week, so there is hardly anyone here. Which gives us the privacy I was hoping for. Maybe Ash and I can skinny dip in the lake.

Heat floods my body as the memory of our ocean escapade enters my mind. "Kate, I've got to go. Jordan just pulled up with Asher and Gus."

"Alright, good luck. Give me the deets later, Mistress."

"Shut up." I laugh, saying goodbye and hanging up the phone, cutting off Kate's cackles. In the quiet, I hear Jordan outside asking if Asher needs any help with his bags, but he says no.

The sound of my man's voice zips through my body, and my excitement at seeing him builds. It's only been a month, but it's a month too long.

As I told Kate, after we got together at Melissa's wedding, we had to get serious about what would happen. There were times during the discussion of our future where everything felt like it was moving too fast but at the same time moving too slow. In the end, I terminated my lease at the apartment and moved into Winnie.

To quote Ash: There was never another option.

When I thought he was selling Winnie and moving to London, I knew this was what I wanted. It may feel a little scary sometimes that we both went all in so fast, but it's what we both wanted. Again, there was never another option, at least for us.

For the last month, I've been alone in the RV. It's been nice, just lonely. I got a little taste of the life Asher lived for so long, but I'm glad he's home now.

However, just because we've been apart doesn't mean we haven't spent as much time together as possible. If sex over video chat had been on my bucket list, I would have checked that off the list ten times over.

We've also had very non-sexy chats about what we want out of life. I told him about why I don't think I want children, and we talked at length about it. He's happy with building a family any way we choose to, and that's perfect for now.

We're taking everything day by day, and we've made plans to travel to areas of the South, see the world, and spend time together before we decide what we want in the future.

The future. With Asher. Something I know I'll never regret choosing.

"Honey, I'm home!"

My skin prickles, and a smile breaks out over my face at Ash's greeting. A moment later, a cat is bounding through the RV and jumps up on the bed, the bed that once was Asher's but now belongs to us both. I forget I'm wearing a sexy outfit and greet the little cat I missed.

"Hi, GusGus," I coo. He purrs as I scratch his head and down his back. "Did you miss me?"

He meows, and I chuckle, giving him a few more pets until I feel hands grip my waist. "Well, well, well. What do we have here?" Ash's lips attach to my neck, and he sucks on my pulse.

A near moan leaves my lips, and I tilt my head to the side to give him better access. "Surprise." I whimper as he sucks harder.

"All for me?" he asks between licks and sucks.

"It's not for the cat."

Asher chuckles. "Hmm, welcome home to me, then."

Fighting the feeling to sink into his touch and forget my objective for the evening, I turn in his arms. We're so close, our noses bump, and I pull back to look into the brown eyes I've missed.

"Hi," I whisper.

"Hi, Jesse girl." He tucks a strand of my styled hair behind my ear. "I love the outfit."

"I got it special, just for you."

He kisses my eyelids and then my nose and finally my lips. "I love it. But I'll love it even more on the floor."

"You're such a man," I tease.

He plants a kiss on my lips again and walks me back toward the bed. When the backs of my knees bump the mattress, GusGus jumps off and runs to the back room where I used to sleep—now his cat domain and my office.

But before Ash can push me back, I lay my hand on his chest. "No," I say simply.

Ash quirks a brow. "No?"

My eyes cast down to the bed, and Asher follows my gaze. I hear him suck in a breath when he sees what I've laid out: his brown tie.

"Oh," he smirks. "Really?" Ash adds an eyebrow waggle for effect.

I smile back. "If you want."

"I want."

I press my hand on his chest so he's forced to step back and channel my inner goddess. I can do this. I *want* to do this. And it has nothing to do with checking it off a bucket list.

"Strip." My command is simple, and Ash blinks at me.

I smile demurely, digging my nails gently into his pec beneath his clothes. "Strip, or I'll tie you to the bed and make you watch me touch myself."

"That doesn't sound half bad," he teases.

I pinch his skin and smirk when he hisses. "Not if I leave you there after I'm done."

"For how long?"

"All night."

The knot in Asher's throat bobs, and his hands go to the hem of the T-shirt he's wearing, pulling it up and over his head.

"Good boy," I say. The words feel foreign, and for a second, I want to flush in embarrassment. But Asher's nipples tighten, and his breath grows heavier at the praise. That reaction alone makes me want to keep going.

"Now the rest," I say. "Don't keep me waiting."

Asher continues to strip until he's naked before me, his dick nearly at full mast already. Eager myself, I grab the tie off the bed while he watches my every movement. I hold out the fabric, and like the good boy he is, he offers his wrists.

I tut. "Kneel with your hands at your sides."

Asher's naked body drops to the ground, and I praise him again. I take a step forward, pleased his mouth is at the right height for what I want. He continues to watch me as I slip the tie around his neck and knot it. Once I'm satisfied with how it looks, I tug on it.

"Too tight?" He shakes his head. "Use your words."

Ash's eyes are filled with near awe as he says, "No, it feels good."

I nod and pull on it so his face is near my sex. "Make me come."

"With pleasure," he responds. "May I use my fingers?"

I shake my head, dropping the fabric for a moment to push my sheer underwear down my legs before stepping out of them. I grip his tie in one hand then spread my legs a touch. "If the tie gets too tight, let me know."

"I will," he says huskily.

I smile down at him, using my free hand to run my fingers through his curls before tugging sharply on them, forcing his face up to look at me directly.

A moan escapes his lips, and I don't miss the pearl of pre-cum on the tip of his now straining dick.

"Make me come with only your tongue, and I'll give you a reward." Before he can respond, I shove his head between my legs. The power I feel from the action alone nearly makes me come before his mouth is even on me. I've imagined this moment, dreamed of it even, and now it's happening. And it's happening with a man I almost walked away from.

His tongue swirls around my clit, and I'm brought back to the first time I had him between my thighs. Was it really only three months ago we had our first night together? That he laid me out and made me feel things I'd never felt before?

I moan as his mouth suctions over my sensitive nerves. I miss the feel of his hands on me, but I like that he's listening. That I'm the one in complete and utter control.

I've felt so out of control since my first heart attack, like my life and my body wasn't my own, that I was a servant to the repercussions of my disease. I realize now that, even with the bucket list, I was serving it, checking off the items because it felt like I was in a race against the clock.

And while I might be, I see now that nothing's guaranteed. Life is precious, and I want to live. I want to experience every moment of it with those I love. I don't want to die with regrets, and I know I could never regret anything with Asher.

"*Yes*," I chant, pushing his head further into my pussy. He licks and sucks, using every motion and trick he knows. "Harder," I command. "I need more." His lips suction, and I look down at the top of his curls. He's staring up at me, heat in his eyes and nose wet from my arousal.

I tug the knot up on the tie a little more, putting slight pressure on his throat. At the motion, he hums around my clit, and I spread my legs a bit wider. His tongue travels down to my entrance, sweeping inside and tasting me.

I run my nails through his scalp, tugging the tie so he's buried between my thighs. He moans again, licking inside me before I direct him back to my clit. Our eyes connect once more. "Be a good boy, and get me off."

Asher's dark eyes sparkle, and his tongue flicks in small motions over my swollen clit, shattering me into a million pieces. I throw my head back, calling out his name and holding him to my sensitive sex. I ride his face through my orgasm, my hips undulating against his mouth as white sparks flash behind my eyelids.

My heart pounds in my ears, and when I finally look down, his face is still between my thighs, waiting for me to move him. I gently tug his head away and drop the tie, running a shaky finger over his wet beard until I'm tracing his swollen lips.

"Do you want your reward now?"

"Yes," he replies. His tone is gritty, sending a shiver up my spine.

I tug at the tie, and he stands up, stiff cock bobbing as he straightens. I grip my hand around his shaft and pump him, watching his eyes nearly roll into the back of his head.

I spin us so his back is now facing the bed before I push him gently backward. He bounces on the mattress, and I smile down at him. There's a thin sheen of sweat on his forehead. The tie I wrapped around his neck is lying askew on his chest. He's perfect, and he's all mine.

"I was thinking of tying you up and giving you the best blowjob of your life," I say with newfound confidence. "But I think I'll ride you instead."

Asher licks the taste of me off his lips. "Anything you want, Jesse girl."

My nickname sets my skin ablaze, and I grab a condom from the nightstand. I get up on the bed and straddle him, wrapping my fist around his cock. He watches me with hooded eyes as I roll it down and secure it.

"Since you were so good, I'll let you pick." I run my hand down my corset top. "Top on or off?"

"Leave it on. I want to see your tits bounce in it."

If I wasn't wet before, I would be now. I slyly grin before I get into the cowgirl position. It's my first time ever having sex this way, and I can't think of a better moment or person to do it with.

I brace one hand on the pec with his rune tattoo and keep the other around his dick, placing him at my entrance. We both hiss in pleasure when I sink down onto his length. "God, Ash," I moan. "You feel so good."

"Please, Jesse, can I touch you? I don't think I can stop myself."

I vigorously nod, knowing I can't deny him. I want his hands on me, too. "Please."

His hands grip my hips, fingers digging into the soft flesh. Not wanting to hold back, I slide up and down his shaft, using his chest for stability and leverage.

"So fucking beautiful," he moans. "So fucking mine."

I lower down to kiss him, his hands moving to my ass and squeezing. I continue to bounce up and down until my needs grows.

"Give me more, Ash. I want to feel you deep."

His hips lift off the bed as I move down, the added friction and pressure making us both cry out. The burn and stretch of him nearly undoes me.

"I'm not gonna last, baby."

Baby. He's never called me that before. I seek his lips and kiss him, our tongues battling together so I feel him everywhere—in my mouth, inside me, on my skin. A moment later, I pull back, grabbing the tie around his neck with one hand and placing the other on my clit. The added sensation makes my inner walls squeeze around his cock.

"Fuck, I'm gonna come," he nearly whimpers.

"Wait for me," I command.

"I'll wait forever for you."

My eyes sting, and I put strong pressure on my clit before rubbing small circles over it. "Fuck!" I cry. "I'm coming."

I crest over the edge, insides fluttering and squeezing him. Asher thrusts up into me, a groan leaving his lips along with chants of my name as he comes. His hands hold my hips, strong enough to leave bruises, ones I'll gladly wear until they fade. Then we'll replace them with new ones. *Not hard to do with all the blood thinners I'm on.*

I smile at the silly thought, and Asher smiles back at me. When my thighs shake with exertion and our breaths have calmed, I roll off him and reach to grab the box of tissues from the nightstand. After I dispose of the condom and wipe between my legs, I curl into his side, playing with the tie still around his neck.

When silence falls between us for too long, I look up at him. Ash is looking down at me with awe, and his eyes are wet. "What's wrong?" I panic. "Did I hurt you?" I ask, leaning over to study his neck.

He grabs my hand and squeezes it. "No, no. I'm good. Perfect, actually."

"Then why are you crying?"

"Because you're here."

The stinging in my eyes turns to tears of my own, and I cup his cheek, the hairs of his beard scratching my palm. "I'm here. I'll be here until you don't want me anymore."

"Then you'll be here forever, Jesse girl."

My heart beats in my chest so loudly I can hear it in my ears. I slide my hand from his cheek to his chest, resting it over his heart. Its rapid beat mirrors my own, and I lower my lips to the rune tattoo etched on his skin—a silent promise to love him. Forever.

"Good," I whisper with a smile. "Because that's how long I plan to stay."

Acknowledgements

I HAVE TO ADMIT, this book was one of the hardest books I've ever written. I've known for a while that I've wanted to write about Kawasaki disease, not only because it's rare and to bring awareness, but because it's so much a part of my everyday life experience. While my experience isn't exactly Jesse's, I gave her so much of me that sometimes it was hard to write. I can only hope I did her and other KD survivors and ICD warriors justice.

I have to give some massive shoutouts to the people who believed in me and cheered me on every step of the way. My friend, Nic, my alpha reader, Taylor, my friend, Bailey, and my therapist, Nicole. I also have to thank my late friend, Sally. She died of cancer in early 2023. When I had my first heart attack, she checked on me daily. We went on walks together and talked about our health struggles. Sally's life was taken from us by cancer way too soon, and I miss her every day. She taught me to keep going, to stay strong, and to live life to the fullest. I hope this book makes her proud.

This book would also not be what it is without the help and support of my incredible alpha, beta, and sensitivity readers. Thank you again to Taylor, Nic, Kylie, Emily, Jennifer, Siobhan, Sara, Brittney, Shay, Starleisha, and Kamisha. Your insights into your own personal experiences and thoughts on the book truly helped shape it into what it is. Then, of course, I also have to thank my editor, Mason Frey. We did another book! WOO!

It's also important that I thank you, my readers. Thank you for reading this book and for giving me a platform to not only share stories about plus-size people living their best lives but a platform to give Kawasaki disease a voice. It's not well-known, and if this book can help one person save a child from what I've had to experience in my life, it would mean the world to me. If you'd like to learn more about KD or donate to important research, you can visit: https://kdfoundation.org/.

I also covered Asher's ADHD in this book, which is another very important disorder that many, many people live with. If you'd like to learn more about ADHD, get help and support, or donate to research, visit: https://chadd.org/.

Thanks again for reading, and I hope you enjoyed Jesse & Asher's love story. Till next time...

Xoxo,

Kayla

P.S. Don't think I forgot my House of Smut members over on Patreon. THANK YOU. Thank you for your endless love and support of my work. I could not and would not want to do what I do without you. Special thanks to my Smut Obsessed and Smut VIP members: Michelle Culver, Tracy Christianson, Lilly Naughton, MoonViolet33, Glow Lariego, Crystal Ingle, Amanda Summerfield, Natalie Del Rio, Raquel M., Danielle Piepho, Blair Nicole, Leeanna Johnson, Tamara Schnüriger, Alyssa Cates, Roksy, Holly Daymude, Breana, Miranda, Hollyn Alyse, Necia M, SeeCherylRead, MGN, Jessica Mincey, Jackie Braam, Jee Kwon, Jenn, Lindsey Morrison, Sarah V Smith, Kasandra Raux, and Carlee Rhodaback.

Want More Jesse & Asher?
Get Their Bonus Chapter At
www.patreon.com/kaylagrosse

More Books by Kayla Grosse

AXES & O'S
a super spicy MMF snowed-in lumbersnack romance

WHIRLWIND
a spicy age gap, storm chasers novella with a plus-size female lead
and her hot forbidden professor

SILVER FOXED
a dad's best friend, spicy age gap novella with a plus-size female
lead and her sexy silver fox

TRICK SHOT (BROTHER PUCKERS BOOK #1)
a spicy MMF novella with a plus-size female lead and male
lead...and their hot hockey player

PUCK SHY (BROTHER PUCKERS BOOK #2)
a spicy novella with a plus-size female lead and her golden
retriever hockey player

REIN ME IN (THE COWBOYS OF NIGHT HAWK #1)
a late brother's best friend, small town, cowboy romance with a
plus-size cowgirl

ROPE ME IN (THE COWBOYS OF NIGHT HAWK #2)

a small town, country boy meets city girl romance with a plus-size female lead

I LIKE YOU LIKE THAT
a second chance, rock star romance with a plus-size female lead

FALLING FOR THE MANNY
a single mom, contemporary romance by author duo Kayla Nicole

For Exclusive Bonus Stories, Artwork, and More Visit:
www.patreon.com/kaylagrosse

Find Kayla:
Website: http://www.kaylagrosse.com/
Instagram: @kaylawriteslife
Facebook: Kaylaholics Facebook Group
TikTok: @kaylagrossewriter
Twitter: @kaylagrosse

About the Author

Kayla Grosse, author of the international best-seller Trick Shot: A Spicy Christmas Novella and a collection of sweet and spicy plus-size romances, grew up in a suburb of Madison, Wisconsin. Though she lived near a big college town, her backyard was a cornfield, and her favorite hobby was riding her horse and imagining herself flying through the fields with a cape on her back  and a sword in her hand. Her overactive imagination led to writing lots of FanFiction, scripts, and publishing several books. When not writing, Kayla can often be found riding horses or drinking fancy espresso. She lives in Los Angeles, CA with her cockatiel, Fiyero, and Quarter Horse, Atlas.